Hamilton Aïdé

Rita: an Autobiography

Hamilton Aïdé

Rita: an Autobiography

ISBN/EAN: 9783337074913

Printed in Europe, USA, Canada, Australia, Japan

Cover: Foto ©Raphael Reischuk / pixelio.de

More available books at **www.hansebooks.com**

RITA: AN AUTOBIOGRAPHY.

CHAPTER I.

My earliest recollection of home is the fourth story of a house in a dusky street in Paris, where we lived when I was a child. We moved afterwards to a brighter apartment, near the Champs Elysées; but it is with this gloomy abode that the first joys and sorrows of my childhood are associated.

It used to make me giddy to look out of window upon the top of the people's heads below, and on our return from a walk, how often and how wearily have I counted the hundred and thirteen steps we had to climb!

I was the first-born of English parents; and born on undeniably English ground, — within the Tower of London, where my father, Colonel Percival, was then quartered in the Guards. After the birth of a second child, he sold out and came abroad, overwhelmed with debt, and chose Paris — of all places — to commence his career of economy. But I must go back yet a little further, to say a few words of my mother and her family, and explain how I came to be born at all.

My mother was the fourth daughter of the Honorable Ernest Rossborough, and as all the world knew, had not a penny. She had been the belle of a season, as her three sisters had been before her (all but one of whom were dead), and it was thought she might have done better for

herself than marry Jack Percival, with little besides his
good looks and his gay reputation. Perhaps my mother's
vanity was gratified at the idea of carrying off the handsomest man about town, who had flirted and jilted through
so many seasons. Yet it was not believed to be a love-
match — on my father's side at least — but rather the result
of some pique and disappointment. However this may
have been (I now know the true and the false), I will
plainly say, that so long as I remember any thing, their
married life was the reverse of happy.

And here let me draw the reader aside for a few minutes,
that he may understand my object in sitting down to recall,
as faithfully as I can, some passages of my past life. Mon-
taigne says of his admirable Essays: Ce sont mes gestes,
c'est moy, c'est mon essence." Every autobiography should
fulfil these conditions in some measure. It is that inner
world, of which the outward life is but a faint reflection,
which it behooves the self-historian to lay bare to the view
of his readers. If the narrative of an obscure life can be
of any interest, it must be by speaking "the *whole* truth and
nothing but the truth;" if it can serve any good purpose
to retrace one's steps over the battle-field, marking the
struggle here, the victory or defeat there, assuredly this
can only be done satisfactorily by considering also the
past generalship, and its secret tactics which we alone can
divulge.

The lives that most directly influence our own are those
of our parents. In speaking of mine, therefore, however
painful the task, I shall not consider myself justified in
withholding any circumstance that, in its results, shall seem
to have affected my character, my actions, or my after life.
But I shall be fully as candid about myself, I hope: avoiding the error of those recently published Memoirs (would
I could emulate their grace and charm!) in which the
gifted authoress holds up her mother's weakness to the

world's mirror, while she carefully veils the full-face reflection of her own.

My father was the handsomest man I have ever seen; and he kept his looks marvellously, for years. He had been brought up in the ways of his fathers, and was no more vicious, I suppose, than most of the young men of the Regent period. He was by nature *débonnaire* — what is called "*good*-natured" by the world, where he was certainly a popular man upon the whole. But he was selfish and sensual, and though he had one absorbing passion which will be touched on hereafter, his temperament was lukewarm. He was incapable of a strong and deep affection such as redeems, in our poor human sight, a world of sin. He had, indeed, once in his life, loved "wisely," but not well enough to save him from his weaker self. Early habits of self-indulgence, without any controlling principle, vitiate the character eventually more than the fiercest passions. From the ashes of such, when subdued, rise the strongest characters; my father's was essentially weak. With years, indeed, and the life he led, together with the harass of his accumulated debts, he became irritable, and even violent at times. We children seldom saw him; he was very little at home. But there is a moral intuition, often far in advance of the intellect. I was not four years old when I felt that my father was, somehow or other, the cause of my mother's frequent tears. I have a distinct recollection of one terrible scene — a storm of sobs, reproaches, oaths, that sent me cowering to the window-curtains, where I hid and trembled, and which visited me at night again in strange and terrible dreams. I cannot remember when it was I first became aware that a want of money was the evil (after that primary one of want of unity in its heads) that tended to depress the family thermometer. I must have been still very young; for one of my earliest recollections is my mother's lament over an empty purse, and her subterfuges to escape paying the week's washing. I speculated thereon in secret, and hid three sous away very carefully in a hole in the floor.

My dear mother was not a wise woman. She wanted energy to master the position of our affairs, and to try and better them ; and tact to gain an influence over her husband. I never saw her out of temper in my life ; and she was sorely tried. But upon the other hand tears and reproaches from a sofa were the least available arguments for a man of my father's temperament, who, after a night's dissipation, rose up ready as a lion to run his course. And that course was often fatal to domestic unity. My mother lay on the sofa, and mended our clothes ; receiving the few fine ladies who still, for the sake of old acquaintance, took the trouble, when they came to Paris, of climbing up four pair of stairs to see "that poor Mrs. Percival," with a courtly grace that would not have ill-fitted some royal lady conferring the honors of the *tabouret* on her distinguished visitors in the old palace yonder.

Ill health very early compelled my mother to give up going into society ; but I well remember my wonder and admiration once at seeing her dressed for a ball ; and my creeping up to touch the soft white satin, and thinking she must be like Cinderella. She soon grew large and unwieldy, from lying so constantly on the sofa, but her face remained beautiful to the very last, and at fifty her hand might have served as a model for a sculptor. She deserved great credit for her endeavors "to make both ends meet," and as far as herself and children were concerned the expenditure was small indeed ; but she wept over the extravagances that reduced our wardrobe to bare, *thread*-bare necessaries, and our attendants to one poor English nurse-girl.

We were five in number. Rose, my only sister, was a year younger than I, and took after my mother's family, as I was thought to resemble my father's. She early gave promise of great beauty, and was, not unnaturally, my mother's favorite. So radiant a looking child I never saw; her complexion brilliant, her eyes large and liquid, her long hair full of light and sunshine. She inherited, moreover, the grace that was immortalized in a picture of our great-grandmother, Lady Rossborough, by Sir Joshua Reynolds, of which an engraving hung in the drawing-room, in a gilt frame, surmounted by a coronet on a fat cushion.

My brother Ernest came next; a handsome boy, possessed of good natural abilities, alternately petted and neglected by my father, till he threatened to become completely unmanageable, and was a perfect firebrand in the nursery.

The family group closed with my twin-brothers, Arthur and Roger, whom my father never forgave for making their unexpected appearance in this world together, after an interval of six years. They were so sickly that it was thought at first they could not live; but having struggled through their teething, and other ills of cradlehood, contrary to the prophecy of all the English nurses in Paris, they began to assert their intention of remaining upon this "shifting scene" with very strong lungs indeed. It was, no doubt, owing to my mother's unremitting care that my twin-brothers were reared; and this devotion, which was intended to compensate for my father's unnatural aversion, endeared them to her twofold, especially Arthur, who was singularly plain to come of such handsome parents, and on whom I can positively affirm I never saw my father bestow a single kind word or a caress.

My father, as I have said, was immersed in the dissipations of Paris. Often have I heard him come home at four or five in the morning: the heavy step, the click of the latch-key in the door, the stumbling through the rooms in the dim light of a perishing lamp, and the curse if it suddenly went out! — I seem to hear it all again as distinctly as when I lay in my little bed against the wall, and trembled. Jean Paul asks, " Who would not become a child again!" Ah!

no one whose childhood has been overshadowed by the heavy cloud that mine was.

How little any of the grand ladies we occasionally saw, guessed all the shifts to which we children were often put for a dinner. How little did they think that the bonbons they brought would serve probably to silence my hunger at bedtime! Speaking of this reminds me of a circumstance which occurred when I was about five years old. I had been taken by my nurse to see Lady Greybrook, who was a very fine lady, and a friend of my father's rather than of my mother's. She lived in the place Vendôme. I remember there was a great stone staircase, and a powdered footman, who relieved Betsy of her charge, and desired the "young woman" in a patronizing way to sit down, while he carried me through a suite of gilded *salons* to my lady's boudoir. My imagination was much impressed, and it was with some feeling of awe that I found myself in the great lady's presence. She eyed me attentively, took me on her lap, and praised my long eyelashes. I was fully sensible of the compliment, and being reassured, ventured to look up into her face. She declared I was the image of my father. I thought her like the beautiful dolls I always coveted in the shop-windows.

"And now, little Marguerite, tell me what you would like best to have in the whole world?"

I colored and hesitated. If her ladyship expected that I should say a *cornet de dragées* (I saw the corner of one ready in ambush behind the sofa-cushion), she was mistaken. I hesitated, but only for a moment, then replied boldly,

"A pair of new shoes!"

Her ladyship burst out laughing, glanced down at my well-worn boots, through which the toes were beginning to appear, and cried,

"*Qu'elle est originale, la petite!* You shall have a pair tomorrow, Marguerite — the smartest I can find. In the mean time, here are some chocolate boots, and heaven knows what besides."

I did not see that lady again for many a long year, but she was always connected in my mind with a certain pair of blue kid shoes.

My education, until I was about eight years old, was as completely neglected as it is possible to conceive. In the matter of religion, my very grand godfather and godmothers having undertaken to be responsible for my sins, it seems to have been thought that all had been done that was necessary. I received the name of Marguerite — abbreviated very soon into Rita — from one of these godmothers, whom, in consideration to her feelings, I shall not more particularly name, seeing that from the hour she stood by me at the font she never troubled her head further about me. A certain conventional religion overtook us on Sunday afternoons, moving us to certain forms. I also repeated the Lord's Prayer every night and morning — when I was not too sleepy, or too late and lazy — and was instructed to say grace (which my mother remembered to have been done always in the schoolroom at Rossborough) before and after every meal, and as they were often scanty, I am afraid I seldom felt properly grateful. So far went our faith, and no further.

I never remember learning to read. That I did so, somehow or other, is clear, and the use I soon made of the accomplishment was to devour all the books (seldom very healthy ones) I could find. Of that respectable course of instruction which comprises "writing, arithmetic, geography, with the use of the globes," through which every farmer's daughter of ten years old in England passes, my sister and I knew nothing when long past that age.

But I am running on too fast. A death occurred in my mother's family when I was only nine, which considerably changed the aspect of our affairs. I say *aspect*, for it was perhaps more in appearance than reality, as the state of

ignorance we children were still left in proved. Yet the drop
from a fourth floor to a first is, after all, an important event
in life, and as such claims especial notice.

I was alone in the drawing-room, when my father burst
open the door.

"Rita, where is your mother?"

"Lying down."

"Come, off with my boots, old Queen of Tarts!" (a form
of address which always argued well for my father's temper,
and which originated in the historical ballad of the " Queen
of Hearts," etc., for which I had early shown a predilection).
"That frock's monstrous shabby. You must have a new one
—a black silk one," he added, holding out his foot. I
knelt down to unbutton the boot, then looked up into his
face.

"Papa, what is it?   Is Uncle Rossborough coming?"

This was the event to which I knew my parents were
always anxiously looking forward, and I could conceive no
other cause for my father's elation.   He laughed aloud.

"Better than that, old Queen of Tarts! better than that!
The old curmudgeon's *dead*. Fetch me my slippers." And
he kicked his boot to the other end of the room.

I ran for the slippers, then flew to my mother's room, and
such was my anxiety to be the first to communicate the
intelligence, that it oozed out before I got half-way to the
bed.

"Mamma! mamma! Uncle Rossborough is dead!"

She started from her pillow. " Good God, child! what do
you mean?"

I repeated the words, and my father, following me, cor-
roborated them. She pressed her hands to her eyes. "Poor
old Uncle John!" Then after a pause, raising them to my
father's face, she looked into it eagerly, inquiringly.

"Four thousand pounds!"

CHAPTER II.

John, fourth Baron Rossborough, was my mother's uncle, being her father's eldest brother. He was rich ; and certainly not prodigal : he never married, and as none of his brothers had a son, the title, at his death, became extinct. Nieces, however, there were in abundance, who used to overwhelm him with knitted purses, mufflees, and the like, but as he seldom gave any thing in return, I do not think his loss was mourned in proportion to the affection that had been manifested for him in his lifetime. My mother had indulged in the most absurd dreams of his making Ernest his heir. The old gentleman had taken a fancy to him as a baby, when the former once passed through Paris, years before, and my mother's hopes fed on the vague promise he then made of repeating his visit. She kept up a regular correspondence with him, and he answered her letters with great exactitude, at the same time politely evading the advance of a shilling towards the liquidation of my father's debts. My mother felt shocked, and mildly affected, at my uncle's sudden demise, and considered herself aggrieved that the bulk of his fortune should be left to a cousin (to the annihilation of her Spanish castle) ; but finally consoling herself with the comfortable reality of the legacy — so sorely needed in our condition — she and my father sat down to talk over matters together more serenely than I ever remember to have seen them.

I retained a clear recollection of Lord Rossborough as an old gentleman in a scratch wig. He had presented me, upon that memorable visit, with an English pocket-book adorned

with choice engravings, and amongst them one of a Grecian
temple in an umbrageous park, with very large deer and a
lady with a parasol in the foreground, under which, "Rossborough Hall, Suffolk, the seat of Baron Rossborough," the
whole bound in red leather, value one and sixpence. This
was all I had known of my great uncle. The following day,
there was an unusual number of visitors, none of whom were
admitted, though my mother was at home, and in the enjoyment of far better spirits than usual. I wondered, therefore,
exceedingly, as I stood in the ante-room, to hear one lady
inquire, "How poor Mrs. Percival was?" to which Betsy,
coming to the rescue of her one fellow-servant at this trying
juncture responded, with great gravity,

"As well as can be 'speeted, ma'am, hunder her 'fliction."

The social position of the deceased called forth this universal sympathy, I suppose; and as to my mother, she was
only following the well-known conventions of society. It was
my first initiation into the "forms, modes, shows of grief."

My parents agreed that the first thing to be done was to
move to a more commodious and airy apartment. My father
paid his creditors, whose claims amounted to upwards of
fifteen hundred pounds; my mother restocked our wardrobe;
and a man-servant was added to the establishment, who
united in his person the offices of butler and housemaid.
Betsy, thereupon, became our exclusive property, and hard
enough work she had, now that "Master Hernest" was of an
age to imitate the young gamins in the street, and insist upon
standing on his head in the bath, in spite of nurse's entreaties
that he would assume a more becoming posture. What a
life he led her and the French girl who was now installed as
her coadjutor!

The first Sunday after our "sad loss" my mother came
down resplendent in black satin, like a complete suit of
court-plaister, and armed cap-à-pie with crape and bugles.
She went to church, which she had not done for an age, and

we dined that day, for the first time, like honest British children, on roast-beef and plum-pudding, having our loins girt
with sable sashes of inordinate width.

Our new apartment was pleasantly situated, having a side-
long glance at the green alleys of the Champs Elysées, and
at the everflowing tide of pedestrians that flock thitherward,
especially on Sundays. It took a holiday view of the world,
just as our former abode, in the grim narrow street of tall
houses, with a tinker living in the back-court, and a dyer
opposite, saw life in its work-a-day aspect. As it was here
that I was destined to pass so many years, I may as well
describe our new home. It was spacious enough. The
ante-room, three sides of which were studded with doors
and the fourth with windows, served also as our dining-room.
It communicated, on one side, with our nursery department
and the servants' domain; on the other with the drawing-
room, my mother's bedroom (used as a second *salon* for the
reception of privileged visitors), and my father's dressing-
room. The last was a territory I never penetrated as a
child. Glimpses of boots, ranged with military precision
along the wall (the only thing in the room that seemed or-
derly); a table strewed with papers, razors, spurs, and
brushes; coats left, as they had been thrown off on the
chair, or on the ground; and everywhere bills, and cards,
and shreds of " Bell's Life," — glimpses of these I had occasionally through the half-open door, but the room itself was
strictly interdicted. So much for the new home; now for
the inmates, our new neighbors.

Over us lived a little old French general and his wife,
with whom I very soon struck up an intimacy. He had belonged to Napoleon's army, and had been present on every
battle-field, from Lodi to Waterloo. I loved to sit upon his
knee, and get him to describe how " mon empereur" presented him with such an order on such a day; what he said,
and how his curt praise was more than whole speeches from

other men; together with anecdotes of the fair Beauharnais and Tallien, and of the times when they of the camp relaxed the pressure of their iron harness for a breathing-space, under the softening influence of beauty. Not that my idea of a warrior at all resembled that yellow old gentleman, profuse in snuff, and sparing of pocket-handkerchief; but then he had lost two fingers, and had a gallant wound right across his forehead, which compensated, in a great measure, for his not being dressed up to my idea of the part. Every thing about him was old and yellow. An old yellow valet, with an older and much yellower coachman, who drove the oldest and yellowest of chariots, more scarred and plaistered up than the General himself. These he was pleased to term, "mes gens" and "mon équipage;" for he was a little pompous, sometimes, was General Gobemouche, save upon the battle-field of the past, which, being a true thing, needed no bombast, as the false airs of nobility did. He seemed to grow twenty years younger when he got on the old ground : his voice cleared, his eye brightened, his whole manner underwent a pleasant change. And wasn't it worth while to hear him, were it only to watch Madame Gobemouche, listening with never-flagging eager interest, as though she now heard the recital for the first time with unmingled wonder? Wasn't it a pardonable fiction, and a pleasant one (*I* thought so, I know. though I foresaw it coming every time), by which she always pretended to have her understanding darkened at certain parts of the narrative, and to need enlightenment upon such points, as "*where* Blücher stood, when, etc. etc."

Were they not, in fine, admirably suited to each other? At what period of her existence this good and faithful ally signed the solemn treaty that united her to her General, I know not. Her antecedents were shrouded in mystery : and there were not wanting ill-natured stories. Some said she had been a vivandière, and knew quite as much about the

General's battles as he did himself. Some declared that she had been the personal property of several generals in turn, until, at last, she married a commissary, and that it was with the wealth of that deceased functionary she endowed the General upon her second marriage. The latter part of this I believe to have been true: but I always thought her personal appearance the most powerful refutation of the scandal. The irregularities of her face forbade the thought of any in her conduct. She was deeply pitted with smallpox: her complexion more like a coarse cheap sponge than any thing else; the features having lost all clear articulation of outline, and presenting a generally indistinct and bruised appearance. She dressed rather with an eye to strong coloring than pleasing combination, and, altogether, I must confess there was a decided flavor of camps in her aspect and demeanor. But one could not see her, as I saw her, without knowing what a kind, generous heart beat beneath this unpromising exterior. Somewhat touchy, perhaps, more for the General's dignity than her own; irritable, but always easily restored to good humor. She had two large teeth — I should be more correct if I said *tusks* — when I first knew her, which kept her mouth ajar. And, curious to say, it was a circumstance in connection with these, soon after I knew them, which was the means of cementing my friendship with madame. I went up, one rainy afternoon, on some pretence or other, and found her rocking herself to and fro, and declaring that she was "at the point to die." Suffering all night from toothache; dentist sent for, and not yet arrived. Vain was the help of man, meaning, in this case, the General, whose efforts to soothe her were, of course, unavailing.

"Ça — ça, viens donc, ma biche — calme-toi — ça va mieux à présent, n'est-ce pas, Cocotte?"

But Cocotte refused to be comforted, and only rocked herself the more, declaring that it was "un enfer insupportable."

The old man's face wore a comical look of puzzled distress
and dismay. He had stood unmoved on battle-fields, surrounded by dead and dying. He was not proof against Cocotte's face-ache.

He walked up and down the room, wiped his forehead,
looked out of window — no signs of dentist — walked up and
down again. I began to think I had better retire.

"*Mais, diable!*" he cried, in his excitement whipping off
the yellow bandanna he always wore at this hour knotted
round his head — but the door opened at the same moment,
and the dentist was announced.

He proceeded to examine the mouth in the regular professional way, as if he were opening an oyster, amid the violent
contortions of the sufferer. There was an awful pause. No
one spoke. Then sentence was pronounced in case Jaw *v*.
Left Tusk. The doom of the offender was sealed. The days
of stopping were past. Justice had, at last, overtaken the
notorious criminal — he was condemned to be drawn, though
not quartered.

Some one must hold the head.

At this the General started up, declaring No! he could
not — positively could not stand *that* — he was sure he could
not — any thing but that. It was absurd — *mais que roulez-
vous?* his nerves were not strong now. Cocotte must spare
him — and yet some one *must* perform the dreadful office.
What was to be done? The General's hand was on the bell
to summon the yellow old valet. " Here," thought I. " is a
fine opportunity to display my courage before the General.
It is disagreeable, certainly, having to hold that greasy black
wig, and to see that man tugging away, and to hear her
screams — but then I can shut my eyes, if not my ears " —
and so, with some trepidation, I offered my services.

The dentist looked dubiously at me, as if he thought I
was not strong enough for the place; but I assured him I
was a female infant Hercules, though so small, and that I

would hold tight, and not flinch, or turn faint, or otherwise misconduct myself. The General was delighted at the idea, wrung my hand, had a fit of hysteria between laughing and his other emotions, and made for the door as fast as he could. The victim was then ordered to place herself on a low stool; I stood behind to give myself more purchase. Off went the cap, the wigged head fell heavily between my knees. Now then! I swooped down upon my prey, and clutched it firmly in my talons.

The operator bends over, instrument in hand. A lurch, as of a ship in a heavy sea — then a pause — groans and stifled shrieks — " Is it over ? "

" Not yet — coming."

Another lurch, more violent than the last; the well-oiled wig slips about under my fingers, like a Roman gladiator from the grasp of his foe — I can hardly hold it. Redoubled groans and shrieks, and then a third and prolonged wrench — and all is over! I sink back for a moment, quite exhausted, but when I look up cannot help laughing at the sight of Madame Gobemouche's bald and polished head, the wig, during the last desperate struggle, having remained in my tenacious grasp. Then she falls to, embracing me; the dentist holds up three fangs in triumph, and we congratulate each other mutually on our several performances.

After this signal service I rose greatly in the estimation of the old couple. Hardly a day elapsed without my seeing them; frequent were the little presents I received, and in all moments of distress or ennui it was to them I had recourse.

But there was another inmate of that house of whom, in process of time, I saw as much, nay more. This was Monsieur Barac, the proprietor, who lived on the ground-floor — an obese old gentleman, generally believed to be of the Hebrew persuasion. With that, however, I had nothing

to do; nor is it probable that I should ever have had any
thing to do with him, but for a ruling taste which had early
shown itself in me. Whenever I was fractious as a baby,
I have been told, they used to hoist me on a level with some
colored prints that hung round my mother's room, and I
began to crow with unaccountable delight. And as I grew
in childhood a pencil and the back of a letter kept me quiet
in a corner for hours, while my brother and sister were at
play. I created all sorts of fantastic groups, which meant
something for *me*, however unintelligible to others; made,
as I imagined, a correct copy of our grandmother in Sir
Joshua's engraving; and often forgot little miseries in the
solace my love of art afforded me.

Now Monsieur Barac was a connoisseur and speculator
in pictures. He made a journey once or twice a year to
Holland and Belgium, or the North of Italy, and his
tobacco-smoked apartment was always rich in old masters,
often disappearing as rapidly as they came, but ready to
spring up, hydra-headed, in some other form, so soon as the
wall showed a blank. He took a fancy to the little dark-
eyed girl who stood on the threshold and peeped in one day,
and who, after the first invitation, came so readily to look
at his Rubenses and Rembrandts, and showed such a ready
apprehension of their beauties. He was very kind to me;
never tired of my questions, always pleased at my delight
when a gleam of sunshine brought out some hidden beauty,
patient to explain in what the painter's art was most cunning; careful to discriminate and compare the various
gradations of excellence. Sometimes there were visitors
with him, strange bearded-looking men, who talked in
foreign tongues on matters connected with the pictures, as I
gathered; but when I found these men there I never staid.
I liked old Barac alone, and alone I generally found him,
with a greasy velvet cap, a meerschaum pipe, and an enormous sapphire on his fore-finger, with apparently no other

occupation in life than to walk up and down the room, and pass his silk handkerchief over the face of a Gerard Dow, should he, haply, find a speck of dust there, and then to stand with his back to the stove, as if in a constant state of preparation for something or other.

At last, one day when I was admiring a little chalk sketch of Rubens's, he suddenly suggested that I should try and copy it. "You will not succeed — never mind that — must make a beginning — all artists have failed at first." This was the substance of his words. So I fetched my pencil and a sheet of coarse gray paper, and, nothing daunted by the difficulty of the task, sat down full of vanity and determination. Of course, as he had predicted, nothing could be worse than it was — my cherub had a foot three times the size of his head; but I tried again and again, and under the old man's careful eye at last produced a copy which he pronounced very fair for a beginner. With what triumph I carried it up to my mother I well remember; and how she said "she was glad of any thing to keep me out of mischief," and took no further notice; and what wonder the production of my full-blown cherub produced in the nursery. From that time I generally spent an hour or two of every day in Monsieur Barac's room; drawing, with little success it is true, but with unflagging ardor and perseverance. Few parents, probably, would have given me this unrestricted license, but I might have made a pilgrimage to Rome and back without my father's discovering my absence, and my mother, with four other children to think of, was only too glad, as she said, to have me out of the way, and where she knew I was safe.

For our education still fared ill. There had been a talk of sending my sister and me to some cheap French school; but two years had rolled by and this was not done, and my father's affairs, meantime, were gradually returning to pretty much the state they were in before that windfall of a legacy came to us. Duns again poured in with the old regularity; for though my father's income was improved by the investment of the 2500*l.* that remained after the payment of his debts, he had largely exceeded it each of the following years, so my mother was obliged to abandon the idea of a school for us girls. But something must soon be done about Ernest, who was now nine, and becoming quite unmanageable at school. If he was to go to India — and my father had the promise of a cadetship — he must receive some preparatory education. "As to us girls, we must get on as well as we could, and should certainly have some dancing lessons by and by." This was my father's decision, and general view of the importance of education.

How long matters might have gone on so it is hard to say; indeed I suppose I should never have written these passages in my life, but for an event which happened just as I entered my thirteenth year, and which was destined to have a lasting influence over my whole future.

CHAPTER III.

"Your aunt Mary is coming here on her way to Italy," said my mother one morning, holding a letter in her hand. "She inquires a great deal about you, Rita. Do you remember her when you were quite a little thing at grandpapa's, in London?"

"No, mamma, not the least."

"Well, to be sure, you were only two years old, I believe. Emily, I know, was a year older, and no bigger than you were. Poor Emily! Your aunt writes that she is as tall as herself now. I'm afraid she has been growing too fast, for the doctors have sent her to a warm climate; but you are terribly short for your age. I wonder *when* you will grow, my dear child?"

"Ah! I remember Emily's face," said I, somewhat nettled, "she had red hair and freckles." In fact I retained a very distinct recollection of my grandpapa's gloomy house in Pall-Mall, and some of its inmates, among them my little cousin.

"Poor child! Her mother seems very uneasy about her."

"Has she no brothers or sisters, mamma?"

"None; she is your aunt's only child, and a great heiress." (A sigh.)

"What is an heiress?"

"A rich woman, dear." (My mother's definitions were not generic.) "Her father, Sir Nicholas, died when she was very young, and left all his fortune to your aunt for her life; afterwards, of course, it goes to Emily. Dreadful thing if she

dies! the fortune, of course, goes to some distant branch of
the Dacre family. Poor Mary!" sighed she, aside to herself; "and after all she has gone through!"

"What makes her unhappy? Have all her other children
died?"

"People can be unhappy in other ways besides their children dying. Every one has n't as many brothers and sisters
as you. Emily never had any. Heigh-ho!"

"What's the use of money, then, if it can't make people
happy? I thought that we — I 've heard you say that if you
and papa were rich, we should have every thing we want;
but if aunt is so unhappy, I don't see that this big fortune is
of much use to her."

"Little girls can't understand these sort of things. Money,
Rita, is worth rank, and talent, and beauty, and every thing
else; by-and-by you 'll know that. It won't make a sick
child, like Emily, well — that, you ought to be aware, God
alone can do; but it enables your aunt to undertake an expensive journey to attain that object. Were she as poor as
we are" (with a touch of bitterness) "Emily must die.
Thank God, my dear, you are all strong, and don't require
much care."

It was seldom my mother spoke with so much energy.
Seldom, too, the logic of her answers reached me as clearly
as this. The power of money seemed doubled in my eyes.

About a fortnight after this Lady Dacre and Emily
arrived in Paris. I remember the circumstances of that
arrival as if it were yesterday. My aunt wrote to say she
would drive to our house first, to know whether we had taken
apartments for her at Meurice's or elsewhere. It was early
in November, but the afternoon was raw and foggy; the outer
world from our windows looked very cheerless as we stood
and watched down the Champs Elysées, each anxious to be
the first to see and to announce the expected arrival. My
father and mother were both in the room; she upon the

sofa, he with his back to the fire, apparently engaged in no very pleasant reflections. As no one spoke — for our remarks to each other on the passers-by were carried on in whispers — the silence, in the twilight, became quite oppressive; it was mine to break the spell. " Here they are ! " The faint cracking of a whip in the distance, that prolonged " crick-crack " of the postilion caught my ear, and in another minute the jack-boots, feathers, and tassels of the noisy performers came bumping through the fog upon their steaming horses, which they pulled up with a great jerk before our *porte cochère.* I heard the drawing-room door bang — my father had left the room. I thought he was gone down to receive my aunt; but the steps of the well-mudded chariot were lowered by an undeniable English footman, and two figures descended without the assistance of my father's arm.

My mother was uncoiling herself from her shawls on the sofa as my aunt entered; she had not time to accomplish her purpose before the arms of the latter were round her. As for us we fell upon our cousin in a phalanx, so that it was a wonder how she stood the charge. It was quite dusk, we could only see each other's faces by the fitful light of the wood-fire, as we stood tugging away at Emily's bonnet, cloak, boa, and gloves, and meeting with a good deal of quiet resistance, though she seemed very tired and incapable of active demonstration of any kind. When Roger had succeeded in taking off her bonnet, after nearly throttling her, and Arthur had dispossessed her of her cloak, we saw a tall, very slight girl, with a profusion of auburn hair that hung, out of curl, round her face, and almost completely hid it. There was not a sound from the sofa ; the sisters lay locked in each other's arms quite silently, and we instinctively drew my cousin away to the further end of the room, Rose holding one hand, I the other. Had she liked her journey? Had she had any adventures? Was she hungry? Had she given up dolls? (As men are asked, if they have given up smok-

ing?) What sort of place was her home in England? Was
it like — the Tuileries, for instance? By-the-by, did she
like chocolate? Roger was despatched for our last box, and
I saw my father's shadow on the half-open door at the same
moment. As he entered and crossed to the fireplace, the
light fell for an instant on his face. Was I mistaken, or did
it seem strangely moved? He approached Lady Dacre, hurriedly, and poured forth a volley of common-places about
her journey, etc., in a nervous manner, as it seemed to me.
It made a strong impression, for I remember I left the remainder of the interrogatory in Rose's hands, and sat still
and listened. My aunt answered in a low voice, rather
coldly I thought ; immediately afterwards she turned, called
us to her and kissed us kindly, while my father continued,

"I have taken apartments for you at the ' Bristol,' my dear
Lady Dacre, and I hope you will like them. Unfortunately
Lady Aylesford has the best suite, or you should have had
them. Comfortable hotel; good *cuisine*, etc. We are only
so sorry we have n't room for you here."

" Thank you. We shall only be here for a few days,
otherwise the ' Bristol ' would be too expensive an hotel for
me. I am anxious to get on to Nice before the very cold
weather."

" Sorry to hear you intend running away from us so soon
—not your own health, I hope? Ah! your daughter's, I
forgot. 'Pon my soul she 's as tall as you are, and quite the
Grandisson coloring, I see. What a *chevelure!* You must
positively bring her out in Paris next year. She will create
quite a sensation. Fair English beauty is here — "

" My daughter is no beauty, and will never create a sensation, as you will see by a better light. Fortunately it is
the thing I least desire for her. But she is tired now, and we
must leave you, dear Kate ; besides, it is not fair to keep
those poor horses. We shall be with you early to-morrow,
and I shall call upon my nieces to do the honors of Paris to

us. Come, Emmy, put on your cloak. Good-by, my dears." And a minute afterwards they were gone. My father now conducted them to the door of the carriage, and stood bowing gracefully as the postilions cracked their whips once more and sent up the mud into his indignant face. I stood wondering and musing by the window for nearly an hour afterwards.

Thus began my acquaintance, though not my affection for, or real knowledge of, my aunt Mary. It was a hard character to read. Few guessed that a warm heart beat beneath that cold exterior, for there were depths in it that the world knew not, but where the sun lay always. I was afraid of her at first. Her grave, severe expression of face, and the way in which her faded eyes looked through and through one as she spoke, made me uncomfortable. She had, moreover, the lines of a bad temper, or of some heavy sorrow written about her mouth and brow. I thought the former (like the world). How differently I learnt, in time, to judge this noble woman. Emily was as unlike her as possible; her mother had said truly that she was no beauty, nor was she ever to me very interesting, though the freckles I remembered as a child had been succeeded by a brilliant hectic flush that accounted only too well for her mother's anxiety, and made her very nearly a pretty girl. But she was so remarkably childish for her age (and yet more for her height), so feeble and common-place in mind to be the daughter of my lofty aunt, and the only child on whom she lavished all her care, that it was a puzzle to me then, though I now know that it is no uncommon thing for the greatest pains in education to produce very poor results. It is true she told me herself that she had learnt the Latin grammar, and had Magnal's questions by heart; had been through quadrations (whatever that may be), and knew the names of all the rivers in North and South America, and I forget how much besides; yet I failed to trace the elevating influence of all this learning, at the same time that I felt my own ignorance the more. I had long ceased to take an interest in doll's feasts, and here was Emily, my senior by a year, entering into all Rose's games with a zest for which I could not help entertaining a secret contempt. It humbled me to think that, spite of my fancied superiority, she knew so much more than I did, and my mortification reached its culminating point a few days after the arrival of my new relations.

During these few days my curiosity had been kept perpetually awake to the strange position Lady Dacre assumed in our family. Silently, apparently without an effort, it seemed to be accepted throughout the house, that her will should be law. Naturally an acute observer, I could not help remarking that my father never was at ease in her presence. His manners towards her were obsequious, but so forced and overdone that I always felt relieved when one or other left the room. On my aunt's side, the chilling reserve, habitual to her in general society, but which thawed at once with those she loved, she never broke through with my father. You can hardly fancy any thing so uncomfortable as seeing these two people together, each of whom I knew *could* be so different, and *would* be so, when the other left the room. Yet, strange to say, the second morning after her arrival, I knew perfectly well that she was closeted with him in his dressing-room for nearly half an hour. Later in the day, when they met in the drawing-room, there was no change perceptible in their separate demeanors — the same servility on one side, the same freezing laconism on the other. But there were other changes in my father far more important than that of his manner (which I confess I hardly thought an improvement on his ordinary off-hand style, highly seasoned though it sometimes was). We were no longer disturbed from our sleep by his return home at three and four in the morning; he seldom went out at night, and wore the semblance, at least, of a respectable domestic character. That my aunt's presence had wrought this change I could not doubt; but how? I soon saw that one of her first objects was to find out all she could of our interior economy; the nursery, the kitchen, the wardrobe, nothing escaped her, and very singular discoveries I have no doubt she made. For she met with no obstacles; on the contrary, every facility was afforded her of probing silently and skilfully, as she did, all the hidden wounds of the establishment. My father, indeed, knew little enough about them; had he done so, perhaps his pride might have led him to endeavor to conceal them from the searching eye of his sister-in-law. As for my mother, she seemed to lean with implicit confidence and affection upon her strong minded sister; there is nothing, I am sure, she would have concealed from her, and many were the long hours they passed together, seldom conversing of the past, I suspect, but rather of the complexities of the present and the future.

A wet afternoon — the boys away at their daily school — Emily and Rose buried in a corner of the drawing-room, exchanging confidences in state whispers — my aunt and mother together and alone in the adjoining room. A French novel had fallen into my hands that morning, having been left on the table by my father the night before. This was the only literature he affected; and when he was out, I knew I might, with safety, possess myself of a volume. Accordingly, with the one in question under my arm, I slipped out of the room, and ran into the nursery, now cold and deserted, for the fire had gone out. I sat down by the window with the book upon my knee. In the morning I had but dipped into its pages, now I became absorbed: it was deeply, terribly exciting, beyond any thing I had yet perused — no matter that I did not understand two thirds of its insidious immorality. The heroine was a married lady, a giddy sort of person, but tossed upon such a perfect sea

of troubles, poor thing, that I felt very much interested in
her fate.   I had a dim apprehension that she had better not
meet her husband's friend quite so often, at uncertain hours
of the night.   There were long passages, too, about "l'âme
pure" and "l'union sympathique des cœurs," that I skipped,
because I found them dull; but the story itself, ah! that
was cunningly and thrillingly told! incidents threaded on
close and thick, like beads — a murder, a mystery, a dis-
closure, a false marriage, another murder — all so wrought
up, that my blood ran hot and cold by turns.   How long I
had been reading I know not: the thick gray evening was
closing in, and I had to press my head against the spattered
window-pane, to catch the fading light, upon my book.   So
absorbed was I, that I did not hear the door open.   I
started, and almost screamed with terror, when a hand was
laid upon my shoulder.   An involuntary impulse made me
scramble the book into my pocket as I turned round and
met my aunt's kind, but grave face bent over me.

"Why are you here all alone, Rita, in this cold room?
Rose and Emmy are in the drawing-room — don't you like
playing with them?"

"No."

"What are you doing here?"

"Reading."

"I am glad to find you are so fond of reading; but it is
getting too dark now, so sit down and talk to me.   What
sort of books do you like best?"

"Amusing books — interesting, I mean."

"Stories, I suppose — ghost stories, or fairy tales?"

"Oh, no (contemptuously); real things — and horrible —
I like the most horrible ones best."

"Then the book I saw you reading, as I entered, was a
true story.   Will you tell me what it was about?"

"Oh! I don't know that it's true.   I meant books about
real men and women — not ghosts and that sort of nonsense,

that is told to frighten children. (Twelve-and-a-quarter fancied itself a woman.) Do you ever read French novels, aunt?"

"No; I suppose you have. Is that one?"

"Yes; I find one sometimes, when papa is out, on the table. Mamma says I oughtn't to read them, she's sure; but, then, as mamma doesn't read French, I don't see how she can tell. And then, I've got nothing but stupid old books I know by heart. Every Sunday I read Dr. Horne's ' Life of Abel,' to mamma, and I have been through it three times, and I don't see what is the good of reading the best book over and over again."

"Would you mind letting me see this book?" said my aunt, holding out her hand.

I pulled it from my pocket, and gave it her. She drew closer to the window, and bent her head over the fly-leaf, till it almost touched the paper. I watched her countenance, but could make nothing of it. Presently she left the window, and said abruptly,

" The little I have seen of you makes me think you are a sensible girl, with some natural ability, and good reasoning faculties, which are more valuable still. Above all, I like your frankness about the book. I should not have pressed the question, I assure you. Now I am going to be equally frank with you. This book I know well by name: it is a bad book, though you may not think so; one I would not let Emily read for the world. All the evil it contains you are not capable of understanding now: how soon you might do so, I cannot tell; for you are beyond your age in some things, though sadly behind in most. Your ignorance is greater than that of many children of seven years old. (I told you I should be frank.) Do you know this, Rita? and do you feel the importance of education? the desire to improve? My dear child, I am aware that it is not from any fault of yours that you are so backward. I do not blame you, but I wish you to *feel* that 'Knowledge is Power,' as the old copy says; though in fact, it is the use we make of knowledge, in maturing our judgment and reflection, that is power, and not knowledge itself, if we cannot turn it to account; for many learned men have been but poor thinkers and reasoners. That is not, however, what I was going to say. To you, education is especially important. Do you know why?"

"Because I am the eldest, to begin with."

"Just so: because your father is very poor, and you must learn, in order to teach your sister and your brothers. You may be of the greatest service to them: indeed, who knows but that their future may, in a measure, depend on you, besides your own success and happiness in after life, when you may have to struggle through the world alone? French novels never assisted any one to do so. Will you promise me not to read one again, for the next six years, if I undertake to provide you with books? You shall have plenty, so there will be no longer that plea, and there will also be some one to superintend your reading, and whom, I hope you may learn to regard not as a governess, but a friend."

I threw my arms around her neck, and thanked her with what eloquence I could command at the moment. My tears ran down my cheeks, as I assured her I felt too proud of her good opinion not to promise much more than she asked. My aunt seemed pleased, and said she should make immediate arrangements with an English lady she knew to come to us daily in the capacity of governess. She hoped I should work very hard to make up for lost time.

It would have been difficult for me to do otherwise, under Miss Lateward's system. Fortunately, I was strong; and disposed, as much from real thirst for the springs that had hitherto been denied me, as from vanity, and the desire of satisfying my aunt's expectations, to study eight or nine hours a day. But poor Rose, after the first week, gave way completely; neither her health nor spirits would stand the long hours of confinement and attention, and the day's lessons always came to an abrupt close with a headache and a fit of crying. Miss Lateward did not understand such things as nerves, tears, and headaches. She thought Rose spoilt (as, indeed, she was by my mother), frivolous — and how was it to be expected she should be otherwise, with her beauty, and brought up as she had been? — deceitful and affected — which she never was. My harder nature suited Miss Lateward much better; and my desire for knowledge, with an indefatigable power of questioning, enabled her to be oracular, which she liked. She was a person of the most solid attainments, and the soundest theology; the opposite, in short, of all I had been accustomed to see and hear, in superficial Paris. Every useful and legitimate subject of information, from Parliament to pin-making, received, in turn, a due share of attention at her hands; and, as far as information went, she was complete in it, and downright. When she had spoken, you knew all about it, and nothing remained to be said. If it was a moot-point (as would occur sometimes in reading history), or a case in which acute discrimination and a careful balance of judgment were requisite, her opinion seldom satisfied me. Remarkable in her was the absence of all imagination and humor, a disregard of the graces and flowers of life, and a love of depriving even history of its legends, and the poetry that clings to it. Yet we were soon fast friends; for it was impossible to know her long and not feel a respect for the conscientious manner in which she fulfilled all her duties by us, the scrupulous justice with which she measured to us praise or blame, and the general consistency and faithfulness of her character. If she lacked that delicacy of perception, which is a sixth sense, that penetration into character which every leader, whether of minds or armies, should have, she possessed another quality that was invaluable in our family, that of prudence. She

had eyes, and saw not; ears had she, and heard not. I
never could tell how much she knew of what went on in the
house; about the strange scenes of which she was often an
involuntary witness she never threw out question or observation. I am inclined now to think that this quality, more
than any other, decided my aunt in her choice of Miss Lateward as our governess; she had known her long, and saw
how necessary certain characteristics were for the position
she was to hold; and Miss Lateward had these, in which
many more accomplished governesses might have been
wanting.

My aunt left Paris very soon afterwards; but she promised, upon her return in the spring, to spend a month there.
I took to my studies, firmly resolved to astonish her by un-
heard-of progress during her absence. The ambition that
had long slumbered in me was now kindled; it supplied a
motive to exertion, and concentrated my energies on one
point. I had no lack of self-confidence; I would shine; I
would no longer be called " ignorant," but more than justify
my aunt's expectations. And musing thus, in my nursery
corner, with my elbows on my knees, and the empire of
Rome between them, I pressed the fingers tighter in my
ears, and bent down with the determination of a Cæsar to
conquer every difficulty.

The six months passed rapidly in my new course of life.
I was less than ever in the drawing-room, and never saw
any of the visitors my mother received in the afternoon,
though Rose was generally sent for. In short, when Miss
Lateward was not with us I was allowed, as formerly, to do
very much as I liked; and often instead of going out with
my brothers and sister, I stole down to old Barae's apartment, and revisited my friends, the Rembrandts and Gerard
Dows. Between these and my books the short gray days
went swiftly by; and this world of my own in which I had
begun to live rendered me very happy, and almost indiffer-

ent to the many little troubles of our inquiet home. The unexplained influence for good which my aunt had exercised over my father passed away, alas! with her presence. I seldom saw him; I never willingly witnessed the scenes that often agitated my mother; but Rose would run in and whisper, " Poor mamma is crying, and there's some man out there — an ugly, dirty fellow, who wants something, and papa is so angry, so dreadfully angry. it made me quite tremble. What can it be all about, Ritey?"

So passed the winter.

3

CHAPTER IV.

"Not," said Miss Lateward, "that I hold with those who deem dancing to be a reprehensible relaxation under certain conditions. Have we not high scriptural authority for it? David danced before the ark; so did Miriam and Jephthah's daughter. Allusions are made to it as a legitimate expression of joyful emotion in various parts of the Sacred Writings. No, my dear young friend, it is not to the use, in moderation, but to the *abuse* of it that I direct my observations." (Here she looked very hard across the table at Rose.) "When it ministers to the vanity and absorbs the thoughts both beforehand and afterwards, it is never sufficiently to be reprehended."

The event that gave occasion to this peroration was a children's ball at the Tuileries, to which my father took Rose and me. Some fine ladies had made him promise to bring "his beautiful little girl," and so I was to accompany her, though much against my inclination. I was pale, and my eyes red in consequence of the little exercise I had taken lately, and my father declared he was "ashamed to be seen with such a white-faced fright," which I found to be perfectly true when he left me alone on the scarlet benches, and took Rose round to all his aristocratic friends. She soon became the centre of a knot of youthful partners; two of the young princes danced with her, and the queen herself complimented my father on his beautiful child. I watched her for some time with pride, and I think I may say without the smallest touch of envy; but I felt rather lonely and deserted, and

the ball seemed to me mighty dull, and that there were a
great many too many lights, which danced before my eyes,
until in spite of every effort I fell asleep.

It was my first and only experience in juvenile dissipation. There were other entertainments given for the youthful world of fashion, to some of which Rose went, but I ob-
stinately declined them all, returning to my books with even
greater assiduity than before. Whether wounded vanity
may not have been a better governess than Miss Lateward
in stimulating my exertions, I leave the reader to determine.
The pleasure Rose took in her little toilette arrangements
beforehand, and her excitement and garrulity afterwards,
joined to the impossibility of getting her to sit down to her
book the whole of the next day, caused Miss Lateward to
deliver herself of many a thorny didactic sentence like the
one I have quoted.

In May the Dacres returned to Paris. Emily's health
was improved, and they were to spend the summer in England. Our meeting was a very happy one. My aunt was
pleased to find the progress I had made in my studies,
though she was shocked to see how pale and thin I was
grown.

" She must have change of air," said my aunt, turning to
my mother.

The latter shook her head. " Impossible, my dear. Percival goes to London next week, on business " (a sigh), " and
we cannot afford to go to Anteuil as we did last year. There
is no hope for it. Indeed, as far as I am concerned, I prefer
our own apartment, when I can be *quiet*, you know, to the
trouble of going into strange houses, where one has n't one's
own things about one ; and then the children, and altogether — "

So my aunt determined that Rose and I, under Miss
Lateward's charge, should accompany her to Boulogne,
where she had been advised to take Emily for a few weeks

before returning home. My mother was delighted with the idea on all accounts. I was delighted to get anywhere away from the feverish streets in this hot spring time, and to be with my aunt. Rose was delighted with the idea of a change, and the prospect of Emily's society. Every one was well pleased, and an early day was named for our departure. Before that event, however, the family spirits experienced another unexpected " rise ; " though I was less elated in consequence of a little circumstance that preceded it.

My father had been more gloomy and preoccupied of late than I had ever seen him. He appeared now to avoid my aunt, and I suppose the salutary or restraining effect of her first visit had passed away, for he was out night after night, and when she was of our party he hardly ever even dined at home.

One morning my mother sent me into her bedroom to look for something in a wardrobe that stood near my father's dressing-room door. While I was yet in the middle of the room, I could hear his voice, through that door, speaking rapidly, and apparently with great earnestness. I approached the wardrobe and began my search. Another voice answered, and this time it was so clear and distinct that I could not avoid hearing whole sentences. The speaker was my aunt.

" Oblige me, Colonel Percival, by not alluding to the past. Let bygones *be* bygones, if you please — I did not come here to listen —— And the recollection, you cannot suppose is flattering or agreeable to me. We will return to the question of the present and the future, if you please. I ask you again, what is your position now ? and how have you kept your promise ? You are mistaken if you suppose I shall continue to supply you with the means of indulging your vicious habits. I was weak enough to believe you. I thought you were really anxious to lead a new life, and lift up your head amongst honest men. While your children have been almost wanting the necessaries of life, *how* has this money been applied? Percival, if you persist in this course you will bring down God's wrath upon you. Not alone will your family be reduced to beggary — far, far worse than that! The disgraceful, shameless life you are leading ——"

" Mary! — Lady Dacre, hear me! You do not know — I can explain ——"

" Stop, Percival! do not attempt to explain. *I know more than you are aware of*, I had nearly said *all*, but who can say they know all the sin and folly one man is capable of committing? Do not add to it by trying to deceive me further. I tell you frankly, I have lost all hope in you. I had the folly to nurture some, a few months back — worse than folly, as I now see, for you have sunk instead of risen since then. I pray God to bring you to a better sense, for He alone can do it — to make you amend your ways ere it be too late. Any words of mine must be weak and powerless, they were so in that ' long ago ' to which you have referred — doubly so, now. For you, therefore, individually, I will do nothing further. The consequences of your sins fall on your own head! Henceforward, what I do shall be for my poor sister and your children only. Your eldest girl, Rita ——"

But I had already heard too much. I had really not *intended* to listen: but the intense interest of that conversation, which came so clearly through the door in the excited voices of the speakers, had made me completely forget myself, and the fact that I was standing before the open wardrobe, motionless. The sound of my own name suddenly startled me into a recollection of the unworthy part I was playing; my brain throbbed, my cheek burned — I turned and fled from the room. I buried my head in my pillow. " Not alone will your family be reduced to beggary, far, far worse than that!" the words rang in my ears. I believe, were I to tell you all my thoughts, you would think them strange ones for a mere child, as I still was. But my childhood — if I can be said ever to have had one — was already gone from me. That blissful ignorance of self — that frank and joyous confidence in every thing around — that bounding exuberance of spirit that should belong, and can belong *only* to life's first Olympiad — these had withered in the damp and sunless atmosphere of our home, long, long ago; but now the shadow of the future, like a hand, seemed weighing on my brow. I had eaten of the tree of knowledge, and the fruit thereof was bitter: not alone in that hour, but in many a subsequent one, sharp and acid did the taste remain. There were moments, indeed, when I cared not for any thing or anybody; when, my heart turning as it were to stone, I said that out of that very material would I hew and set up a wall between the world and myself. But the next minute I remembered my true-hearted and noble aunt, towards whom I was beginning to feel all the enthusiastic love of a lower nature for a loftier one, with which it can, nevertheless, sympathize; and a better frame of mind came, though something of this indurating quality, perhaps, characterized me thenceforward.

The door of my father's dressing-room remained closed until dinner-time, when he came out, scrupulously dressed, and in uncommonly brilliant spirits. He dined at home, and my aunt was there; and I could perceive no trace of that agitating interview in the manner of either. My mother, too, seemed so happy and tranquil, that I began to wonder whether it were possible that I had dreampt it all. Presently my father called Ernest to him, and asked him whether he shouldn't like very much to go to a big school in England — lots of boys, and plenty of fun? Ernest responded by taking a somersault (such as he had seen lately at Franconi's, and had been practising ever since), and alighted with his head on the fender. The pain, I am sure, must have been great; but, under the circumstances, Ernest would have died sooner than utter a sound: so as soon as the commotion caused by this little incident had passed away, my father proceeded to explain that he intended taking him over to England with him in a few days: his aunt had been kind enough to find a school, where he would be very happy, and where she could occasionally come and see him; and his long holidays he should certainly spend at home. The boy was wild with delight, and very nearly performed another acrobatic feat, but recollections of the last restrained him. Home had, indeed, long been too tame for his high spirit; he had no companions of his own age and strength, and lorded it over his little twin-brothers and Rose, and such of the household as would submit to his authority, like a true tyrant as he was. Among the number I never enrolled myself. The contest between us was often renewed; on his side physical strength (not unfrequently a word or a blow), on mine the weight of nearly three years' seniority, an obstinacy fully equal to his own, and the set-off of a manner far beyond my age, which especially irritated him, for, as he said, "that girl, Rita, gives herself the airs of a grown-up woman!" And yet I loved him; only it was somewhat as I might have loved a pet young tiger, of whom, even in its most sportive moments, one may be supposed to feel some latent mistrust and apprehension. We had latterly been the best friends; our dominions, since the arrival of Miss Lateward, were separated: he went to his daily school and I saw little of him; my father often making him his companion at times and places when he would certainly have been better elsewhere. I felt, therefore, in common with the rest of the family, rejoiced at the idea of his leaving home; where, from having his own way, and with the force of bad example, he must soon be completely spoilt.

"It is high time," — Betsy is the speaker — "that Master Hernest should 'ave some manners-like, and 'havior put into him."

"He is almost getting too much for me," sighed my mother, over a pair of rent garments, and wondered who there would be to mend them for him at school.

We left Paris three days afterwards. My father and Ernest were to start for England the following week; thus my mother would be left alone with the twins; but when I pointed this out to her, she assured me that she considered it quite a holiday, and looked forward to this season of respite as much as we did to our sea-side trip. So we kissed her, without more repining, and as our carriage rolled away, my father took off his hat with a most gentlemanlike grace, which Ernest imitated; then my father stretched his arms and lit a cigar, which as Ernest could n't imitate, and found his hands in his way, he began pelting a vendor of lemonade and *gauffres*. And this was the last thing I saw, my head strained out of window, as the carriage turned a corner.

Instead of one, we spent three very happy months at Boulogne. I cannot refrain from lingering over this portion of my early life, for many years were to elapse before I again enjoyed so wise and peaceful and happy an existence, as far removed from "that unrest which men miscall delight," as our walks on the ribbed sea-sand from the hot pavements of the noisy city. Here, too, I learnt more of the depth and loftiness of my aunt's noble character, which was, in reality, known to so few, even of her own family, though all felt its influence; like those mountaintarns, enveloped in cold mists, that only descend by secret channels to refresh the plains below. Her wisdom was of a nature that has been admirably described by a modern writer as "that exercise of the reason into which the heart enters, a structure of the understanding rising out of the moral and spiritual nature;" her knowledge was an intuition, enlarged by suffering and experience. So penetrating an insight into the minds of others I have never since met in any woman. Her opinions were sometimes severe; but it was the expression of a mind which had no sympathy with the little and common-place, and expected, perhaps, too much from poor erring human nature. In proportion to my knowledge of her grew the influence she exercised over me. I wondered that I should ever have felt repulsed at her cold manner; they seemed to me a part of her; I would not have exchanged them for the warmth of more impulsive natures. I had felt the heat of the inward fire, and knew that the spirit burned no less brightly for all the lamp that held it was of alabaster.

Lady Dacre had a strong memory and affection for the lays of that border-minstrelsy, among which she had lived so long in her northern home; and she fostered in me a love of these fine, soul-stirring old ballads, full of chivalry and elevation of sentiment. My delight, when we walked out upon the distant pier, was to get her to repeat one of these, or some of the proud passages in her family history — gallant sieges and defences, rescues, and the like — while the echo of our feet over the hollow wood seemed to me like the tramp of warhorses in battle. With what pride did she warm in the recital! Sometimes, in a fervor of enthusiasm, I longed to have been a man, and to have lived and fought in those days; and then my aunt would say, gravely, "Ah! dear child, you will learn that life has still its battles for every one of us, and harder to be won than these!" But I was not always in so belligerent a frame of mind. As we sat on the sand of an evening, and watched the sun dip down into the sea, scarcely one ripple on the water and not a cloud upon the red-gold sky, I said:

"A fisherman's life, aunt, must be a pleasant one, with his cottage on the shore, watching the beautiful sunrise and sunset in the sea. After all, I think I should like to be a fisherman as well as any thing."

"Have you thought of the long, cold, hungry days,

watching for fish that won't come to your net? — the stormy nights at sea, Rita? You must take the fisherman's hard life, with his sunsets and his cottage on the shore."

"Oh! I couldn't bear the *sea*. You know how sick I was the other day, aunt. I was only thinking how delightful the repose of this scene is, after crowded streets, and all the bustle of a town."

"There is no such thing as *repose* in this life, Rita; you must not expect it. The street is a better type of life than this quiet shore — an earnest struggle forwards."

"And yet are there not many very peaceful, quiet lives?"

"Not without their round of toils and duties. Small it may be, but without them no one can be happy, for they are not doing the work they were appointed here to do. Rest — that is inaction, is *decay*. We are always either going forwards or backwards; we cannot remain as we *are*. Remember this. Even the world we live in is always changing — passing from one state to another, beside revolving, as you know, daily on its axis, and making its annual course round the sun. That sun, itself, which we are apt to consider stationary, astronomers tell us is now advancing on a vast journey, in which the earth and her sister planets must accompany him; in short, all the heavenly bodies are incessantly in motion, and none are at rest. It is so with our lives. Do you think we are the only creatures God has put into this fair world to do nothing? With our minds, or with our hands, we must all of us work, some more, some less; otherwise we sink below the condition of the brutes of the field."

It was always this same note she rang. Whether her tale was of the past or the present; of the knightly arm wielding its battleaxe, or the peasant's at his plough; statesmen in their closets, women at their looms — the oldest and the youngest, the richest and the poorest — one note for all: that man should live by the sweat of his brow, and that this earth is not our abiding place.

Rose and Emily seldom took part in, or indeed listened to, these conversations. They were generally a few paces behind us, with their arms entwined, and making a very pretty picture, as some of the Boulognese young gentlemen seemed to think, from the remarkable frequency with which we met the same faces, go in which direction we would. Rose certainly did not love my aunt as I did, and the latter, on the other hand, was rather severe on my sister's innocent love of dress — at least, I thought so then, and that she did not make sufficient allowance for the training she had had. Was it a merit in me, whom no one flattered or admired, that I cared little if my hair was out of curl with the sea air when we went out walking in our new pink bonnets on Sundays? And yet I had enough vanity in other ways, as my aunt well knew. But she looked to the future, I believe, and the danger of these frivolous tendencies being encouraged in Rose's position. On one occasion, when the latter had been suffering from violent headache, and was feverish, my aunt took a pair of scissors, and, with her own hands, cut off a quantity of the long golden hair that hung down her back. As far as the fever went, I do believe the remedy was worse than the disease, such a storm of tears and indignant reproaches as it entailed. She kept her bed for a whole day, and, like Rachel, refused to be comforted, nor did she for long afterwards forgive my aunt's "cruelty," as she termed it.

Those pleasant summer days, whose sunshine still remains with us, while their shadows have long since fleeted and are forgotten, came at last to rather a sudden close. The limit originally fixed for our visit was long since past, when a letter was put into my aunt's hands one morning which made her anxious to reach England, as soon as possible, she

said, and fixed her departure for the following day. She
was evidently preoccupied, uneasy, and spent the whole
morning, which was a very sad one for us, in close colloquy
with Miss Lateward. This may have had reference to us,
and to our education, for in the evening she said :

"I have asked Miss Lateward, on your return to Paris,
to procure for you a good drawing-master, Rita. I always
intended you should have one, for you have a decided talent,
which it is right you should cultivate. Besides, you really
deserve this little reward for your hard work at more
important studies, of which Miss Lateward gives such a
good report. Write to me regularly and constantly, my
child, and never be afraid of telling me the most trivial
things. Letters are always the most valuable when they
are true reflections of the writer's life and mind. Do not
try to write clever letters, or amusing letters, or any thing
but the simple transcript of what is going on in you and
around you — as much of yourself, in short, as you can give
me. Above all, in any difficulty from within, or from
without, write to me at once, fully and openly. If I can
serve you in no other way, you may at least depend on
having my best counsel."

But it was evident that matters of moment weighed on
my aunt's mind, and this threw an additional gloom upon
our parting, which was effected with many choking tears on
my part, and many a kind word on hers. She held out no
hope of a return. Nothing but Emily's health would bring
her abroad again ; but some future year I should come over
and pay her a visit in England. And so we parted. The
bell rang, and the boiler began to spit out its indignant
steam at us, and we had only time to run across the plank
back upon the crowded quay before it was withdrawn, and
the faces we loved upon deck began to glide away, slowly —
slowly — from our tearful eyes. We ran down the pier,
and waved our wet handkerchiefs as long as the steamer

was in sight; and when the smoke had faded quite away, and our straining sight could no longer distinguish it from the foggy cliffs of old England, we turned back with heavy hearts to the diligence-office, and took our places for Paris.

CHAPTER V.

I SHALL pass over the next three or four years in almost as many pages. Should any middle-aged critic (the young and the old will be more lenient) feel disposed to resent the unreasonable time I have detained him over these recollections of my childhood, I can but humbly beg his pardon. I know beforehand all he would say of " that puerile affectation which authors now adopt of describing minutely every event that happened in the hero's or heroine's nursery." He will refer me to many admirable works, in which the ladies and gentlemen step from the author's brain, Minerva-like, upon the scene, full dressed, and ready for action; models, in their several ways, well-developed and ever sufficient for the exigencies of the situation. Alas! my dear sir, I am nothing of the kind. That is my excuse for noting down, as memory serves, the small events that seem to have influenced in a great measure all my subsequent life.

On our return to Paris, we found our mother in bed, ill and miserable. The secret cause of this I was far from guessing, but it oozed out some days afterwards in an unguarded moment. My father was in trouble again. He was in a place they called the " King's Bench," in England —no uncomfortable seat, one would have thought; but his being there was evidently a calamity. Long letters arrived, and I heard my aunt's name more than once in the conversations that passed between my mother and Miss Lateward. The latter never abused the dangerous post of a confidante, to which she was now raised; her good sense and prudence made her a valuable friend to my mother, which she remained, from this time forwards. I had written to my aunt more than once, and was a little mortified at these epistolary compositions, upon which I had spent considerable time and labor, remaining unacknowledged, save by a message at the end of one of her letters to my mother: "Thank Rita for hers. The style is better than the orthography. *Apartment* is spelt, in English, with one *p*, and *fulfil*, with two *l*'s, and not four. I am much too busy, as you know, to write to her just at present, but hope to do so before long."

At last, it came out that Lady Dacre had once more paid my father's debts; and after endless trouble with law and lawyers, had got him liberated. A month or two later, he returned; my aunt's name was never mentioned by him, but, for a time, things went on better. The winter passed, bringing its storms and rains and intermittent sun-gleams, in our inner world, as in the world without. My mother's health was evidently much shattered, and in proportion as she became incapacitated from superintending the domestic arrangements, I began to assume a more prominent position in the household. Those insignia of office, the keys, were transmitted to me; I ordered dinner; I came into personal contact with butchers and bakers; and, in course of time, I had to devise humiliating subterfuges for deferring payments long since due, and for keeping clamorous creditors in tolerable humor. Before the year was out, I had but too much ground for fearing that my father's affairs were again deeply involved. The applications I was obliged to make for money to meet the most pressing bills were generally fruitless. Occasionally, if I chose a lucky morning, and found him in good spirits, his dressing-table strewed with loose notes and silver, he would toss me one of the former, with a recommendation to make it go as far as I could. A strange sensation it was, for a girl of fourteen, the relief I felt at such a moment, as I snatched up the money, and hurried out of the room! I had, fortunately, very buoyant

spirits; and for the many miserable hours I spent, enjoyed
some of true and lively pleasure. My drawing-lesson was
always sure to bring me one. It was proper "high art;"
not the glazed card and B. B. pencil style of thing, but
casts of hands and feet, anatomical sketches, and sections;
until at last, in a proud moment, I was promoted to the bust
itself, helmeted and Hyperion-locked. These progressive
studies had one drawback. The history of Rome began to
be illustrated all over with my conceptions of its heroes;
there every variety of the Roman nose was to be seen, and
was seen by Miss Lateward, to that lady's just indignation.
In vain she called the practice "vulgar and unladylike."
Sometimes, as I yawned over Cæsar, dying with decent
dignity, it was irresistible to try and portray his venerable
head, bowed beneath the folds of the toga. This was one of
the few causes of serious complaint my good governess ever
made against me. In other respects, I was an exemplary
pupil, and began to assist her in teaching my little brothers.

I very rarely saw the General now, or Madame. Every
Sunday afternoon, however, I made a point of paying them
a visit, as well as old Barac. It was as great a deprivation
to the latter as to myself that my visits to his den were now
so few and rare; but I was no longer a neglected child whose
time was at her own disposal. On the Jour de l'An he sent
me a box of oil-colors and brushes, and, to my satisfaction,
a few months later, I was able to present him with the first
fruits of his present in a tolerable copy of a favorite little
picture of his, which, after years of repose by his mantelpiece,
with a green curtain over it, had found a purchaser, and was
going to adorn some brilliant boudoir in the Faubourg. I
had a double satisfaction, therefore, in replacing, however
inadequately, the old man's departing Penates, for such it
almost seemed from long association. I carried it myself
(under protest from Miss Lateward against a "young lady's
infringing the usages of society in so marked a manner as to

pay visits to unmarried gentlemen "), and I remember distinctly the pleasurable excitement, and the full beating of my heart as I stood and tapped gently at the battered face of the door, from which the paint was torn and blistered. There was a murmur of voices within — then I thought I would go away; but remembering I might not have a few spare minutes again that day, I gathered courage, and knocked yet louder. The old Jew greeted me warmly.

"Mein Gott! Mees Marguerite! come in. Not often I see you now. The leetle 'mädchen' has grown out fine young lady. Comes no more for to draw in de old man's room. I have new tings — etwas wunderschönes — take a stool, liebes Fräulein, and see." Whereupon he dusted a chair with his pocket-handkerchief, and offered it to me.

There was a heavy, black-bearded man standing in the centre of the room, his hands thrust behind his coat-tails, in a contemplative manner, his eyes fixed upon a picture that rested against a chair in the window, when the light fell on it to the best advantage. The amount of jewelry which this person carried about him was dazzling. Chains and rings of Newgate dimensions hung over a velvet waistcoat embroidered in rosebuds, and sparkled upon very dirty hands. The expression of his features was as anomalous as the rest of his appearance. Eyes sharp and cunning as a fox's; a low, receding brow, balanced by a full, hood-tempered mouth, lined with white, fierce-looking teeth; manner at once shrewd, familiar, obsequious; language (in every tongue, I subsequently learnt) more fluent than accurate, so that his nation was always an unsolved problem, except inasmuch as he was of Hebrew persuasion.

This was the great Ismael, agent to the Emperor of all the Russias, dealer in pictures, and in objects of vertù, "doer of bills," performer of any kind and quantity of dirty-work for great men, and of some acts of kindness, in extremity, to small ones. Do not forget the last: it is held to be an impossibility in his class. Though of the same trade" as Barac, that they *did* "agree," in contradiction to the popular adage, probably arose from the fact that there was a difference in their ostensible position in the world, and that their interests did not clash. Monsieur Barac, as I have already said, was by way of being "a gentleman." His buyings and sellings were all under the rose. You were not supposed to know how the pictures came upon his walls, or where they suddenly disappeared — the truth being that his was a sort of secret repository for the great world-known dealers, such as Ismael, whom I now found closeted with him.

" What is this here?" exclaimed Monsieur Barac, as he took the picture I placed in his hand — "copy of my Isabey? Lieber Gott! Miss Marguerite, why, is this your doing? Capital! I had no idea — but then it is many months that I your work have not seen. Ah! mees, you will for to be one Elizabetta Sirani, or Angelica Kaufmann, some day."

" I am so glad you don't think my copy very bad, Monsieur Barac, because I did it for you."

" My dear little mees, I thank you. It will be one veritable treasure, and I will value it as the orange of my eye" (a variation of the Eastern hyperbole well suited to the organ in question).

" Sagen sie mal, Ismael, ist es nicht eine vortreffliche copie? The young lady is daughter to Colonel Percival, up there, whom you know."

" Sans doute, je le connais ce pon colonel," said the other, with a singular expression of face, as he approached and took my picture out of Barac's hand. " Brava! je fous en fais mes complimens, mam'selle. I have de plaisir to acquaint many ladies who paint demselves. Dere is Princesse Chiararosso, one vast amiable lady, wid a fine talent after nature, and your compatriote, Lady Waterloo, also; but, barole d'honneur, I have seen none at your years expose a more rich sensibility for art. Dis sea here is zo clear and zo good color as you may see de fishes a sporting almost underneat. Ah! pity you not have to study as artiste, instead of peing porn in de luxury." (Was it my fancy, or was there an expression of mockery in his eye as he said this?) "You would make fortune if you were like dat poor deffle whom I gif to copy 'La Pelle Jardinière' for Prince Doppledorff — entre nous — pure charity. He cannot draw zo well dan dis. No warm — no color; his eye not full of juices like yours."

I thanked him, with a smile; and feeling that I had intruded long enough on old Barac's time, as he was evidently "doing business" with Ismael, under pretext of a friendly chat, I was preparing to leave the room, when the latter exclaimed,

"Bermit me, Mamzelle, to offer my cart. If never, zome day you should turn *artiste* —" Here he broke into a smile that showed all the fierce teeth, and, with an elaborate bow, placed in my hand a glazed card, on which the name and address of Felicien Ismael lay embedded in a labyrinth of flourishes, conceived in the boldest style of ornamental printing. The curl of the F swept all round the word, till its convolutions terminated in a griffin's head; and the tail of the L kept up a balancing movement, of a serpentine nature, at the other end. Is there not character in a visiting-card? I have thought so, and held certain theories of my own on the subject ever since I beheld the one in question. Now that the public is satiated with its interpreters of caligraphy, why does no "professor of *cartography*" advertise in the *Times?* I throw out the suggestion to any needy gentlewoman.

As I bowed to the jewelled waistcoat and left the room, I caught, through the closing door, "Diable, Barac, mais elle sera pelle, cette petite."

It was probably about nine months after the circumstance just related — I was just sixteen — when I was called out of the room one morning to speak to a man, whom my father, as usual, finding he was a tradesman, would not see. The man, I was told, refused to leave the house without speaking to some member of the family, and as Betsy announced her conviction that he would stand there " all the blessed day, he do look so dogged-like," and, further, that he was " English — somethink of the groom," I determined to see him ; not without a dim hope that there might be some mistake.

I found, as Betsy had indicated, a broad, sandy-haired, obstinate English face, and a pair of brown cloth gaiters, accompanied by a strong smell of the stables.

" You cannot see Colonel Percival. He is not out of his room ; but I am his daughter and can tell him any thing you have to say."

" Not much use a-*saying* anythink, I suppose ; only I jist come to tell the Colonel as I 'm not agoing to stand it any longer. I 'm a poor man, 'ard up for the money. My bill 's of near two years standing. So long as he kep' to me, I couldn't do no more than ax him to pay some part of it on account. which I did, scores of times — no use. And now he 's taken to ridin' an 'orse of Smith's, in the *Havenou Noully*, because *mine* ain't good enough, p'rhaps, and 'ow is a poor man to — ? "

" Stop ! are you not mistaking some other person for my father ? He seldom rides ; when he does a friend lends him a horse."

" Ho, miss ! there ain't no mistake unfort'nately. 'As n't the Colonel been to my stable 'is self ? and 'ave n't I led the 'orses, him and the Countess's, up and down the street there, a-waitin' for 'em, and tuk the 'orses agin when they come back, over and over agin, miss ? Besides, I suppose you know the Colonel's writin'. I 've got a 'alf-dozen orders, signed with 'is name. After a bit, when I see he were so shy of payin', I kep' some on 'em." And he pulled out of his pocket a soiled and crumpled paper, the handwriting upon which I only recognized too well.

"What is the amount of your bill?"

"Four hundred and twenty francs." (Poor mother! and you were ill and wanting so many necessary comforts!) "I've been served the like trick by so many *gen'lemen* — calls themselves sich — and some on 'em has been and cut; and now I'm gettin' a bit sharper, and," he continued, in a louder voice, and thumping his fist down on the table, "I'm not agoin' to be done out of my money, and so you may tell the Colonel; and as I see 'e don't intend to pay me if 'e can 'elp it, why I'll jist see if I can't make 'im."

"Wait!" said I, hurriedly, and alarmed at the idea of more law, "pray wait, do nothing until — until I can see my father. If this debt is just and right I am sure he will pay you — but have a little patience."

I spoke with a confidence I was far from feeling, which probably the man guessed, for he rejoined, with a determined shake of the head, as he stuffed his hands far down into his breeches pockets, "Very well, miss, then if *you* please, I'll just wait till you *can* see the Colonel, and 'ear what 'e says, and then I can act according*ly*. I pre:fer waitin', if *you* please."

Seeing that the man was resolved, there was nothing for it but to hazard an interview with my father, and try and induce him to pay some part of the bill, which I could no longer doubt was a just one. I knocked at his door.

"May I come in, papa?"

"What the deuce do you want? I'm busy."

"I want to speak to you particularly." Here I opened the door ajar.

"Well, come in, and make haste."

I entered; my father was seated with a cup of chocolate, a cigar, and *Galignani's Messenger*, between which his attention seemed equally divided. The table was covered with bills and papers. Among these, my eye rested more than once in the course of the interview on a letter directed in a small, foreign hand, "A Monsieur Edouard Brown." It made an impression on me — perhaps from the combination of a French with an English name — and I found myself unconsciously repeating them over several times that day. I laid the bill before my father.

"There is a man outside who insists upon seeing you, or having an answer about this bill. He is very importunate for the money. He —"

"D—n his importunity; he's an infernal cheat. He knows he can't prove a single item. If he'd brought in a decent bill, perhaps I might have paid him. Last June twelvemonth! The scoundrel! How am I to remember so far back? Why didn't he bring in his bill before, I should like to know? Not had a horse from him for months; horrid screws they were too."

"He says he asked you for the money very often, but that he did not think of insisting on the payment of it until you gave up dealing with him some short time back."

"Confound these blackguards! they really are too cool — so ungrateful, too, after my having patronized and recommended him! *Insist!* What can he prove? not one quarter of this bill, I am sure."

"You do not deny that *some* of it is just?"

"Well — perhaps — 'pon my life, at this distance of time —"

"It is immaterial. *Fortunately* — for the man — he has orders in your hand, to show that these horses *were* for you. Now, I am very sure, from his determined manner, that he will go to law, and spare no means of making you pay this bill. Is it not better to pay, at least, a part of it? Don't let me aggravate him, by sending him away without a hope of getting any thing."

"I know something more of French law than he does, I

suspect. He can't produce more than three or four orders in my hand. The court will ask him why he didn't sue me for his rascally bill a year ago. They always take one's part against the *canaille*. It won't be the first time I have known them to do so. Tell the fellow to wait, and not to bother me, and some day I shall pay him."

" What, even for what you say you do not owe ? "

" Eh ? Well, it is more than the fellow deserves ; but as to paying him now, it is out of the question ; I haven't got it, and so you may tell him ; and I really cannot be bothered in this way. But if he remains quiet I'll recommend him, I really will, and he knows I have got him lots of custom already."

I checked the suggestion which rose to my lips, that these recommendations might have proved but doubtful benefits. My father took up the *Galignani* and I left the room in silence. What was to be done ?

I sat down in the drawing-room, to think what I could say to the man. It was extraordinary how my father, with his worldly experience, should be so short-sighted — should blind himself in this way to immediate consequences. Careless for the morrow, it seemed sufficient for him that he should elude the difficulties of the day any how. As to the dishonesty of such conduct, of course I did not expect him to consider *that.*

But the business was pressing ; something must be done. I had not a five-franc piece in my possession. To apply to my poor mother was worse than useless ; it was to cause her additional anxiety and agitation. On the other hand, to send the man away exasperated, to carry his threat into execution, seemed madness — any thing rather than that. Suddenly an idea flashed across me. "Absurd! Well! I can but try ;" and I started up. I did not stop to consider the feasibility of the plan, but ran into the next room, with my cheeks very red, gasping out —

"Will you wait for a few hours? I promise that a part of your money, at least, shall be paid this evening. You will trust me?"

The man, who was evidently prepared for a very different answer, looked astonished, but finally consented to return again at six o'clock.

As soon as he was gone, I called Betsy, desired her to put on her bonnet, and come out with me immediately. So unusual a proceeding, as we never walked but in a family phalanx headed by Miss Lateward, called for remonstrance.

"Why, law, Miss Rita, you ain't a-going by ourselves, sure*ly*?"

"And why not? I am not a child. I am old enough and plain enough to take care of myself; if you can't do the same I must take care of *you*, that is all, Betsy. So come" (in my most authoritative manner), "put on your bonnet directly, if you please, and don't say a word to anybody."

With some difficulty I got the little maid under weigh. I tied a thick veil over my bonnet, and, with a paper parcel under my arm, may have passed for one of those mysterious and all-powerful "assistants" of the female form, who are to be seen hurrying through the fashionable *quartiers* of Paris in the early morning. It was a hard frost. The sun had not yet thawed the ice in the gutters, and we scudded along the slippery streets, as fast as we could, until, emerging in the great thoroughfare, I slackened my pace as we approached a large shop, in the window of which were exhibited water-color sketches, heads in chalk and pastel, and two or three small oil pictures upon easels. A man was arranging these for the day and studying the general effect, as I entered. A second shopman "bearded like the pard," was at the counter; he looked up from the greasy novel over which he was lounging; but neither of them seemed to think it worth while to discontinue their occupations for the shabby-looking women who darkened the doorway. The man who was arranging pictures just looked over his shoulder and asked what I wanted, while I proceeded to untie my parcel with trembling hands.

" Here are two small pictures; I thought, perhaps — you would buy — I have seen such in your window, in passing, sir, and being anxious to sell these — "

" What do you want for them?" said the man, abruptly. At the same time he took them up and examined them attentively. I was afraid of saying less, and ashamed of saying more than the man might think them worth; so I adopted the diplomacy of true cowardice, and took refuge in silence.

" I will give you twenty francs each for them."

Twenty francs only! I could hardly restrain my tears. They were my last performances, on which my master had bestowed considerable praise, and I had expected, at least, a hundred francs. But it was not altogether disappointed vanity, for that horrid bill was uppermost in my mind; to which twenty francs was as a drop in the ocean. I began to wrap up my children again, indignantly.

" No, if that is all you will give, I will take them elsewhere; but I think they are worth as much as the daub on that easel, which I see marked a hundred and fifty francs."

" Possibly that is your opinion. Now, the gentleman who did that, wanted three hundred francs for it. Artists are not always the best judges of what their works are worth, mademoiselle."

" I shall take mine to some one I consider a better judge than you, sir."

" Come, mademoiselle, by way of encouragement, I don't care if I make it thirty francs — sixty for the pair; though it is really more than they are worth."

I hesitated. Time was precious; and as I revolved in my mind the impossibility of carrying my pictures about

Paris for sale, I reluctantly concluded what I knew to be a very bad bargain for me. As the man leant over and put the money into my hands, he looked into my face, and said, with an air of impudent familiarity,

"Je ne l'ai fait que pour l'amour de vos beaux yeux."

I was too angry to say any thing, and was leaving the shop without taking any further notice of the man, when he called out,

"Happy to see you, mademoiselle, when you have any thing else to bring us." And so terminated my first transaction in trade.

We walked rapidly and silently home; Betsy dumb with astonishment at the scene of which she had just been a spectator, until, as we reached our door, I turned to her and said,

"Remember, Betsy, not a word of this. I know I can trust you."

In the evening the liveryman came, and I gave him the sixty francs, saying I hoped he would be satisfied with that for the present. I was confident of being able to pay him the remainder, by instalments, in the course of two or three months.

"Call again this day fortnight and ask for me, not for my father, or any one but myself. I have kept my word with you this evening, so far as this small sum goes. You will continue to trust me, will you not?"

And the man did; saying in his rough, dogged way, that he didn't think I wished to cheat him, and that he would leave it in my hands, for the present.

It will be sufficiently obvious why I was anxious that my secret should be strictly kept. Miss Lateward was the only person whom I should have thought of consulting in the matter; and I knew, however much she might have approved of the intention, her rigid ideas would have been shocked at the manner of its execution; and her sense of propriety would have compelled her to make known the circumstance to my mother. That was the last thing I wished; unless, indeed, it was, that my father should become acquainted with the fact of his daughter's turning her talent to pecuniary profit. He would have regarded it as a disgrace, even though it were for the payment of his own debts. Therefore, acting on my own unassisted judgment, I determined to follow the course I had commenced that morning, until I should make up the sum required. I thought, at one moment, of writing to my aunt Mary, that ever faithful counsellor and friend; but a fear that she would reply by sending me the money herself, deterred me; for I blushed to think what a burden we had been to her; how she had paid my father's debts over and over again, and was now entirely educating us children. No; I would tell her all, and ask her advice for the future *after* I had followed my own, in this case; which was only doing what the world generally does.

Old Barac, who would have been of such material assistance to me, was unfortunately absent on a picture-hunting tour in Germany, and was not expected back for two or three months. I had no one I could ask to assist me in disposing of my pictures; and when, after several mornings' early rising, I had finished three small landscapes, I remembered with repugnance that I must undergo a repetition of the disagreeable interview I have described, or take them elsewhere. I went to two other shops, and found one of them more civil, but neither of them more liberal in their offers. I then returned to the first, sorry at heart, but firm and forbidding of aspect. My two former productions had disappeared. The man tried to have those I now brought on the same terms, but finally agreed to pay me ten francs more for each, which gave me an additional sum of eighty francs.

A few days after this, a young French girl, Cécile de

Beaucroi, whose aquaintance we had lately made, called with
her governess to ask me to walk with her. We were walking down the Rue ——, when, as we passed the drawing
shop I so well knew, I caught sight of two of my pictures,
upon easels, near the door. An idea suddenly struck me,
and I said, laughing,

"Cécile, do me a favor. Go into that shop, and ask
the price of two small pictures you will see facing you
— one with peasants and cows in the foreground — the
other, a towing-path, with a barge and horses — you can't
mistake it."

Cécile skipped into the shop, without paying any attention
to her governess's "Mais où allez-vous donc, mademoiselle?"
and before that lady's feeble mind had recovered from its
astonishment sufficiently to follow her, Cécile returned, shrugging her shoulders,

"Ma bourse est bien malade, chère petite, or I would buy
them for you; they are a hundred and fifty francs; the work
of a young artist, and only so *cheap*, the man says, on that
account, though I think them very dear."

"Ah! no doubt. I don't want to buy them," I replied,
with a kind of gloomy satisfaction; for though it was clear
the man was making a profit of seventy francs out of my
labor, it was also clear that the market value of that labor
was more than I had latterly brought myself to believe or
hope; and I determined to find some other method of turning it to the best account.

I was now engaged upon a more ambitious subject than I
had yet attempted, a Holy Family, the design of which
originated in a sketch of Rose and our two small brothers,
as they sat under the strong light of a lamp one evening,
Arthur on Rose's knee, and Roger nestled at her feet. My
sister had grown up suddenly to be almost a woman in appearance. She was fully an inch taller than I, and though
very slight, she had none of the awkwardness of a young

girl. It required very little to make her the Virgin of my imagination, and I was so much pleased with the sketch, that I went to work with immense ardor, though in fear and trembling, to paint my first composition in oils. It was a great proof of my improvement — though I did not then know it — the disgust I often felt, during the progress of this picture, at my own performance. I had regarded former productions with a complacency which now amazed and shocked me ; indeed, with a less powerful motive to continue my labor, I should probably have thrown aside the brushes altogether. At last, such as it was, the picture was finished ; and, after leaving it a day or two to dry, I proceeded boldly to carry into execution a resolution I had come to, after some deliberation. I had not forgotten Felicien Ismael : there lay his card, each time I opened my desk, staring me in the face, through the trellis of red tape that held my aunt's letters and a few other documents. I could not help seeing it ; and if I could not but remember the disagreeable impression his general manner and appearance had made on me, neither could I forget the favor with which he had regarded my first oil sketch, now nearly a year ago. Certainly, he was the best person to whom I could apply. There could be no harm in just taking him my picture. If I did not find him agreeable I need not return. I grew familiar with the idea ; arranged the interview in my own mind — what I should say, and what he would answer — until it seemed extraordinary I should not have thought of going to the Jew dealer in the first instance.

I could not hope to keep this visit a secret. Ismael lived in a distant part of Paris, and I knew I should be absent at least two hours, and must be missed by Miss Lateward at all events. I desired Rose, therefore, to inform that lady, upon her arrival (she only came at half-past nine), that "business of importance" had obliged me to go out, and that

I should not be home for some time. I laughed at Rose's look of wonderment, and refusing to gratify her curiosity about my "business of importance," I kissed her, and hurried out of the house with Betsy.

After three quarters of an hour's walk, we came to a narrow street, whose five-storied houses must have rendered the sun's daily visit but of short duration. The houses were large and handsome; had once been hotels of some of the old aristocracy; now the glory of their day was departed. Under the archway of one we entered, where sat, in eternal twilight, an old woman over a pan of charcoal, at an open glass door leading into a black hole, the air exuding from which was a heavy abomination, of which fried lard, cabbage-water and stale tobacco were by no means the worst ingredients.

" Is Monsieur Felicien Ismael at home ? "

" Up three pair of stairs — first door to the left — pull the string."

" Miss Rita, mum," said Betsy, as we ascended the great stone stairs, with the traces of gilding still upon the banisters, and of long-faded frescoes on the walls, " Miss Rita, mum, I have it on my conshins your coming to these strange outlandish kind of places. Wherever are we going now ? As long as you goes only to shops and in the open streets, and I don't say nothink, though I ain't clear in my mind *that's* right; but up these dark places, right away at the other hend of Paris, then into strange houses — we might be murdered and all, before —— "

I pulled the 'bell; its loud tingle drowned Betsy's remonstrance. But, to say the truth, I began to feel not quite so bold myself; and a certain nervousness in my manner did not escape the keen eyes of my little maid. A man, with strong Jewis'n features, opened the door. " Monsieur Ismael was engaged. What was my business ? Would I walk in and wait ?"

"I say, Miss Rita, *do* let us go back," says Betsy, *sotto voce*, pulling at my cloak.

I hesitated. No; I would go in, after coming so far, and wait a little, at all events. We were shown into a room literally filled with pictures, and with nothing else, save two or three threadbare satin chairs, on one of which I sat, while Betsy stood, transfixed with horror, gazing round her on the walls. I confess I was somewhat startled myself as I glanced at the pictures which decorated them. They were Venuses, more or less, by whatever denomination it might have pleased the painters to style them — "Susannas," "Eves," or "Lucretias." I knew enough of painting now to see that none of these were original, and few even good copies. The frames, however, were very gorgeous. There was a vile edition of Titian's famous Venus — that remarkably plain woman on a couch, whose attendants in the background are rummaging through a chest after some not-uncalled-for garment. The expression of Betsy's face, and her exclamation of horror, as she looked at this picture, was really comical, and made me laugh, though I seriously began to fear that Monsieur Ismael's taste was not for pure-looking virgins, plentifully clothed, such as I had to offer. Two or thee minutes elapsed, then a door creaked on its hinges, and the *portière* that hung over it was stirred. I could see no one, but guessed rightly that an inspection of us was taking place, for a moment after the portly form of Félicien Ismael, lustrous, jewelled, in a brocaded dressing-gown, emerged from the scarlet curtains and stood before me.

"Ha! ma betite demoiselle, is it you? I no forget your face — ravished to see you again. In what will you use me? Always your humble serviteur. Have de kindth to follow me. It makes cold in dis piece."

So saying, he ushered us into an adjoining room, which wore a far more comfortable air than the one we had left.

A large wood fire burnt in the chimney, before which the
remnants of the Jew's breakfast and his easy-chair were
drawn. A table with writing materials; a table covered
with snuff-boxes, enamels, rings, carved ivory, and valuable
rubbish of all kinds; a glass cabinet, occupying one end of
the room, and filled with rare china; several pictures,
smaller, better painted, and less exceptional in subject than
those I had already seen,—these caught my eye in the
hasty glance I gave round the apartment as we entered.
Ismael handed me a chair, and began at once, with a very
knowing grin :

"I tink I prophesied right, mademoiselle. You bring me
tableaux to dispose? And how is my gut friend, your papa
—gay and merry as ever? Dat is gut. Now, let us see.
Ha! original, I see—une Sainte Famille; and not after
de Raffael, nor de Corrège, but after the Nature, straight—
gut—var gut—capital! Vere find you de model for dat
head? Blein de grace. Je fous en fais mes complimens.
I tink I know one gentleman who like—bah! dat make
you noting. You want de monish, at once. How much?
You shakes de head—dat will say, 'Monsieur Ismael,
give me so much as you can afford.'" And the Jew
laughed while I signified my assent, and waited in trepidation to hear what he would give me. I was getting as
greedy for money as Ismael himself could be.

We all speak of people as we find them, not as they really
are, otherwise History must be rewritten. At the expense
of gratitude we should gain consistency, but whether the
exchange would be for the better I doubt. Imagine, for
instance, hearing a man say, 'So-and-so has been very kind
and generous to me, but, from all I hear, he must be one of
the greatest rascals unhung.'" Of Felicien Ismael, I speak
not from my after knowledge of his character, but as he
behaved then to a struggling, unfriended girl, generously
and kindly. His offer was more liberal than I had dared

hope, and the bargain being thus speedily concluded, I rose to depart.

"Will you for to see de gut picshur? I show you into number dree. Not every one is admit to number dree — ma ponne demoiselle. Number one chamber be for de old gentlemen what wants for to puy de grand historic tableaux for dere salles-à-manger. Noting too bad for dem. Here be number two, for dem what knows a little more, and tinks dey knows a great deal. Are dey satisfaits in number one, dey come not to number two. Vere I see dey really know the gut over de bat, den I opens number dree; but dat is var selten. Tiens! je fous mettrai au courant de tout cela!" and he opened a small door, over which hung a tapestry-curtain. We entered a much smaller room — indeed, hardly more than a closet — but filled with pictures, of which several stood on easels, and had curtains before them. Ismael drew back one, and bade me admire the Raffael it jealously protected. An exquisite little picture it was, and I remained lost in admiration before it for some minutes, during which the servant entered, and said something to his master in a low voice.

"Show him in here," said the latter aloud. "I have no mystères from the gut young gentleman. Make him for to come in here."

My back was to the door, so that I could not see the person who entered, while Betsy, in a strongly objective attitude, took up a position beside me, scowling at Raffael, scowling at Ismael, scowling at the new-comer.

"Good morning, Ismael. I came to speak to you about that Ghirlandajo for my uncle. What have you done about it? He is afraid of its escaping him, and says you are to secure it on the best terms you can."

"Tank your var gut uncle for de confidence he place in me. He know me — dat I always does de ting —"

"Yes, yes; he knows all that. Now about that Majolica

you were speaking of the other day. Some of the Guas-
tagni family, I think you said, wanted to part with it. My
mother is very fond of China, and if this is really good, as
I am going over to England next week, I would take it.
But how many plates are there? and what are they likely
to cost? I am not like my uncle, you know, Ismael, who
doesn't care what he gives for these things — so you must
find out for me first."

"I have procurated dis to show you for specimen, my
gut sar. *Véritable* Maestro Giorgio, you see — dere be his
mark." And, he reversed a dish that stood on the table:
whereupon the two fell into a discussion as to its merits,
which, not understanding much of, I suddenly recollected
that the business which brought me had been concluded
some time, and that I had no longer any excuse for being
here. I turned round, but felt shy of interrupting the
learned disquisition on clays. The stranger was a young
man, above the middle height, with very remarkable eyes,
and a brow upon which the light fell broadly and evenly.
Otherwise, he struck me as rather the reverse of handsome;
but certainly not common-place-looking; a head to single
out and remember from a crowd.

" Good morning, Monsieur Ismael," said I, moving
towards the door; " don't let me disturb you — good
morning."

"Ah! ma betite demoiselle! You no leave, sans foir de
Corrège, et tous mes trésors? You not see noting —"

" I must go, indeed. I am sure you have a great many
things I should like to see but I cannot stay ; I ought to be
at home. Be kind enough," I added, in a low voice, as he
held open the door, " not to mention my name — *you understand.*"

My eyes for an instant met those of the stranger, and I
was struck with their very peculiar expression. Whether
he had heard, or guessed what I had said, I know not. A

minute afterwards I was in the street, feeling lighter at
heart than I had done for many a long day.

But my morning's adventures were not over. There was
a curiosity-shop at the corner of a narrow street that lay in
our way home. I stopped for a moment at the door, at-
tracted by the picturesque effect of armor and old lace,
carved oak and Venice glass, grouped together in studied
confusion — one of the haunts of artists and lovers of *bric-à
brac*, so common in Paris. Suddenly I remained transfixed
by a face within. I could not move or take my eyes from
it. Not that it was beautiful — at least it was a very faded
beauty — but so intensely wretched, so expressive of the
deepest heart-misery, that neither before or since have I
ever seen a face that so powerfully told its tale. It belonged to a young woman, shabbily dressed in black, who
was addressing the ill-favored old dame at the counter ; nor
was it difficult to gather that the former was endeavoring
to dispose of some singular-shaped vases she held in her
hand.

"Bah!" said the old woman, "see, they are cracked!
And as to their being real Bernard de Palissy, I don't believe
it. It may be or may not — my husband would know, but
he is not at home. If you like it, I will give you twenty
francs, or you can leave them and call again."

"But, mon Dieu! I must have the money at once, or it
will be too late, and they are worth fifty francs each, at least.
madame, perhaps much more, but I would not part with them
for any money, if I were not in such distress. Indeed,
madame, it is the truth. I have kept them to the last, and
now —"

"I have offered you all I can — you may take it or not,"
said the woman, brutally. Then turning to me, as I stood
upon the threshold, already half in the shop, "Is there any
thing I can show you, mademoiselle?"

"Ah! young lady," said the woman in black, clasping

her hands suddenly, "have pity on an unfortunate woman.
You are young and happy — may you never know such
misery as mine. My child is dying, and I have no money.
Buy my beautiful vases of me. I have kept them through
all these years, for my mother's sake, and only now —"

Here her voice was choked with sobs, and she sank upon
a chair, in a perfect convulsion of grief. I longed to slip into
her hand one of the gold pieces I had just received, but I
reflected that the money was not mine; that I must be just
before I could afford the luxury of benevolence; and I therefore did the only thing that occurred to me at the moment to
do. I wrote with a pencil, on the back of Ismael's card,
"The bearer, who is in distress, is sent to you by M. P."

"Go immediately to this address, and take the vases with
you. If the china is good, a person you will see there is sure
to give you a fair price for it. Show him this paper. If he
should not purchase it — where do you live?"

She put into my hand a card, on which was written,
"Marie Dumont, Brodeuse," and her face thanked me far
beyond words.

"You are a *brodeuse?* Perhaps I may be able to get you
some work; at all events, I will come and see you. Do not
despair. I am sure you will sell your vases, if they are what
you say."

The woman of the shop, who saw that she was losing a
good bargain, I suppose, here changed her tone, and struck
in with a bland voice,

"I am sure my husband will offer as much as any one, if
you will leave the vases, as I said, until —"

"No, no," cried the other impetuously, and seizing my
hand; "this young lady — God reward you, mademoiselle!
— I go at once." She took up the vases, and covering them
carefully with her shawl, "Whatever is the result, I shall
remember your kindness; and I believe now that God will
not desert me, since he has sent me one friend."

I watched her hurry down the street until she was out of
sight, and then walked rapidly home. Betsy was actually
frothing with indignation. The visit to the Jew was bad
enough, but this last little scene, which had passed in much
less time than I have taken to tell it, irritated her almost more.
She pronounced it to be the greatest ridic'lousness she ever
seed; moreover, that she did n't know what ever had come
over me, but I did now the queerest things any one ever *heerd*
tell of, with many other exordiums which I will spare the
reader.

"Betsy," said I, turning to her at last, "choose how I am
to behave in future towards you. If you wish to retain my
confidence, you must be faithful, silent, and obedient; but
I warn you, you will find me doing many things you don't
approve of. Is it to be war or peace between us? Shall I
bring Fanchette the *bonne* with me next time?"

The little woman's eyes filled with tears, and she was
silent the remainder of the way home.

CHAPTER VI.

I found Miss Lateward seated, like Urania, before her globe in the school-room; and her greeting had something of the lofty solemnity that might have belonged to that goddess. I took hold of both her hands.

"You are, of course, surprised, dear Miss Lateward, at my having gone out for the whole morning, without letting you know, and with only Betsy. You will expect to hear where I have been, and demand a promise of me not to repeat the offence. Well, I will tell you as much as I can, and promise nothing, until you have heard me fairly. On the other hand, your telling papa and mamma will do no good, but a great deal of harm, as you will judge."

Thereupon, I related as much of the whole affair, from the commencement, as was necessary for the right understanding of my conduct; informing her of my unsuccessful attempts to obtain money from my father, which part of the story evidently caused Miss Lateward no surprise. It was the part *I* had played throughout which puzzled her. She had not *envisagéd* the position, as the French say. It was a new and almost unexampled one. What was the right thing to be said? She cleared her throat, and hardly knew how to begin.

"Really, I am a good deal surprised — a good deal," she said, at last. "This is a most extraordinary step. I cannot but honor your motives, Marguerite, which are laudable; yet I should be but ill performing my duty, did I fail to point out to what unpleasant, nay, dangerous consequences, a repetition of such conduct might lead. You say you are no longer a child — true; that is the more reason for being circumspect in your behavior. This Jew *may* be a respectable character — far be it from me to say he is *not* — only, really, *you* can know nothing of him. And just imagine, now, any one by chance seeing you there in his house, it would have a very odd effect." (I was so glad now I had not mentioned the stranger at Ismael's.) "If any one recognized you as Colonel Percival's daughter, he would think it very strange, to say the least. The world is not lenient in its judgments, my young friend. The purest actions are often misinterpreted. Then, as regards the fact of your disposing of your paintings unknown to your parents, it is not what many persons would approve of, certainly. Still, the circumstances are peculiar, and I only advise your asking Lady Daere's opinion. If you have her sanction, I can say nothing; but until then, I must desire that you will not repeat these clandestine visits, under pain of my revealing the whole circumstance to Mrs. Percival."

"I promise the more readily, that I hope there may be no further necessity for them. The sum I received this morning very nearly clears this odious livery-stable bill. There are only twenty francs left, and I hope no more bills may come in."

"If there are, we must devise other means of meeting the difficulty, until you hear from you aunt, at all events." And my good governess, putting her hand into her leather reticule, drew from it twenty francs, and laid them on the table. "There, my love, say nothing about it to any one: it will make your mind easy for the present, and at some future time you will repay me. I have no need for the money, I assure you, and I greatly prefer employing it in aiding you to do an honest action."

And so I kissed her, which I very rarely did, and sat down once again as the child before my good governess, the

old respect and esteem having warmed within me into something more, in those few minutes.

I said to my mother that afternoon, " May I take some of
that jelly you had made yesterday to a poor woman whose
child is ill ? "

" Ill ! why, good gracious, my dear, where did you hear
of her ? I never see any poor people about ; those things
are so well managed here. Her child ill did you say ? Poor
thing ! have you seen her ? "

" Yes, this morning, and I promised to go and visit her.
She is a *brodeuse*, and I have been up to Madame Gobemouche, who has given me some work for her. May I take
her the jelly ? "

" Oh ! certainly ; do. dear ; only I hope there is no chance
of fever or any thing of that kind — smallpox, you know —
I have a horror of it ; and then for Rose and the boys, do
you think it is a clean place ? "

" I don't know, mamma, it may be very dirty ; but Aunt
Mary goes about among dirty cottages when she is at home,
and if one never goes into any but clean houses, it seems to
me one can know very little about the poor. There are
plenty here, only they are kept out of sight."

" Ah ! well, that may be true, but in the country, you
know, it is a different sort of thing ; poking about in that
way, into all sorts of places, in a town where no one knows
who you are, doesn't do. But I suppose there *is* a good
deal of distress here, after all. I remember," she added,
thoughtfully, " the bishop used to have a charity sermon,
every now and then, for the poor of Paris, but I never heard
of any one going about to visit them. I don't think it is the
thing. I don't think it is done, really."

" Miss Lateward will go with me," said I, not noticing the
last observation, but adroitly taking the question for granted ;
" you have such confidence in her, mamma."

" Oh, yes, a most excellent person. I really don't know

what we should do without her now." And so the conversation ended.

Miss Lateward and I found out, with some difficulty, the address Marie Dumont had given. She lived in a narrow court, and on the sixth floor of a large house, the walls of which had a peeled, scorbutic look, with large slops of water on the stairs, and children in all states of *déshabille* swarming about the banisters. Pots of flowers were at several of the windows, and lines, with linen to dry, crossed the court, which was also pervaded by a general smell of ironing and vegetables.

Marie opened the door to us herself, and when she saw me, a bright smile lit up her pale features as she begged us to walk in.

"Mon Dieu! mademoiselle, how shall I ever thank you. Rather let me thank le bon Dieu for having sent you, in my distress, as His good angel. If I had not met you where should I be now? Ah, the vile woman, who wanted to cheat me, and to-morrow, or next day, with her twenty francs, I should have been as badly off as ever! And that good, noble gentleman has not only given a hundred and fifty francs for my vases, he has been here himself to see my child, and brought a doctor with him, and finding that the story I had told him was true, he has promised to come again, and says I shall not want for work."

"Indeed? Has Monsieur Ismael done all this? I am delighted; but in truth, Marie, I did not expect him to do more than buy your vases."

"It was not Monsieur Ismael, mademoiselle, but a tall, younger gentleman, who happened to be there when I was admitted to Monsieur Ismael after sending in your paper, and when they had seen my vases, the English gentleman — for I saw he was English — said he would buy them, and that Monsieur Ismael should name their price, and they talked for some time, and Monsieur Ismael said that if they were

not cracked they would be worth five hundred francs; as
they were, he would say a hundred, and *that* he would give
himself; whereupon the other said he would add fifty more,
for he was sure he could not get them for that money in a
shop, and so I came back a rich woman, and am now a happy
one too, for my boy is much better. The doctor gave him
some cooling draught, and, indeed, I believe he never was
as ill as I feared. Ah, mademoiselle, a mother's fears with
only one child, you will know them some day, only," she
added, with a peculiarly sad expression, "not as I have
known them. Will you see the little angel?" And she
took me up to a crib where a pale child of five years old
was lying fast asleep.

"He is a pretty boy, but he does not look strong."

"Yes, mademoiselle; the doctor says he wants nothing
now but good nourishment, and, thank God! I have money
enough to buy him plenty now. And since I know he
will live, *I* have strength to live also, and fight on," she
added, with a low sigh, as she stooped to kiss the boy's pale
brow.

"I have brought you some jelly, which I think the child
will like; also some work, which you can do at your leisure.
The lady for whom it is, is in no hurry, and we shall be calling to see you again before long."

"Thank you again, mademoiselle, for all your kindness.
I told the gentleman about my speaking to you, because of
your kind face; and how I was sure you would come, or
send, as you promised; and he listened to it all, mademoiselle, for he is not like these gentlemen generally, frivolous and wild, but has something serious and thoughtful,
which makes one able to say any thing to him. He promised to mention me to a lady, who would give me work, he
said, and to whom I am to apply if I am again in distress,
for he is leaving Paris shortly."

I was on the point of asking the gentleman's name, when

Miss Lateward, who had hitherto maintained a solemn silence, said, dryly,

"How was it you kept those china ornaments so long, if you were in such distress? Why did you not sell them before?"

"My old grandmother, who valued them more than any thing else, lived with me until she died, three months ago. I kept them for her sake as long as I could. They had come into her family years ago, through some descendant of the Palissys, and she kept them in all her poverty, and would sooner have starved, I believe, than have sold them."

"You have been living alone since then?" pursued Miss Lateward.

"Yes."

"I presume you are a widow — only this child?"

"Only this child — thank God!" and she burst into tears.

I was provoked with Miss Lateward for interrogating Marie in this way, and opening old wounds, so I hastened to say,

"You have found it hard work, no doubt, supporting yourself and child in this great city."

"The curé of the parish knows your case, I suppose?" persisted Miss Lateward, in the same impassible way. "If I apply to him, he will be able to certify to the truth of your statements?"

Marie stooped over the crib, as if to arrange the pillow, and her cheek flushed crimson, as she stood up, and said,

"Yes. Apply to him. He *will* certify to the truth of what I have told you; and though he will tell you somewhat else besides, if you are Christian women, as you profess to be —"

"*Pardon!*" interrupted my governess, with a short, dry cough, "I think, as the object of our visit is accomplished, Marguerite, we had better be going, if you please. *I* shall call and see you again. Good morning." And Miss Lateward walked out, gathering up her petticoats preparatory to a descent.

Marie caught hold of my hand and kissed it. The tears rushed to her eyes again as she said,

" Forgive me, mademoiselle ; I do not know what I say sometimes — but, oh ! do not think too badly of me. I shall never see you again, perhaps — but I shall pray for you often, and I know now that God does hear the prayers, even of such as I am !"

The door closed on her, and when we stood in the street, Miss Lateward turned to me, and said,

" You must be careful whom you pick up in this kind of romantic way about the streets, Marguerite. I shall make every inquiry concerning this person, and I hope I may discover that she is a worthy recipient of your bounty ; but I confess I very much fear it. I do not disbelieve her story, indeed, *so far as it goes ;* but her manner is strangely confused, and really altogether unsatisfactory, and I must positively forbid your repeating this visit until I shall have some more certain knowledge concerning her character. In the mean time, any communication upon the subject of the work you have left with her can be made through me."

I thought Miss Lateward really cruel and unjust, and I said to myself, " How strange that people who are generally kind-hearted, can sometimes be so hard on others !" But I knew this was a sort of point — any thing connected with "propriety"—upon which Miss Lateward would be unyielding as stone and iron, so I said nothing until some days subsequently, when I ventured to ask, as we were going out to walk :

" Have you made the inquiries you promised about poor Madame Dumont, Miss Lateward ? because Cécile de Beaucroi has given me an order for some pocket-handkerchiefs, and I should like to take them to-day."

"I will take it, my love, if you please."

"Why can't I go? What have you heard about her — any thing?"

"Yes; and from what I have heard, I think it is advisable you should abstain from visiting her; though, understand me, I believe she is very much *to be pitied*, and I am far from wishing to withdraw assistance from her. Therefore, as I said before, I will be the bearer of any thing you may have to send."

"I do not understand these distinctions. Either she is a good and honest woman, or she is not. If she *is* a worthy object of interest, why should I not be allowed to go and see her?"

"These are questions, my dear, you cannot be expected to understand. When you are older you will know."

"Nonsense! Miss Lateward. You treat me as if I were a child. You forget that I am sixteen, and that I have seen and know a good deal more of the world than most young ladies of my age."

"You have not learnt to govern your impetuosity, my dear," said my governess, with a mildness which touched me. "However, I will go so far as to say that, as this person's past life has not been immaculate, though I believe she is sincerely repentant, and desirous to be honest and well-conducted, still, there is a certain deference to be paid to the world's opinion, as I told you the other day, and I think it far from desirable that you should visit her. In my case, as an elderly person, it is very different."

I only replied: "The world's opinion, dear Miss Lateward, seems to me in direct opposition to the opinion of a much higher Judge, of whom you read to me last Sunday, that he said that there was 'more joy in Heaven over one sinner that repenteth, than over ninety and nine just persons that need no repentance.' I hope we are not of the ninety and nine, that is all."

I did not press the matter further; and Miss Lateward, on her return, said very little of her visit, except that the child was now quite well, and that the mother seemed in no want of any thing, as a lady had interested herself about her, and had given her employment. Months passed before I again saw or heard of Marie Dumont. I had, happily, no further occasion that spring to apply to Felicien Ismael, or any one else in the matter of my pictures, for no very pressing bills of my father's came to my knowledge. In the mean time, however, I received a sanction, upon which I was not slow to act, in a letter from my aunt, of which I give an extract:

"I applaud heartily the determination to devote your talent to a really worthy purpose — making it something better than a young lady's accomplishment. I cannot see any objection to your paying your father's debts, even without his sanction, in this way. Many people would think differently. They would say that, however ill-founded, Colonel Percival's objection to his daughter's selling her drawings should be sufficient for her. I cannot think so. The one obligation seems to me a far higher one than the other — what we owe to God's law of honesty, before the debt of obedience to man, even though it be your own father. My dear, it is a dangerous thing to counsel a child to disobey or to disregard its parent. What shall I say to you? You are now of an age to know something of the difficulties and dangers of your position. It is useless to ignore them — to write as if they *were not*. You must face them boldly — face them with earnest prayer, remembering the words of that true philosopher who said, 'though God is so great that the Heaven of Heavens cannot contain him, yet he dwells *here*' — pointing at the same time to his breast. You have that counsellor: the weakest among us may have him who earnestly seeks him. This is the only advice I can give you, my dear niece, which will suit all emergencies and all seasons in life. But there is that other and lower wisdom, called ‘worldly,’ which you must try and gain. You are too impulsive. I foresee that it will lead you among thorns and briars, unless you put a strong curb on that impetuous charger of yours. Why, even in your letter to me he snorts, and kicks, and champs his bit, upon the subject of that poor French woman, whom you seem to think Miss Lateward treats coldly and unjustly, while she seems to *me* to have behaved with great prudence and good sense. And to return to the subject of your pictures, understand me, I utterly disapprove of the method in which you carried out your good intentions. In the first place, I hate mysteries — underhand transactions of any kind — not only because they destroy the freshness and ingenuousness of the character; but in the world-wise point of view, nothing for a woman is so ill-advised. The most innocent actions, when masked, can wear the look of guilt. I had a friend who used to go to market with such a ridiculous air of mystery, stealth and precaution, carefully avoiding every one, and thickly veiled, that I was not surprised when I heard it whispered, with a shake of the head, that she had an assignation every morning. Now, I am very glad that your visit to Monsieur Ismael turned out so well; but it was a mistake, and must not be repeated. What I advise you to do, since you find you can turn your talent to such profitable account, is to tell your mother *all*, in the first place. Say that I see no objection to your selling your pictures — on the contrary, that I approve of it. Miss Lateward will, I am sure (having your mother’s sanction), consent to be the medium through whom you can negotiate with Ismael, or any other dealer. I am so much a friend to openness that I wish it were possible for you to tell your father: but, if he did not actually *forbid* it, I foresee that it would frustrate the good results that may arise from your having this small fund at hand for any exigency. Write to me fully, and at once, should such occur. I promise, for the present, I will *not* send you any money, should such scrupulous fears deter you, as in this instance, from asking my advice. To say the truth, this has been a very hard winter with us; as I have had to do more for our poor people than any former year, and have had no rents, I do not find my pocket very heavy. These severe March winds have been very trying to Emmy. She has a cough which makes me anxious, and I fear we must spend next winter abroad. A friend of ours is going in his yacht to the Mediterranean in August, and has offered to take us, but nothing is determined on, till I have taken Emmy up to London to see Sir James Clark," etc.

I followed my aunt's advice strictly, and during the ensuing summer, many were the little comforts I was able to procure for my mother, many the petty annoyances I was able to relieve by the sale of my sketches and pictures, which under Miss Lateward's able management, produced very fair sums. She did not apply to Felicien Ismael; he lived so far off, and my good governess seemed to have such an unconquerable dislike to the idea, that I did not urge it. At length Barae returned, ostensibly from visiting some members of the house of Barae, in Amsterdam; in reality, as I knew perfectly well, from negotiating important business connected with tobacco and the fine arts, half over Germany. I found him very ready, as I knew he would be, to assist me in every way, and from that time forward the occasional sale of my pictures was both more easily and more profitably conducted.

CHAPTER VII.

ONE afternoon in the December following, I was going into the drawing-room to sit with my mother, as I always did towards dusk, when on opening the door, I heard the voice of a visitor, and according to my wont was retreating, when my mother called out.

"Is that you, Rita? Come here. I want to introduce you to Lady Greybrook, who has not seen you since you were eight years old."

"I suppose you don't remember me," said a shadow in the twilight, drawing, with soft-gloved fingers my hand into a nest of sable fur.

"Yes, I do. I remember perfectly going to see you in the Place Vendôme, and your giving me a pair of shoes."

"Only think of your remembering that! But how tall she is grown, Mrs. Percival! Do you know, when Colonel Percival told me last night at the Embassy that my little friend was grown up and ready to come out, I could hardly believe it. How old it makes one! It seems only the other day. Why, she can't be more than fifteen, surely?"

"Seventeen, last month. She has grown very much this last year and improved; she promised at one time to be very short. But I must really ring for the lamp, that you may see her."

"Do: I hate talking to people without knowing what they are like. I am a great physiognomist, and make up my mind about characters at once, and never change. That is the way I used to choose my Bedouins, when I crossed the Desert."

"Ah, really; curious! You've been a great traveller, by-the-by, since we saw you. How did you like the East? Very hot you must have found it, and living under a tent, and altogether, so odd?"

"I liked it immensely, except the fever, which nearly carried me off; but I have a charmed life, I believe, and nine of them, like a cat. In my *Juive errante* life, I have had so many miraculous escapes! Returning to civilized life, at first, seemed horridly tame. I broke myself in at Naples for a year, which is better than any other capital, more exciting. Then I tried returning to London; but I could not endure the state of social fog for more than one season. I should have committed suicide, or done something shocking, if I had stayed."

"Where have you been since then?"

"Oh, travelling about. In the summer at Baden or some other German spa; in the winter at Rome or Florence; and last winter at St. Petersburg, where my brother Clarendel is ambassador, you know."

"Ah! that must have made it pleasant; but do tell me how you liked the society?"

"Oh! it is just what one would expect. The women have the most *recherchées* toilettes, the most splendid diamonds, and the most charming manners in the world; but with all its outward refinement there is a good deal of barbarism *au fond*. Like the icicles hanging round one's window, the conversation is very glittering and pointed; in reality nothing but frozen water. Then the men are often such brutes, and one hears of such barbarities, that take away one's appetite for breakfast, which, as I never have a large one, is a bore. I amused myself for a short time until the novelty of the thing wore off, and then I came away."

The lamp was now brought in, and while Lady Grey-orook proceeded with Russian *sang froid* to examine me from head to foot, I will do the same by her, for the reader's future recognition.

I remembered a woman fair and brilliant: I beheld one faded, withered up, and worn, with eyes whose fire seemed to have burnt down into their sockets, and to have consumed, as it were, the whole upper part of the face, though still the embers smouldered at the further end of those dark caverns, sending out sparks ever and anon, and lighting up the sharp, but still handsome features, with a feverish flash. Those features were seldom in repose; a sort of restless eagerness possessed the mouth, even when she was not speaking; and though the eye no longer gleamed and shone and sparkled with the brilliancy that had been so remarkable in youth, it was never still an instant; the most fatiguing eye to watch, and giving one an impression that it never could relax its vigilance for a single moment, or succumb under the influence of sleep. She talked with a hit-or-miss kind of cleverness, which, while it is less alarming than actual wit, often passes for such, when assisted by a natural off-hand manner. Hers, which was partly natural to her, partly the result of the atmosphere in which she lived, was particularly agreeable: it was said, indeed, that her "success" had always been greatly owing to this charm. What this "success" was, I shall presently inform the reader. I will only add now, that she was magnificently dressed; and I had time to observe that her hands and feet were remarkably small and well-shaped. Suddenly turning to my mother, she exclaimed:

"Much more like her father than you, and I see she has none of the *mauvaise honte* of sixteen. She has been examining *me* as curiously and narrowly as I have *her!* Bravo! that unblushing face is a paternal inheritance, also, dear Mrs. Percival! You Russboroughs are a modest race," she added, laughing. "But what do you mean by not bringing her out? Your husband and I must talk about it. These youthful roses and lilies go by so soon" (with a sigh), "that it is a perfect sin the world should lose a whole year of them! She is quite old enough to make her *début*."

My mother smiled languidly, and said something about her health, and my fondness for books; and Rose entering at that moment, Lady Greybrook proceeded to inspect her, as she had done me; but, curious to say, the great lady did not appear to admire my beautiful sister as much as I had expected. She only remarked, that she looked delicate, and was very like my mother — quite a Russborough. Yet, in my eyes, every month had but added to my sister's grace and loveliness. She seemed to me the very creature to make what I had heard called "a sensation" in the world. She was not clever; she had not even a great variety of expression, it is true; but for ball-room triumphs I could not conceive this to be necessary. I was surprised, therefore, that she did not make a greater impression on Lady Greybrook — and so, I saw, was my mother.

"Good-by," said the former, at length, rising from the sofa; "I hope you will let me see a great deal of your daughter. I am so fond of young people. Will you come, Marguerite, and see me to-morrow morning? I dare say your father will bring you." Then, without waiting for an answer, she swept out into the ante-room, where her *chasseur* was looking supremely contemptuous, in green and gold, and glowering at our meek domestic's endeavors to unbolt the obstinate half of a folding-door, which, in honor of so magnificent a visitor, he wished to open to its full extent. I watched the flutter of the *chasseur's* plumes down the stairs, followed by her ladyship's graceful form, in its heavy draperies of velvet, until both were out of sight.

"What an amusing original person Lady Greybrook is,

mamma — so off-hand. But what a life of excitement. One sees it at once, in her whole manner. I rather like her, though."

"Do you, my love?" My mother said no more, until she presently remarked, very pertinently, "I am sure I don't know *what* to do about your clothes. There is that black gown of mine can be turned and shortened, and will do for common wear, but you will want a best gown for —"

Here my father entered, and the conversation, if it could be called such, dropped. He appeared in the schoolroom about noon next day, much to my astonishment, and bade me "get on my bonnet immediately."

"What is the matter, papa? Where are we going?"

"Why, did n't you promise to go to Lady Greybrook's this morning? She told me so when I met her last night."

"Lady Greybrook said something about it, certainly; but I did not promise — for you know I am always with Miss Lateward of a morning, and never pay visits."

"You will break through these good rules in future. Come, get yourself ready, as fast as you can — don't stay talking, and make yourself look as decent as you can, too — not with all your hair tucked back in that absurd manner."

I obeyed, and presently we were walking, for the first time in my life, my father and I, alone, and arm in arm, down the Rue de Rivoli. My father was in remarkably good humor, and the visit passed off, I believe, to the satisfaction of all parties. As for me, at least, I thought Lady Greybrook even more entertaining than I had done the previous day. I had not time, indeed, to analyze what she said, and I found that the greater part of it had passed from me when I tried to recall it afterwards; but the general effect of her conversation was to dazzle and pleasantly bewilder me. She confessed, in the most naïve way, impressions which I had felt myself, but to which I had never dreampt of giving form in words; and we are all of us, more or less, captivated by this kind of apparent spontaneity, until we find it out. She kissed me when I got up to go away, called back my father, just as we had reached the ante-room, whispered something in which I heard my mother's name more than once, and so the visit ended. My father bought me a bunch of violets, I remember, at a stall on our way home, and was very talkative. These were strange signs and wonders.

I was accustomed, of an evening, to draw in my own little room (which opened into the *salon*), where my table, with its litter of chalks, etc., was unmolested, and where my brothers could read and talk without disturbing my father, when he was taking his after-dinner nap, as he generally did, before dressing to go out. The door was left open, and sometimes Rose, who now played extremely well on the piano, was summoned by my father to play one of his favorite waltzes. She had done so this evening; and it had ended in her treating the boys to some " magical music," while they hid things under the chairs and sofas, but very quietly; they knew the ground too well to indulge in any boisterous demonstrations of mirth, for my father and mother were talking together near the fire; and while I drew under the shade of the lamp, and the boys glided about like shadows, and the music alternately swelled and died away, my father's voice rose and fell almost in unison with it (he was the principal speaker), until I became excitedly curious to know what could be the subject of his eager conversation. At last Betsy summoned the boys, and Rose soon after kissed me, and said she should go to bed also, feeling tired. Then, when she had closed the door, the silence was only broken by the scraping of the knife as I cut my chalks, and by the voices in the adjoining room, which, though somewhat lowered, I could now hear distinctly. There was a long pause: at last my mother said,

" Well, Percival, I know Mary will disapprove of it very much. I remember her saying, years ago, that I ought not to know her — that I ought not, on any account, to encourage intimacy with her. She may be very fashionable and that sort of thing *here*, but you know she is not received in London. Indeed, she said herself, she found it so dull there she could not stay — which meant as much. She is very pleasant and good-natured, but —"

" But women are jealous of her! just because she manages to keep men round her, by being so monstrous agreeable, when younger and handsomer women are deserted. She is at the head of every thing here."

" Well, you mustn't forget how much we owe to Mary, and I know she will —"

" Stuff! Lady Dacre knows as well as you do that the girl *must* be married, and those prudish, old-fashioned English notions don't do in Paris. She has taken an amazing fancy to the girl, says she knows she will make a brilliant match, and I am not such a fool as to let any confounded humbug stand in the way."

" What is Lady Greybrook's object in wanting to take Rita out? She is by way of being a beauty still herself. I should have thought a young girl would have interfered."

" She likes having a court of men round her, and the addition of a good-looking girl, who has some brains and conversation, is a great attraction. She is too sharp to fancy herself any longer sought for her own personal charms. Men like talking to her because she is such fun, and she knows that, so she generally manages to take out some girl, whom she makes the fashion, and has the pleasant excitement into the bargain of looking out for catches. Oh! I know my lady as well as possible, and don't consider myself under any obligation to her for this. It is a mere matter of business. If she takes out the girl she must pay for her clothes, I suppose, and even then we are quits."

"She is so very young — and doesn't wish to go out herself, I know," said my mother, hesitatingly.

"I tell you," rejoined my father, vehemently, "she *must* be married. I have explained to you a dozen times that we must get her off at once, if possible. And I should like to know *how*, if she is not to go out?"

"But why don't you, then, take her out yourself? Surely it would be much better."

"I should make a deuced bad chaperone; besides, I don't know all these French people — that rich Faubourg St. Germain set, where, I am told, there are some capital *parties*. Lady Greybrook is very intimate in all these houses — it is quite another thing."

"Well," said my mother, after a pause, in a low voice, "it would be a great thing if she was well married, I confess. But why not to an Englishman, Percival? Why do you talk so much about Frenchmen?"

"For best of reasons — that Englishmen do not come to Paris to marry — they come here to amuse themselves — opera-dancers and ball-room flirtations — and every girl here they consider fair game. No, no. I understand my respected countrymen pretty well, I believe. You won't catch them committing a *folie* here, as you might a middle-aged marquis, who has survived his first *marriage de covenance*, and considers himself at liberty to choose the first pretty face that takes his fancy. There is a ball at Marshal S——'s next week — the first great fête of the season. Lady Greybrook proposes her making her début there; so prepare her, and see that she is properly got up — you know —"

My mother was silent: and soon afterwards I heard my father leave the room. I sat there for nearly an hour longer; but my thoughts were not with the little plaster Cupid before me. They had wandered far away into the dim future. I seemed to be looking down a deep gulf, on the brink of which I stood. My childhood had passed away; a new world of sensations and vicissitudes was opening out beneath my feet; and with the consciousness of this, throbbed that bitter thought — that I must *be got rid of* — no matter how, or where — at any price! — no, I am wrong — to the highest bidder, and on the best terms the market could afford.

The world excuses this, and says it is "very natural." Well I suppose it is, for the same thing has been going on for thousands of years, from Bible patriarchs, haggling over their children's dowries of flocks and herds, through long lines of kings and humbler folk, bartering hearts for crowns, or power, or wealth: it is the same old story, uninfluenced by nation, age, or circumstance. Will it be so to the end?

Even my gentle mother had said it would be "a great thing" to see me married. That, henceforth, was to be the object of my life; all my looks and actions were to have reference to it. My home, God knows, had not been a happy one; with few of the joys and little of the sweet influence belonging to that name; and it may seem strange that I viewed with such horror the prospect of going forth into the world and making for myself new ties. But here, at least, I was *free.* Here, if anywhere, I felt that I was of some use in my generation; for more and more had I taken my mother's place in the family of late; and in numberless ways I stood between her and the shadows that pressed on us from without. How could the little household get on without me? I asked myself. Our pliant Rose would bend before the storms that I had weathered; nor had she capacity or inclination to take the reins when they fell from my hands. Why would they not let me pursue my own quiet path, and leave to my beautiful sister, in due course of time, the triumphs of that world for which she was so suited?

I felt by turns indignant and miserable as I asked myself, "Is it for this I was brought into the world? Am I a thing, then, of so little value to those who gave me birth, that their only anxiety is to sell me, like a slave in the market? From my father I had no reason to expect otherwise, but from *you*, mother —"

The whole head was sick and the whole heart faint, when I lay down in my little bed that night.

CHAPTER VIII.

WHEN it was officially notified in the family that I was
shortly to make my appearance in the world of balls and
parties, the intelligence was variously received by three of
its members. My faithful Betsy was overjoyed, and
plunged forthwith into a turmoil of crape and lace flounces
(the latter being the remnants of my mother's wedding-
dress). Rose looked despondingly on at these preparations.
She sighed heavily, and I rather think a tear fell upon her
English Grammar; but I am not sure. Miss Lateward
heard the announcement, as the Sphinx might have done,
with a stony gloom, which sent a chill to the hearts of the
beholders. Mine was depressed enough as it was. I put
my arms round her, and said,

"I am very ignorant, dear Miss Lateward; no one can
feel it more than I do. I am quite unfit to go into society
— I told mamma so — but I am determined to work on still
at my books, just the same, if you please. It shall make no
difference."

"No, Marguerite, that is impossible. The exciting atmosphere in which you will move, and the demands upon
your time and thoughts, will render any attempt at serious
study, for the present, perfectly fruitless."

I thought she was quite wrong, and that it showed she
very little understood me; but I said nothing, and only sat
down beside her, full of silent resolves.

Lady Greybrook greeted me most affectionately, when
next we met; and in spite of what I had heard my mother

say of her, I believe, if any thing could have overcome my repugnance to the idea of entering society, it would have been the prospect of having so original, entertaining, and good-natured a chaperone. The truth is, that having heard some evil spoken of half the people whose names were mentioned in my mother's drawing-room — whose society, I knew, was eagerly sought after, and who, in their turn, possibly paid their visits, and abused those who had preceded them — the bloom having thus been very early rubbed off my impressions of the world in general, my thoughts upon the subject were pretty much as follows :

"I dare say Lady Greybrook is no worse than the rest of the world. She is evidently a very natural person, and those who are so always show their worst side. Then, again, every one seems to me to speak ill of every one else. I am sorry, however, my Aunt Mary doesn't like her; but she has probably heard some of these ill-natured stories, and people imbibe prejudices and false impressions so easily. I remember Madame Gobemouche's pitying me for being sent to Boulogne with my aunt, because she had such a bad temper! Ah! happy days, will they ever return? shall I ever see that sweet, wise face again ?"

What the world said of Lady Greybrook was this, though I did not know it for long afterwards. That she had married the late lord when she was a perfect child, and he an old man of dissolute habits and ungovernable temper. That he had treated her like a brute, and that she had borne it like an angel, until, in an evil hour, she had allowed some one to tell her so. That before any steps were taken to procure a divorce, her lord had died of *delirium tremens*, and she was left a rich widow, of five-and-twenty. That, soon after this, the carriage of one of the royal dukes began to be seen regularly every afternoon at her door, and that the virtuous Queen Charlotte had turned her back upon her at a drawing-room. That she had then come over to

Paris, where she became immensely the fashion, and was the cause of a duel between two well-known noblemen. That, at Naples, her "cavaliere servente," was a young Russian prince, with whom, it was positively affirmed, she subsequently travelled in the East, and that she followed him to St. Petersburg, where, for some unknown cause, she was but coldly received.

Finally, that after an illness which had done more towards destroying her beauty than the ravages of time, she had adopted two or three nieces in succession, and had succeeded in marrying them all to foreigners of rank.

Such was the world's opinion of the person to whom my parents entrusted their child, upon her introduction into that censorious arena. Such was the atmosphere in which they consented she should move, for the sake of present, and yet more (as they hoped) future advantages.

Lady Greybrook at once assumed her position as sponsor for my appearance in society. She questioned me as to my dress, and summarily pronounced against Betsy's well-meant efforts.

" What! blue and blonde for such a child as you! What can dear Mrs. Percival be thinking of? Tell her to leave it all to me. I shall desire Palmire to come to me to-morrow: pure white, and not a flower or ornament! With a certain amount of distinction nothing makes such an effect in a crowd as perfect simplicity."

So Lady Greybrook arranged it all, and it was an understood thing that I was to be dressed as she chose, and (not the *least* important part) entirely at her expense.

The evening came that was to see me launched upon the world. My mother had been very ill all day; and I felt a depression at heart I endeavored in vain to shake off. It had been arranged that Lady Greybrook's carriage should call for me rather early, and that I should repair to that lady's house, so as to enable her to "inspect" me before we

went to the ball. The family all crowded into my little
room when I was dressed: there was a great running to
and fro with hair-pins and pomatum for an hour before that,
and I was thankful when it was over, and the general result
approved of (on the whole), though Betsy said it was very
"plain-like," and clearly preferred her unfinished cerulean
structure. My father, however, cast a satisfied glance over
me, and when, at last, her ladyship's chariot was heard
rumbling under the *porte-cochère*, he actually offered me his
arm; an honor I felt I owed as much to the chasseur and
coachman as to my own merits.

"I shall meet you at the ball, by-and-by," he said, as he
handed me in. The chasseur clapped the door to, with a
sharp report, and sprang up behind; the carriage heaved for
a moment, and then rolled smoothly out into the night.

I felt a loneliness as I sat there, with the carriage-lamps
shining brightly in my face, which was quite indescribable.
It sounds foolish, but it required a strong effort to prevent
my bursting into tears, and yet tears with me were not common. I looked out upon the wet pavement, where the long
shadows of the gas-lights were reflected, and where, here
and there, the figure of a woman pattered along in her
sabots, under the ample wing of a scarlet cotton umbrella.
There was a momentary stoppage at the corner of a street.
A man and woman — evidently his wife — with their little
girl, were just coming out of a grocer's shop. The man had
some candles and two or three parcels under his arm. He
stooped and gave one to the child to carry. She looked up
proudly in his face. They were going home to their pleasant fireside, that happy trio! — "The mother will put her
child to bed — then she and the father will sit down together
over their homely supper." I saw it all, and I envied them.
At the same instant the woman looked up; perhaps she, in
her turn, felt a momentary pang as she saw the occupant of
that brilliant equipage, and thought of hard work and poverty.

When I arrived at the Place Vendôme, I was shown into Lady Greybrook's dressing-room. I found her seated before the Psyché; her maid putting the last touches to her attire.

"Your dress, my dear Marguerite, is *irréprouchable*," said her Ladyship, examining me from head to foot; "but you look dreadfully pale — as if you had had a *tête-à-tête* with Mephistophiles, like your German namesake. Come here; kneel down, I want to arrange something. Take care not to crush your gown — so —"

She held a small casket on her knees, and took from it what looked like a piece of jeweller's cotton. I had no conception of what she was going to do, until I felt something swiftly and lightly passed over both cheeks. I started up, and ran to the glass.

"Don't be alarmed, my dear — nothing more than the delicate tinge you always have when you walk here in the morning. You won't detect it yourself. Nothing in the world is so impertinent as to interfere clumsily with Nature."

"Oh! nonsense, Lady Greybrook; it makes no difference whether it is clumsily or well done — it is an acted lie, wearing a complexion God has not given one, and I hate it. I hope my cheeks are red enough now to please you, for it makes me feel perfectly hot and scarlet to think of entering a room —"

"Brava!" cried she laughing, as her maid threw the bernous over her shoulders; "you see, after all, I only restored the complexion God *has* given you. It was 'a word to the wise,' and Nature immediately took the hint. Come along, we shall be late;" and before I had time to expostulate further, and beg for a sponge and water, she had drawn my arm through hers, and was leading me down stairs.

The first thing I can remember when we entered the ball-room and made our way through the crowd round the door-ways, was the painful consciousness of being stared at. I thought my cheeks were attracting general attention, and that was sufficient, of course, to dye them the deepest crimson. Lady Greybrook made her way forward with that balancing movement on the toes which has now become so common, but was then confined to a noble few. Her whole body rose, sank, and vibrated in that sea of gold-embroidered epaulettes, amply-padded chests a-blaze with orders, diamonded necks and stomachers, adroitly cleaving, where she could, the less material waves of gauze and tulle, and bowing almost incessantly, right and left.

"There goes Lady Greybrook," I heard a little fat woman say in English to a man near her. "What is it she has got with her?"

"Don't know — something raw — dressed quite *au naturel*, you see."

"For shame! The chaperone, at least, has plenty of *sauce piquante*."

We reached the top of the room. I remember making a low courtesy to an old gentleman, and being taken up to a knot of magnificent-looking matrons on an ottoman. I appeared to be in a dream; the room literally swam round with me. I knew that eye-glasses were raised, that something complimentary was said to Lady Greybrook about me, and that one of the magnificent-looking matrons addressed me. I answered at random, and there was an audible titter — a whisper of "Au moins, elle est bien bête!"

Lady Greybrook bowed, nodded, laughed, shook hands, inquired after the health of her "chère Duchesse," and had a *petit mot* for each of the great ladies in turn. Several men came forward: to some she extended a finger, with all she seemed, more or less, on terms of intimacy; and a rapid fire of jokes passed, evidently requiring a key to understand. I felt much like a shipwrecked mariner, who hears an unknown tongue and sees no friendly, no familiar face to bid him welcome to an inhospitable shore. My chaperone suddenly turned round and introduced some one to me whose name I did not catch. I saw and heard at once he was an Englishman, in spite of a black beard, which our country-men seldom wore in those days. He was tall, and certainly handsome, but with a disagreeable, forbidding expression of face — at least I thought so, at first sight; and, as his manner did not prepossess me more than his appearance, I said, what was the truth,

"Thank you — I feel too giddy to waltz."

"Nonsense, my dear," said Lady Greybrook, rather sharply, "that will pass away; sit down here. Come and claim her when the waltz begins;" then, in a whisper, as the bearded gentleman sauntered away, "A great thing to be seen dancing with him — you have no idea what an honor it is! He never dances with any one but a married woman, and that very rarely. It will make you the fashion among the men at once. Ah, mon Prince, comment ça va?"

A young man, with a face like a sheet of white blotting-paper, hair white, eyelashes white, a flat nose and thick white lips, the whole strapped up immovably into the stiffest of white stocks, with a head so lifeless, in short, that all the blood seemed to have trickled out of it down into the scarlet riband of an order he wore round his neck — this young man approached, and bringing his feet with a sudden click together into the fourth position, made Lady Greybrook a profound obeisance. I was sufficiently at ease now, being seated, and left to my own observations, to derive some amusement from watching this inane figure, as, in a penny-trumpet voice and the purest French, he jerked out a few questions to her ladyship, who received them with the bland-est smile and responded with a sparkling little flow of talk. It is true there were two other men standing by her who benefited by her brilliant conversation; still I thought, in my ignorance, "How can she like to talk to that creature?

A clever woman like Lady Greybrook to waste her breath upon that glove-and-boot-tree! He has evidently not two ideas — a perfect automaton, and such an ugly one, too!" But I did not know the automaton was his Serene Highness the Prince of Pultowa.

The pale little eye-balls of the serene countenance twinkled under their frosty lashes towards me, and to avoid looking any longer at so disagreeable an object, I turned my head in an opposite direction. The crowd had not yet done arriving: there was still a stream of people coming up the room, to pay their respects to their veteran host, and among these I suddenly perceived a little figure in cramoisie velvet, with a turban and bird of Paradise on its head, lurching to and fro, like a boat with a top-heavy sail. It was a familiar face, connected with my childhood, but one I had not seen for two or three years, at least. It brought a rush of pleasurable feelings, in the midst of that stranger-world, and from an irrepressible impulse, as she came within a few yards of me, I started up, ran forwards, and seized her hand.

"Dear Madame Gobemouche! don't you know me? Marguerite, whom you used to be so kind to. I little thought to see you here: I thought you had left Paris for ever. How long have you been back? Where is the General? Do you find me altered? This is my first ball," &c., with a good deal more in the same style, which I will spare the reader. Indeed, my tongue, which had so long seemed tied, now took its revenge: I was again the child, chattering away with the kind little woman, who answered with corresponding volubility. We talked over the old times; there were many inquiries to be made and answered. Oh! they had only been in Paris two days — come up on business from madame's château, where they were now residing. The General's old friend, Marshal S—, had invited them here, but, unfortunately, the General was not able to come, owing to — whereupon Madame entered into certain medical details, which I would fain have been spared, seeing that the bystanders appeared to be deriving more amusement than I did from the recital. A fan tapped me on the shoulder. It was Lady Greybrook, looking exceedingly annoyed.

"When you have finished that interesting conversation." she said, in a tone of concealed disgust. "the Prince de Pultowa wishes to be presented to you. What on earth is that thing you are talking to?" she added, hardly lowering her tone.

"Au revoir, my dear old friend!" said I, turning to the little woman, whose angry eyes betrayed that she guessed but too well the nature of her ladyship's remarks, though made in English — indeed it was impossible to mistake the look she had bestowed upon the bird of Paradise — "au revoir! pray come and see us to-morrow, and give my best love to the General. I am going to dance, you see, so I must leave you now. Adieu!"

"I must inform you," said Lady Greybrook, when we returned to the ottoman, "as you know nothing of the convenances de société, my dear, that it is not usual for young ladies to start off upon voyages of discovery away from their chaperones across a ball-room. When *did* you pick up that eccentric acquaintance of yours? Any thing so fearfully and wonderfully made I never saw let loose upon society — and then her voice! *Je voyais l'instant* when there would be a ring formed round you to listen to her revelations! I never felt more uncomfortable — there was that sofa full of old French dowagers, looking through their glasses and cackling. Really, my dear, you must — Ah! mon Prince, vous voilà! — ma petite protégé Mademoiselle Percival."

"How shall I ever get through a quadrille with that stiff-necked phantom?" I thought to myself. But the princely arm was rounded, and we took our places.

I will give a sample of the conversation, prefacing that
the reader may perfectly well skip it, if he is so disposed.

Our vis-à-vis has just taken his place.

"Connaissez-vous, Madame de B—, mademoiselle?"

"Non, monsieur, je ne connais personne."

"Hein? cependant c'est une personne que tout le monde
connait.   Comment trouvez-vous la toilette de Mademoiselle
T.?"

"Laquelle, monsieur? j'ai déjà eu l'honneur de vous dire
que je ne connais personne."

"Vraiment?   Tenez, c'est la demoiselle aux roses, en
face.   Préférez-vous le rose ou le bleu, mademoiselle?"

"J'aime tout ce qui n'est pas blanc, monsieur."

"Hein? c'est drôle. J'aurais dit — " He glanced at
my white dress, but the exigencies of the figure lost for me
the remainder, and by the time I returned to my place he
commenced a new interrogatory.

"Aimez-vous Verdi? c'est joli ce morceau, n'est-ce pas?"

"Vert quoi, monsieur? quel morceau?"

"Je parlais de la musique. Ah!   Est-ce vrai qu'en An-
gleterre on ne danse que des *reels*, danse sauvage qu'on a
conservé des anciens habitants du pays? Quelle idée!
Oh! qu'un homme doit avoir l'air bête en dansant comme
ça."

"Il y a des bêtes parmi toutes les nations."

*　　*　　*　　*　　*　　*

"This is our waltz, I believe, Miss Percival," said the
dark Englishman, coming up, as I was being conducted back
to Lady Greybrook.   "I see," he added, as he gave me his
arm, "you have not been adopting the best means to cure
your giddiness. A quadrille with Pultowa is said to turn
most young ladies' heads."

I looked up in astonishment.

"Of course you know every one here, though it *is* your
first ball? You live in Paris, don't you?"

"Yes, but I know nothing of its society. I had to tell my last partner three times that I knew no one, not even by sight, and I suppose I shall pass the evening in repeating this."

"Exactly: I understand; and you have dressed the part admirably. Youth — innocence — first introduction into the world — all that sort of thing. But I thought I saw you rush into the arms of a plethoric dame in scarlet just now — a visitant, perhaps, from the *other* world, eh?"

"A different world from this," said I, amused at the very peculiar manner of my companion, "and a lower and warmer world too — though hardly in your sense — a more kind-hearted and less mocking world than this one seems."

"Is that intended for me? Thank you. You're wrong, though, for all the world is alike. I have seen something of it, and it is all equally worthless — from the palace to the poor-house; but if you retain any illusions on the subject, I beg your pardon for having disturbed them."

"Oh! I should not think of lowering my opinion of the world from an individual instance."

The dark man smiled oddly.

"Miss Percival, you are a female Chesterfield for politeness. Confess, now, that you have heard a very bad character of me."

"I am sorry that I cannot gratify you, but I never heard of you in my life that I am aware of."

"Then, I suppose, seeing what you do of me," said my strange partner, "you would positively object to become my wife if I were to ask you?"

I now made up my mind that he was slightly deranged, but I did not feel disconcerted, as he seemed quiet, and I answered, composedly enough,

"You are right. I should positively object to become your wife under any circumstances."

"Good!" he rejoined, with an expression of great relief. "Now, then, we can talk at our ease, which I very rarely do with a young lady. I wonder how this seems to you? To me it is all very empty."

"I beg your pardon — empty?"

"I mean hollow — how hollow it all is!"

"I was beginning to think it rather pleasanter, now my first nervousness has worn away. But where are we going? It seems to me we have left the music behind us. Here, we are in the *Orangerie*."

"Are we? Oh! it is all the same" (abstractedly).

"Not if we are to waltz — we must go where the music is."

"Oh! we are going to waltz, are we?" And an expression almost irritable crossed his face as he turned short round.

"Not unless you wish it, pray. I will return to Lady Greybrook."

"No, no!" And a minute afterwards we were whirling round in a small circle of waltzers. There was a pleasurable excitement in the music and the movement which was new to me. When we stopped at last, and as I leant, somewhat out of breath, on my partner's arm, I was conscious, by that magnetic influence which every one has experienced in a crowd, at some time or other, that a pair of eyes were intently fixed on me. Each time I glanced over the thick serried mass of head opposite, I flashed fire, as it were, against these same eyes. They seemed familiar to me, strange to say. I knew the head, but where and when I could not remember.

"Who is —" I stopped and hesitated — "that — that girl with fair hair, waltzing?"

"That girl is a grandmother, aged thirty-seven — the Marchesa Boschi; that inexhaustible waltzer in blue is her daughter — both *lionnes*. The mother has been separated from her husband for the last fourteen years. He only returned to Paris lately, after a long absence — saw his wife in a box at the opera, and did n't know her. 'Chi sarà mai quella bella donna?' he asked his daughter. 'Non conoscete Mama?' she answered; whereupon the old gentleman, I suppose, jerked his glass in some other direction; for the only thing that is not permitted to a man in Paris is to admire his own wife — curious, eh? is n't it, Miss Percival?"

We floated off again to the sound of Strauss, but the waltz was coming to an end. With its last strain the crowd began to circle freely through the room, and I caught sight of the magnetic eyes still bent on me, as my partner led me away.

In the doorway we were arrested by a large woman in a head-dress of mingled spectacles and diamonds, a belt of the latter dividing her forehead into two hemispheres, from which pended a spike, which, uniting with the spectacles, was as once dazzling and peculiar. This lady had a remarkable way of arching her neck, like a swan, and as soon as the fancy struck me, I could not help thinking the two pale little girls with fluffy curls, who swam close after her, were not unlike cygnets.

"Naughty man! why did n't you come and doine with us last night? Quite a *congtre-tong*. The girls were so disappointed! We had a very select little party — a few literary people," etc.

"I 'm not literary, unfortunately, Mrs. Fisher, and my worst enemies never accused me of being select."

"Ah! foi, now! I wish you were a little more so — sad *maurais soojet*, I 'm afraid — but then, as I say, you are *onfong gatté* — and with your refoined moind, you are sure to marry some day, and settle down into a respectable member of society. That is what I always tell Lady Janet — but the Oglevies are all so narrow-moinded!"

"So they are, in spite of their connection with you. They don't recognize my good qualities, for which I cannot say how grateful I feel, and how I respect their judgment," and gliding adroitly through Mrs. Fisher's clutches, he continued to me, "There is a specimen of our charming *compatriotes* abroad, whose vulgarities are too often mistaken for British eccentricities by the natives. And they're right, for such a woman as that could only be British. She worships a Jupiter *Bifrons* — rank, however dull — literary notoriety, however ill-conducted. She would fain drag Virtue, and make a Trinity of it, but she can't. Virtue won't have it at any price: for it finds that, instead of being worshipped, it is sacrificed at the altar of the other two. I assure you there is nothing she won't admit provided it fulfils one of these required conditions. I lose no opportunity of pointing out to her my numerous little weaknesses, but she persists in viewing them leniently. I am perfectly bombarded with little pink notes, and the worst of it is, you see, I can't believe it is for any merit of my own."

"That is fortunate: as your opinion of yourself does not appear to be characterized by any extravagant modesty. I do not understand how a man can talk of the attention he receives, in the way you do."

"You cannot tell what it is to be sick to death of all their horrid worldliness — the same people — the very same who would barely acknowledge me some four or five years ago, when I was a penniless captain in the Cape Mounted Rifles. But, after all, you are right, Miss Percival. The reproof is not undeserved: I shall be more careful, in future, with *you* to —"

"Which of her own conditions does Mrs. Fisher fulfil?" I interrupted, "harking back" in sportsman's language, to the former topic, from this personal ground. "Is she aristocratic, or is she a blue?"

"In her own person, neither. She was an Irish heiress,

and will tell you, no doubt, that she is descended from the kings of Munster—"

"Ah! I see—King-Fisher; on the banks of Boyne the family still exists, I dare say. I thought she had an aquatic look."

"The deceased Fisher was connected with the Oglevies; a nephew of Lady Janet's, that is where she gets her aristocracy, and she loses no opportunity of giving you the benefit of it. As to her learning, we all suffered severely last year at Baden, from her attempts to 'combine instruction with amusement,' as she informed us, in a series of historical charades, which with the aid of 'Maunder's Treasury,' she used to compose and produce nightly at the *thés* among the English with a hydra-headed facility—no sooner was one disposed of than another sprang up! The old Sphinx, at last, could get no one but her own daughters to listen to her riddles and unriddle them."

"The offspring of this learned lady—the daughters, I mean, not the riddles—are clever, I suppose?"

"It makes one's brain ache to think of the mental gymnastics those girls go through. They talk divers tongues, of which it may truly be said there is neither speech nor language, though their voices are heard among them. They play *études* for the left hand on the piano, while they stipple chalk heads with the right. In short, they are frightfully accomplished. They do every thing, and do nothing well; and are innocent of any single original idea."

"What a picture! it is enough to prevent one's ever learning any thing."

"Here is your chaperone—but will you dance the next quadrille with me?"

I bowed, and Lady Greybrook made room for me on the sofa beside her. Some foreigners were grouped round: and a recital of her ladyship's, about which they all seemed very merry, was brought to rather an abrupt termination, I believe, on my approach.

"Well! how are you amusing yourself?" said she, turning round with that change of manner which tells you that the past conversation was not for *you*, and that the speaker is about to enter on a new field, solely on your account. "Engaged very deep, I hope? I'll do a violence to my feelings, and stay the cotillon, if you like it. Your father has been doing the paternal, my dear, and inquiring after you; when he heard you were dancing with Rawdon, he seemed to think you were wasting your time, and —"

"Is that the eccentric Englishman I have just been dancing with? What a very strange man! — but amusing and original certainly."

"Didn't you know it was Lord Rawdon? who is so *épandu* in Paris, in many different ways. Most people think him a little mad, though I doubt his being as much so, as he wishes to *make* them think. He is so impertinent and sarcastic, and does give himself such airs. He amuses me, though, and we are tolerably good friends."

"I suppose I may consider that we are, too, for I had not talked with him ten minutes before he asked me whether I should object to become his wife. I must confess, however, he seemed very much relieved when I said I should object."

"How odd! Why he has a perfect horror of matrimony. That, combined with the insanity (which really does, I believe, exist in his mother's family), has made most of the mammas give up the desperate chase — Mrs. Oglevie Fisher, and one or two others excepted, in whose houses I always say the police should insist on a placard being placed, to warn the public against man-traps. Lord Rawdon is so dreadfully extravagant, however, that I doubt his being any longer a great catch, but he is very much the fashion, and he so seldom speaks to any girl that you may consider yourself wonderfully honored."

"I could not make him out, but he amused me. At first I thought he was mad, and then I thought he was making fun of me, so I answered him in his own tone, as well as I could; but now and then he says things that make one fancy he has more feeling than — that surprise one, in short."

" And he does things that surprise people too," said Lady Greybrook, with a peculiar smile. " However, there are allowances to be made for him. He was left without any near relations when he was very young; cheated by a guardian, I believe, and went out in some regiment to the Cape. Unexpectedly, in consequence of the death of several intermediate heirs, he succeeded to the title and estates — woke one morning and found himself famous in the great world, surrounded, flattered, worshipped, where before he was hardly noticed. It was enough to make a peculiar nature like his sarcastic and capricious, wasn't it ? "

Two or three men came up to Lady Greybrook at that moment, and several introductions followed. I do not think they much admired me before, or liked me after, they had danced with me; but I was *new* — I was chaperoned by a " grande dame " — and, on the whole, it seemed to be considered the thing to dance with me. I soon became confused between the black beards and the red — the well-shorn chins and silken moustaches — and behaved as young ladies generally do, under like circumstances, engaging myself to two or three men for one dance. The fact is impressed on my mind from the recollection of Lord Rawdon's scowl at a dapper little Frenchman who was leading me away, and his stepping before another who was mildly asserting his claim to this particular quadrille.

" I beg your pardon ; but this is *my* dance."

" Mademoiselle is the person to decide that, I believe," fired out the little Gaul, his face growing scarlet.

I really felt frightened, and endeavored to explain and to pacify ; and of course it ended in my impetuous countryman carrying the day, — and the Frenchman never forgave me.

Lord Rawdon afterwards took me in to supper, Lady Greybrook being conducted, at the same time, in great pomp, by
a white-haired old marshal, with a breast full of orders.   I
found the conversation of my new acquaintance not only
amusing, it even became interesting, when, dropping his
cynical tone, he described some of the scenes of his wild
life among the Kaffres.   His experiences were striking and
varied, and he told some of them in very graphic language.
His reading had evidently been of men, not of books, and he
spoke only of what he knew.   If the result had not been
to raise his opinion of the species, it at least bore no common fruit in his conversation, which, with all its abruptness
and fierce bitterness at times, had a strange fascination for
me.   His touches of character showed rare discrimination;
and I began, after nearly an hour's conversation, to feel
uncomfortably conscious that he saw further into my
thoughts than I intended, and that my efforts to veil myself,
Olympus-like, in cloud and mist, were futile.   Twice in the
course of my conversation at the supper-table I turned
round and found those same mysterious eyes I had before
observed, fixed on me through the crowd.   I could not
recall where I had seen them: it was the vaguest ghost of
a memory.   They made me almost uncomfortable for a
moment, but I soon forgot them in my companion's entertaining discourse.   Lady Greybrook at last interrupted it.

"Rita, my dear, sorry to disturb you; but Mr. Murray
has been persecuting me to be introduced.   You must try
and give him a dance.   Here, Mr. Murray! — "Miss Percival."

The very type of a healthy, clean young Englishman
came up, smooth cheeked and bright eyed, with a pleasant
briskness of demeanor that betokened a happy home, a good
temper, and a love of field sports.   He danced with a vigor
which was quite exhilarating to behold.   He talked of every
thing with the keen relish of enjoyment, unimpaired by criti-

cal acumen; no witty, worldwise aphorisms —no sharp-sighted arrows of observation—it was all clear, honest, straight-forward, and without evincing any great powers of mind, was pleasant and as refreshing, after a good deal I had listened to that evening, as healthful country breezes after the rich but noxious perfumes of a conservatory.

"Miss Percival and I have struck up a relationship," said he laughing, to Lady Greybrook, when our quadrille was over. "We find we are nearly connected. My aunt's husband's brother married—"

"Stop! for mercy's sake! I have not a strong head. Why, it is as bad as that dreadful thing about Tom's father and Jack's son, which I never yet could make out. Only think of finding a relation at a ball! 'Tis the very foundation for a romance. Cœlebs, or Japhet is it, who goes over the world in search of a wife? I see it all before me; perilous adventures, through three volumes, and a marriage at the end of the third! I hope you're not within the pro-hibited degrees of consanguinity? that would spoil it all, you know."

I was relieved at my new connection's laughing heartily, for I felt slightly uncomfortable at her ladyship's witticisms. The young man asked leave to call on my mother next day, and went off to dance, and as soon as he was gone, Lady Greybrook said:

"You might do much worse than *that*, my dear. Sir Charles Murray's only son; heir to eight thousand a year, and a nice place in Huntingdonshire. A sort of man, too, that *you* would twist round your finger."

"Thank you for the compliment, if it is one," I answered, laughing; "but I have no talent and less ambition for that sort of work. I should be afraid of entangling myself inex-tricably."

We did not wait for the cotillon. I told the truth when I said I was tired, having danced a great deal, and amused myself far better than I ever expected to do. I was proof against the prayers of three heart-broken gentlemen, but I allowed one the consolation of putting on my cloak for me, and of handing me to the carriage. In the crowd on the stairs was my father, with a handsome woman on his arm.

"Who is that lady?" I whispered to Lady Greybrook.

"Is it possible you don't know the fair one whom your father so constantly rides with?"

A sharp pain shot across my heart. My father nodded, and we passed on. His companion gave me an impertinent stare. I heard nothing of all the nonsense the garrulous Frenchman was pouring forth as a libation to me on my way down stairs. Lord Rawdon was standing near the carriage-door in a sort of brigand's cloak and hat. Lady Greybrook bent forward, after she was in the carriage, to beg him to come to her Opera-box the next night. He signified his assent, and as we drove away, he stood there erect and solemn, slightly raising the large beaver from his head, while all the Frenchmen round broke into a fever of little bows.

"Do you know her?" I asked, suddenly, as we drove along.

"Who, my dear? What are you talking about?"

"The person whom you said — the lady my father was with."

"Oh, no! I don't even remember her name. Not one of our set at all. One meets her at these sort of places, great crowds, where all Paris manages to get — but never in good society. Handsome, don't you think so? but shocking style, so very *décolletée*. We always laugh at the colonel very much about his fair friend."

"Do you?" said I, as the carriage stopped.

CHAPTER IX.

I received a letter from my aunt Mary the following morning, in which, by a curious coincidence, mention was made of two persons, one of whom I had heard of for the first time the previous evening; the other, whose acquaintance I had then made.

"I grieve to hear that you are so soon to be introduced into the Paris world," she wrote. "With your father, you will be placed in many situations of difficulty, requiring all that world-wisdom to steer you safely, which, at your age, you cannot have. If you had one wise female friend near you, I should be happier; good Miss Lateward being of no use in this case. There is a lady spending the winter in Paris, of whom the little I know induces me to think she would be a safe and useful friend, if you can make her such. Her name is Lady Janet Oglevie. Neither her appearance nor manners are particularly prepossessing; you must not be discouraged by that, if the opportunity should offer of becoming acquainted. I know some excellent actions of this woman, though I am personally but slightly acquainted with her . . . Here we are living under orange-blossoms and summer skies, while you, no doubt, are shivering in Paris; and Emmy has benefited by the change no less than by the voyage here, which we performed very prosperously in our friend's yacht, touching at Cadiz, Gibraltar, etc. We shall probably remain here till March, when the winds are said to become cold; then, if Mr. Follet should ask us, we may perhaps cruise about a little to

Naples and so on, before returning to England.   But I fear
the long journey through France for Emmy, and therefore
must relinquish the hope of seeing you this spring, dear
child, for we shall certainly make the journey by sea. . . . .
P. S. There is a young connection of mine, by marriage,
Mr. Charles Murray, going to Paris.   Tell your mother he
is a son of our old acquaintance, when we were girls.   Sir
Gilbert will probably tell him to call on her.   Charles
Murray has been well brought up, I believe, and is probably superior to most of the young men you will meet in
society.   By-the-by, if your father should throw you in the
company of a certain Lady Greybrook, remember *to avoid
her* in every possible way."

I lay in bed, revolving this and other advice equally
difficult to follow, which my dear aunt's letter contained,
until, to my horror, the clock struck eleven.   Miss Lateward pointed to her watch on the table, and I held out my
open letter when I entered her territory ; but I sat down at
once to my books, and tried to banish in them the strange
confusion of thoughts and sounds and shapes that rose there.
It was hard work.   The sun streamed upon Miss Lateward's spectacles — they glittered like Mrs. Fisher's last
night ; then an organ in the street struck up the waltz I had
danced with that strange partner.   I looked out : a hard
frost, and the boys sliding in the gutters, just as we had
glided over the polished *parquet* of the ball-room — What !
my head actually turned by my first ball ?   Come, to work.

That afternoon, Rose and I sat by our mother's sofa, all
three working ; I relating my last evening's adventures, they
listening and questioning and demanding further detail, and
my memory was sadly perplexed to remember how all the
notable beauties were dressed.

" I shall have no visitors to-day," said my mother, looking out upon the blinding snow which for the last hour had
been driving steadily against the window.

"Yes, mother, I think you will have one;" and almost at the same moment came a ring at the bell. "It is Mr. Murray. He is not a Paris dandy. He said he would call, and is not likely to be kept away by a snowstorm."

I was right, he came in with glowing cheeks, sending a stream of frosty breath before him.

My mother received the son of her old acquaintance with her usual graceful manner, into which, perhaps, additional warmth was infused from the fact of my aunt's special recommendation. The tinge of British shyness, which did not sit badly on him, gradually wore off. He talked of his home — oh! it was much changed since my mother's time: the governor had added two wings; he was pretty well, but suffered from the gout — it prevented his hunting; this weather would stop the hunting. Was there any skating on the Seine? He thought Frenchmen great muffs, for his part, but he liked Paris — thought he should spend some time here — and so on.

"Have you known Lady Greybrook long?" asked my mother, when there was a pause in the conversation.

"No; I was introduced to her at the Embassy the other night. She seems such a good-natured person."

"Oh, very," said my mother, after a pause, thinking it necessary to say something; "she was one of the Dalkeiths, you know." (As if that accounted for it.)

"By-the-by, Miss Percival, are you going to act in these theatricals at the Embassy?"

"I did not know there were going to be any. Have you heard who the actors are?"

"Mrs. Fisher told me one of her daughters was to perform, but I believe she has got nothing to say. Borridge, of the Blues, is the great star. He is a very good-looking fellow, you know, and does the sentimental parts."

"Acting must be very pleasant if one has any talent that way, which I certainly have not. Who is the prima donna?

I suppose there is some lady who *does* speak in the course of the piece ? "

" Oh, yes — Miss Wright; clever, they say — an awfully sharp, witty young lady. Borridge is very much smitten, so the love-scenes will be quite natural, you know. Did you hear the impertinent speech Rawdon made her? — advising her not to throw away her birth-Wright for a mess of Borridge! They wanted Rawdon to act, but, of course, he refused."

" Is he a good actor, then? And why ' of course?' "

" Oh! because he can do any thing if he chooses, only he never does choose. Capital voice — but no one can ever get him to sing; and you should see him at billiards! — but he scarcely ever plays. Are you musical, Miss Percival?"

" No, not all."

" But very fond of music, I suppose?"

" It would be hardly true to say ' very fond.' Sometimes I am, but not always. My sister has all the musical talent."

" Really! Do you play or sing?" turning to Rose.

" Yes — no — play — only a little," she stammered out, with a pretty, blushing confusion.

" She plays with great feeling, and will have a very good voice, I think," said my mother. " We are very quiet people and never entertain, but if you should ever feel inclined to drop in of an evening, before one of your late parties, I should be very glad, and we might have some music."

This, though apparently no very great act of hospitality, was a most unexpected move of my mother's. Her ill health and my father's irregular habits had obliged her, many years ago, to give up receiving visits after dinner, according to the foreign fashion. The drawing-room then often wore the appearance of a stage at the close of a bloody tragedy, strewed with bodies in every attitude and state of *déshabille:* my father (if he chanced to be at home) snoring in slippers by the fire; my mother, in curl-papers, stretched on the sofa with a pocket-handkerchief over her face; and we juniors sprawled about the floor like ninepins. This must now be changed. Henceforward we must literally, as well as morally, keep our lamps trimmed in expectation of this visitor's possible advent.

Charles Murray thanked my mother, shook hands with us all round (as none but an Englishman would have done, God bless him!), and took his leave. No sooner was he gone than each took up his note, and loud was the trio we sang in this young gentleman's praise. Mine was a steady-sustained bass of amiability and general pleasantness; my mother kept up a running passage of birth and breeding, as evinced in the resemblance to his father's nose, and such well-shaped feet; while Rose indulged in long flights and cadences, always returning to the original *motivo*, "Such beautiful eyes!"

So Mr. Charles Murray made a favorable impression; and my father announced that evening that he should call on him, and even hinted at the possibility of asking him to dinner; whereat my mother looked grave, as knowing the state of our culinary establishment, and yet did not altogether oppose the idea, as I expected.

Looking over the journal I kept very carefully in those days, I am amused to see what my first impressions of an opera were on that same evening. How unnatural I thought it that people should sing elaborate airs, or, indeed, any airs at all, when they were being led to execution, stabbing their rivals, and in such-like positions. Above all, how irritated I was when the lover, instead of escaping, as he ought (every moment being precious), came forward to the footlights, and began some juggling tricks with his voice, throwing it up out of sight, and catching it again with great dexterity; which argued, I am afraid, that I had but little natural taste for the lyrical drama.

An old gentleman, whom Lady Greybrook introduced as the Marquis d'Ofort, came into the box very soon after us, and seated himself behind me. There was something particularly repulsive to me about this old man, and I instinctively shrank away as he leaned over my chair and began pouring out some faded compliments of the date of the Empire. His hair, which was dyed, was brushed up into a sort of sheaf at the top of his head, intended, no doubt, to add height to a very short figure. He had evidently had recourse to art to conceal the ravages of time and dissipation on his face, which I suppose had once been handsome, judged by a hairdresser's standard. He was a type of the elderly French Hyperion ; *jabots* and jewelled snuff-box, the eternal red ribbon in the button-hole, and the gold-headed cane ; with a reputation still for gallantry, and of a flowery speech, but lacking wisdom and wit to know the true graces that belong to threescore years and ten.

Presently Lord Rawdon came into our box, and was at no pains to conceal his annoyance at finding the place he had intended to occupy already filled. Lady Greybrook opened a fire of wit on him, which he hardly answered, but sat in the back of the box for a few minutes, and then walked out.

In the mean time the first act was over ; and to avoid answering all the nonsense the old marquis talked, I had been reconnoitring the house with Lady Greybrook's glass. The box immediately opposite was occupied by a very pale woman, with some magnificent jewels, and behind her chair two or three men, to whom she occasionally spoke, directing their attention, as it appeared, towards our box. My curiosity was sufficiently excited to ask Lady Greybrook who it was.

"Lord Rawdon will tell you, my dear. Oh, he is gone ! —probably to her box, no great loss, for he is unbearable to-night — so rude. It is a great friend of his, or rather, perhaps, a great admirer — Madame Galoffska — a most charming woman, so spirituelle — pity she stammers, though — and *such* a musician! only she is so affected. She was handsome, too, when I first knew her at St. Petersburg — but she has always some desperate '*passion*' for some one or other, and nothing wears a woman out like that."

" Is she a widow, then ? "

" Ya — as. Oh ! yes ; or separated from her husband, which is the same thing. The Emperor admired her very much, and sent the husband off on some special mission — to Siberia, probably. Her present infatuation is for Lord Rawdon, but he seems extremely cool about it. She was dying of jealousy all the time he was here, I know. Look ! there, he has just gone into her box — now she'll be happy for the night. Just watch him — he is not listening to a word she says, but looking over here all the time. I know I could easily get him back. What fun it would be ! "

At the end of the next act, " Cher marquis," she said, " would you mind asking for my carriage? I doubt whether I shall remain to the end of the next act, for we have to go on to the Austrian embassy."

The Marquis tottered nimbly to his feet, and bowed ; but looked, nevertheless, as if he did very much mind being sent out into the cold, and as if he thought her ladyship ought to keep some young *attaché* in waiting for such services. He seized his opera-hat, however, and velvet-lined cloak, and when he was gone Lady Greybrook, making an almost imperceptible movement with her fan towards the Galoffska box, said,

" You will be relieved from the bore of the old Marquis, my love, for the remainder of the evening ; but you must be more patient under the infliction in future. If he only *would* fancy you, my dear, you have no idea what a thing it would be. The richest *pair de France*, and one of the highest families."

Lord Rawdon entered the box and sat down beside me.

"How is the Galoffska?" began Lady Greybrook. "Un-
feeling monster that you are! She will go home and admin-
ister the knout to her maid out of rage at your desertion.
Not that I believe all the stories about her; but she really
does look so ghastly to-night — whether it is that wreath or
what: and I know, by the movement of her head, she has
been stammering so desperately in her efforts to be agreeable to you that I should not be surprised to hear —"

"In short, you think that the woman who hesitates is lost.
Miss Percival, why don't you smile? You look bored. Is
Roger, the tenor, or I the culprit?"

"He is a wretched actor — perhaps you are a good one.
I heard so to-day, at least — but I am tired, and longing to
get home."

In fact, I did not much fancy the sort of rivalship in which
Lady Greybrook had placed me with Madame Galoffska,
and I was glad when the Marquis at last reappeared to say
the carriage was ready. The opera was nearly over, and
many boxes were already empty. Lord Rawdon offered me
his arm, and in the lobby we met the Russian, leaning on
one of her attendant cavaliers. Lady Greybrook and she
greeted each other as cordially as two jealous ladies generally do, congratulating each other on their looks and their
toilettes with edifying warmth.

"Vous êtes ravissante avec cette coiffure, chère comtesse;
c'est à en perdre la tête!"

"Et vous, chère Lady Greybrook, c-c-c-comme vous avez
b-b-b-b-bonne mine! C'est votre fille?"

Of course she knew who I was, and my estimate of her
general sincerity was not altered when I heard her whisper
to her companion as she passed us,

"Mon Dieu! c-c-comme elle est fardée cette vieille Anglaise!"

In going down the stairs I found I had dropped my fan in

the crowd, which had begun to pour out. I begged Lord Rawdon to go back and look for it. A little old lady in a grey cloak brushed by us at the same moment, gathering up her garments as she passed Lady Greybrook, with a look that might have become the days of the Plague.

A minute or two afterwards, a hand — whose I could not see — was stretched out to me from the crowd of heads. There was my fan, and twisted between its sticks a small piece of paper, apparently a leaf torn out of a pocket-book, with something written on it in pencil. As I stood under a lamp, I could read these words: " You are in a dangerous position — trust the gray mantle who passed you just now." I thrust the paper into my bosom.

" I have found my fan, Lord Rawdon," said I, as he came back. " Some one picked it up. And now tell me, if you can, who is that lady in a grey cloak — there, just getting into her carriage?"

" Lady Janet Oglevie — one of the few honest women in Paris; and she hates me."

As we were driving home, Lady Greybrook unexpectedly began talking of the very person who was in my thoughts.

" I hope that odious woman, Lady Janet, won't be at Mr. Griffith's déjeûner on Saturday. She is quite enough to spoil any thing — a sort of skeleton at a feast — and his are such pleasant little parties, when she is not there. A connection of his, I believe."

" Does she go much into the world? Has she any daughters?"

" Oh, no — never had any children. That absurd woman, Mrs. Oglevie Fisher, is the widow of her step-son; and they don't exactly suit, I should think, as Lady Janet is the most straight-laced old Scotchwoman, and far too righteous, to belong to the set the Fishers do. I wonder, indeed, at seeing her at the Opera. She is one of those people who rail against English residents abroad, and calls Paris ‘ a den of iniquity.'"

" Rather inconsistent, is it not, her coming here herself?"

" Those inconsistencies are remarkably common, and I suppose she would tell you she had some good reason.   But here we are at your door. Good night, dear. Go and dream of a marquis's coronet and an hotel in the Faubourg St. Germain."

Instead of dreaming, I lay awake a great part of the night, thinking of the strange communication I had received, until I had made up my mind that it was probably written by the little old lady herself, between whom and Lady Greybrook there was evidently no love lost.   As to the counsel itself, I was perfectly ready to make a friend of the " Gray Mantle " —the more so at my aunt's special recommendation — should the opportunity offer.   In the mean time, my position was none of my own choosing. I could not alter it, if I would.

Would I, if I could?

How we play the hypocrite with our own hearts! Perhaps, after all my self-protestations, it would have cost me something to withdraw from the brilliant world into which I was now launched.

CHAPTER X

Mr. Griffiths was an old bachelor of good fortune, and of what Mrs. Oglevie Fisher termed a "refoined mind." That is, he was fond of pictures and good dinners, and in his small hotel every thing was in perfect taste — as irreproachable as was the smooth and polished old gentleman who presided there. He chose his company with no less fastidiousness than the rest of his furniture. At his small morning parties only what was pleasant and attractive, either in looks or conversation, was assembled — if I except such necessary bores as his connections, the Fishers, and such lions as are held privileged to be dull or sulky in society, when, like their brethren of the forest, they are indisposed to roar.

Lady Greybrook and I entered Mr. Griffiths' miniature picture-gallery, and found some twenty people there. A knot of men in the centre of the room talking the learned jargon of art. A knot of dowagers in juvenile attire, among whom Mrs. Fisher was conspicuous, falling into ecstasies over some Sévres cups and saucers. A flirtation was being carried on opposite a Magdalene of Guido's, and another, a little further off, at the piano, over an unsung duet of Gabussi's. A cloud of young ladies were hovering about, like Zephyrs, between the statues and large baskets of flowers that stood at distances down the room, and made altogether a very pretty picture. One figure only sat in solitary dignity on a sofa near the fire, looking rigid and stony to the last degree, in a slate-colored dress. It was Lady Janet.

Mr. Griffiths received us with that mixture of cordiality

and courtliness which belongs to a past day. Lord Rawdon's shake of the hand just after formed a notable contrast to it. Not that his was by any means the limp grasp — the unstiffening of the knee-joints and collapse of the whole person which young England so much affects now, but rather the free and easy greeting of a man who is confident of being well received.

Mrs. Fisher, followed by one of her cygnets, swam forwards, and, arching her neck, expressed " the deloight " she felt at meeting Lady Greybrook, and begged I might be presented to her, whereupon she presented her cygnet, and we talked young ladies' platitudes with becoming imbecility.

Madame Galoffska was announced soon after this, and entered with a sweet infantine grace, acknowledging the salutations of her friends. Lady Janet, meantime, apparently took no cognizance of the outer world, but stared straight before her at a buhl cabinet in the corner, as who should say, " Nothing shall induce me to lean back or otherwise compromise myself." I was lost in contemplation of this unprepossessing figure, when I heard Mr. Griffiths say to a gentleman, whose back was towards me,

" Here, Hubert, I want to introduce you to Lady Greybrook. Allow me to present my nephew to you: Lady Greybrook — Mr. Rochford; Miss Percival — Mr. Rochford."

I almost started when I recognized those strange, searching eyes. He smiled slightly.

" I believe you are fond of pictures, Miss Percival." (How does he know that? I thought, but answered, of course, something very different.) " Let me do the honors of my uncle's collection, which is a small, but very good one. Here we begin with the early Italian and German schools, of which there are some very good specimens, and go round the walls." And, thereupon, he led me down the room gradually, telling an anecdote of one painter, pointing out the subtle beauties of another — crude Siennese, on gold grounds — early Florentines, full of a poetry of their own; grand and individual types. There was no ostentation of learning in his conversation: it had been a labor of love with him to know something about these men and their works, and he spoke of them in the inartificial language of honest appreciation, not in the sliced phrases of a pedant. His manner was grave and earnest; the expression of his face habitually severe, but when he smiled, the whole face was lit with sunshine, and, like the words of a silent person, these smiles gained value from their rarity. Lord Rawdon sauntered up just as I was hearing something of the portrait of a Riccardi, by Lippo Lippi.

"His name was Giorgio, so, by a license common in his day, Lippo made a saint of him, put him on his best suit of Milan steel, and he is handed down to posterity as Saint George."

"Fra Lippo did not succeed as well in making a saint of *himself*, in spite of his Carmelite hood," said Rawdon.

"We have nothing to do with the artist's life," said Hubert Rochford; "that he was a great painter ought to be enough for us."

"Can you really separate the man from his works?" I said. "I always feel so curious to know every thing that concerns the author or painter who really gives me pleasure, and I have thought that such an interesting book might be written, showing how often outward influences have affected different men's works — a sort of philosophy of art."

"So treated, it might be instructive, as well as interesting, to trace the workings of the Flemish and Italian minds, for instance, and compare them in any one century — how realistic the one always was, even in the treatment of sacred subjects, and how singular that the other should never have painted a domestic scene — nothing but mythology, when they were not employed on Holy Families for their convents and churches; and yet the Italian peasantry of the fourteenth century must have been wonderfully picturesque. But all this is different from the mania for biography, which does infinitely more harm than good, I think, in the present day. We are bound to accept what is great in the man with thankfulness, not to rake up all the wretched scandals of a life. It can do no one any good."

"The shades of Brantôme and all illustrious gossips confound you, Rochford," said Rawdon. "You would do away with all the romance of history — all the '*mémoires secrètes pour servir*,' etc. Well, for my part, I like to know what kind of soap Maria Antoinette used; and Louis Quartorze's shirt, and Mrs. Masham's basin of water, are more interesting to me than Marlborough's and Condé's battles. I am by no means a great reader, Miss Percival, but these details make me feel that the illustrious dead were flesh and blood, like myself. The scandalous chronicle of Fair Rosamond is positively the only thing I remember about our own Henry, and —— "

"Pardon me, my dear lord!" interrupted Mrs. Fisher, who had been watching her opportunity to fasten on her prey, "the best authorities are agreed in desoiding that story to be apocryphal."

"I hate all authorities, ma'am!" growled Rawdon, with an amusing assumption of the savage Johnsonian manner. "If the bones of Henry Plantagenet were to rise and contradict me, ma'am, I should still believe what I learnt in my nursery."

We left him in the toils of the Fisher, and walked on.

"Now-a-days," said Rochford, "no sooner is a great man dead — nay, before he is dead, sometimes — than all his secret weaknesses and miseries are dragged into the light. Nothing is held sacred. There is an eminent composer still living, whose early career of vice is already published for the world's benefit. Suppose a memoir of Shakespeare (whose life we know less of than almost any other great poet, except Homer), were to turn up, and that we found the man fall far short of the poet, the world would hail it, of course, as an invaluable literary treasure, but would it really be such a gain? I doubt it. Byron's private life, which he himself ostentatiously paraded to the world, made men imagine, for a time, that mental power and moral depravity were almost inseparable; and the consequence was, that for years, as Carlyle says, 'some transcript of Milton's Devil' was the universal *béau idéal*. The fashion for it has passed, as all fashions do; but we still occasionally see traces of such an evil influence" (and he said this, I thought, with marked emphasis), "for, if true of the very meanest life, that its workings are felt through all eternity, doubly true is it of such a man's. The less we hear of its unedifying details, the better."

We had wandered, as our conversation had done, from the pictures, and were standing in a doorway, when Mr. Griffiths came up, bringing with him Lady Greybrook and Mrs. Fisher, from whom Rawdon had broken away.

"Here are a few modern masters in this room, Mesdames, if you care for them."

"Modern pictures! me dear Mr. Griffiths, with gems of ancient art around me! I have the bad taste only to care for the old mausters."

"You will find one or two good things, though they *are* by modern painters, in there, I think," said the old gentleman, good-humoredly; and, as we all followed him, "Here is a Wilkie," he continued, "what do you say to that? And here is a Decamps that has been very much admired; and here a Bonnington and a Constable, side by side — the two English artists who have had such an influence over the modern French school. Here is a little sketch from ' Faust' by Ary Scheffer — what do you say to that?"

"Ha! very sweet, indeed! *chiaro scuro* perfect," said the swan, doubling up her fist before her eyes, with the airs of connoisseurship. "Me dear Sir, I stand corrected before this great work — as foine as Raffaelle, 't is indeed — truly the mellifluence of pictorial harmony!"

"And what is this?" said Lady Greybrook, who had followed us, and was standing before a small easel with its back to me. "Pretty little thing — very. Whose is it, Mr. Griffiths?"

"Oh! that is by a young artist in great distress, I believe. My nephew bought it some time ago — wants force, but there is a nice feeling for color in it, is n't there?"

"Charming!" cried Mrs. Fisher, who seemed suddenly to have found a taste for modern art; "quite charming! What's his name? — in distress, did you say? Would give lessons cheap, no doubt. Just the style I should like me daughters to paint in."

I had gone round, and was leaning over the mighty sweep of the lady's shoulder. My cheeks were very red; for the reader will have guessed the fact that I recognized my own performance, which I sold to Ismael. A light suddenly broke in upon me. I glanced up, and found Rochford's eye fixed on me, after his peculiar fashion. Then, for the first time, I remembered where it was I had seen them before.

"I can tell you nothing about him myself, my dear Madam," said the old gentleman. "I believe my nephew knows the artist's name, but there was a foolish mystery made about it when I asked Ismael. He said something about a distressed wife and ten children, so I conclude the poor fellow would be glad enough to give lessons."

The eyes never released their hold on me. "He knows the truth," I said to myself, "and is wondering whether I should have moral courage, before all these fine people, to confess that I was the poor artist. There was no obligation, certainly, and yet I should like to show him that I am perfectly indifferent to their opinion."

No doubt there was a good deal of bravado in this, for the company had most of them flocked into the room, and it required some assurance to raise one's voice at all in such an assembly. There was Captain Borrage, that burly Life-Guardsman, handling his moustaches with a supercilious air over the back of the easel; two or three tittering misses, ready-armed with javelins; and Madame Galoffska, with her double-barrelled glass levelled full at me.

"I am the best able to answer any questions about this picture, Mr. Griffiths," I said at last, in a distinct voice, "as it was painted and *sold* by me. I am sorry Monsieur Ismael thought it necessary to tell any stories about it, though he was not at liberty to mention my name."

Lady Greybrook turned sharply round, colored, and seemed about to speak, but did not. There was an awful pause. Most of the women stared at each other as if they thought I had gone mad. To commit, and then to confess such an outrage on their class! One or two only, looked at me with well-bred astonishment, and said something about its being wonderful for a person who was not an *artiste*. Hubert Rochford's eyes betrayed no surprise; but, if I read their expression aright, something of pleasure and approval. Our courtly host, as soon as he had recovered from the shock caused by my announcement, delivered himself of a neatly-turned speech, in which his surprise was conveyed in flattering terms, and terminated with this flowery figure: —

"It requires only the forcing-bed of necessity to bring your talent to full fruit, my dear young lady. Brutal as it may seem, therefore, I am almost tempted to regret the distressed mother and ten children."

This happy turn gave the company an opportunity of laughing, and relieved the uncomfortable silence. Mrs. Fisher, indeed, turned round, and solemnly assured me she considered it "a most creditable performance for an amateur;" but this had not the effect so gloomy a compliment might have been expected to produce, for, following as it did her late extravagant praise, it was very merrily received by Lord Rawdon and one or two others.

"Me dear Lord," she hissed into his ear — not so low but that I caught every word — "*Ongtre nous*, it's all out of drawing. Look at the Infant's thumb! the articulation of the muscles in the Virgin's neck — all the loins —"

"Loins, Mrs. Fisher? It is fortunate there is no American here!"

"Loins of the neck, you wicked man. You know, *unfortunately*, I have such a critical eye."

"Winkleman was a joke to you," said his Lordship. I am afraid he intended it for a pun.

The company began to move off to the breakfast-room.

"Young woman," said a harsh voice, and Lady Janet Oglevie held out her hand, "I respect you. You do right in turning God's talent to account, and you do better in not being ashamed to own it."

I was taken so completely by surprise that I had not a word to say. She continued :

"Most lasses would have shrunk from telling the truth. They all looked queerly at you, did n't they? Vain, empty-headed things ! — you 're worth them all put together. What brings you here? What have you got to do with any one of them? Bad company — very bad company for a young thing like you. The Miss Oglevie Fishers ! — yes; but they 've got their mother — and a wise one she is, too ! I have nothing to say to *their* way of going on. Did n't I see you come into the room with that —? Hem ! Perhaps after all, you *are* very poor — that story about the distress, not far wrong, eh? Well, never mind, don't be angry. I like your modest looks. What 's your name? I 'll be your friend."

It is impossible to give an idea of the sharp, irritable, inquisitive look and manner, that accompanied these questions and remarks.

"I am much obliged to you, Lady Janet. My name is Percival. I have no relations here; but you know my aunt, Lady Dacre, I think?"

"Very little — good woman, I believe — had a fool of a husband, whom she managed capitally. Where is she? Why don't she keep you out of all this mud, eh?"

"She is in Italy. I am just come out, and my mother being an invalid, her friend, Lady Greybrook, is kind enough —"

"Friend! friend!" she muttered. "Better a millstone were hanged about your neck, child. Percival — daughter of Colonel Percival's? — hem? thought so." Then, after a moment's reflection, "I shall call on your mother to-morrow."

She took my arm, and led me into the breakfast-room, where most of the guests were already seated at a table artistically laid out with fruit and flowers in gold vessels of all forms and sizes; rare jars of Venice glass, containing Eastern preserves, and figures of old Dresden, laden with baskets of *bon-bons*. The admiration of all this, and the expectation of a good breakfast, had put every one into good humor, and they were laughing very heartily when we appeared; but Lady Janet soon put a stop to *that;* a blight immediately fell upon the conversation at our end of the table, which visibly drooped and died away in fragments. I sat between her and the Life-Guardsman, who confined his attentions to a lady upon the other side of him — Miss Wright, as I afterwards learnt — nor addressed a word to me, beyond mere bread-and-salt civilities. As Lady Janet did not open her lips either, I should have had a meal of Trappist character, but for the amusement I found in watching my opposite neighbors. Madame Galoffska had managed that Lord Rawdon should sit next her. She was employing all the artillery of her charms, by turns languid, infantine, impassioned. But on the other side of the noble Lord, Mrs. Fisher, by a dexterous manœuvre, had planted herself, and showed no disposition to abandon the field to the Russian. She opened the attack with vigor, and the struggle between these ladies lasted nearly an hour, until her antagonist made a bold stroke, and carried the day by a *coup de main.*

"Milord," putting back her long curls and half closing her eyes, "Je me sens défaillante — c-c-c-conduisez-moi, je vous en prie, au s-s-s —"

"Au sacrifice?" suggested Rawdon.

"Au salon, milord."

What could he do but offer his arm? When we entered the drawing-room a quarter of an hour after, Madame Galoffska was at the piano, and Rawdon leaning on the back of a chair at her side. She knew that here she was omnipotent; no one with a soul for music could resist the charm of her playing, and once upon her throne, she feared no rival. As she very seldom played, the world treated the performance with a respect seldom paid to piano-forte playing. Not a word was spoken when she was at the instrument. No! Mistress Fisher, even you must be silent awhile, or you will be hissed down.

The syren made a feint of rising, but being duly entreated, began rubbing her large white hands, while we gathered round her in a circle. Then her eyes wandered vaguely over the group, as if seeking inspiration — wrapt in a vision of far-off things — until they lighted on me with an expression that made me shiver. Rawdon had given me his chair, but still leaned on the back of it.

"Don't look at her face," he said, in a low voice, "and you'll fancy it is an angel playing."

When she bent her eyes, and their cold expression was

veiled, I thought he was wrong. The marble-cut face, with lips slightly parted, was almost divine, presiding over the grand and heavenly melodies of Beethoven and Mozart. Then, after some of Chopin's wild mazourkas, she began to give specimens of the modern "Romantic School," as it calls itself; mental aberrations they appeared to me, without rhyme or reason. This, however, she told us, was the music that would ultimately triumph over every other — the perfect marriage of melody and verse; each word in the text with its proper musical synonyme. As she went on with her little impediment of speech, to explain the theory, it was, indeed, a very pretty piece of German mysticism. We had outlived antiquated forms — these were the days for straight-to-the-heartedness — for throwing aside all that was false — for the worship of the true and the earnest.

"Enfin," she added, "cette musique-là r-r-remplit un b-b-b — "

"Bal? — Bête? — Bain chaud?" inquired Rawdon.

"Un besoin métaphysique de l'âme, milord."

There was a good deal more in the same style, which the company understanding but imperfectly, and finding rather dull, her audience gradually oozed away. Mrs. Fisher was one of the first to rise.

"Had Praxiteles been a pianist," said she, "he would have played like that, at once refoined and chaste!" and having done what this virtuous woman considered to be her duty, she "took the stage," as actors say, and swept to the further end of the room, with an air that said plainly, "Come, we have had enough of that to last some time."

Only three or four remained near the piano. "Did any one sing?" it was asked. Now, I am fortunately or unfortunately, as it may happen — gifted with uncommonly sharp ears. The reader has already had evidence of this, and I warn him that he will constantly find me overhearing what was never intended for me.

"Ask her — I dare say she does," I heard a young lady whisper to Captain Borrage. "Who knows? Perhaps she has sung at one of those *cafés* in the Champs Elysées — *décollettée*, you know, in pink, on a stage — I shouldn't be surprised. It would be quite in character with so independent a young lady. Don't you see her, screaming ' Robert, toi que j'aime ' to an enraptured audience?"

Something very like an oath, I think, broke from his lordship's black beard, behind my chair.

" Such *effronterie* in a girl of that age," resumed the fair speaker. When, a few minutes afterwards, Captain Borrage came up, and asked me to "favor the company" — he was sure I sang ; I replied, very quietly, that I only did so when I was paid.

" Brava ! " growled the black beard. Then suddenly turning to the lady, " By-the-by, Miss Wright, *à propos* of effrontery — I heard you use the word, I think — (Wright grew scarlet), do you know if the story is true that is told all over Paris of an English girl going to the bal masqué the other night, with her mamma, and making an appointment with her own papa in the *foyer ?* They even say she kept it, and enjoyed the old gentleman's consternation when she pulled off her mask. We want to find out who it was, and you, as a great authority in these matters, perhaps can tell us."

No one who watched the lady's face could doubt to whom the story referred.

"I am obliged to you," she said, with a ghastly smile, for supposing that I know all the scandal of Paris.

" Scandal ! Heaven forbid ! it is purely as a matter of fact, an historical anecdote characteristic of the times we live in."

" ' Pon my soul, you 're too bad, Rawdon " flared up the

Guardsman. "I believe you invent these stories, and pretend you've heard them—I really do." And thus the sword went on, slashing impotently at the coronet, while I walked to a distant window, out of reach of the disputants. Rochford came up soon after, but no allusion was made on either side to that first meeting of ours, and we fell into a desultory conversation, of which I only remember part.

"You seem surrounded in this house by every thing that makes life pleasant. I can't fancy a more charming home."

"Do you think so? I wouldn't live in Paris for all the world. I come here generally every winter, for a month or two, to see my uncle, for I hate Paris."

"It is hardly civil, do you know, to say that, as I live here. It is plain you have not been brought up in Paris, at all events. I am *obliged* to live here, and, fortunately, am contented."

"You would probably find a quiet English life very flat after it, which *I*, on the contrary, think the only enviable existence. Here, leading the sort of life they do in society, people have no time for thought. The perpetual excitement of the wheel going round prevents people's seeing how far they are on the great high-road. They lose sight of the aim of their existence, till suddenly the wheel stops, and they are jerked out. Isn't it so?"

"Perhaps. I have seen very little of the life you are talking of, yet. My recollection of England is of a foggy-looking house in Pall-mall, with spikes all round it, where my grandfather lived, and where I was once staying, as a child. The sun never shone in. I used to stand upon a chair, and look over the wire blinds and through the very dirty windows of the dining-room. That is all I know of England. Do you wonder at my preferring bright and sunny Paris? Then, as to the people, you will be shocked, Mr. Rochford, but the manners of my countrymen and women seem to me very bad; often, instead of courtesy and

kindness, arrogance, impertinence, flippancy.   For instance —
but do you agree with me? or are you disposed to defend
even your country's manners, like a true patriot?"

"Certainly I am," said he, smiling.   "You are describing
the manners of a particular set — the fast and fashionable.
Nothing so well-bred as an English lady — nothing so ill-
bred as a fashionable English woman.   You must not confound the two.   Your experience, I fear —"

But Lady Greybrook here announced that it was time to
go.   She had a dinner engagement, and must take some
"repose" beforehand.   I was astonished, for it was difficult
to imagine her otherwise than restless and excited, even in
bed.   However, I now know that certain terms mean very
different things in different mouths, and "repose," in her
ladyship's case, meant milk of roses, and a bath of amandine
and eau de Cologne.

CHAPTER XI.

This is not a fashionable novel. I have given the reader one or two specimens of the society into which I was now introduced, and I have no intention of detailing for him all the balls and parties to which I went nightly. An extract or two from my journal, linked together by a few words, will tell the story of weeks.

Lady Janet did not call on my mother the following day, having been taken ill the same night, as I afterwards learnt, and confined to her bed for a fortnight. She was so exceedingly unattractive to me, that I cannot say I had any poignant regret at not seeing her again, only, perhaps, a curiosity to know why she should have felt sufficient interest in a stranger to write that mysterious little note, and offer me her friendship. In the whirl of dissipation into which I was now plunged I had nearly forgotten the old lady, when one day, on my return from driving with Lady Greybrook. I found from my mother that Lady Janet had called. The visit, apparently, had been of no very pleasant nature, judging from the state of my mother's nerves that evening, and her repeatedly asserting that *some* people couldn't put themselves into *other* people's position, and that it was all very fine talking, but how was it to be helped? with other remarks of a similarly tangible nature. Poor dear mother! I guessed at once what had been the subject of Lady Janet's conversation, and almost resented the interference. For I enjoyed myself exceedingly well in the life I led, owing, no doubt, to the fact that I felt an increasing interest in two persons whom I was in the habit of constantly meeting.

Lord Rawdon had established himself as a constant, almost daily, visitor at our house. My father did not encourage his intimacy as much as I expected, considering his position and reputed fortune, but my mother declared he was charming. Let others call him what they pleased — bearish, bitterly sarcastic, mad — for her he was only wise and witty — to her he was always courteous and kind. And what woman could withstand this? A man has but to make himself disagreeable to the many to be doubly appreciated by the few to whom he is civil. And how amusing we find satire when the satirist makes us distinctly feel that under no circumstances can his fangs be sharpened upon ourselves! Lord Rawdon, whose manner towards me had undergone a gradual change since our first acquaintance, was very different in our house to the man he showed himself for the world. He was often sarcastic; but there were moments when one caught a glimpse into some unexpected abyss of tenderness that took one by surprise. This was especially the case when alluding to his own mother once; and I could not help fancying that some indefinable association with her was the cause of his tender deference to *my* mother. Silent he was, too, and gloomy at times; but it was when touching on serious subjects that the strange wildness of his manner startled me into the belief that there really was a touch of insanity about him. It was as if in that one chamber of the brain all was darkness and chaos.

If I ever asked myself what my feeling towards him was, I must have found it difficult to answer. It was less any one sentiment than a compound of many anomalous ones. He interested me. That very unexpectedness and difficulty of reconciling the various sides of his character that were constantly turning up, stimulated curiosity, and had for me a considerable charm. My vanity was pleased that he should prefer my society to that of the many handsome and clever women who smiled on him. I did not believe such a *blasé* man of the world could fall in love (as I understood the term); but I enjoyed the influence which I began to see I had over him. It was like mounting a wild horse, which is only tractable under the light hand of a woman; an exciting amusement enough. And yet it might be dangerous, too, for his was a passionate nature, difficult, perhaps, to rein in, after a certain time. I pitied him sincerely, for I felt sure that he had never been a happy man; but I had no respect for him, since it was plain he had none for himself.

Hubert Rochford I saw less of, though he asked permission to call on my mother, and came. She did not much fancy him. Too solemn and priggish for a young man — no doubt he would make a very good clergyman — for her part, she liked something a little more lively. But I never could look on him in the light of a common acquaintance. The peculiar circumstances under which we first met must always have prevented that, had I not instinctively felt that he took a deeper interest in me than word or look ever told; for the expression of those eyes was more keen and searching than tender, and his language was always singularly guarded — nay, even cold, at times.

It almost invariably happened that he found Lord Rawdon with us when he called, and even my mother, who was not sharp-sighted, remarked that a cloud passed over his face when such was the case. In truth, it was plain how antagonistic these two men were in all their habits of thought and conduct. If Lord Rawdon's was the more aggressive, Rochford's was not a less deep-rooted aversion. The former was always peculiarly disagreeable and sarcastic when Rochford was present; while he, on the other hand, generally made as though he heard him not, and when absent, avoided, with obvious purpose, all mention of Lord Rawdon. The orbits of these gentlemen were not the same.

When they came dangerously near each other, I was constantly thinking of the disastrous result should two planets, by some celestial derangement fall foul of one another!

The following extract from my journal is dated about three weeks after Mr. Griffiths' *déjeûner:*

Poor old Lateward is laid up with a cold — not seen her for two or three days — the schoolroom seems quite lost without her. Lady Greybrook having very good-naturedly given me an order for Marie Dumont, who was out of employment when Miss Lateward called on her last week, I determined to take Betsy with me, and carry the order myself, as it may be some days before L. is able to go out, and poor Marie might be starving in the mean time. I was properly punished for my disobedience of orders by meeting there the very person of all others I would most have avoided — Mr. Rochford! It did not occur to me that on his return to Paris this year he would probably call and inquire after the poor sempstress, whom he was so kind to last winter; which it seems he did some days ago, and procured her work at once. He was any thing but agreeably surprised at seeing me, I think; as little so as I was at meeting him. But Marie was enchanted, and the child ran up and held his rosy cheek to my face. Rochford moved away to the window while I explained to Marie what the work was I had brought for her. I would not sit down. I felt anxious to be gone as soon as possible, and was not quite comfortable, to say the truth, with that stern and silent man there all the time.

"Good-by! I mustn't stay. How the child is grown, Marie! Almost big enough to go to school, is n't he?"

"Yes, mademoiselle ; and, next summer, this good gentleman has generously promised —"

Rochford turned impatiently round. "Mademoiselle did not come here to listen to all that, Marie." Then, as I prepared to leave the room, he added, in English, "Miss Percival, if you are going, allow me to conduct you down stairs. They are dark and slippery. Have you been here before?"

"Only once."

"You met her, I think, accidentally, a year ago?"

"I did; and was the indirect means of saving her from starvation — through you."

"Do your friends approve of your visiting her?"

"No one knows of my coming to-day. Why do you ask? Is there any crime in visiting a poor woman?"

"I am afraid, in the opinion of the world in which you live, 'c'est plus qu'un crime — c'est une faute,' for a young lady to be seen wandering up and down dark alleys like these. You have learned enough of society by this time, Miss Percival, to know that it is not very good-natured."

I felt myself coloring as I replied, "Thank you for reminding me of it particularly at this moment. We are in the street, Mr. Rochford, and my road lies this way. Good morning."

I bowed and left him. I would not shake hands, for I was indignant with what I thought at the moment was his impertinent interference; and yet I rather like him for it, too, now I come to be cool over it. He is very unlike all the other men I meet; certainly I always feel the most perfect confidence that he is in earnest, that he does not talk for the sake of talking, but that what he says he really means. He makes no fine speeches — there is none of the silent and subtle flattery of a certain person in his intercourse with me. He is stern and uncompromising. I know he does not approve of me very often, and I enjoy defending the society and life here against his severe strictures. I even pretend to like it all much better than I really do, for I would not have him suppose —

Interrupted by a long visit from that tiresome old Marquis. My mother sent for me, so I was obliged to go; otherwise I always avoid him when I can. His conversation is perfectly insupportable to me, and I was so glad when Charles Murray came in and made a diversion in my favor. The latter often drops in now of an evening for an hour, though I do not see much of him, as I am generally dressing to go out; but Rose plays to him on the piano, and he is easily amused. A good-natured fellow.

(Two days afterwards is the following entry:)

Last evening we had a small dinner at Lady Greybrook's. Mr. Rochford sat next to me. I said to him:

"How is it that you think so much about the conventions of society, you who talk of the purposeless existence of the fashionable world, etc.?"

"I think the world's opinion, as regards women especially, is entitled to respect. A thing may be harmless in itself, Miss Percival, nay, even right, and yet —"

"No, no, no, Mr. Rochford! There is but one right and one wrong. Don't attempt to make me think otherwise. Understand me: I generally do the latter, but it is because I want moral courage, not because I succeed in persuading myself it is better *not* to do the right thing — in short, to leave well alone!"

He smiled. "And yet, surely, you must see that a virtue proper for one, is not, of necessity, proper for all."

"As, for instance, visiting the poor is not a proper virtue for a town young lady, though proper enough for a country young lady, with a basket on her arm, and a pair of pattens? Oh, nonsense, Mr. Rochford! it is all a matter of conventionality."

"I should rather say a matter of judgment."

"Is not conscience judgment? If one feels sure that what one does is right, what does it signify what all the world says?"

"I am afraid you will find that it signifies, sometimes, a

great deal — but this leads to a whole set of questions rather difficult to discuss with you. The Roman doctrine of expediency is so far wise, inasmuch as it admits of the judgment's being exercised in matters of principle. You look surprised. It is not true, as you said just now, that there is only one right and one wrong. There are often conflicting duties. What your judgment then points to as the most expedient thing becomes the rightest."

"And what if it be opposed to the opinion of those whom you ought to respect and obey?"

"If it be a matter of judgment — not impulse — act on it."

"And I act entirely on impulse, I'm afraid."

"Your impulses, I feel sure, are always good and womanly," said Rochford, with unusual warmth; "but do not trust them too far, or let them carry you away. Life is not the easy thing — the long summer's day — some people try and make themselves believe. I speak to you, Miss Percival, as young men do not generally speak; but I have been peculiarly brought up — taught to have a stern reprobation for things I here see smiled over. I cannot shape my speech and manners to suit this society, and I cannot talk foolish nonsense to you. I feel you are worth something better than that. Surely, this life you are leading, the people with whom you are thrown, are not congenial to you?"

"Very often not. But as Shakespeare says, 'What is without a remedy should be without regard.' The position is not of my own seeking. I only make the best of what I can't help."

"There are positions so serious, so disastrous in their results on our whole after-life, that any thing is better than submitting to them."

"It is easy to say that, Mr. Rochford," I replied, somewhat bitterly. "You do not know all the difficulties of opposition in such a case. Besides which, I think you are very prejudiced against Lady Greybrook. There are things I don't approve of in her, and particularly in the people who surround her, but she is very good-natured — even kind and generous to those who are in distress."

"Tanto buono che non val niente," muttered Rochford, with a sarcastic expression, very foreign to his face, as we rose from table. "It is an old Italian proverb, full of meaning."

"Why do you come here, Mr. Rochford, if it is only to find fault with everybody and every thing?"

He looked at me for a moment; then replied, carelessly,

"I come to study character."

"And, apparently, what you find is not to your liking."

The old Marquis came up just then, and there was an end of all conversation, of course. A sense of sleep always steals over me when he approaches. I feel, "If I were as tedious as a king, I could find in my heart to bestow it all upon him;" and the worst of it is, Lady Greybrook persists in telling me I ought to consider myself particularly honored, and that it is evident the old gentleman is *épris*. I hope she does not talk to any one else in this sort of way; but I observed Madame Galoffska last night directing Lord Rawdon's attention to where the Marquis sat brooding over me. I am sure if woman ever showed her dislike, I make my sentiments evident enough. *A propos* of Madame G., I don't think she likes me. Why? I have never done her any harm that I know of. Rawdon, and some others, were looking over a book of sketches which Lady Greybrook had asked me to bring (very much against my wish), when Madame G. walked up. Rawdon handed the book to her, with some extravagant words of praise. I heard them, though I was quite at the other end of the room; and I also heard the rejoinder, accompanied by the most malignant glance, as she tossed the book aside:

"Ah? ça — elle dessine bien? Je lui ferai fair le portrait de m-m-mon chien!"

Late in the evening, when nearly every one was gone (there was a small evening party), I saw Mr. Rochford sit down with my sketches, and begin looking over them alone. There was one of a window in the Hôtel Cluny, which he examined for some time; at last, I walked up to the table and said,

"What attraction is there in that sketch, Mr. Rochford? You have been looking at it for five minutes, and it is very ill done."

"It might be better," he answered, quietly. "It is not, architecturally, very correct: but yet correct enough for my purpose. Do you know if there is any print of this?"

"I dare say there is; but what *is* your purpose?"

"I am building a school-house at home, and want a window of this sort. I was struck with this one the other day when I was at the Hôtel Cluny; but, unfortunately, I am no draughtsman. I can be critical, you see, like Mrs. Oglevie Fisher, but I can do nothing myself."

"I will copy the sketch for you, if you like it."

(A fortnight later, the following entry :)

My father came into my room most unexpectedly this morning.

"I have come to speak to you, Rita, about that fellow Rawdon. It is perfectly absurd his coming here in the way he does, and you encourage him. Every one knows that he means nothing — he is not a marrying man; and if he was, I am told he is so deucedly in debt, that —"

"Make your mind perfectly easy, father. Lord Rawdon has not the least intention of asking me; and I have n't the least intention of accepting him, if he did."

"It is all very fine talking in that way, but it keeps off other men. I know that the Marquis d'Ofort is only waiting for the least encouragement to come forward."

“Then he will have to wait long enough.”

“Your head has been turned by success, you foolish girl. You won’t have many such offers, and marry you *must* before long, that’s all. Do you think that puritanical fellow, Rochford, means any thing? I hear he has a tolerable rent-roll, and Lady Greybrook says she encourages him, as a *pis-aller*.”

“Perhaps you would wish me to ask him?”

“I am not certain I sha’n’t do so myself. He is certainly behaving very badly, if he doesn’t intend to propose.”

“You are not in earnest, father. You could not think seriously of doing such a thing. I should never be able to speak to Mr. Rochford again. His conduct towards me has always been studiously guarded.”

“Has he never said any thing that would lead you to suppose —”

“Never! He has never said any thing that a true and honorable Englishman might not say to any girl in whom he felt some interest, without meaning —”

“Sentimental stuff!” said my father, turning on his heel. “This comes from Lady Dacre, I suppose, this sort of twaddle about ‘true and honorable Englishmen.’ I know the style of thing.”

“So does she,” I answered, quietly enough.

“Very well,” said he, getting very red. “You understand, honorable or not, the first eligible offer you have, by G—d, you shall accept it!”

CHAPTER XII.

In spite of my defence of Lady Greybrook, as recorded in
the last chapter, I am afraid I must confess that she did not
improve on increasing intimacy. Little by little I began to
see that all the brilliancy was false lacquer — the good-
nature flavored by a far-sighted prudence based upon an
adage touching those who dwell in glass houses. She seldom
said an ill-natured thing, unless it would have been at the
sacrifice of a witty one, and she often did what was kind,
when it did not entail any personal inconvenience. Her
money she would give away right and left; but that is what
certain natures find it easiest to be generous of. Her heart
was too saturated with worldliness to be able to expend
much sympathy or real solicitude on objects that did not
touch her personally in some way. Her craving for excitement was a perfect malady; I often thought she *dreaded* to
be left alone — that the secret monitor whose voice is heard
in the still-night season, made himself heard even to her
sometimes, poor, restless, uneasy woman! Whatever she
once had been, this the world had now left her. During all
the hours I sat beside her in that green chariot, day after
day, and night after night, we never got nearer to each
other. But I had the advantage — if advantage it was —
of knowing gradually every corner of her character; for,
indeed, the veil was transparent enough; while "she never
could make me out — such an odd compound" (as I heard
her once say) "of effrontery and shyness, cleverness and
10

stupidity, vanity and want of common womanly coquetry, as that girl is, I never met."

The Marquis d'Ofort now constantly dined at Lady Greybrook's, and I was lost in astonishment at her capacity for making herself agreeable to that old bore, until I observed the dexterity with which she always managed to collect a small auditory of men round her, before she began to be brilliant, ostensibly for the Marquis's sole edification. Truth compels me to add, that sometimes, when the spirits of these little coteries ran away with them, the bounds of decorum were not very rigidly regarded in their speech, and the mirth of the old marquis on these occasions always rose exceedingly. A number of equivocal jokes and *mots à double entente* used to pass between her ladyship and some of the Frenchmen who were in the habit of coming often to her house, the point of which I sometimes did not, and always appeared not, to understand the least in the world.

I received a letter from my aunt about this time — the last one, alas! that I was ever to receive from her — which opened my eyes still more to the nature of Lady Greybrook's character. She wrote to my mother, and also, I am inclined to think, to my father, imploring them not to allow me to be the constant companion of a person whose reputation was so entirely ruined. She offered to take the care and responsibility of me on her return to England, though she strongly disapproved of such a separation from home ties. Any thing, however, she said, was better than my being sacrificed in this cruel way. To me she pointed out some of the dangers of my position, and entreated me not to be carried away by the fascinations of the life I was leading. Of Lady Greybrook she spoke pityingly, but with uncompromising truth. She besought me, by the love I bore her, to see as little of that lady as possible; to resist her influence in every possible way, and, above all, as regarded any marriage in which my heart was not concerned.

It was a curious confirmation of my aunt's far-seeing wisdom, when, as we drove along to a ball that same evening, Lady Greybrook urged on me more vehemently than ever the expediency of encouraging the Marquis d'Ofort's suit.

"Never mind, my dear; though he *is* dull, you may depend on it a man of that sort makes the best husband. My experience has taught me so." (A sigh.) "Clever men are only fit to marry fools. They've no idea of giving us the rein. Now, the woman d'Ofort marries will make him do just what she likes — particularly if she is young. You had much better try and think of him, instead of that sad, wild fellow, Rawdon. He will only get you talked about. Remember, *I* wash my hands of all responsibility as regards him. Besides, you know as well as I do the state of your father's affairs, and that his only hope is in your making a brilliant marriage to extricate him from his difficulties. He will immediately borrow a thousand or two from his son-in-law; and old d'Ofort fulfils all the requisite conditions for that post, being a good-tempered old goose, with one of the largest fortunes in France."

I was silent, feeling less disposed than ever to discuss these matters with my companion, and after a time she continued:

"I knew, my dear, you were ill-off; but I had no idea, until that little discovery about your picture, of the state your family affairs were in. Shockingly reduced, indeed, to come to *that!* Fortunately, you have a manner that carried it off — that unpleasant scene, I mean — and Griffiths, and that old cat, Lady Janet, and other people, chose to look at it in a very fine light; but, as I told you afterwards, it made me horribly nervous, and I should n't wish you to repeat the little eccentricity while you are going out with me. If you want any money, you know you can go to Eugénie, my maid, who keeps my purse, and I dare say, if it is not a large sum, she will give it you."

I thanked Lady Greybrook for her kind offer, while I mentally wondered by what process her feelings of delicacy had become sufficiently blunted to make it in such terms.

" My dear, you haven't the *position* that is required to do those things. It does very well in a certain rank of life. We all know that Lady Adelaide Wilder sold oranges in the street for a bet, and the Duchesse de Cazes went on the boards of the Opera in the masquerade scene in *Gustavus;* but that, you see, is quite a different thing."

" Quite," I repeated, too much amused to be indignant.

" For people whose position is perfectly well assured in society can do any thing — absolutely any thing — short of running away from their husbands."

" Do you know I am afraid, if I were married to Marquis d'Ofort, that is exactly what I *should* do? "

" Don't talk such nonsense! Well, at all events, you will have to make haste and do *something*, my dear; for, between you and me, I think affairs are getting desperate with your father. He has been borrowing largely, I hear, from Ismael, besides other entanglements, perhaps, even *worse;* and I shall be going away in a few weeks now, for the season will be over, — so you have really no time to lose."

In spite of all the sickening apprehensions and anxieties that crowded on me, I could hardly help laughing at her ladyship's breathless injunctions to marry, and general view of that institution; but we drove under the *porte cochère* of the Embassy just then, and all further conversation was stopped.

I was out of spirits. The ball seemed to me almost as dull and wearisome as that court-ball in the days of my childhood; and I wondered how people could find any amusement in such a crowd and heat, forgetting how extremely well I had amused myself in several such scenes. I sat down, and said it was too hot to dance. My thoughts reverted to my aunt's letter, and I thought if she could but see me now! It was an unexpected pleasure when Mr. Rochford came up and shook hands with me. He seldom went to these large entertainments; I had not seen him for two days. What brought him here to-night?

"You rarely honor balls with your company, Mr. Rochford. I wonder a philanthropist like yourself does not come and see people enjoy themselves."

"When people really enjoy themselves, I like to see them," he replied, smiling; "but in ball-rooms the number is small. Look round: do you see many happy faces? I confess I can't. Vanity — jealousy — the mania for 'getting on,' — I see all this, and it makes me rather melancholy. If you ask why more here than in any other congregation of human beings, it is that women's weaknesses come out stronger here than anywhere. A ball-room belle is not my *beau-idéal* — her head completely turned for a time, until she is deserted for something new."

"Rather rude," I thought. "He fancies I come under the deserted class, because I am not dancing, and look unhappy, as I feel, indeed!" His Serene Highness the Prince of Pultowa approached just then, brought his heels sharply together with a click, and requested the honor, etc.

I regretted that I felt too tired to dance.

"I have a note for you, Miss Percival," said Rochford, drawing from his pocket a little three-cornered billet. "I was dining with Lady Janet Oglevie this evening, and as I knew I should meet you here, she begged me to give you this."

"Oh! Lady Janet? I have not seen her since that morning she made my acquaintance at Mr. Griffiths'. She called on my mother a short time ago, but I was out; and I am ashamed to say I have never been to see her."

The note, written in a clear crabbed hand, ran thus:

"Will Miss Percival drink tea with Lady Janet Oglevie to-morrow evening? She will meet the Rev. Mr. Kennedy, a friend of her aunt's" (it had been "your," and was scratched through), "and one or two more; but there is no party. Miss Perceival will please to remember that. Mrs. Kennedy would call for her at eight o'clock, and set her home at night."

And little as this invitation sounds tempting I was anxious to accept it. But it was difficult, for I was to dine out with Lady Greybrook, at the rich Mr. P.'s, and it would be nearly eight o'clock before we sat down to dinner. I reflected, however, that, according to Paris fashion, the party would, probably, disperse very early. I turned to Lady Greybrook, and explained the case, saying that I wished very much to go to Lady Janet's if possible.

"I'd advise you not. You'll be bored to death; but if you insist on it, I will drop you there on my way to Madame Galoffska's, where, by-the-by, you are not invited — so it will do very well. When I said to her I should bring you, she said she was sorry that her rooms were too full. Odd, ain't it?"

As Rochford offered to take any message to Lady Janet, I begged him to say, that though I could not come at the hour she named, I hoped to do so later.

"Do you know her well? She is a very singular person; certainly rather terrific."

"She is excellent, for all that. There is no one for whom I have so great a respect in Paris."

The observation was a simple one. What was there in the manner with which it was said that irritated me?

"For so very excellent a person, apparently she can be very bitter. When people grow old and ugly, and have lost their taste for the pomps and vanities of the world, it seems to me that just the one temptation they should most guard against is that of the tongue."

He appeared annoyed. "You are mistaken if you suppose she generally troubles herself about her neighbors' concerns. She is no gossip; but her shrewd judgment, her honesty, and strong good sense make her a valuable friend to any one — a friend not lightly to be rejected among the pitfalls of Paris society."

I looked up suddenly into his face. This too, was a simple observation, like the last, but it produced a different effect on me. A thought flashed like lightning through my mind, bringing both pleasure and excited curiosity with it. I began tearing up Lady Janet's note into little bits.

"Have you known her long, that you speak of her in such terms?"

"Ever since I was a boy. She is my mother's oldest friend."

"Really! Ah, how stupid of me! I have torn up her note, and I actually don't know where she lives! Would you write down the address for me?"

He tore a leaf out of his pocket-book and wrote down street and number.

That night, as soon as I was at home and alone, I ran to my desk and took from it a small piece of crumpled paper, on which some writing in pencil was now almost effaced.

"Yes," said I, comparing it with the piece I held in my hand, "it is a leaf from the same book, and — there is no doubt about it — it is the same handwriting!"

CHAPTER XIII.

I THOUGHT the dinner at Mr. P.'s would never be over, but I was in a state of happy excitement, so that not even the dulness of this great entertainment was able to depress me. I did not ask myself why this was. I did not confess how anxiously I looked forward now to the evening at Lady Janet's, or how differently I regarded her since I had discovered — or thought I had discovered — what was the secret spring of her conduct towards me.

A gentleman with a very red face surrounded by a great deal of white, sat next me at dinner. His conversation was not of a nature to distract my thoughts from the subject which engrossed them. Indeed, little was talked of at table but the dishes as they succeeded each other, with an occasional anecdote about the number of years this Madeira had been in bottle and the vintage of that claret. With the second course, there was a slight diversion in favor of politics, and our host became eloquent about bullion and the Stock exchange. Lady Greybrook was seated next to a capacious Italian nobleman on the other side of the table, and, judging from their merriment, I am inclined to think their talk was *not* of the Stock exchange.

At last it was over, and the same red face (a good deal redder now) handed me back to the *salon*, where we ladies sat upon blue satin sofas for the space of twenty minutes, while the men stood and sipped their coffee round us ; then, one by one, the latter slunk out of the room to their cigars, and to

(152)

their opera-stalls or elsewhere, as the custom is at these sociable entertainments. Lady Greybrook, following their example (but with more of ceremony), then rose and took her leave.

"Now, my dear, where is it I am to drop you?" said she, as we got into the carriage.

"Rue de l'——, Number — let me see, I think it is Number Five," said I to the chasseur, and away we rolled.

"Past ten o'clock!" said Lady Greybrook, striking her repeater, as we drove along, "you'll be late for the *tartines* and the distribution of tracts. I am afraid you won't get any of the 'Crumbs of Comfort for Chickens in Distress.' Fortunately you have had a good dinner to support you under the disappointment. How capital that *salade d'ananas au vin de Champagne* was, was n't it?"

The carriage drew up before a house where two or three other carriages were standing.

"Why, positively the old lady has a large party!" cried her Ladyship, as the chasseur fired open the door and shot down the steps. "There, make haste, my dear, and don't keep me — I can't stay in the cold. François can just go up-stairs with you, but I really can't wait; there — good night."

"Quel étage?" roared he of the green plume, through the porter's glass door.

"Premier," growled a voice; and up the stairs I ran after the chasseur, who pulled a bell on the first floor.

"Merci — cela suffit — n'attendez pas," said I, thinking of Lady Greybrook shivering in her carriage; and downwards disappeared the green plumes four steps at a time.

The door was opened by a tiger.

I was rather surprised, but a grave-looking man in black (probably Lady Janet's Scotch butler) came forward and silently took my cloak. We passed through an ante-room, where, to my amazement, were several hats and canes.

The grave man did not ask me my name, but threw open
the *battants* at the further end of this apartment.

I stepped into a large and brilliantly lighted drawing-
room, and the doors closed behind me. Never, as long as I
live, shall I forget my bewilderment, — bewilderment growing into terror every moment, as I stood and looked round
me : hesitating whether to advance, and with retreat cut off.

Where was I? Where was Lady Janet? Who were all
these people lying about on sofas and divans, playing at
cards : smoking, laughing loudly, and rattling small boxes
on a green-baize table? Men and women, but no face I
had ever seen before !

Yes, one ! That lady in white with camelias in her hair, I
knew full well, from seeing her drive daily in the Champs
Elysées : I used to recognize the carriage from the camelias
in her horses' heads, and I had been told, alas ! that she had
a melancholy notoriety. She was half-sitting, half-lying on
a sofa, upon the back of which a young man leaned, and
passed his hand familiarly over the smooth bandeaux of her
hair. A handsome, greasy-looking woman stood, smoking a
cigarette, near the fire. Another was seated before a piano,
and lightly passed the fingers of one hand over the keys.

My eyes rapidly seized every detail of that strange scene
in the few seconds, which seemed indeed years, that I stood
transfixed there, at the door. Suddenly I became conscious
that my appearance had created scarcely less sensation in
the assembly itself. All eyes were turned on me.

" Tiens, Madeleine, qui est-ce ? — comme elle a l'air
effarouchée ! "

" Mais qui est-ce donc ? "

" D'où vient-elle ? "

The large, greasy-looking woman came towards me.
Two or three men started up from their sofas. It was as
the sudden breaking of a spell. I turned and fled. How
I managed to get out of the room, — how I flew past the

grave man in black, and seizing my cloak, bounded out of the door and down stairs, — by what sudden power I was enabled to do this, in less time than it takes to tell, I know not. Thank God! I *did* it: but it was only when I stood in the court, and felt the cool night air blowing upon my face, that I fully regained my consciousness.

I ran to the porter's glass door; and shook it.

"Une dame Anglaise, Oglevie, ne demeure-t-elle pas ici?"

"Connais pas le nom."

What on earth was I to do? I heard the door of the first floor apartment burst open: a confused uproar of men's voices, laughing, and one, louder than the rest, that called out,

"Elle est descendue — suivons-la."

They were coming down stairs. Not a moment was to be lost: I ran into the street.

Good God! What a position. Which way to turn? should I trust to speed in evading my pursuers? Alone in the middle of Paris, at night, with bare head and arms, in evening dress, flying along the street — my heart and my limbs alike failed me. Two or three coachmen were asleep on their boxes. The thought occurred to me of taking refuge inside one of these carriages, but then they were the property of some of these very people — perhaps of my pursuers themselves. No! that would not do.

I had had the presence of mind to pull the large door close after me. I now held its handle tightly with both hands. It was a few seconds gained at least — while I strained my despairing eyes up and down the dark, silent street. Steps came running down the court, and a voice cried out, "Cordon!" The string was jerked, but I pulled with all my strength, and the door remained shut.

"Diable! qu'est-ce qu'elle a cette porte? — Cordon!"

The string was jerked violently again.

“Help! Help! Help!”

Not a living soul in sight, except the coachmen, who start up from sleep and stare at me. No help from them.

The string is jerked a third time — they have discovered, by my screams, that I am holding the door.

“Help! Help!”—and just then a brougham turns into the street a little lower down. Thank God! it is coming this way. The door is forced open, but at the same instant the carriage drives up straight to this very house. A gentleman jumps out, — I spring towards him, with redoubled cries, — but a pair of strong arms are thrown round me from behind, lifting me off my feet, and a loud laughing voice cries,

“Pourquoi être si cruelle, mademoiselle, de nous priver de votre société?”

Another moment, and a grasp of iron seized the arms of the man who held me, and, strong as he was, sent him reeling against the wall.

“Good God! Miss Percival, what do I see?”

I was too overjoyed to be astonished at recognizing Lord Rawdon; I clung hold of him, and gasped out,

“Oh! save me — save me from those dreadful men! I —I mistook ——”

“Parbleu, milord, c’est fort joli ce que vous faites là!” roared my aggressor, truculently.

“Messieurs, par quelques apparences, quelques circonstances, peut-être, que je ne connais pas, vous vous êtes trompés. Monsieur le comte, cette demoiselle est sous ma protection. Qui que ce soit qui l’insulte m’en répondra. Vous connaissez mon adresse.”

What effect this speech produced on the young man he had called Count, I hardly know : I was too frightened to look or listen. His companions seemed to treat the thing as a good joke. Lord Rawdon said something to one of them ; then turned and handed me into his brougham as composedly as if nothing had happened.

" Miss Percival, where may I have the honor of conducting you?"

" May I — will you — ask your coachman to drive me home."

Agitated as I was, I had not completely lost my presence of mind. I sat close to the door, and held it with one hand, as I extended the other through the window.

" I shall be better able to thank you to-morrow, Lord Rawdon. Good night!" And I drew up the glass.

He did not hesitate a moment, but jumped upon the box, and seized the reins from his coachman's hand.

" Le jeu de l'amour et du hasard!" laughed one of the group, as we drove off. A man passed along the street at the same moment. The light from the gas-lamp fell upon his face, as it did into the carriage upon mine. He looked at me, and I recognized him. It was Hubert Rochford.

The coincidence was so singular that I almost doubted my own eyes. I had a strong inclination to call after him, but what excuse had I? — what would be the use of it? — I was going home. All would be explained to Lady Janet and to him to-morrow. Had he recognized *him*, Lord Rawdon, to be sure he must think it very strange. Was he on his way to Lady Janet's? As to *my* going there now, of course, it was out of the question. My brain was in a feverish whirl: my hair had fallen about my shoulders. I leaned back, and covered my face with my hands.

Those few minutes had been more eventful than many entire lives. What a fatality that I should have forgotten a number, for almost the first time in my life, just when such a mistake was of real consequence! More strange still, considering that the address was written, and *how* its writing was impressed upon my mind. And that I should never have thought of asking if Lady Janet lived there! I had had a glimpse into society of which most young ladies probably do not know the existence, — a glance into that

depraved world which is the secret sore of all great cities
like Paris. I shuddered when I thought of that fair and
gentle-looking girl, with camelias. Did one but know them,
how many terrible unwritten histories that one room contained!

It was a providential escape. But was it *chance* that
brought Rawdon down the street at that moment? His
brougham had driven straight up to the very door — there
was evidently a recognition between him and those men.
Was this the society in which report said he spent so much
of his time?

Then my thoughts returned again with secret uneasiness
to the vision of Rochford. What must he be thinking of me
at this moment!

The carriage stopped: I was at home. Rawdon opened
the door and handed me out.

"You will come and see us to-morrow," I said. "I cannot explain it all to you now. In the mean time, try and
prevent this affair from getting talked of. Do not let my
name appear if you can help it."

"I promise your name shall not appear — none of them
know you — and if — "

He held my hand for an instant, as if about to add something, then dropped it, merely adding,

"Good night. I hope to see you to-morrow."

I little thought it would be many to-morrows ere we
should meet again.

CHAPTER XIV.

"And now, dear mother, I have told you all, and it will be better to say nothing about last night's business to any one. Nobody but Lord Rawdon and one other person knew me —"

"And about Lady Greybrook, dear, don't you mean to tell her?"

"Above all, mother, not a word to her. Lady Janet is the only exception I shall make, and am going there presently. I was only waiting to see Lord Rawdon, when he calls."

"What must he have thought, my love? — so distressing and disagreeable that kind of thing, eh?"

As we were talking, Lady Greybrook was announced. She put her head into my mother's bedroom, where we were.

"Will you accord me *les petites entrées*? Astonished to see me so *matinale*, ain't you? Not yet two o'clock! Couldn't resist coming to ask if you'd heard the news. No? Well I'm really lucky. What *do* you think has happened? *Je vous le donne en dix — je vous le donne en vingt*, as Madame de Sévigné says. All Paris will be talking of nothing else for the next three days. It has put me quite into an agitation!"

"Good gracious! Lady Greybrook, do tell us at once what it is," said my mother. "I can't bear this sort of suspense."

" It concerns some one you know well," said her ladyship, fixing her eyes on me. " Guess."

I felt a choking tightness at my chest, and could actually hear my heart beating.

" We can't," said my mother plaintively. " Oh! do tell us."

" Are you really prepared? Well, then, it appears that this morning, Lord Rawdon fought a duel with Count M., and is severely wounded!"

My mother gave a loud cry. Some involuntary sound escaped my lips, and I leaned back in my chair.

" Heavens, Rita! what is the matter? You're as white as a sheet. Don't faint, pray. Why, you did n't care for that gay Lothario, I hope? I was afraid you saw too much of him. Mrs. Percival, I think it is quite fortunate that he will be *hors de combat* in this or any other way for some time to come," and she gave a little rippling laugh.

" Is the cause of the meeting known?" asked my mother, tremulously.

" Not exactly — a woman at the bottom of it, of course. Such a *mauvais sujet*. Poor fellow!"

" Ah me!" said my mother, wiping her eyes; " but he has his good points. Oh dear, I wish I could go and nurse him!"

" The post is already filled. Make yourself easy, dear Mrs. Percival; the Galoffska will watch over him better than any *sœur de charité*. I called in the Rue St. Florentin on my way, just to ask how he was going on. She drove up at the same moment, having just heard of it, admirably got up for the part: white *peignoir* — black veil — hair dishevelled."

" Do you think she really cares for him?"

" Yes, I suppose so, or she would n't set the world at defiance in that way. By-the-by, last night at her reception, you know, Rita, he was not there. She was dreadfully an-

noyed, and kept looking towards the door the whole evening.
Then she suddenly became very anxious to know where
you-were. I dare say it has something to do with this silly
affair that kept him away."

My mother cast an uneasy glance at me.

" Is it," I contrived to gasp out — " is it a serious wound?"

" Yes, I believe it is. They seemed to be afraid of his
arm — couldn't extract the ball, or something of the sort.
Very shocking, ain't it? Well, I mustn't stay any longer;
to-night I'll call for you at ten, my dear, for the Apponys."

" I shall not be able to go to-night, thank you; I am not
well."

Lady Greybrook protested loudly against my " doing sentimental;" said the world would begin to talk, and couple
my sudden retirement from its gay scenes with Lord Rawdon's " little accident;" used every argument, in short, she
could think of, and finally got quite angry when I said that
nothing should induce me to alter my intention of remaining
at home.

As soon as she was gone, I threw myself into my mother's
arms. " Oh! mother, I am so wretched! Think if he were
to die, and on my account! Even to be the involuntary
cause of this, is something too dreadful. Never ask me,
mother, to go out, as long as he is ill. It isn't that I care
for him — you know that, mother — but it is too heartless;
and to hear that woman talking in her light, careless way of
it! Has the world really such a petrifying effect on every
one? I don't care what *she* says, I will not be dragged
into the world until he is out of danger."

" Well, my darling — there, calm yourself — do; and
we'll talk over it quietly."

*   *   *   *   *   *

An hour afterwards I sat by Lady Janet on the sofa in
her drawing-room. We were alone, and I related all the
circumstances of the previous night faithfully and minutely.

She listened with a grim composure, manifesting neither horror nor astonishment.

"Just what one might expect, of course. I'm not such a fool as to blame you. No fault of yours that you were pitched out at that house, like a bale of goods, by that woman — nice care to take of a girl! — but I do say it serves your mother right for sending you out with that creature — what could she expect? *I* warned her. *I* told her what would come of this fashion hunting — better have kept you darning stockings at home, instead. Why, do you suppose any respectable man would marry — pah! I tell you she is known from Dan to Beersheba for a disreputable jade — all false about her : heart, and tongue, and cheeks, and teeth, and all — pah!"

The expression of "fuming" is the only one that gives any idea of the manner in which the old lady delivered herself of this exordium. I felt it best to be silent. Without entering into domestic details, which I thought myself hardly justified in doing, it was impossible to show her all the difficulty my poor mother had in resisting the stream of circumstance. After a while she continued, with somewhat less asperity,

"I believe you 're naturally a good girl — horribly brought up, of course ; but I think well of you, otherwise I should n't take the trouble of talking to you now. Pray do you think you can touch pitch and not be defiled? Do you suppose you can have for a companion such a woman as that, and surrounded by such a set as she is, and not become hardened to evil? There is that lord, for instance, of course he thinks himself privileged to play the fool with a girl he sees in company with such a woman as Lady Greybrook — pah! — one of the most profligate men in Paris, I'm told. And now you 'll be more intimate than ever with him, from gratitude and so forth, after last night. Pah! — the worst thing that could happen to you."

My cheeks burned scarlet.

"Your fears, as regards Lord Rawdon at least, are groundless. There is, I grieve to say, no chance of my seeing him for a very long time, if ever. The unfortunate consequence of his chivalrous conduct last night was a duel — a duel with one of those men, and he — Lord Rawdon — is severely wounded."

"May the Lord have mercy on him!" she said, in a low tone, "and lead him to repent of his ways! This is very bad — very bad indeed. I thought these horrid fights had gone out of fashion. How carelessly these men rush into the jaws of death, without a thought on the awful fiery torments that await the unprepared!"

There was no doctrine of her church which this really kind woman would not sooner have given up, I believe, than that of a state of future punishment.

"I bore him no love, as you know, but I am sincerely sorry: so will Hubert Rochford be, I am sure, when —"

"I am afraid," said I, gaining courage, and clearing my throat to get at the point I anxiously waited for — "I am afraid Mr. Rochford must have had a very strange opinion of me when he saw me in Lord Rawdon's carriage, and alone. He spoke of it — what did he say?"

"Mr. Rochford was shocked to see any young woman in such a position, under the protection of a bad man," said Lady Janet, with her old rigidity and dryness; "otherwise, of course, it did n't concern him."

"I hoped to have explained to Mr. Rochford how I came to be in such an extraordinary position. As I shall not see him perhaps — for some days — will you — will you —"

"Tell him the long story you have been telling me? Well, it is but right I should do so. He shall know every particular. I will write to him by to-night's post."

"I thought you saw him nearly every day?"

"I did so while he was here," she answered, looking

at me intently, "but he left Paris an hour ago, for England."

How I stood the old lady's scrutiny I know not. I remember, when I got home, locking myself into my room, and sitting down on the bed, feeling incapable of any exertion. I first learnt then the full force of that scriptural phrase the "bruised in spirit." I tried to shake off the wretchedness that weighed on me; I argued with myself, called up my pride — in vain. The whole of Lady Janet's conversation had hurt and grieved me far more than I allowed her to see. And she was the only link I had now! Why had I not taken my aunt's advice, and sought her long ago — made her my friend? She was *his* friend; had she prejudiced him against me? No, I did not believe that. With all her asperity, she meant kindly by me — But he was gone! Whatever he might have felt — whether it amounted to any thing more than pity for my youth and position — he was gone! He had not even waited to hear the explanation of my conduct; he had departed, taking with him more than a doubt, perhaps, about me. "A letter from his mother that morning had hurried his departure; pressing business," she said. Cruel! and yet what right had I to say so? Had he ever, by so much as a word, given encouragement to this wild hope that had been growing up, unknown to myself, in my heart of hearts? Might he not, in truth, despise me? Had he not seen me enjoying to exercise my influence over a man of whom he had the worst opinion, encouraging his attention, living in daily intimacy with a woman of indifferent character, and resisting the proffered friendship of a wise, though stern, unflinching one?

Then, if my thoughts turned to the wounded man, there was nothing but misery in that direction. The phantasmagoria by which I had been surrounded during the last few weeks seemed to have utterly faded away, and to have left two bare facts standing out with terrible distinctness. I had gone through a fiery ordeal, and if unscathed at heart, was not so perhaps in name. I knew that a warm breath had passed over me; the first blush of the heart had died away, and the wings of that angel whose name is Happiness had swept by, perhaps never to return.

Some days elapsed. We sent constantly to inquire for Lord Rawdon; the ball, after great agony, was extracted from the shoulder, and he was pronounced to be safe. I cannot describe the relief and thankfulness I felt; but the trouble and anxiety of the last few days had left me very weak and irritable. Even my father, when he came to urge me (in no very mild terms) to go out, was shocked to see me looking so ill, and told Lady Greybrook it was impossible I could do so for some days. That lady I positively declined receiving. I could not have stood her raillery. She sent me several graceful little notes, full of the *on dits* of the day, touched in her gossamer style; assured me that every one was *désolé* at my illness, particularly the Marquis d'Offort (who, by the way, left endless cards ornamented with a very big coronet), and protested that she felt quite lonely, going out without her darling Rita! It was a relief to find that my name had never been connected in any way with the cause of the duel; had it been so, Lady Greybrook would have been the first to inform me.

I tried to employ myself, as of old, in those pursuits which (spite of all my resolutions) had been abandoned of late. But I found my thoughts constantly wandering, and good Miss Lateward complained that I had "quite lost that power of concentration, which is the most valuable habit of the mind." I could not explain to her, excellent woman that she was! how the feverish restlessness with which I turned from one subject to another, was the result of "a mind diseased" not by the excitements of the world, but by the bitter thoughts that crowded on my brain. These were not to be translated into a language she could understand. I doubt, indeed, whether at that time I could have confided them to any one. I tried to begin a letter to my aunt, but even that was now a difficult task to me; and there it lay, half-finished, when —

One day, about a week after the events I have been recording, my father sent for me into his room. I found him seated before a heap of letters, and he held the *Galignani* of that morning in his hand. He looked up as I entered, and it seemed to me that his features were working with some unusual emotion. A bracelet lay on the table before him; he snatched it up with an oath, and thrust it into his pocket.

" Come in — and read that." He handed me the paper. " May n't be true, you know — but — you must break it to her — I can't."

I seized the paper. My eye fastened on the paragraph to which he pointed, and I had sufficient strength to read it to an end. It was headed,

" DISTRESSING AND FATAL CATASTROPHE. MAR-SEILLES. — The melancholy intelligence has just reached this town of the loss of an English yacht, the *Seagull* schooner, 120 tons, the property of Mr. Follet. Besides the owner, there were on board Lady Dacre, her daughter, to whom Mr. Follet is said to have been engaged, and the crew, amounting to eighteen persons. We have, as yet, received no particulars of this terrible catastrophe. The steamer from Genoa states that she passed the timbers of the wreck, but the yacht had evidently gone down some hours before, and there is but too much reason to fear that all hands on board have perished."

I read it word for word, and then the blood seemed to rush violently to my ears, and eyes, and brain. I fell into the chair my father placed for me, and knew nothing for some minutes. I remember his pouring out a glass of cold water, and walking to the window. I drank a little, and tried to collect my thoughts. Did I doubt it? Oh no! I *knew* it to be true. The overwhelming horror of the event was there alone — ghastly — spectral, yet real: I never doubted. At last the bursting springs gave way, and a cry broke from the desolate heart, for that faithful counsellor and friend, the only real guardian of my life, snatched from me for ever! I threw myself upon my knees, in a frenzy of wild and passionate sobs.

My father never spoke. With rare tact, he saw it was better to let the full storm of grief have its course, though my whole being seemed shaken to its very foundation. He had never seen me cry, probably, in his whole life before; and now he guessed that "great nature" was "more wise than" he: so he stood there silently at the window.

I will not dwell upon the misery of that day. In my mother's weak state of health, break the news as gently as I could, the effect could not be otherwise than terrible. She had a succession of fainting and hysterical fits: then, towards evening, grew feverish and light-headed. She talked in a wild, rambling way of her sister; upbraided herself for having wronged her; referred to days and things long past, and to people of whom I knew nothing. Miss Lateward and I, who sat beside her, at last became so uneasy, that we sent for the doctor. He said I need not be alarmed: that it was the effect of a shock on the nervous system, which would soon pass, and he ordered some calming medicines, which had the desired effect of putting her to sleep. But the next day, and the day after that, in spite of the doctor's predictions, my mother did not rally from the shock. She was visibly weaker. Calm, indeed, she now was, but it was the calmness of prostration.

We received confirmation of the terrible news two days afterwards. The yacht had been caught in one of those fierce Mediterranean storms and driven upon some rocks. Two of the crew only were saved, having been picked up by

a Spanish vessel, after drifting many hours on a spar; and
if any faint glimmer of hope yet lived in any of us, it was
now extinguished forever.

My father never once spoke upon the subject. What he
may have felt none of us ever knew. He went once or
twice into my mother's room, but avoided, I fancied, being
left alone with her. Rose, who surprised me by the thought
and care she showed, was in almost constant attendance on
my mother, and appeared to me to have stepped suddenly
into the woman. I forgot that the prominent position I had
always taken in the house had prevented Rose from exercising these dormant qualities; but now I was often obliged
to go and lie down for hours in a darkened room: my
nerves had been so much overtaxed of late, that it had
begun to tell on my general health; and thus my sister
came more forward. She supplied my place by my mother's
bedside; and saw any necessary visitors who called.

Thus a melancholy month passed. The spring. that
saddest of all seasons when the heart is out of tune, was
beginning to push forth its tips of tender green upon the
branches in the Champs Elysées. The air of the street was
heavy with the scent of wall-flowers from open windows;
birds, too, were already singing, though, as yet, they were
but solitary messengers from warmer lands. Half the
English had left Paris; Lady Janet was gone, and I had
not strength to go and wish her good-by. Lady Greybrook
still lingered, and I forced myself to receive her once or
twice, after which, finding what dull company I was, she did
not call again.

One morning my father was closeted with my mother for
some little time, after which she sent for me. It was found,
she said, that my aunt had left two wills: the last executed
just before she went abroad. The greater part of Lady
Dacre's fortune was not in her own power: it would have
devolved naturally to her daughter, and now passed in due

course of succession to the present baronet, who was a distant cousin. In the earlier will, dated some ten years back, my aunt bequeathed five hundred pounds to each of us children, and a thousand pounds to my mother. In the latter will, however, some trinkets and papers only were left to my mother, and to myself was bequeathed an annuity of a hundred pounds, to be paid quarterly, from the date of my aunt's death. The same legacies, as in the former will, were left to my brothers and sister, to be paid on their coming of age, or, under sanction of the trustees, to be devoted to an Indian outfit, or other object promoting their worldly interest, during their minority. The trustees were both barrister-friends of my aunt, to us personally unknown.

"The reason of this change in your dear aunt's disposal of her property," said my mother, in a low voice. "you must not misunderstand, dear. We were always — I mean latterly — always the same, thank God!" Here she broke down, but recovering herself, continued: "I may say it was my request — yes, *request*, when she said she was making her will. that she would leave me nothing — but rather to you. *I* should have been able to do so little. you see — I knew how it would all *go* — like the rest! whereas you, I hope. will do a great deal with this, my child, — and you'll be *firmer about it* than I could be, won't you, dear?"

I pressed her hand silently; my heart was too sick and weary for words. She seemed about to add something, but changed her mind. "No, later — some other time," she muttered to herself. and changed the conversation. My father was much disappointed at the tenor of the will. He talked of sending Ernest to India at once, now that his outfit, etc., was provided for, as he had the promise of a direct appointment, and his schooling was such an expense. The others, too, must go to school; and he talked (my mother said) of trying to persuade the trustees to devote the boys' legacies to that purpose.

"And now, Rita, I want to talk about yourself. You are looking very ill, darling. The doctor was speaking of you yesterday, and said you ought to have change of air, and that nothing else will set you up. Now, curiously enough, here is a note I have just got from Madame Gobemouche, saying they go back to their *campagne*, near T—, to-morrow, and asking if I would let you go with them, and stay there for a month or two. What do you say? As it happens that owing to this — this —" her voice faltered — "mourning, your father can't expect you to go out now, I don't suppose he will object."

My heart yearned for the quiet of the country — for a complete change of scene and association. The only drawback was leaving my mother. I asked if she did not feel that a change would do her good herself.

"My love, no change would do me any good. I have long felt that it is only an affair of some months more or less with me. My malady, I know, is incurable. I am sorry to grieve you, Rita, but it is right you should know this. I have often thought I would tell you, but now — You must go away and get quite strong and well, dear. Think if you were to fall seriously ill too, how much worse it would make things! You will have plenty of trouble, I am afraid, darling, without bad health to fight against!"

I knew my mother's spirits were so low, and she had often before spoken so despondingly of herself, that I did not attach the serious importance to her words they indicated. I threw my arms round her, and assured her she was looking better than she had done for some days, and my good governess — who would not have told a story to save any one's life — fortunately entered just then to corroborate the assertion. Indeed, later in that same day I was surprised to hear that my mother had received Mr. Murray when he called. Natures, however, are differently constituted; mine partakes of the savageness of wild beasts, who, in sickness, shun their kind, and retire to moan out their hearts in solitude.   My mother, on the contrary, when suffering, derived comfort from the society of those she liked, and among that number was certainly Charles Murray : she generally saw him when he called.

As my father made no objection, I accepted General and Madame Gobemouche's invitation that afternoon ; and the following morning found me seated in the *coupé* of the T— diligence between the old couple.

CHAPTER XV.

I HAD to make an exertion to meet the conversational demands of my two friends, who, attributing my depression to physical rather than moral causes, sought to "distract" me (in French phrase). And this exertion was the best thing for me in the state I was. Perhaps the necessity of coming out of ourselves is good for us under any circumstances. Certainly I believe it is so in trouble. Had I been alone all those weeks in the midst of my unhappy family, I should have brooded reproachfully over the past, despondingly over the future. My mind, as it was, regained a comparatively healthy tone at Grandregard. Of the complexity of sore troubles that overshadowed me, Madame Gobemouche knew but one. My aunt was dead — that stern Englishwoman in a green veil whom she remembered to have occasionally seen and dreaded. " C'est bien une tante," she said, with a shrug; but she little guessed all the loss was to me; as little as she knew how the burden of that sorrow was increased by all that had preceded it.

The Château de Grandregard, as Madame Gobemouche took occasion to inform me, was her own property, where she had lived in dignified retirement during the period of her widowhood, and which she had embellished according to her own unassisted taste. It was a very white house, with intensely green shutters, and a great many of them, standing on a slight elevation, as its ambitious title indicated, just outside the town of T—. The garden was surrounded by a wall, having stone pots upon it. The iron gate was of an elaborate construction and gilt, as were the weathercocks on the top of the very high roof, sparkling like minarets in the summer sun. The whole place managed to look bright and cheerful even on a rainy day. It was also, I must confess, a specimen of the worst French taste, which — like persons habitually good — when it takes to vicious courses, becomes incurable and outrageous. There was a cow of painted canvas with dead props, forever waiting to be milked on the grass-plot before the door. This was supposed to give the place a rural look, which, from its vicinity to the town, might have been wanting. I have always had a weakness for statues in a garden, but the number of white Venuses and Fauns set up, like ninepins, in that small quadrangle, used to make my eyes ache, and almost sickened me of the plastic art for life. The flower-beds were mostly guarded by rows of sharp, distorted little rocks, like teeth; and there was a grotto of shells, with a marine view at the further end (which latter, not being stretched tight enough, had some diagonal waves across the sky), upon which madame especially prided herself, and where she generally insisted on our taking coffee after dinner. The interior of the château corresponded with its external decorations. A general atmosphere of yellow satin pervaded it; mirrors and gilding, and engravings from the emperor's battles, round the walls, and so many ormolu and alabaster clocks in all the rooms, that one might have thought the computation of time was the sole enjoyment of the household. And a household of busy idleness, in truth, it was, from the bowl of gold and silver fish, the monkey, cockatoo, and cageful of canaries, upwards, to madame herself running about all day long with lumps of sugar for her birds. Life, and song, and sunshine filled the house; and its excellent old owners did their best to infuse some of the latter into me. I exerted myself to meet their kindness by not appearing indifferent to all that interested them. After the first few days I succeeded in getting up the poultry statistics, and in keeping my attention alive to the sleek little Abbé's gossip; he being our daily visitor, and a general favorite with madame.

But when I was alone, and oftenest in the long night hours, I lived again through the past few months, retalked whole conversations, and thought how differently I should have spoken and acted now, in many cases. Above all, with what vividness did *his* looks and words return! How all my irritability and little vanities faded away in the memory of his gracious presence! He was far above me; but I loved to think that in some hereafter time — perhaps when we were both old, or even beyond that again — he would know that there were moments when my heart had beat in perfect sympathy to his true and noble words. I believed that he did *not* know me now, and I was content to accept it. Our natures were widely different.

> Unlike are we, unlike O princely Heart!
> Unlike our uses and our destinies;
> Our ministering two Angels look surprise
> On one another, as they strike athwart
> Their wings in passing.*

Perhaps he could never have learnt to understand one so impulsive and inconsistent. "And yet," whispered my heart, "*could* he have known —" and vainly woman's pride recalled his studied coldness — his careful indifference. Every one can struggle successfully against the outward demonstration of a passion; the secret image in its shrine of shrines is not so easily displaced. When I looked into my heart, I was startled to find this image there — immovable, unbroken! Strange to say, it was only now, when all was past and gone — forever, perhaps — that I awakened to this self-knowledge. The turmoil of a crowd of feelings had swept by, and left the footprints of one alone upon my heart.

* E. Barrett Browning.

Concerning the enigmatical Rawdon, that strange compound of good and evil, I was now, comparatively, at ease. I received a letter from my mother, the week after my arrival at Grandregard, which mentioned his being sufficiently recovered to leave Paris for some German baths. Madame Galoffska, it is supposed, accompanied him. Lady Greybrook had also left Paris. Ernest had come home, grown tall, and much improved mentally as physically; with a prize from school, and a good character. He was to go out to India in six weeks. My mother said little of herself, and a great deal of Charles Murray, and of his numberless kind attentions; she wrote, altogether, in much better spirits than I could have hoped, but her letter contained one piece of intelligence which grieved me much. My father had decreed that, as my little brothers must be sent to school, and as Rose was now of an age "to have done with lessons," Miss Lateward's services could no longer be retained; Lady Dacre having left no provision for her salary. The loss to us all would be irreparable, I knew; and so did my mother.

"I told your father," she wrote, "I was sure you would consider part of your annuity well employed in paying Miss Lateward, but he got very angry at the idea, and said there was plenty for you to do with it; and, in short, he saw Miss Lateward, and told her that we could not keep her any longer: and the boys are to go to Brighton on the 15th, and I am sure I don't know how we are to get on without her. It is said to be a very good school. Lord Inverearty's son is there. I wish we could hear of a good place for her; but most of the English have left, and then she has no accomplishments, poor dear!"

Miss Lateward herself wrote to me a few days later, and as I have her letter still by me, I will give it. For many a long hour in the quiet moonlight, after I had blown out my candle that night, I sat by the window, pondering over part of the contents of that letter.

"The communication, my dear Marguerite, which will have been made to you by Mrs. Percival, will not have been unproductive of pain, I feel confident. Believe me, the concern you may feel at the dissolution of our partnership is fully participated in by myself. Had it been practicable, I would gladly have remained a few months longer, upon any terms; but your papa gave me to understand that my services were not required. Indeed, your sister, whose education, as you are aware, is very incomplete, is now so much occupied between attendance on your mamma and the reception of visitors, that, as regards her, I cannot but feel that the withdrawal of those services is wholly unimportant. Your young brothers are about to be promoted to a higher arena of learning than our humble schoolroom. For educational purposes, therefore, my vocation among you was nearly at an end (though we never finished the 'Thirty Years' War,' if you remember, and I *did* hope to have gone through the 'Wealth of Nations' with you this summer); but I am principally concerned at bidding you 'farewell,' my dear pupil, when I recollect that in many little difficulties, from time to time, you have applied to me for advice — advice always cheerfully tendered, and which, I trust, may have been of service. Bear in mind, however, that in Tabitha Lateward you have a sincere friend, who, as far as she is able, will ever give you her best counsel, whether present or absent.

"You will be pleased to hear that a most generous offer has been made me by a friend of *yours* — an offer which, in my circumstances, I should not be justified in declining. The friend to whom I refer is lady Janet Oglevie — a lady evidently of strong judgment and a benevolent nature, though lacking, perhaps, that polish of manner one might anticipate from her station. I was taking ambulatory exercise with your brothers when I first encountered her ladyship. She had just returned to Paris from Vichy, and said she was only here for a few days, on her road to England. She recognized me, as having seen me walking with you; and accosted me with an inquiry as to your health. This led to further conversation. She appears to have conceived a lively interest in you, and questioned me much and closely; doing me the honor, at last, to desire that I would wait upon her. Since then I have had several interviews with her ladyship, and she has spoken to me, with great candor, as to all the difficulties of your position. Let me caution you *seriously* as to what *intimacies* you form, my dear Marguerite. I saw that her ladyship thought you rash in this respect: yet she was inclined to believe all I said of your excellent disposition, and is, I believe, sincerely your friend. In the course of my visit, I mentioned that circumstances had unfortunately arisen which necessitated our parting. It was then her ladyship kindly said she knew of a situation which she thought would suit me — the care of a young lady, the daughter of a friend of her ladyship's, in England. The name is Rochford. There is only a mother and this daughter, besides the son, who is the head of the family. They live in a very retired district in one of the northern counties. As Mrs. Rochford is (most justly) very particular in the choice of the person who is to superintend her daughter's education, and will engage no one without a personal interview, Lady Janet has most generously offered to take me to England as her companion, in which capacity I am to accompany her on a visit to Rochford Court. The arrangement is a highly satisfactory one for *both* parties. I cannot sufficiently express my sense of her ladyship's great kindness to a stranger as I am; but any expression of it annoys her, for she is peculiar — and who are without their idiosyncrasies? It was arranged yesterday that I am to leave Paris with her ladyship in the course of a few days; consequently, I grieve to say, my dear Marguerite, we shall not meet again; for I apprehend that you will yet be some

weeks longer a guest of the gallant general's. With the
expression of my esteem and regard, and in the hope of
hearing very often from you,

> " Believe me,
> " Ever to remain,
> " Your sincere friend,
> " Tabitha Lateward."

How strange the coincidence appeared to me that my old
governess should leave us to become Hubert Rochford's
guest — to live in the same house with him day after day —
to learn the hourly routine of his life — to see him in sunshine and in shade! It seemed to me impossible. I read
the name over and over again wherever it occurred, to be
sure I had not mistaken it. There was no mistaking Miss
Lateward's hand: it was upright, hard, and honestly clear as
was her character. Might it not be some other branch of
the same family? That was hardly likely. I remembered
Rochford's having spoken of his young sister: I knew that
his father was long since dead, and that the mother lived
with her son. Still, I could hardly realize to myself that
here was a link, established between us — that I should occasionally hear of him — and that, if he were so minded, he
might also hear of me. I felt strangely elated. It was the
first ray of sunshine that had visited me for weeks; and I
caught myself in the glass, smiling out on the bright sun-cas-
tles I was building from it.

The days slipped by more fleetly after this. An incident,
which I shall presently relate, was one of the very few, during my stay at Grandregard, that broke the monotony of
morning visits from the Abbé, with an occasional one after
dinner from the doctor, or some old military gentleman in
the neighborhood. I am inclined to think that the great
ladies of T— (for they *were* great, I presume) did not
affect Madame Gobemouche. She viewed them with great

scorn, and tossed her ostrich plumes defiantly whenever we passed them in the carriage. Whether the occupants reciprocated these bitter feelings, I have, of course, no means of judging; but they never called, or otherwise took cognizance of the inhabitants of Grandregard.

After dinner there was always a game of piquet. It was madame's favorite amusement, and the general, like a noble old soldier as he was, devoted himself to it, without having a natural gift, or the smallest inclination, that way; and as, when he was not on the field of Austerlitz, he often took a siesta at odd hours in the day, it sometimes happened that the unlucky habit overtook him in the middle of a game. Now, nothing made madame so irritable as this; and with a view to soothing her, as well as to enabling the general to snore in peace, I humbly offered " to try and learn " the game, if she would teach me. The offer was accepted, and proved a master-stroke of policy. Madame believed that she was conferring a lasting benefit on me, and was in the very best humor, as people always are who think they do a magnanimous action. Whenever I played a wrong card — and I must confess that my wandering thoughts made this too often the case — Madame pointed it out with a mild reproof; and the general drowsed on, undisturbed in his chair, with the yellow bandanna handkerchief over his face. Sometimes I read the *feuilleton* of the *Patrie* aloud; or narrated, with such amplifications and alterations as my imagination suggested, any story that I thought likely to suit the taste of my auditors — moving incidents by flood and field — and if with Macbeth they "supped full of horrors," the better they were pleased. In the morning, I sometimes helped madame in making strawberry preserve, or in preparing sundry creams (for both of which she conceived she had a special vocation), and we afterwards occasionally drove out in the old yellow carriage, — a state observance I particularly disliked. In short, I tried to make myself as useful and pleasant as I could to the old couple, and in this way forgot many of my own troubles.

One June morning I was returning from the garden for our noonday breakfast, when, passing about a hundred yards from the gate, I saw the Abbé run in, with a somewhat perturbed face. On perceiving me, he trotted across the grass.

"Dear mademoiselle, there is a lady outside there, who is ill — an English lady, I think. Will you let me have a chair and a glass of water? — a little *fleur d'orange*, perhaps?"

I told the Abbé to run and fetch some, while I begged the lady to come in. I found her just outside the gate, leaning on the arm of a little old gentleman, and looking very faint. With his assistance, I got her to a bench under some trees in the garden. She was middle-aged, rather plain, and scrupulously neat; such a person as you may meet any day in an English country neighborhood. Her bonnet itself said as much as a bonnet can about its wearer: the straw, cleanliness; the form, modest retirement; the strings and curtain, not the "pink" but the dust-color "of propriety." The face under it was sensible, kind, but somewhat obstinate. The little old gentleman wore a buff waistcoat, such as I remembered to have seen on Lord Russborough in my childhood, and brown gaiters. He called the lady "my love," and was so nervously solicitous about her, that I made up my mind they were a long married couple, without children — a sort of refined British edition of my host and hostess. They contradicted each other, too, in the most affectionately positive manner, which confirmed me in this opinion, at which I arrived (always forming mine hastily), while the usual process of bathing the face, untying the bonnet-strings, etc., was gone through.

"Thank you," said the lady, with a faint smile, looking up at me. "I feel so much better. I am sure we cannot sufficiently thank this young lady for her kindness, can we, my dear? The fact is, the heat —"

" No, my love, the hill. I told you so. I begged you not, if you remember. I was afraid of your walking, and — "

"My dear, you know Dr. Roberts *ordered* me to walk. He did, indeed. I feel so much better now, I can walk back, *quite* well" (in a very weak voice).

" Stuff and nonsense, my dear! — more than a mile back to the inn."

" A mile? Why, I'm 'sure, love, it isn't further than from the Hall down to the school, where you know I walked every day."

" And much good you did yourself, my dear! If this lady will kindly allow you to remain here, I will run down and get a carriage, and shall be back here in a quarter of an hour."

Much expostulation followed, in which I thought myself called on to side with the stronger party; and finally, the lady was persuaded to sit still until a carriage should be brought. When I was left alone with her — for I had begged the Abbé to go and apprise Madame Gobemouche of my detention — our conversation was confined at first to a few common-place words of kindness on both sides; then, from remarks, we got to questions.

" I think I understood you were at an inn? Travelling, I suppose ? "

" Yes. We have only been a day in T—. We are going on this afternoon."

" You will not think of travelling to-day, will you? Had you not better rest ? "

" Oh dear, no. I want to get on as fast as I can. It is so very tiresome for John. We are going on to the Pyrenees. Have you ever been there ? "

" No, never. I know nothing of the pleasures of travelling."

"As to pleasure, we should never have left our own dear home for *that*. My health, unfortunately, is the cause of our coming abroad. Dr. Roberts wished me to have spent last winter at Nice, but I was so unwilling to leave home. You don't know, perhaps," she added, with a smile, "how hard it is to leave a place you are very fond of? Those who live abroad can't feel the same thing."

"I think not: but is this the first time you have been abroad?"

"Yes; and I hope it will be the last. Dr. Roberts thought if I were to spend a year in a warm climate, I should return quite restored."

"Do you dislike it, then, so very much?"

"Oh! it's very well, only the people seem to me so dirty, and such odd habits — never dressed of a morning — all the women in curl-papers and slipshod, which to our English ideas —"

At this moment, the vision of madame in a green dressing-gown, with the very curl-papers in question, surmounted by one of the general's yellow bandannas, appeared, much to my confusion, at the dining-room window. I had even some fears as to what effect this spectacle might produce on the weak nerves of the stranger; especially so, when madame, apparently with the intention of joining us, advanced one tapestried slipper, down at heel, over the window-sill, upon the terrace. She thought better of it, however; and — discouraged by the *très Britannique* air of the lady, I believe — retired, leaving us undisturbed.

With the tact of a true gentlewoman, my companion made no remark on this apparition; she could not, however, repress an indirect question, which showed her curiosity concerning the establishment. Looking round the garden, she said,

"What beautiful roses! It reminds me of my own dear garden — they must be just coming into bloom now. Do you take much interest in your flowers?"

"I am only on a visit here. I am sorry to say I live in a town, and have never had a garden; but perhaps it makes one prize it the more. Cockneys are said to be the truest lovers of the country, and I believe it."

"No," said the lady, positively, "that is certainly not true. How can they have all the varied interests *we* have — with our farms, and our schools, and our poor people — not to speak of watching the growth of every thing from month to month? They can have none of these pleasures."

"Oh, of course; I only spoke of the delight we town-bred feel at getting into the country, and breathing pure air — and all the sights and sounds of the country, which are so new to us. If I were a man — "

"Ah! for a man accustomed to an active life in the country, a life in towns is killing. John always has a fit of the gout when he has been in London a week. You may fancy, therefore, what a sacrifice it is to him coming abroad with me, and leading this stupid life — but he is the best of brothers — "

" Brother ? "

"And pretends he likes it. I resisted his coming as long as I could, but it was no use; and, as I say, *how* is the country to get on in his absence? There are his magisterial duties (such a head — you've no idea — so clear), and his farming (so very practical), and his general influence in the parish (no one such influence as he) — really it is terrible to think how his loss will be felt ! "

A carriage drove up, and this great public character jumped out, hurried up to us, and thanked me again for my attention to his sister. I had so persuaded myself that he was her husband, it seemed quite unnatural to find he was only her brother. There was no plea for their remaining longer, and the lady rose.

"Our acquaintance had progressed so rapidly in half an hour," said she, "that I feel as if we were old friends. I must tell you our name — it is Bissett. Will you let us know by what name we may recall our kind young friend at T — ? ”

“ My name is Marguerite Percival.”

“ Percival ? Was n’t that the name of the people, brother, who took Cloud Castle last year ? ”

“ Pooh ! my love ; nothing at all like it. It began with a B.”

“ Oh, my dear, I ’m confident it began with a P. If it was n’t Percival, it was something very like it ; — not that it much signifies. The name *now*, at all events, my dear Miss Percival, we shall not forget.”

And so Miss Bissett and I shook hands, and mutually expressed a hope that we might, some day, meet again : — which I thought very unlikely.

The following morning the Abbé had every particular by heart of the rich old English traveller at the Lion d’Or ; how the Bissett arms — to wit, a squirrel rampant — were emblazoned on the panel of the dark-green chariot ; how the interior of the carriage was filled with air-cushions, medicine-chests, and Murray’s Handbooks ; how two servants reclined in great state in the rumble of the same ; and how, on leaving, the gentleman had deemed fit to harangue the landlady, in very tortuous French, upon the softness of the beds, the smallness of the basins, and the dearness of the bill.

It served for a morning’s gossip, and was then forgotten.

CHAPTER XVI.

A few days later I received some most unexpected news from my mother, which obliged me to return to Paris. Her letter ran as follows:

"My dear Child,—I have only time for a few lines to-day, but cannot let the post go out without letting you know the happy news! I am in such a flutter I can hardly write! I dare say you guess what it is. I dare say you saw it all along. I never mentioned the subject to you, or in my letters, for fear it was a delusion; but I *thought* I saw it from the beginning. Do you remember the day he first called? Since you left, he has been here *every day*, and this morning he has actually *proposed* in due form. Think of little Rose as Mrs. Charles Murray! Only seventeen! She really fancies herself desperately in love with him, even if he had not a farthing, instead of such magnificent prospects! Fancy how delighted your father is! He wrote— I mean Charles Murray—to his father, and obtained his consent before he proposed, which is very gratifying and satisfactory. They are gone out together. She looks so beautiful in her half-mourning (I got her a white bonnet last week, for her black was getting so shabby). I don't wonder at his falling in love with her. Do you know, he says he was always rather afraid of you! Ah! my darling, nothing men *are* so afraid of as a clever wife—but only think, after all, of your not being the *first!* I hope the

country air has brought back the roses to your cheeks. The
dear boys went to school yesterday; it was a sad parting for
me, for I could not help feeling " — (here followed something that had been blotted out) — " but this has put me
into such good spirits to-day, I am quite another person.
Ernest remains with us until after the wedding (which is to
take place as soon as possible); then your father will go
with him to England, and see him on board his ship for
India — poor dear fellow! You must come back *at once*,
dear. I have quantities for you to do. Now that our good
Lateward is gone, I have no one, you know, for Rose is so
much occupied, going about with him. Heaven bless you,
my darling !

" Ever your affectionate mother,

" C. P."

In spite of my mother's assumption that I was fully prepared for the intelligence her letter contained, it was a great
surprise. — I had almost written *shock*. I was glad : I was
very glad, of course. But what a child she was ! At least
I had been accustomed to consider and treat her as such,
until quite lately : and even then, was so completely and
selfishly engrossed, that whenever the image of my sister
crossed my thoughts, it was only as a gleam of sunshine in
the home-picture — a morning gleam, as yet far removed
from the glare and heat of mid-day passions. She had not
made a confidante of me — she had never poured into my
ear the secret tale of fluttering hopes and fears; and I had
no right to expect it. It was very natural : my mother had,
in fact, been more of a sister to her. And yet I was very
fond of Rose, though there was so little sympathy between
us; but when I thought of what this last year had been to
me, I felt inexpressibly thankful she should be spared all
that I had gone through, and be safely havened from all
future storms by the quiet hearthstone of an English home.

True, I knew little of Charles Murray, but all the man was written in such clear, open characters, that whatever might be thought of his mental powers, his candor and true heart it was impossible to doubt.

I began folding up my dresses and laying them in my trunk. My kind old friends received the announcement that I must leave them with loud regrets. Notwithstanding the wide disparity of our years, and the wider disparity of our tastes and feelings, they were *friends ;* I could not leave them without the sorrowful reflection that I had few just now, and these I might not see again for years! We all three mingled our tears over an early breakfast the following morning, and I was publicly embraced outside the gilt gates by both the general and madame, in the face of the crowded diligence; after which, being given over, with many injunctions, to the care of a steady old shopkeeper, Paris-bound, I was stuffed into the bowels of the *intérieur,* with a large bunch of flowers on my knee, which, soon fading, left the fine aroma of ham-sandwiches in my bag predominant. I had rather a pleasant journey, as my old gentleman was obliging enough to drop asleep, and leave me in undisturbed possession of my own thoughts, during the greater part of the way. The only other occupant of this portion of the diligence was a young priest, who shrank into his corner upon my entering, and appeared to think there was contamination in my aspect, so studiously did he avoid me, his eyes fixed upon his breviary. I looked out of window, for my part; and found much interest and amusement in watching the haymakers in the fields, as we passed, and in studying character at inn doors, when we stopped to change horses. It was my first journey alone. I felt very independent, and thought how I should like to be travelling in an English stage-coach (which I knew by sight from a colored print in my father's room of one driving down a hill in a great cloud of dust). This stage-coach should be bound for the north of England — *where*, I was not exactly clear; but a certain face should be at the window when we stopped, waiting there to meet me ——

Instead of which (foolish diligence-dream!) comes the handsome face of my father, when we drive into the Messageries' courtyard in Paris; not without a cloud upon it, though, for we are half an hour behind our time, and he expresses his disgust in very forcible language at having had to wait so long.

Beside him stands a tall fair young man, who bows distantly, but whose bold laughing eyes I recognize at once, and throw my arms round his neck.

" Why, Ernest, what a giant you are grown! How long is it since we have seen you? It must be surely more than two years? "

" Just two, Queen of Tarts, since we had our last quarrel."

" Last holidays I spent at Dacre.   And now, may it please your Majesty, is there to be peace or war between us? "

" Oh, peace by all means, since you are only a visitor in my dominions — and your size, too, rather alarms me. You're very much improved in appearance; I hope equally so in other ways."

" Thank you: ditto to you. 'Pon my soul! you're a devilish sight better looking than I expected. What one may almost call a 'fine-looking girl.' "

" Yes, grown fat, I see, and actually got some color in your cheeks," said my father; then jocosely added, as we all three walked away together, leaving my trunk to follow with a porter, " Well, the filly's cut you out, Rita: won in a canter, you see! You've got to wear the yellow shoes, and all your own fault, Lady Greybrook told me."

" There, father, we will not talk about that. Dear Rose's marriage ought to satisfy you for a long time to come. I'm so glad. He just seems made for her. If I am any judge of physiognomy, he has a fine disposition — frank and free."

"It is more than his father has, then, if by 'free' you mean *liberal*. Sir Charles is n't so in purse, any more than politics."

"I am a friend to conservative principles," said I, dryly.

"He gives Charles a most paltry allowance, considering his fortune ; and the settlement he makes on Rose would be mean for his own steward. However, one must n't quarrel with one's bread and butter, I suppose, and the entail is a clear eight thousand a year."

"How do you like our new brother, Ernest ? "

"Oh, a capital fellow ; given me such a splendid gun to take out to India. Tiger-shooting, I suppose, is the only thing to be done in that cursed country."

"I should think there was a good deal else to be done, if you looked about you. But don't you like the idea of going out ? "

He shrugged his shoulders.

" As the governor said just now, one must n't quarrel with one's own bread and butter."

" I hope you 've been getting on with your Hindostanee ? "

" I 've worked at it — I have, indeed — but it 's so deuced hard."

" Well, I hope you 've learnt something at school besides swearing ? "

" Meaning that I could have done that at home, eh ? " he whispered, laughing, as my father stopped to speak to some one. " I say, the governor's hard up, again, Rita. He asked Charlie Murray to lend him a hundred this morning, and Charlie told him he had n't a hundred at his banker's. That's why he's so savage about it. Charlie's very wide awake about money."

I sighed, and walked on in silence. Here was this boy, already *rusé* in the world's ways — all the freshness, the delightful *gullibility* of youth gone! You would n't " catch him napping," as he informed me ; and I believed him. But

I felt the sooner he went out to India, and away from my father's influence, the better.

I was shocked to find how ill my mother was looking. The brilliant spirit she was in could not conceal the ravages of illness. But she spoke more cheeringly of herself and I was too willing to believe that the worn face was only the result of some sleepless nights, following days of excitement. Those that followed my return were busy and uneventful, except for the two persons on whom all thoughts were now centred, and for whom each hour, now, brought felicitations and marriage-gifts — plans for the future, openly or secretly discussed — tête-à-tête walks in the shady alleys of the Tuileries. No two lovers ever looked more radiant and happy than they.

My brother often took me out walking of an evening, and we became great friends. With all his faults — and he had still plenty — there was something to me very attractive about him; and he returned the compliment so far as to receive that cheapest of all presents — advice, at my hands.

"Mother," I said one day, when the important question of Rose's *trousseau* was being discussed, "if you have no objection, I should like to give some of the fine linen to Marie Dumont to do. Ernest would take me there. Have you heard any thing of her lately?"

"I believe Miss Lateward saw her, but I forget. I know there was something about Lady Janet's having been very kind to her, but really it has all gone out of my head."

That evening my brother and I walked down the narrow alley where Marie lived. Ernest was indignant at my bringing him to such a place, and disgusted at the cabbage-stalks and bones on the door-steps, and other less savory odors. We mounted four pair of dirty stairs, my brother growling all the way up, like a fine young mastiff-gentleman of sixteen as he was. I knocked, and Marie opened the door herself. She gave a cry of delight, seized my hands, kissed them, and began, with French volubility, pouring forth her gratitude for the visit, when she caught my brother's face behind my shoulder.   She started and turned pale.

"Who is that? — who is that with you?"   Her gaze seemed fascinated.

"My brother.   Why?"

"Strange!" she muttered, as she drew me in, and presented me a chair.   "Pardon, monsieur, walk in, pray." From time to time during our visit she glanced uneasily and furtively at him, but generally seemed to avoid looking that way, as though it distracted her attention from what she was saying.   And she had a great *deal* to say about the English lady who had been so kind to her in consequence of that excellent young gentleman's recommendation; how she had given her large commissions of work, and had put her boy to a day-school, and had even asked her how she should like to go to England, and said she could get her plenty of employment there in teaching *broderie* and French — for (I forget if I have before mentioned that) Marie's French was particularly pure and good.   That good lady had left her some work, and had promised Marie should hear from her further in England.

"I am glad to find you have been doing so well, Marie. And how is the child?   I suppose he is at his day-school?"

She dragged him forwards from behind a chair, where he was playing with a kitten — a noble-looking boy, with bright, glossy hair, and the rosy hue of health on his well-washed cheeks.   But suddenly, as I looked at him, I caught an expression in his eyes that had never struck me before, so like — No, no; that was imagination — but it made me shiver.

"Is he good?   Does he give you no trouble?"

"S'il est sage?   Oh! c'est un ange!" and she impressed a resonant kiss on his head.   "Tenez, si le bon Dieu en a beaucoup comme lui, il doit être content!"

"Have you time to do any more work, Marie, or are your hands full?   My sister is to be married in three weeks, and these collars and chemisettes *must* be finished before that time, if you undertake them.   Perhaps Lady Janet's work has to be done also by a certain time; if so — "

" Ça ne presse pas. Vous pouvez compter sur moi, mademoiselle."   And she took them with a confident smile, promising to bring the work home, as I should be too busy to send or come again.

The next fortnight was a very busy one. I had no time to think of Marie ; for every arrangement devolved upon me, and, to add to the bustle, a few days before the wedding Sir Charles Murray arrived. He was a fine old constitutional gentleman, with the old constitutional blue coat and gilt buttons, and the constitutional touch of gout every year ; with a rheumy eye, a cheek like a winter-apple, and a hearty voice. He had not been in Paris for five-and-twenty years, from which epoch he dated every event. "When I was in Paris at the time of the Peace," etc.; or, "I remember so and so, for it was not very long after I returned from Paris, at the time of the Peace," etc.

He and my mother talked a good deal over past days, and he secretly confided to me that, beautiful as he found his future daughter-in-law, she was not equal to her mother, as he remembered her, in the days when she was the toast of the county.

" I was very sweet upon her in those days, but I was a younger son — though a good bit older than her — and a poor country squire wouldn't ha' done for her. Jove ! she used to make us young fellows mad, when she came to our county assemblies, and danced all night with fine London sparks — guardsmen, and lords, and so on — and wouldn't look at us. How time does fly, Miss Margaret ! It's near thirty years ago ; for, after that, I came over here with my father — at the time of the Peace — and then poor Jack, my eldest brother, died, and in course of time I married, and have never seen your mother since."

"Charlie's, then, is a sort of inherited admiration?—the sins of the fathers visited on the children! No wonder at his falling in love at first sight, as he says he did. It really was n't fair. The infatuation was in his blood, poor fellow!"

Sir Charles chuckled.

"Lord bless you! they 're a cold set of young dogs now—a different sort to what they were in *my* day. Look at Charlie, there, sitting as demure by the side of his sweetheart as if she were an old 'oman o' seventy! *I* should n't ha' sat so when *I* was two-and-twenty."

It was the night before the wedding that Sir Charles delivered himself of the above sentiments. They were all sitting by the open windows, I remember, and I kept running in and out, devoting myself as much as I could to the old gentleman, for I found that he and my father did not get on too well together. Sir Charles was exceedingly shrewd. He knew the sort of a man my father was by report, and I have no doubt he warned his son, even before there was any idea of an engagement with Rose, to be prepared against attempts to borrow money. Whatever may have passed between them, certain it is that my father was very much disappointed, and he always spoke of Sir Charles as "mean and close-fisted." In vain I represented that few fathers would welcome as kindly as Sir Charles a daughter-in-law who came to him in the same state as she entered the world—save the clothes on her back. My father refused to take any other view of Sir Charles's conduct, and the intercourse between them was not of the most cordial, in consequence. So I had enough to do in keeping up the ball of conversation (a soft, elastic one, that could hurt no one), being called out of the room fifty times in the course of the hour; for, like Martha, my mind was troubled about many things. There was the packing of the boxes, and the preparations for the break-

fast; the cards and the carriages; tradesmen bringing home
forgotten orders at the eleventh hour; ridiculous little notes
from the merest acquaintances, requiring answers; lastly, a
sharp skirmish between Betsy and Rose's new maid, in
which I had to act as peacemaker. What an evening of
confusion it was! And there sat Rose herself, smiling
alternately at Charles and at his father, as she sewed on the
tassels to a purse she had been knitting for the latter.
How clearly every little incident of that July evening returns to me!

And I linger over them, reader, for very loathness to
approach a certain short passage in my life's story to which
I am rapidly coming. But it must be done. I know I cannot give any faithful picture of that life's subsequent journey — its weary desert stages, toilsome ascents, and pleasant
garden-halts, without passing boldly across this dark and
narrow bridge.

I was putting the last dresses into my sister's boxes late that night, when Betsy suddenly exclaimed,

"O Lor', Miss Rita, why if we ain't bin and forgot all about the collars and things as that Frenchwoman were to have brung home. What *hever* are we to do?"

"How provoking. It can't be helped now. It's too late to send, and there's no one, I'm sure, we can spare in the morning. Perhaps she'll bring them; fortunately there are plenty here. It is very tiresome of her — she promised so faithfully, too!"

It was long past midnight before we were in bed; but all the bridal party were dressed and ready the following morning by ten o'clock. It was a full-blown, cloudless day at the end of July — one of the hottest in the year: the windows open, and green shutters close; the atmosphere of the house heavy with the scent of flowers, which no breath of air stirred. Our beautiful Rose stands there, in a mist of tulle and orange-blossom, perfectly calm and collected. Why not? Before her all is sunshine — behind her gloom. She has no doubts or regrets — a few natural tears, perhaps, at leaving us all — nothing more.

We had read over the marriage-service together, at my earnest request, very early that morning. I sought to impress on her the solemn nature of the compact she was about to enter into, and my own view of a woman's obligations in matrimony. I ended by saying, "And therefore, dear Rose,

I would sooner beg my bread than be married to a man I could not '*love, honor, and obey.*' Not all the rank and the riches — not all the persuasion in the world, shall tempt me to do this. You have been so fortunate, darling, as to meet with a companion and protector for whom you can really feel thus, at the very outset of your life. Few *are* so fortunate; never be ungrateful for this — never trifle with the happiness which is yours to-day, but cherish it, try and keep it fresh and unspoiled through life."

" Oh yes, dear, of course : and you'll be as happy as I am very soon, I know. A certain person, who I'm sure adores you, will return, and it will be all right, and then you'll come to England. *Happier* than I am you can't be — it's impossible. Charles is such a darling! and I can say any thing to him I like, and he doesn't think it nonsense. I never felt that about anybody before, except mamma, and I'm sure I never, never could love any one as I do Charles ! "

I liked to hear her reiterate the assurance of her entire love and confidence in him. I knew that she was not capable of the strong life-and-death attachment of more passionate natures ; I knew that had Charles died, or the marriage from some cause been broken off, her weak, affectionate heart would have clung and bound round something else in a year or two : but I liked to hear her declare her belief in the unalterable, immortal nature of her love ; and she would be a tender, good little wife, I knew.

There was a large assemblage of persons in the British Embassy chapel, for whom we none of us cared, but who were asked, as being the only members of the *beau monde* left in Paris at that season. I stood near my sister, and once again, as I listened to those impressive words, I breathed a secret vow that never would I stand before God's altar, as a bride, but when I could make those solemn responses with my whole heart and soul.

The wedding and the breakfast passed off much as those things usually do. My father and Sir Charles each made a speech, which they had constructed on the regular conventional models. My father said, with effusion, that sad as the parting with his daughter was, he was consoled in remembering into what excellent hands he gave her; that she had always been perfect in her conduct as a daughter, and that he doubted not that she would prove so in every other relation of life; finally, that he begged to congratulate the man whose wife she became. Sir Charles observed that, coming of such parents, it was impossible to doubt the amiable character of the lady whom he had the happiness to call his daughter that day; his excellent friend Colonel Percival's acquaintance he had only lately had the happiness of making, but Mrs. Percival he had long known; and he could only say, that if her daughter but emulated the admirable example she had always had before her, etc. etc. etc.

My mother did not cry, as I expected. She looked flushed, and so handsome in her gray dress, with its soft, white lace, that I heard several people say she might be taken for our elder sister. When Rose retired to change her dress, we accompanied her, and even then my mother did not give way. She seemed sustained by the strong excitement to exertion as long as the necessity for it lasted.

And now the carriage with the white-favored postilions is at the door; the last package has been carried down stairs; the maid is already in the rumble. Rose, with a few tears on her cheeks, kisses all round two or three times, then passes through the drawing-room, shaking hands with those who are near her, and hurries down stairs, leaning on my father's arm. Charles and the old baronet follow.

"God bless 'ee, Charlie, my boy!" cries the latter; "write to me from Geneva, and let me hear how you are getting on. Confounded dull place, unless it's changed since I was there, with your mother, in '15, when we toured it, after the Peace. Confounded dull work, travelling. I advise you to come home soon. God bless 'ee both!"

He wrings his son's hand through the carriage window, and now the young couple are off. We all crowd on the balcony, and kiss our hands: a little white glove waves in answer. Betsy rushes forth, and to the astonishment of the Parisian mob, flings an old satin shoe after the carriage as it whirls away, and a great cloud of dust receives it out of our sight.

They are to spend the remainder of that summer and autumn in Switzerland, and the winter in Italy. They will pass through Paris on their way home in the spring, when Mrs. Charles Murray will be presented "on her marriage." I hear people talking of these things as they stand in the balcony, or hover in knots about the room, spinning the light gossamer-web of small-talk — but I seem as one in a dream. I look towards my mother, who has borne up bravely hitherto, and I observe that she begins to grow pale, and her face has a weary, worn expression about it. How I wish all these people were gone! but they are beginning only slowly to disperse. It is desperate work keeping up an appearance of liveliness now.

I seat myself at the window at last, feeling incapable of further exertion. Two or three men only remain, and they are talking about the Chantilly races with my father and Sir Charles, so I can be quiet. I recall the engraving of Newton's " Bridesmaid," and fancy I feel as much as she may have done. But this is not a time for vain regrets: I have enough to do in the " living present." Nay, a moment of action is even now at hand. I get up to attend to my mother, whom I can see in the perspective of the second room, stretched, completely exhausted, on her sofa, when I am stopped by a servant.

" There is a person outside who wishes to speak with you, mademoiselle."

"What sort of person?"

"A woman."

"It must be Marie Dumont;" and upon the staircase outside our door I found her indeed, but looking more as I first knew her — pale and very worn.

"Come in, Marie; why do you stand there?"

"Oh, mademoiselle, forgive me! I dare not come in. The child has been very ill, and that is why I was not able to do the work in time. I could not bear you to think —"

"I understand. Well, never mind; it can't be helped. How is the child?"

"Dieu soit béni! he is well now. I thought the bon Dieu would have taken him. For four nights I never left his cradle."

"You look ill yourself — you must take care. What was the matter with him?"

"Smallpox, mademoiselle."

I shrank back, involuntarily, with horror. "Good Heavens, Marie! what could make you think of coming here, then? You don't know how easily infection is brought."

"Dear mademoiselle, the doctor said there was no danger whatever. The house is well purified, none of the lodgers have caught it, and I wanted so much to tell you how it was the things were not done. I would not go *in*, however, and here —"

"Well, at all events I cannot stay talking to you. My father and mother have both a peculiar horror of the disease."

But even as I speak, the sound of voices in loud and laughing discourse come nearer and nearer through the doors. The stair-landing where we stand is dark, and hearing the voices approach, I draw aside to let them pass, when suddenly I feel myself seized by an iron, icy grasp. Marie,

her eyes dilated, her face livid, distorted, drags me yet
further back — back into the shadow of an alcove. I have
no power of resistance; my breath seems suddenly suspended, while she crushes me against the wall. And as she
stands there quivering under some violent emotion, the owners of those merry voices appear, and seeing me apparently
engaged in earnest conversation, pass on down stairs.

" Who — who is that?   How comes he here?" she gasps
out.

"What do you mean?   Don't hold me in that manner,
Marie."

" For the love of God, *what* is that man's real name?"

" Who — which do you mean?"

" The last speaker — there — he who is showing the way
— that tall, fair man."

" That?   Why, that is my father."

" Father!" she shrieked, and threw her arms wildly up.
A glimmering of the horrid truth flashed on me.

" *He is my Edouard Brown.   He is the fa*—" A burst
of hysterical sobs choked her utterance, and she sank in a
heap on the stairs.

*   *   *   *   *   *

CHAPTER XVIII.

I DRAW a veil over the rest of that scene. What I then felt, you can guess, reader, better than I can tell. You have never known, happily, the bitterness of such an hour, but you can imagine something like the revulsion it created in my whole being. I got the poor creature away somehow — I hardly knew how myself. I felt giddy and stunned. I could no more have shed tears than I could have talked over the hideous secret that lay festering at my breast; and I had a sickening dread of meeting my poor, miserable mother. Long afterwards, the recollection of that dread came back to me, as one of those mysterious forebodings that Providence gives us all some time or other in our lives.

At length Betsy came to say my mother had gone to bed, feeling unwell.

All that evening, and far into the night, I was in close attendance on her. She was feverish, with a headache and frequent sickness, and lay tossing and moaning there, unable to get any rest. Oh! that long, sultry night! when the orange-trees on the balcony never stirred a leaf, and the moon shone full into the room through the open window, carving black stone-shadows all about, like those that lay so heavy at my heart! There I sat at the foot of the bed, bathing her face now and then with vinegar, or trying, with a feather fan, to bring a little air about her. Towards morning — it might be two or three o'clock — Betsy insisted

on relieving watch, that I might go to bed. I was indeed
worn out, and thought if I could sleep for a few hours I
should be better fitted to meet the to-morrow, and whatever
it might bring. But sleep would not come; perhaps from
over-exhaustion — perhaps from the striving and longing
after its peaceful oblivion. The birds began to sing, and
clocks struck the wakening hours: sounds of life made themselves heard through the great city. It was useless: I rose
and dressed myself. My mother was no better; and all that
day she remained much in the same state. The next, my
father and Ernest were to leave us, which was an inexpres-
sible relief to me. But in the morning my mother was so
ill, that, after sending for the doctor, I mustered courage to
tell my father that I thought he *ought* to stay (it was a bitter
draught for me!) and that the parting from Ernest would,
I feared, have a terrible effect on my mother in her weak
state.   I was told that the vessel in which my brother's passage to India was taken sailed on a certain day, and that
"the least he could have in London was three days, and the
idea of his losing his passage-money, on account of his
mother's headaches," was quite ridiculous.

So spoke our father; but the tears gathered in Ernest's
eyes, though he tried to conceal what he felt.

"God bless you, dear boy," whispered my mother, raising
herself up in bed with a great effort, and folding her arms
around him. "We shall never see each other again, but
you'll be good, and steady, and all that sort of thing, won't
you, dear, for the sake of poor mamma? and you'll wear
this piece of hair round your neck, and think of her sometimes, when you're getting into any mischief." And so they
parted, to meet in this world no more.

That same evening, when the doctor had seen his patient, he drew me aside with a grave, hesitating air, and
paused, as he fingered the seals on his watch-chain, before
he spoke.

" I am afraid — I am rather afraid, young lady, we have some awkward symptoms this evening. I can't say positively, but I think, all things considered, it would be safer for you to remove to some friend's house, and send for a nurse — a *sœur de charité*, for instance — to attend on your mamma."

" What *do* you mean, doctor? I don't understand. You surely don't suppose I should leave my mother? What is it you are afraid of? "

" Why, I cannot say positively — not *decidedly* — till to-morrow; but, judging from certain symptoms, you see, I should think it safer, for *fear* of infection — "

" Infection? What of? "

" Smallpox."

I trembled, and turned even paler than I was, I suppose, for Dr. T. hastened to add,

" I see you are alarmed, and you had much better take my advice, for nothing disposes so much for infection as fear."

" Do you think it was for myself? " I said, scornfully.

O strange, mysterious dispensation! God only knows whether I was really the medium through which the impalpable poison had been transmitted from that wretched woman, or whether it was seminated in the hot, stagnant atmosphere of the great city. But it was too true. If Dr. T. had any doubts, they were dispelled the following day. It was a confirmed and virulent case. I need not say that I never, for one instant, thought of leaving her, though strongly urged to do so by Betsy, and, last of all, by my poor mother herself. Indeed, I know not where I could have gone, had I been so disposed. I had no friends among the mammon of unrighteousness who would have " received me into their houses." At all events, I never put them to the severe test. My duty was plain: to remain by my mother's bedside as long as strength was given me: if stricken by the hand of that sickness, I should, at least, have the consolation of having done what was right. I cannot deny that I *had* an invincible loathing of the disease, but now that I came into personal contact with this raging demon, whose ravages in some painfully disfigured face had so often made me turn away with disgust, a fortitude, and fearlessness were given me I dared hardly expect. I never left the sick-room : I snatched a few minutes' sleep when I could, Betsy and a *sœur de charité* taking their watch, then, in turns. Thus passed nine anxious, weary days, fluctuating from hope to fear, and fear to hope. I wrote to my father, and his answer was much what I expected. He said it was "a fortunate thing Ernest did not remain after all, as he might have caught that confounded complaint :" that he had "just returned from Southampton, after seeing him off in the *Ganges* — a capital steamer" — that London was already very empty, and he thought of going down for a week to Cowes, as of course he should n't return home until all danger of infection was over, as he could be of no use. He was really very sorry; it was a great bore : and he begged I would see that the house was properly purified before he came back.

Purified before he came back. Hideous mockery! And she lying between life and death the while — all alike to her, now, tenderness or neglect.

Then my impious heart cried aloud in its bitterness, daring to question the decrees of the All-Wise.

" Father! if there be retributive justice on earth, why is *she*, patient-hearted, sinned against, the victim of this loathsome disease, and not *you* ? "

In the delirium of fever my mother's mind recurred, as it had done once before, to other days and scenes. She was quite unconscious of our presence, and often rambled on the whole night, so that it was exhausting even to sit by and listen. On the ninth day the fever abated; she became calmer; her breathing less oppressed; and she knew us — my faithful Betsy and me. My heart grew light in the belief that the danger was now over.

"If she have but strength to rally," said the doctor that night, "she is safe. Unfortunately, we have to contend with a constitutional malady as well, that has been weakening her for years."

But I would listen to nothing but my own hopes, and so five more days slipped by, and I wrote to my father that all danger of *infection* was over — that my mother was only now left very prostrate after her severe illness, but that if she could be strengthened sufficiently to be moved somewhere, I thought change of air would soon set her up.

It was the evening of the 10th of August. My mother had been sleeping, or at least lying so tranquilly for many hours, and I felt so much easier about her, that I had ventured out for the first time to get a little fresh air. On my return she was awake, and made me come and sit close to her pillow. It was then twilight, but I could still distinguish her face plainly.

" Give me that small leather-case, Betsy, and you need n't stay. You must be worn out. Go and rest yourself. Miss Rita will remain with me. — My dear, now we are alone, I have so many things I wish to say, I hardly know how to begin. Whether I shall have time to tell you all, I think you ought to know — before — My child, you know something of what my life has been. I forgive him from my heart, dear: tell him so when I am gone. I hope I am not wrong in speaking to you about him: I wish to do what is best. You will be left alone, *quite* alone with him, when I am gone. You are wiser, dear, and have a stronger head than I — Well, never mind. What I wanted to tell you refers to the past — for her sake who is gone, and also as a warning.

"These are all your Aunt Mary's letters — some written

before I was married — and some of your father's. You never knew that he was once engaged to be married to her? She was very much attached to him: but she herself broke it off, from his inveterate habit of gambling. Nothing could cure him. He promised, but was always induced to play again. It cost her a great deal to give him up, but she did so. She was very young then, and was never the same afterwards. I was a child and at school, and knew nothing of it. Three years afterwards, when Mary found he was paying me attention — I was just come out, and Mary did n't go any longer into the world — she wrote up from the country, sending me these letters of his, and warning me against a confirmed gambler, entreating me not to think of him. She put her own feelings out of the question: it must have cost her a great deal to write this to me. I was a foolish young thing, and thought there was no harm in amusing myself with him, and never dreamt of any thing serious. And a year or two passed, and still, whenever we met, he paid me the same attention, and still we heard that he gambled; but I found, notwithstanding, that I thought oftener of him than of any one else. At last, in spite of all my sister's entreaties, I was selfish and blind enough to accept him! Oh! Mary, not even *you* knew half the trials I have since had — no one will ever know — but I considered it all the just punishment of my folly and ingratitude then — God forgive me!"

She laid her head back, exhausted with the exertion of talking so much. I moistened her lips with some grapes, and then sat down, holding her emaciated hand in mine, my heart too full for words. Presently she raised her head again. I made a sign to her to lie down and not speak, but she shook her head.

"I had been married but a very little while before I discovered that my husband did not care for me. That was my first trial — perhaps my bitterest. God knows why he had married me. I was handsome and run after — it's all one now, I can talk of it — and perhaps it was pique, for it was *she*, and she only, Mary, he really loved — as much as he was able to love any thing. Oh! he would have been a different man if he had married her, I think. She would have had an influence over him I never had. I was foolish — weak. Rita, when you marry, make your husband respect you. Sometimes, since I have been ill, the thought has come over me that I was terribly, wickedly the cause of — O God forgive me! He knows I had much to suffer."

She stopped, gasping for breath; a sharp spasm crossed her face, and her thin hand trembled convulsively in mine.

"Mother, dearest mother, do not agitate yourself in this way — pray do not. Leave the rest of what you wish to say till the morning. Your mind is unnaturally excited now; do not talk any more. I will remain by you all night, only try and sleep now, and when you wake —"

"I must finish what I have to say while I can. Your aunt, after some years, Rita, married Sir Nicholas Dacre. She had a great respect and admiration for her husband; I don't think it was exactly love, but she mourned for him, when he died, as her best friend. And meantime our difficulties began, and got worse and worse, until at last — oh! it was very hard and humbling in my position — I applied to Mary for assistance. I would sooner have done any thing else than *that*. Your father made me."

If my mother could distinguish my face at that moment, she must have seen a strange expression there. I thought my father could not sink lower in my eyes: there was yet another step, I found. How he, with all his false pride, situated so strangely, as I now learnt, with regard to my aunt — how he could have brought himself to beg of her, was more than I could comprehend. Even at that hour, in a tumult of conflicting emotions, I remember my blood boiling with indignation in my veins — it seemed too unnatural to be *possible*. It seems so still, when I think of it at this distance of time.

"It was a system of constant borrowing after that," my mother continued. "Your father was always getting into fresh trouble, alas!— promising and breaking his word— the old story. I need n't tell you, dear, that Mary did all she could to reclaim him: she saw Jews and lawyers, and settled all his affairs twice, besides all she had given him before to pay his debts of honor— that was when she was here. And at last she saw it was of no use, and she determined to do no more; she said the money had better be spent in educating you all, and that is why she left her money— you understand— any legacy or annuity to *me*, he would have had power over." Her voice was growing very faint, but still she went on. "Now I have told you all. Do you know why? Because, dear, you will have to resist your father, I 'm afraid, in many ways, when I 'm gone, and it 's better you should be prepared, and know that his love of gambling is so great, nothing will restrain him. As a young man, he sacrificed the only woman he ever loved for it; as a married one, he has sacrificed his wife and children. He will try to get hold of your little annuity. You must resist it; and watch, too, over the interests of your brothers. You must be a mother to my poor boys, Rita. And I know he will try and persuade you into marrying some one for his money. Don't do it, dear. I was thinking that by-and-by, perhaps, you might go and live with Rose and her husband — not that I would have you desert *him*, if he will really be a father to you; only —"

She broke off, as though her thoughts were in too painful a train even for words, and when she spoke again, her manner was very calm and solemn.

"I think God will not let you come to harm, dearest Rita — if you ask Him. My own trials, perhaps, would have been lighter, if I had 'laid all my care upon Him.' Ain't those the words? Read me that chapter. I thought too little about religion, but God is merciful. I believe *that* from the bottom of my heart."

I lit a candle, and took down the Bible and prayer-book from the shelf. I thought it would tranquillize her mind, and at all events prevent her talking, to read her something; but of the comfort of the Scriptures I practically knew nothing. I was ignorant where the chapter she asked for was to be found; so I looked for the Evening Psalms of the day. I could hardly steady my voice sufficiently to begin; and when I came to that beautiful Fifty-fifth Psalm — I do not know that I had ever read it before — its applicability to the occasion almost overpowered me. It seemed as though the voice of Conscience sighed, "My heart is disquieted within me, and the fear of death has fallen upon me," the wayworn spirit struggling to be free, and exclaiming, "Oh that I had wings like a dove, for then would I flee away and be at rest. Lo, then would I get me away far off, and remain in the wilderness. I would make haste to escape, because of the stormy wind and tempest." But when I came to the words, "For it is not an enemy who hath done me this dishonor, for then I could have borne it; neither was it mine adversary that did magnify himself against me, for then, peradventure, I would have hid myself from him: *But it was even thou, my companion, my guide, and mine own familiar friend.*" — I felt a strange thrill through me. The song of the Hebrew shepherd-king, plaining away, thousands of years ago, seemed the direct echo of our own actual trouble.

After I had done, she repeated softly the words, "Oh cast thy burden upon the Lord, and he shall nourish thee." Then she fell into a fitful, uneasy doze, and I stole from the room on tiptoe. I could not, would not allow myself to believe there was *danger;* but yet — Let a message be taken to the clergyman, requesting him to come as early as

14

he can in the morning. Half an hour afterwards Dr. T.
stood with me by the bed.

"There has been too much excitement here. I am sorry
to tell you I find her much less well than I did this morning.
She *may*, with sleep and perfect quiet — "

I hid my face in my hands. I gave up hope from that
moment.

"The action of the heart is so very feeble. I am inclined to think there must be some strong mental excitement, too, the brain is still so irritated — it is working too
much for the body. I confess the case begins to look very
serious. Still, if you can keep your mamma *perfectly* tranquil for some hours — "

"Tell me the truth; I had rather. Don't deceive me. Is
there any hope?"

He said, in the low, professional voice, "I am afraid, very
little."

The nights that had preceded it were as nothing compared to this. My faculties, I thank God, were not paralyzed: I was able to think of and do all that was necessary
or possible to be done, but I was no longer sustained by any
hope, and I felt that I never had loved my mother so much
as now I was about to lose her. That last confidence and
appeal, in disclosing to me how much she had loved and
struggled and suffered, had drawn me closer to her than I
had been in all these years. Strange, how little we often
know of those who are next us in the battle-ranks through
this long march of life! Sometimes, at the end of the
day — sometimes earlier, should the heavy breastplates of
custom be displaced by accident — we are amazed to find
the warm, sensitive heart, or, it may be, the ghastly wound
that has laid hidden from us until then. I knew my mother
better now. The earth-cloud that dimmed so much that
was true and tender was removed. My heart smote me in a
thousand little things. I thought how I might have been

móre her companion while she was yet with us, and accused myself of not having loved her as I ought.

I opened the window, and put back the curtain. My mother was awake now. She turned her hot, weary head towards it, and I could see her eyes fixed thirstily upon the blue vault of heaven — she was longing for the eternal peace that was beyond that deep, pure sky. And as I looked into the heart of the night, and thought of my desolate position here when she was gone, I murmured again with the Psalmist, "Oh that I had wings like a dove, for then would I flee away, and be at rest."

With the first glimmer of morning I observed that a change had come over her face. She seemed to wish to say something, and motioned that I should lower my head to her lips. She had not once alluded to my father's absence, or expressed a wish for his return. Now she said,

"I have hoped so to see him once more, that I might charge him — with my dying words — to redeem the past — to amend his life — to be a father to his children, as he hopes to have mercy from our Father — hereafter. Tell him so — tell him I forgave him from my heart — and that I died happy, trusting in the mercy of God — to whose care I commend my children — "

At five o'clock the clergyman came, and administered the sacrament. I know her heart joined fervently in the responses, though her lips moved but feebly, and gave forth no sound. Her cold hand lay in mine, and her face was towards that glorious sun that was breaking in the eastern sky.

*   *   *   *   *

Three hours later, I stood with tearless eyes gazing at her as she lay there, beautiful again in the holy serenity of death. I had folded her hands — those perfect hands — meekly on her breast, and placed some white roses in them. The servants were all gone out, on one sad errand or another: I was alone in the apartment. There was a ring at the bell; then another louder than the first. I thought I heard the door opened as if with a latch-key, and a heavy step coming through the rooms. I had been arranging with my dead-cold hands the linen shroud: I drew it hastily over the face, and went towards the door.

It was thrown open suddenly. My father, covered with dust, stood before me.

" Curse those servants. I 've been ringing for an hour. What does it mean? By G—d, Rita, I 'll have them all — Why, what 's the matter? Where — *where* is your mother ?"

I drew back the shroud. " There she lies — at rest, and beyond this world's cruel wrongs."

CHAPTER XIX.

THERE are periodical changes in the moral as in the
physical system. If we look honestly within ourselves, and
then recall what we were a few years back (and since we
came to man's and woman's estate), we see how differently
we then thought and felt. The change may be for the
better, or for worse. The mind, like its material companion,
may generate some hidden disease, the germs of which have
until now lain hidden; or it may outgrow the feebleness of
youth, become less susceptible to the wind and frost, and
strike forth unexpected shoots, full of sap and vigor. But
we all undergo these revolutions, variously produced in
various minds. With some, the reading of a book is sufficient. It sets their thoughts working in a certain train,
with good or bad results, as the autobiography of more than
one criminal tells. Other less impressionable natures require
some strong shock to set the languid pulses of their being
astir in a new direction. And there are some who sigh
with Romeo, " Dry sorrow drinks our blood," on whom the
years have told, by quenching the sacred fire on their young
hearts' altar. The light of their lives went out suddenly,
and no one knew it — not even their best friends!

Some such change as this now took place in me. All I
had learnt and suffered during the past few months made me
feel prematurely old. The bloom — the elasticity of youth —
were gone, never to return. My childhood had not, perhaps,
been very happy; but *then* my pleasures were so little de-

pendent on others, that my girl's spirit had burned on brightly enough — ambition and enthusiasm undimmed. I possessed that keen sense of enjoyment, impalpable and evanescent as the scent of a flower, which a picture, or a pleasant book — nay, sunshine alone — brought with it, and which no one could take from me. A season had intervened since then, in which I had gone out of myself, as it were. The world's smile had dazzled me until I had nearly become one of its frivolous dependents for life. And now I had returned again to the old silent companionship of my own thoughts. The chamber was the same, but dark and cold; the embers only remained of the fire that once warmed it.

The first days of heavy mourning were over. The autumn, which had set in wet and rainy, was succeeded by sharp winter weather. I have little to tell of my outward life during these months; the history of every day would be but the history of my own mind. I lived entirely alone. My father, to do him justice, showed a respect for my mother's memory, and for my grief, which left me as much to myself as I could desire. After the shock — which he felt in a certain way — was over, and two or three weeks had passed, he was out again just as much as ever. I expected, of course, nothing else. Our lives were as distinct and apart, now that we were left alone together out of the large family circle, as when I was a little child shut into the nursery all day long. We lived under the same roof, and that was all. We had nothing in common. My father had never allowed me to love or respect him, and all that had lately come to my knowledge had increased the distance between us four-fold. Still, I never forgot my mother's dying injunctions. Had he shown the least disposition — the very faintest wish for my society — I would have stilled the bitter memories that cried aloud, and have gone to him. But he never did; and for many months my faithful Betsy was my only companion. I took long walks with her before breakfast; the rest of the day I remained in the house : I dreaded so much meeting any of the gay Paris world. People were very kind. Many were the offers to take me out driving, and other little attentions, from ladies whom I had done the injustice to think had already forgotten my existence. Even the tradesmen showed a consideration for my position, when any of the old money difficulties occurred, to which I was now, from long custom, inured. As to Monsieur Barac, there was no measure to the kind thoughts he had for me. He generally waylaid me on my return in the morning, now to press on me a pot of tulips for my window — now to offer me a number of the " Magasin Pitoresque," or the loan of some hazy little Van der Weldt, just imported from its native soil. For I returned to my old occupations, not with the old zest, indeed, but with the determination to give my mind so much hard work as should prevent its preying on itself. I bought an Italian grammar, and set to work to learn that language. Rose wrote that she found it very easy, which made me first think of learning ; and I discovered that nothing occupies the mind more successfully for the time than the exercise of those faculties — not very high, perhaps, half-mechanical ones — necessary to acquire a language. Poor Rose ! the sad news had reached her at Geneva, in the third week of her honeymoon. It was a terrible shock, coming in the midst of their first happiness ; but I was glad they were travelling. Far better than remaining in one place, with nothing to distract the mind from one sad subject. I heard from her constantly, and already her letters showed she had recovered her spirits. I dare say the constant and rapid change of scene made the weeks that had elapsed appear long and many — to me it seemed but yesterday. In December, my little brothers were to come home. I looked forward to it longingly. It would be pleasant to hear their glad young voices about the house again.

I considered for a long time what I should do about that

wretched woman and her child. I could not abandon her, poor creature, but I had an invincible repugnance to seeing her again. Through her I felt as if Death had entered our doors, and, placed in the painful position we were towards each other, personal interviews could only be distressing. I sent Betsy : she was the bearer of an old winter gown or two and some money, and had particular injunctions to find out how Marie and the child were faring. But they were gone, and no one could tell any thing about them. The neighbors said she had left some weeks before : she had paid her rent, that was all the owners of the house knew or cared for : she had never associated much with them. So I had lost all clue to her, and henceforward she must go on her solitary path without such poor assistance as I could offer.

I have not yet mentioned a letter that I received from Miss Lateward just before my mother's death. I could not open it for many days ; I did not answer it for weeks, though my thoughts often reverted to, and speculated on, its contents. It was followed by many kind and sympathetic ones when she learnt my loss, but I give this first letter because it presents a picture in detail, colored by the writer's character-istic pencil, of the household in which she was now domesti-cated :

"Rochford Court, near Ancaster, August 7.

"My dear Marguerite, —

"In accordance with your amiable wish, I seat myself to narrate to you the progress of events since I arrived here. You received my epistle from the metropolis, I trust, giving you tidings of our safety after encountering the perils of the *watery deep*? In that epistle, I expressed my amazement at the intelligence of your sister's approaching nuptials : she is *full young* to assume the responsibilities of the conjugal yoke, and it is to be desired that her *education* were more complete, but from what you say of the gentleman, I trust it may prove a satisfactory alliance.

" You will be happy to learn that my position is *confirmed* as teacher in this highly respectable family. My pupil, Miss Violet Rochford, aged thirteen, is a young lady of docile disposition, with a taste for botany, and rather an *undue* predilection for equestrian exercise. In her mnemonic studies, I find her attention often wandering to a young female horse (filly is, I believe, the generic term) that is allowed to sport in the park under the schoolroom window. I have requested that its gambols may henceforth be confined to some more *distant* portion of the demesne. We have commenced to form an herbarium in our rural walks, and as Miss Rochford's attention has been arrested by the morphological point of view in which I teach her to regard plants, I am hopeful of thus combining *instruction* with *relaxation*. The country here is singularly devoid of timber; the aborigines, I apprehend, having consumed those vast tracts of forests of which we read as having extended throughout Great Britain. There is no *neighborhood* (as it is ungrammatically termed, — meaning that there is but little visiting), and our daily existence is normal in character, with little interruption or variation. The place, you are aware, belongs to Mr. Rochford, but his mother resides with him. Her benevolence is truly edifying: she is daily among the cottagers, by whom she is much feared and respected: indeed, she is, it is plain to see, a woman of very *strong mind*, possessing both *promptitude*, and *firmness*. Mr. Rochford, who seems an amiable young man, has a great veneration for his mother, consults her on all occasions, and seldom decides a question without her sanction, I am told. He is an active magistrate, and often absent for some days at a time on county business. He takes a lively interest in his sister's mental development, and of an evening often reads aloud Shakspeare (a *family* Shakspeare, of course, with all objectionable passages omitted). Mrs. Rochford occasionally plays on the piano: she was a pupil of Clementi, and considered to have a fine

touch for Handel, whom her son calls 'the Milton of music.'
The other night she was so engaged, when a domestic entered
to say that a child in the village was seized with the croup.
A missive had been sent for the country Æsculapius, but he
resides four miles off. Mrs. R. had on her waterproof cloak
in a moment (for it was *raining hard*). A mustard plaister
and some hot preparation were procured without loss of time
from the housekeeper, and with these in her basket she set
out, her son holding an *umbrella* over her! I mention this
little anecdote as illustrating Mrs. R.'s *energy* and active
benevolence. Yet I think I perceive (though she has been
most *kind* to me, I must say) that she has no ordinary degree
of pride. For instance, yesterday, at luncheon, I inquired
the name of a lady whose portrait hangs over the sideboard —
being struck, the fact is, with a certain degree of likeness to
you! A cloud came over Mrs. R.'s brow, and she replied,
rather shortly, 'that it was the Duchess of Portsmouth.' I
most unreflectingly said, 'Oh! an ancestor, I suppose?' To
which she rejoined, 'We have never had a disreputable character, not even a *king's mistress*, in our family, though Rochford Court has been in our possession four hundred years.
My son picked up that picture somewhere for the sake of the
face: I own I was annoyed at it.' (He was not present,
fortunately, when this occurred.) I write all this, my dear
Marguerite, because you are kind enough to say you wish to
know every particular relative to the family in which I am
living, and that you shall consider no amount of detail as
tedious. Lady Janet left this last week for Scotland. Her
ladyship often did me the honor to inquire if I had heard from
you, and when I read to her some passages of your letter, she
appeared *deeply* interested, as did also Mrs. Rochford, who
happened to be present. The latter has questioned me more
than once concerning you, saying that, from what she had
heard, she feared you must be too original and *peculiar* to
be very happy. I believe my dear pupil deserves all I said

of her — But how I am running on! You will think that the garrulity of age has overtaken me. In the words of the blind bard, ' With thee conversing I forget all time! '

"Believe me, with respectful compliments to Mrs. Percival, ever to be,

" My dear Marguerite,
" Your faithful friend,
"TABITHA LATEWARD."

I thought, when I read this letter, what a disagreeable woman Mrs. Rochford must be. How intensely I should dislike her, and how the poor must resent her impertinent interference in their affairs at all hours of the day and night. You will perceive I was angry. It must have been that touch about the picture, — though a flickering hope *did* arise, "Could he have bought it from its likeness to me?" But it was soon dispelled. He had never even mentioned my name. If he had ever spoken of me to his mother, it was only as "original and peculiar." Well, well, it was a bubble, and it had burst. I had no right to expect any thing else, and I ought to feel how unsuited our characters and habits of life were to each other.

Then I took up my journal and read the following entry, made some months before :

" Hubert Rochford said to-day, in reply to an observation of mine, that we should be all much better without our Spanish castles, — that day-dreaming never did any one any good. And yet, who would willingly have been without his? The man who never had any is truly a possessor of that wisdom which is akin to folly. Delusions are to our youth what mists are to the morning, beautiful in themselves, necessary and refreshing to our human nature, but gradually melting before the strong rays of the world, or if you like it better, the sun of knowledge. Natures, like countries where that sun shines too hotly from early morning, are

never very fertile. The longer we can keep our hearts
fresh and untouched by it, the better."

I had had *my* delusions: they had not lasted long, and
they were gone!

You may believe that I often thought over this letter in
my solitary hours. How different that life must be to any
thing I had ever known or conceived! It sounded dull
enough, certainly, that barren country, with Handel and
the herbarium for recreations; but then my heart said
there was the pervading principle in such an existence,
for ever sweetening and elevating it above a life of mere
social pleasures, however refined and intellectual. Yes,
and I knew, too, that I could have lived thus with *one*
companion (no matter *who*, for had I not driven that
phantom of a passion down to the tomb of the Capulets?),
nor coveted aught, from year's end to year's end, but to be
one with him, to share his joys and sorrows, his schemes and
aspirations, to sit down with him in the cheerful firelight of
" home," and work out the great problem of our lives in
unison.

Reader, I was very lonely all those months; lonely and
desolate at heart, which is a far different thing from the
solitude of the eyes and tongue. The latter, in my case,
was voluntary; but though I employed my thoughts as
much as possible in other ways, there were times when they
dwelt gloomily and despondingly on the future. I was far,
very far, from having learned, in all my troubles, that
Christian conviction, that God ordereth all things for the
best, which I hope I now feel. My wild, impatient heart
no longer, indeed, throbbed as it once had done ; but it was
the heaviness of the stone rolled on the door of the sepul-
chre, not God's angel of calmness setting within.

It was in November, I think, that I first began to feel
uneasy again about my father, from a very unusual symptom
in his affairs — a profusion of ready money. Three or four

times, when I applied to him to pay the house-bills (and
had prepared myself for the old evasions, nay, for a direct
retort that I might advance the money from my own
annuity), he had given it me directly. I knew at the time
of my poor mother's funeral he had hardly enough to pay
for that and the doctor's expenses. Where had the money
since come from? The oftener I thought of it, the more I
was afraid he had been again to the Jews.

One morning, about this time, as I was returning home,
I saw Felicien Ismael standing at the door of old Barac's
apartment. He had been waiting for me evidently, for, as
I approached, he came forward with an obsequious bow,
while Barac retired into a distant room.

"Pon chour, mademoiselle. I am proud af de chance dat
make me for to zee you. Will you accord me five minutes'
entertain, my ponne demoiselle?"

He motioned with his hand to signify that Monsieur
Barac's apartment would be a better theatre for the interview. I thanked him; I would listen to what he had to say
there.

"Var gut. You not forget dat I had vonce de plaisir
you a petite service to render?—a mere pagatelle, c'est
vrai."

"I remember your kindness perfectly, Monsieur Ismael.
Is there any thing I can do for you now?"

"Dere is, my dear mees — a trifle — qui ne fous coûtera
rien."

"What is it? If I can, I shall be glad."

"Dere is one var fine artist af my acquaint, who ambitions to produce a pieshur af de Sainte Vierge getting up de
clouds. He want a model for she."

"Well, Monsieur Ismael, and what then?"

"He desire ardently that you would pose to him. Pauvre
diaple! his fortune is made, ven you so gut are."

"What in the world do you mean, Monsieur Ismael?"

"Mein Gott, it is clear, mademoiselle. He zee in you de true pieshur af the Sainte Vierge, and — "

"Nonsense, Monsieur Ismael. You must think me very vain, to make such an extraordinary proposition to me. This is not your friend's only object, I presume: he can find hundreds of models infinitely better suited to his purpose. There must be some other reason for his wishing me to sit to him. What is it? and what is your interest in the business?"

"My gut mees, I am open as de heaven! I selbst puy de pieshur. I make my honest profit on him."

"Well. That is not all? You buy the picture — and then?"

"He go trough my hand. I von day find a puyer for him, if I have de gut luck."

"Perhaps you have *already* found one?"

"It hangs on you, mademoiselle," said Ismael, dropping an additional infusion of oil into the hinges of his discourse.

"I think I begin to understand," I replied. "There is some one you imagine will buy this picture from — from in short, from its likeness to me?"

The Jew smiled an unctuous smile, and rubbed his jewelled fingers, half in perplexity as to how much he should reveal.

"Hé pien, oui, ma ponne demoiselle. Dere is one var great church puilt in de provinces — where one patron of mine — one var gut friend — is de *grand seigneur*. Man seeks now de altar-piece — and I know de fancy of dis great gut gentleman, dat when he zee — "

"Enough! I don't wish to hear who the *grand seigneur* is, or any thing more. I can lend myself to nothing of the sort. I have let you go on so far, for I was curious, I own, to unravel the mystery. I am sorry and surprised, Monsieur Ismael, that you should ever have asked me to do this."

"De gut Colonel, your pappa, make no difficulties. *Il m'a même dit de fous en parler.*"

I could hardly contain my indignation, but said, as quietly as I could, "I am afraid you see too much of my father, Monsieur Ismael. We will talk no more about this foolish business, if you please; but I wanted to speak to you — to implore you not to advance my father any more money. You know the difficulty of his repaying it: what security you have, I cannot imagine."

"I haf not done buishnesh vid your gut pappa, I gif my vord, for var long time. Perhapsh I guesh where he find de monish. Perhapsh, who knowsh?" he added, with a grin, "some soon day you vill be kinder disposhed to gif my gut patron, de Marquis, de pleasure of your face."

I thought this too impertinent to be answered, and, bowing coldly, I left him, and went up-stairs.

CHAPTER XX.

At Christmas the boys came home. My father had, at first, said they must spend their holidays at school. " It was great trouble and expense for six weeks." (I could not help smiling bitterly to hear him talk of expense — when it suited him.) I urged the point, however, so strongly, that he consented, and they came. They were good, tractable boys, very unlike Ernest in every way, and I found it easy to gain an ascendency over them. I was maternal and authoritative as to their daily holiday-tasks; but, these over, they treated me as their friend and companion, to whom they told every thing — their secret thoughts and school-time joys and troubles; above all, their separate ambitions for the future. Roger, the least clever of the two, had a strong predilection for the navy. He was always drawing ships and rigging a little boat he had, and solemnly declared he would never be any thing but a sailor. What my father's views might be, I knew not, but I saw no objection; on the contrary, it was the best thing for him to enter a profession early, make a path for himself, and be independent of every one. The wish of Arthur's heart — to be a clergyman — presented more difficulty of realization. I turned over in my mind for some time how a college education could be accomplished. I was afraid that the trustees of my aunt's will, who were rigid in its interpretation, might object to allow the legacy, due on his coming of age, to be forestalled in paying for the necessary expenses. As much of my small annuity as I could save

(224)

should be devoted to this object; but it would, after all, amount to a trifling sum; and I could not but foresee the probabilities of my having some urgent, imperative call for these savings in the interim. There was nothing to be done, however, but to await the workings of time. Perhaps Rose might do something by-and-by for her favorite brother.

We walked early one morning, my brothers and I, to a certain pond near the Bois de Boulogne, that Roger might launch his boat. It was a mild, still winter's morning. There had been a long frost, and now it had been thawing for two days. The sky was like a dim opal, flecked with thin white clouds; none of the spirit of wind in it. The sun shone out weakly now and then, and a blue veil of mist hung over the distant wood, making the near trees look yet browner. The leaves no longer crackled under one's feet, but lay damp and flattened on the path, in spots of scarlet and yellow.

We were near the pond, and the boys had run forward to find a place where they could thrust out their boats from the bank, when I heard the sharp canter of a horse on the road behind us. His rider apparently reined him in as he approached. I did not turn round, but I was sensible of the fact from the prolonged snort, the chafing of the bit, and the measured click of the hoof in the soft wet road. Just then, a country-girl passed me, laden with violets for the Paris market. Their fragrance was very seductive, and I looked longingly at them, for I had always a passion for violets; but I had not a sou in my pocket, and walked on. The horseman dismounted, and called to the girl. I started. Was it not a voice I knew? He threw the bridle over his arm, and following me, said, in a low tone,

"Will Miss Percival allow me to offer her these flowers?"

It was Lord Rawdon. I stood still, and all power of

speech seemed to leave me. He was pale and haggard, and I saw that his arm was still in a sling. It brought a rush of recollections back, and with them a sense of what was due to him from me. I held out my hand.

"Forgive me, Lord Rawdon. I am not very strong — my nerves have been much shaken of late — and the surprise of seeing you almost paralyzed me, I think. You look ill. I am afraid you have suffered much, and I am very, *very* sorry to see your arm is still disabled."

"It is almost worth having gone through it all to hear you say so, though I suppose it's only a conventional expression of compassion — what you would feel if one of Franconi's men were spilt, eh? Miss Percival, I have been in Paris a fortnight, and during that time I have walked and ridden round and round your house, hoping to see you, till I believe the gendarmes began to suspect me of burglarious intentions. I didn't call, for I heard it was no use — that you wouldn't see any one; and your father is not wrapped up in me, as you are aware. You never left the house, that I could make out, till this morning, when I thought of ordering my horse an hour before the Paris world is awake. I am repaid."

His manner, which was always strange, seemed to me stranger than ever. His voice was hard and hoarse, as one who has known no rest, and there was a tremulousness in certain accents, which, when I looked at his wild, fierce eyes, made me feel any thing but comfortable.

"I am glad you chanced to meet me," said I, not choosing to understand him, but desirous of appearing at my ease. "I have often wished to see you since that disastrous meeting, to explain to you the strange circumstances under which you saw me that night. I do not know — I mean, I am sure, you only thought, at the time, like a chivalrous gentleman, as you proved yourself; but afterwards it must often have occurred to you as strange."

"Not at all. I cleared the mystery for myself. I went back to the house and questioned the porter, and after that wild young fellow, De Vailly, had winged me, he had the good taste to own that he had never seen you before, and had no idea who you were."

"I thank you, Lord Rawdon, sincerely, but you caused me a great deal of misery by that unhappy duel. Do you still suffer much?"

"Suffer!" he exclaimed, looking through me with that burning eye of his. "Come, you shall hear something of what I have suffered — of what I still suffer. Do you remember that first night we met? I believe I am a changed man since then."

"I hope we are both changed since then," I replied, gravely.

"But it is not a change for the better in me, I tell you. I suffer from the fierce torture of a passion I never felt before. I have struggled for months to drive your image from my heart, for I knew you did n't care for me. I thought that absence — and then, fool that I was! — the old reckless life, and the smiles of other women, fairer by far, would force me, in time, to forget you. I wrestled with my passion till it wore my very vitals. It has made me the wretched-looking creature you see — not my wound — don't fancy that. And if this is not enough, know further, that I suffer — though I have never owned it to mortal before — from the torments of an uneasy conscience, and because I believe in so little that is good here — in nothing happy hereafter!"

"God help you, then, for vain is the help of man! Without hope, this life would be insupportable. It is a long and a dark and dreary way to many of us — a succession of falls, as some one says — but we should get up each time trying to see the light at the end brighter."

"Mud we are and unto mud shall we return! That is

the only future we can be certain of. I have no faith now ;
I am a useless mass, cumbering the earth."

"It grieves me to hear you," I said, "disavowing that
imperishable part of yourself, which is no more part of
the earth than the mist yonder is of the hill it colors. You
do yourself great wrong. You have naturally fine qualities of heart — great mental gifts — why waste and abuse
them ? "

"Oh, Marguerite — I must call you so *once* — do you not
feel it is in your power, and yours only, to lift me up from
this mire — to lead me to purer and better things? My
God ! what woman ever had the influence over a man you
would have ? With you, perhaps, I might learn the way to
heaven : without you, I must live out this hell on earth until
I find oblivion in the grave."

"You strangely deceive yourself, Lord Rawdon. I am
too little of a saint to help any one. I need, on the contrary,
a firm, strong hand to prevent me from falling."

"I tell you, there may be other women better, wiser —
you are the only one for me. Marguerite, that first night
we met, I was idiot enough to ask you jestingly the gravest
question a man can put to a woman. God knows, in a very
different spirit — with the strength and fervor of my whole
soul — I now repeat it."

"I answer as I did then."

"Have pity on me, Marguerite. Consider this is all I
live for now. Give me time — give me hope. You said
that without it life was insupportable."

"I spoke of a hope no one can take away. Alas! Lord
Rawdon, as regards myself, I can give you none. You ask
why ? But you supplied the best reason yourself just now
— the only insurmountable one a woman can give — that I
do not love you. I wish I could be to you as a sister,
but that has passed into a conventional phrase, and means
nothing ; or rather, constituted as society is, it means an

impossibility. Friendship and gratitude are cold words, but I shall always feel a true, deep interest in your welfare — I don't mean your worldly welfare, of course — I mean your soul's. I hope and pray that you may become a better and a happier man. I have no right to preach, as I have already said, nor have I the inclination — but I do earnestly hope —"

" Marguerite, Marguerite, you don't know what you are doing, to drive a man like me desperate. Tell me — promise me, at least, that you will not be persuaded into marrying that old Frenchman. I see the web gathering round you: I know the danger that threatens, and the hand that directs all the threads of it; but I shall be there, at hand, watching over, and ready to defend you, if you will only let me."

" There is no danger of my being persuaded to marry the Marquis d'Ofort, or any one whom my heart does not choose, thank you. I can promise you that, safely."

We stood by the glassy pond, on which Roger had already launched his boat, both boys being too much engrossed to pay much attention to my companion. They clapped their hands, exultant, as the keel cleft the waters, and the miniature frigate rode gallantly forwards. Then a little puff of wind caught it, and it drifted towards a mud-bank: its masts got entangled in the reeds and rushes, and it capsized.

" Is not that an emblem of my life?" said Rawdon, gloomily. " Look there, the toy will fill with water, and must sink."

" Come," I answered, smiling, " walk round to that point, and stretch out your riding-whip. You will easily set it right. The type is not a true one — the poor boat couldn't steer itself, nor extricate itself, when once entangled."

He recovered it, and the boys, in their frank, hearty way, thanked the dark gentleman for his kindness.

"It is nearly eleven o'clock, Roger; we must be going home. Get up on your horse, Lord Rawdon, and oblige me by turning his head in *that* direction. And, if you would not deprive me of the only pleasure I have — my early walks — you will not try and repeat this meeting."

I held out my hand once again: he seized it, and looked into my face with wild, regretful eyes, and before I knew what he was doing, he pressed my fingers passionately to his lips.

He spoke no word, and the next moment was upon his horse, and galloping down a by-road in the wood.

"Who is that gentleman, Rity? and why does he have his arm in a sling?"

"He is a friend who once did me a great service, Roger, and he has been badly wounded."

"What makes him kiss your hand in that funny way?"

"As to that, it is a foolish way some people have of wishing good-by. — Dear boys, I have never asked you to keep a secret, have I? but I have reasons for not wishing you ever to speak about this gentleman, or allude to him in any way. I can depend on you, I know."

But the precaution was vain: exactly what I least wished had come to pass. Half an hour after I returned home my father entered my room. I read in his face immediately that something had occurred to make him angry.

"You are certainly the strangest girl." he began. "I never could understand you." (I thought he had never taken much pains.) "You're a mass of hypocrisy, I believe. Here you pretend to be in such grief that you can't see any one, and I find you are seen out walking, before breakfast, with that d——d fellow Rawdon. What the devil do you mean by it? Have you no regard for the world's opinion? Are you become perfectly indifferent as to what people say of you?"

Time was when I should have replied, " You have shown yourself very indifferent to what the world has said of me already ; " but I only bowed my head.

" Well? What have you to say ?"

" Very little. I was walking, and Lord Rawdon joined me. There was no intention, on my part, of meeting. I greeted him, as I should any one else I know well; and when I asked him to ride on, he did so."

" Not until he had kissed your hand. I have it from an eye-witness. Do you allow all casual acquaintances you meet to do that?"

" No. He is not a casual acquaintance."

" Perhaps, as your father, I may be allowed to ask if — if you're engaged to this madman? — a wild, unprincipled fellow, who has already run through more than half his fortune" — (Oh, world! world!) — "his estates heavily mortgaged, and this year, at Baden, he lost more than twenty thousand pounds at play, I hear."

" That would indeed be enough to deter me from marrying Lord Rawdon, if I had not already refused him," I replied, with an irrepressible touch of sarcasm.

" To be seen with him is enough to ruin all your prospects in life."

" I have none."

He turned away with an impetuous " Pshaw!" then suddenly exclaimed, " How long, may I ask, do you propose remaining shut up in this absurd way, without seeing any one? — except in your morning walks, that is to say. There's reason in every thing. Your poor mother has been dead six months. It's such d—d affectation in a girl of your age pretending you can't go out. But you've no consideration for *me*."

" I would do any thing in the world to make you happy at home, father. I don't think my going out could contribute to your comfort in the least. You didn't think so last year, you know : you preferred my going out with some one else."

"I should like to have two or three friends at dinner sometimes — but you'd go and shut yourself up, I suppose, if I did ? "

"I think, with your means, you can ill afford to give dinner entertainments. We never did so in my dear mother's lifetime, father."

"Oh, my affairs are in a better state now ; the money market is looking up. By-the-by, come out and take a walk with me this afternoon."

Nothing could be more distasteful to me, but I would not refuse ; and, like many a conscientious act in this world — spite of what moralists say — the result did not bring its reward. My father took me up the Champs Elysées just at the hour when it is most crowded ; he bowing, nodding, stopping to *button* some one at every three or four paces. I kept my thick black veil down, looking neither to the right nor to the left, and yet I felt quite giddy and bewildered with the constant tide of faces flowing past me. Presently we met — accidentally, of course — a line of venerable French dandies, midmost among whom was the Marquis d'Ofort. He wore a coat much padded across the chest, and giving occasion for many gilt buttons ; and upon his head a hat exceedingly curled in the brim, and poised at such an inclination over the right ear, that it seemed ready to topple over. If I felt inclined to laugh the first moment I saw him, the feeling very soon gave place to a dead and dreary despair, when, after a cordial greeting to his " bon ami — ce brave Colonel," and an elaborate salutation to me, he left his brethren and joined us in our walk. I thought that walk never would come to an end. I was reduced to such a state of mental nausea and exhaustion at last (at the end of a second hour, I believe), that I was obliged to beg my father would take me home ; and when I heard him request the favor of the Marquis's company at dinner on the following Sunday, I would rather have been condemned to pass that day at the treadmill.

"We shall be *four* at dinner," said my father, as we were going up stairs; "you will make preparations accordingly."

CHAPTER XXI.

Three days after that walk — it was on a Monday or a Tuesday — Arthur ran into my room with a note in his hand.

"Rity, here's something for you. As I was spinning my top outside there, that dark gentleman rode up and gave me this, and told me to be sure and give it to you yourself. And then he said if I was spinning my top to-morrow, he would be sure and bring me something. I hope he won't forget."

The note was written in blotted characters — almost illegible in parts. It ran thus:

"I have spent days and nights of passionate, fevered restlessness since I saw you. I should go mad if I really believed it was my *irrevocable fate* that I learned from your lips. *It shall not be.* Who is there to watch over you, — who is there to lay down his life for you, but I? Oh! worthless and reprobate that I am, yet I love you as never man loved. And I, alone, see all the dark threads weaving round you, poor child! You know nothing of them, and yet you must break through this net, and it cannot be done by sitting still. Let me see you, if it be but for five minutes. You have not walked out these three mornings; perhaps you are not allowed. Your father, I suppose, was warned of our meeting, for, as I rode away, I found I had been followed and watched. *I put a stop to that forever.* It will *not happen again.* I promise not to say a word of *myself* if you will see me, Marguerite. But whether you will or not, you cannot prevent my watching over you: and sooner or later we *must* meet, before the drama is played out.

" R."

The writer's state gave me much more uneasiness, as I read this, than any fears for myself. Painful and annoying as the persecution was to which I was subjected (and of course the "dark threads" could only have reference to this), the days of lock and key and forced marriages were passed. Rawdon's heated imagination invested my position with unnecessary terrors. I wished I had some wise and gentle woman-friend, who would have gone on an errand of mercy from me, and endeavored to soothe the irritated state of his mind. But I had none. I could only sit still and tremble for what I might hear next; and tell my little brother to say there was "no answer," for, of course, I could not see him, and writing was worse than useless.

My father's conduct towards me had undergone a sensible change during these three days. I was no longer completely "lef" to my own 'vices," as Betsy expressed it; and in this she approved (for the first time in her life) of my father's conduct: holding, like most of her class, solitude to be a slow poison, and *any* sort of society a wholesome antidote thereto. My father made me walk with him daily; my only stipulation being that the boys should accompany us; and though he resisted this strongly, saying it was like "taking out a school," he yielded when I reminded him that they had only another week to be at home. I skilfully managed in these walks that the boys should be between me and the Marquis, who invariably joined us; but my father's evident efforts to force the society of that venerable nobleman upon me were not confined to these occasions. The same day that I received Rawdon's note, my father sent for me into

the drawing-room.   I found the Marquis there, come to pay
his "homages," and to place the Minister of State's opera-
box at my disposal that night : it was perfectly "*convenable*,"
he assured me, "to *assister en deuil*."   I thanked him ; I
went out nowhere ; the Grand Opéra I particularly disliked ;
I was occupied just now, would he excuse me ? and I curt-
seyed out of the room.   I flatter myself that I was ladylike
and civil ; but it would be paying my manner a compliment
to call it icy, for ice *will* melt, and nothing would have melted
me.

Five minutes later my father entered my room : he was
pale with anger.

"Upon my life, you treat my friends in the most de haut
en bas manner, Rita.   I can tell you you are very much
mistaken if you think I shall allow it.   Things are not going
on in this way forever."

"I hope not."

"You've had a great deal too much of your own way,
young lady.   Henceforward you will be good enough to understand that you are to receive my friends *civilly*, and just
as many as I choose, or you shall go out again into the
world.   If not, by G—d—"

"Father, father, remember my mother.   I am not fit to
see strangers, or mix in the world in any way just now.   In
the spring, perhaps, when Rose has asked me to go to England on a visit, I may—"

"No ; I tell you that won't do.   It does'nt suit my plans
that you should go to England and marry a country curate
with forty pounds a year, which is just what you would do,
with your romantic ideas.   I shall probably take you to
Baden in the summer, and my friend, d'Ofort, will accompany us.   So, in the mean time, I *desire* that you will curb
that confounded temper of yours, and not be so surly to him.
He is a most liberal old fellow, and quite the *vieille cour*—
one of the oldest families in France—what more do you
want ?"

"Why, even for a mere acquaintance a little more might be desirable; for a husband, a good deal."

"It strikes me you expect a good deal more than you will get, and that you'll be a very hard bargain to whoever you accept at last. The fact is, your head was completely turned last year by that d—d fellow Rawdon, and your puritanical admirer, Mr. Rochford, who filled you with absurd ideas, and then rode off—which showed he was more sensible than I gave him credit for; and I believe, if the truth was known, you're pining after *him*, instead of thinking how you can settle yourself respectably in life."

I looked my father full in the face, though my voice quivered, and I said, "If by settling respectably you mean marrying an old man of the worst character (for whom I feel the most profound disgust and contempt) because he is wealthy and highly born, I do not understand the term as you do. Let it be distinctly understood that the Marquis d'Ofort comes here as your friend, not as having any thing to say to me, and I will try and endure his presence."

"Very filial, really. Now, be so good as to put on your bonnet and come out with me."

My father's mouth was set into that hard and dogged expression I knew it always wore when he was bent on carrying something through, without pity or compunction. When we were in the street, instead of turning, as usual, into the Champs Elysées, he strode out in the opposite direction, into the labyrinths of the Chaussée d'Antin. We stopped at last before the door of a handsome house, and my father pulled the bell.

"Father, where are we going?"

"To pay a visit."

"To whom?"

"To invite our second guest at dinner to-morrow."

"If you please, I will remain in that shop the while."

"But I *don't* please. I insist on your coming up-stairs.

You need'nt be afraid; it is no one who will fall in love with you; but I'd advise you to make yourself as pleasant as you can."

"I never pay visits, and really, father, I beg — to a person I don't know — "

"Don't know? but you *must* know her," almost shouted my father. I was really terrified at the violence of his manner. He grasped my arm, and half dragged me upstairs. Further discussion was useless, and would only have led to greater irritation on his part : there was nothing to be done but to yield with as good grace as I could. A dim suspicion flashed on me as to whom I was brought here to visit. — that mysterious figure in the background, of whom I had more than once had a hint as influencing largely my father's conduct and opinions.

He pulled the bell of the entresol : a servant in livery opened the door. No question was asked, no name mentioned : my father, drawing my arm through his, passed in. We entered a large, low salon, richly decorated in white and gold, at the further end of which sat a lady, who might be described in somewhat similar terms. For she was rather large, and not very tall, and dressed in a white Turkish peignoir, embroidered in gold down the front and sleeves. I instantly recognized her as the person I had seen on my father's arm at Marshal Soult's ball. The countenance was strangely and indelibly impressed on my memory. Depraved Roman empresses had come to me, formerly, over my history, somewhat after this likeness ; the same low brows, and bands of snake-like hair, bold, handsome eyes, hard, aquiline nose, so white and sharply cut, the same overfull sweep of the inferior lip, showing such lines of brilliant teeth when she laughed. It was a magnificent head, certainly, but I should have preferred positive ugliness. There was something in the expression of her eyes that sent a shiver through me, and by the triumph that glittered there,

I know that she saw at a glance what I felt, while her manner became still more sleek and feline. She came forward, holding out both her hands, and drew me to the sofa on which she had been sitting when we entered.

"Madame de Barrènes, I have brought you my daughter, whom you were kind enough to wish to know."

"I have, indeed, long desired it." (She spoke in French.) "That dear colonel promised some time ago to bring you, but you know how faithless he is! I dare say he never said a word to you about it. Dear child! I would not intrude myself on your affliction, knowing — In short, women understand these things better than men, otherwise I would have come and mingled my tears with yours. I hope our friendship may ripen fast; there is something *sympathetic* in our natures, I am sure. I adore books; if it were not for my literary pursuits my life would be very dreary. Would you like to see my article on the ' Expansion of the Soul,' in the *Trois Mondes?* My taste, I confess, is somewhat an abstruse one for a woman, but I occupy myself solely with philosophy and moral development" (my eye caught the words, "par Paul de Kock," on the back of a volume that protruded from a sofa-cushion beside me), "and never read the depraved literature of the day. Have you read Victor Cousin's last work? No? Ah! you have a treat there."

My father looked rather bored while this was going on, as if it was not the sort of thing to which he was accustomed, and that we might be spared it. But madame was not to be baulked of her morality; so I sat at the edge of the sofa, looking very foolish, with my hands in madame's, while she continued:

"Are you fond of the drama, chère petite? Ah! I quite understand,— the plays they give here generally are so unsuited for a young girl. A friend of mine has sent me a box to see the first representation of a comedy of his to-morrow evening at the Théâtre-Français. At the Français, every thing is *irréproachable ;* un peu lourd, peut-être, mais tout ce qu'il y a de plus moral. — Will you do me the pleasure to accompany me?"

"By-the-by," cut in my father, "we came expressly to ask you to dine with us to-morrow, chère Comtesse."

"Enchanted; and the play afterwards. It will be a fête for me, who so seldom go into the world! I lead the life of a recluse, my dear. I hope you will come often to my little hermitage. How like you she is, colonel! Just that proud English air. But you must not remain shut up in this way, dear child; you must conquer your feelings. Ah! I know what that is too well!— but for the sake of *ce cher papa* you must make the exertion. Those cheeks are too pale. I should recommend a little *gris lilac* under the bonnet; all that black is so unbecoming! Ah! by-the-by, cher colonel, have you heard this dreadful report about the Galoffska?— pauvre Galoffska!"

"No. What is it? I had a note from her two or three days ago;" and my father glanced towards me.

"Found poisoned in bed this morning, with the bottle of laudanum in her hand. They say she killed herself partly from jealousy of that roué milord — that she had a terrible scene with him yesterday. Ah! look you, the women who lead these dreadful lives always come to some bad end."

"By G—d! how shocking! I dare say that blackguard Rawdon has been entirely the cause of it."

"Who knows?" responded madame, shrugging her shoulders. "Her debts, *on dit*, are enormous. As milord gambled, and has lost so much, perhaps she supplied him with money, poor thing!"

My indignation here overcame my repugnance to speak.

"I will answer for it that is not true. Lord Rawdon has faults and follies enough, but he is a true gentleman. No one who is such would accept a woman's money for his own vicious pursuits."

Madame de Barrènes gave my father a peculiar look, and a half-inward smile flitted over her features, but they were decently composed the next instant. The latter rose impatiently, and I lost no time in following his example.

"A demain," said the Comtesse, with her most captivating smile. "The marquis of course dines with you. Excellent and benevolent old man! How infinitely preferable is such society as his to that of the wild young men of the day!"

As she spoke, she passed her dimpled white hand over the glossy braids of her hair, and my sharp eye caught sight of a bracelet I recognized as having seen lying in its case upon a certain toilet-table months before.

"My departed husband's hair!" sighed she, intercepting the look I gave it.

Oh! Charlotte Barrènes, you were quick and clever, but did you really think you imposed on me for a single half-minute? I believe my face was a riddle you could not make out, either then or afterwards; a frozen pond, on which you advanced little by little, cautious to tread lightly, uncertain how much it would bear, and quite unconscious what depth of water lay beneath!

This visit was the commencement, the opening chapter, followed by many which I will spare the reader — hours of trial, which I cannot even now recall without its bringing back keenly the kind of sick apprehension I lived under, though all soreness and bitterness have passed away, thank God! with the sharp edge of the actual present.

But if we are permitted hereafter to gratify our curiosity about the accumulated dust of secrets in each other's hearts, I shall look with a painful wonder to see what was passing within yours, Charlotte Barrènes, during those hours! Had you no compunction — no pity? It is hard to believe in the *complete* wickedness of any one. Experience shows that good and evil are scattered through this world in grains, not in cart-loads, as some try to prove. What secret charities this woman may have exercised — what tears she may have dried — what sufferings alleviated, I know not; let us hope there were some. That she carried desolation and misery into many a home — that she was thoroughly hardened and unscrupulous as to what means she adopted to attain her ends, is, alas! too true. And that I suffered, through her, the darkest and stormiest passages in my young life, I cannot *forget*, though I forgive her. She has an account elsewhere beyond my keeping.

I felt a moral conviction about Madame de Barrènes's character which her conversation, far from shaking, only strengthened. That my father should force the intimacy of such a woman on me seemed at first incredible. Viewed simply in a worldly way, the injury he was doing me he knew as well as any one. What was his motive? To render my home so intolerable as to oblige me to exchange it for the Hôtel d'Ofort? It seemed the only possible solution. I foresaw, with terrible distinctness now, whither all this led. I had not lived this past year for nothing. I knew how lightly a woman's name is blown about like a thistle-ball from mouth to mouth in Paris: I must grasp at any thing to save my "respectability." And that my father — my father! — instead of shielding and sustaining his child, should, from some inexplicable cause, thrust me to the very brink of this precipice — it was hard and terrible to bear! I shuddered and turned sick when I looked down the abyss. To be married to an old worn-out debauchee, the touch of whose hand, whose laugh, were insupportable to me, — any thing were better than that. Could I brave the world's gossip? Could I go on living this life, knowing what things must be whispered of me — and loud enough to reach *his* ears? Fool! what did it signify what *he* thought? Ought not my own self-respect be sufficient to sustain me? Was not the knowledge of my own helplessness enough? For the more I thought over it, the more difficult it was to know how to act.

Twice that I attempted to speak to my father he became so excited that I found it hopeless to bring him to reason. His manner was that of a man who has drummed himself to carry through a certain deed. Remonstrance only inflamed him into a sort of temporary insanity. I had no course left me but to yield, and receive the obnoxious visitors my father thrust upon me.

The dinner did not take place next day after all, I believe in consequence of the marquis's sudden indisposition. At all events, I know I was relieved from his society for several days, during which whole hecatombs of flowers were offered up to me, which I dared not refuse, and which were indeed very agreeable substitutes for his presence. But Madame de Barrènes lost no time (as I anticipated) in letting the world see the intimate footing on which we stood. Her beautifully appointed little carriage drew up the following afternoon, as my father and I were walking in the Champs Elysées, and from it she descended (that magnificent hermit!), a glitter of blue velvet and white fur. She joined us, causing a general commotion among the pedestrians by her luminous appearance, and creating in me a strong desire to take to my heels and run home. I can never forget the sense of shame and confusion with which I felt all eyes fixed on us as we walked along; and when, a few minutes afterwards, Lord Rawdon passed us on horseback and raised his hat, I was at no loss to interpret the look he gave me. And every succeeding afternoon, for a fortnight or more, it was the same thing. Madame de Barrènes assiduously drove in the wedge of her acquaintance; she would take no denial when she called, but though assured I was not "visible," said of course the prohibition did not extend to her, and gently thrust past the feeble domestic. My father, at other times, ushered her into my room himself; at other times, again, I was sent for, and found the marquis (resuscitated) with madame in the drawing-room.

Madame, on these occasions, unrepelled by my coldness, talked her very best, which was a pity, for it would have been much better if it had not been quite so good. In her own element, I dare say she could be amusing. But wishing to unite for my benefit the sentimental elegance of a Lamartine with the didactic morality of a Maintenon, the effect was incongruous, like all patchworks, and — to my taste, at least — utterly disagreeable. Her manner of advancing her opinions was subjective, as though her point were to draw *me* out rather than commit herself to any decided view; but I was wise enough to remember that immediately a woman uses her tongue, her judgment no longer remains calm, cool, unbiased. I preferred listening to her, and drawing my own inferences therefrom. And the result showed I was right. At the end of two or three weeks, madame knew as little about me (except that I was a silent, proud, and disagreeable girl) as the first moment we met. And I learned in that time that the dangerous axiom of language being intended to conceal thought demands an astuteness and consistency in lying of which very few are capable. Watch the conversation of the most accomplished of society's actors for a length of time, you shall find some of the essence of their nature oozing out. To lie well requires a good memory: this is lying on the most extended scale, — the whole life and conversation a lie. Madame de Barrènes's accomplishment did not reach the finish of high art; there were constantly little discrepancies between the sentiments of yesterday and to-day. I have said that she rarely advanced a subject boldly: there was one, however; to which she constantly recurred, and on which she never failed to dilate — the excellence, the wisdom, and the wealth of Amédée-Joseph, Marquis d'Ofort.

My little brothers had returned to England. This was but a small addition to my troubles, perhaps, yet their presence had been companionship and something of protection too, however slender, and I felt doubly alone now they were gone.

How I longed that I were a man, to throw off this heavy chain of inaction — to go forth into the world and work my way to honor, if it might be — at least, to independence! And here I was compelled to sit with folded hands, and a restless, fluttering heart, that beat against its cage as though it were like to break. The ground seemed failing beneath my feet. I trusted in my own strength, thinking it a staff, and in the hour of trial it proved a broken reed. For I knew little of the comfort and friendliness of prayer at that time; I asked and gave thanks for physical wants, and I looked forward to the time when I should be united to all those I loved in a happier sphere; but I took no "counsel with God," I did not rely on him alone for guidance and support.

I had heard several times from Miss Lateward — kind letters, containing very little on the only subject that could interest me from that quarter. Mr. Rochford was building a school-house, or Mr. Rochford was gone to stay with his relatives the Nevilles; and once only it was recorded that, on seeing my mother's death in the paper, he had asked Miss Lateward whether she had heard from me. "I was not aware you had ever met him," she wrote. "I suppose the acquaintance was very slight, as you have never named it."

I now sat down to write to that good woman, feeling it a relief to unburden myself, even though it was impossible to enter into more than a sketch of my position. I could not tell her all on paper, as I might have done, alone, into her ear. The letter we write is like a listener to the confidences we would make our friend — we cannot be sure that no other eyes shall see it.

And so three weeks more were gone: each week bringing me into closer contact with the two persons whom I most dreaded in the whole world. At times, my mind was in a state of excitement that bordered on insanity (and then there was no desperate deed of which I felt I could not be guilty), alternating with depression as complete and violent when the flood-gates of my soul gave way. Three weeks, beating and struggling on against the rapidly increasing stream from day to day!

CHAPTER XXII

BETSY set her resolute little back against the door.

"No, mum: very sorry, mum, but it's impossible to-day. Miss Marg'ret's particular unwell, and can't see no one, on no account."

"Betsy," I cried, from the inner room, "beg Madame de Barrènes to walk in. I feel better."

My illness was indeed far more mental than physical. Still, I was very weak, and suffering from a violent headache. But I had suddenly resolved to alter my conduct in some measure as regarded Madame de Barrènes. Let her be admitted: and she entered, glowing with sympathy and the frosty wind.

"I began to think I was never to see you again, petite. Yesterday you shut the door against me—that obstinate little woman had locked it, for I tried—and to-day—"

"Your friendship burst the lock. Thank you, Comtesse. . And now, what object can you have in visiting a dull, melancholy girl every day? Of course, it is very kind of you; but I suppose you have some object. I have too high an opinion of your cleverness to suppose you would bore yourself—and me—without *some* motive."

Madame, for once in her life, was thrown aback. She looked perfectly aghast, never having heard so many words issue from my lips before in the whole course of our acquaintance. She quickly recovered her presence of mind, and said, slowly,

"You are right. I have another motive, which is, my pity for your position, and my wish to improve it, though I see you will not believe in the interest I take in you. The colonel, between you and me, chère enfant, will leave his children only some thousand pounds' worth of *debts*, if he dies to-morrow. What think you? Were it not better to accept the certainty of a high and honorable name, a great fortune, and a worthy husband, instead of — Ah! I shudder to think of it! Le cher colonel is afflicted, too, when he thinks of it. And, remember, no ardent young lover is ever half as much aux petits soins as an old husband. Mine was seventy when I married."

"Was the result satisfactory, madame?"

"Perfectly. Depend on it, for comfort, there is nothing like a husband of a certain age" (d'un age mûr).

"To produce so admirable a wife, I doubt it not. Still, I don't think I shall marry."

"Really? — then you must be in love — ça n'empêche pas," said she, putting her feet on the fender, and drawing up the skirt of her dress. I looked her steadily in the face. She quickly recalled that piece, and made another move. "Of course a charming girl, like you, has *numbers* of lovers."

"But I cannot marry a number, madame; and if I like no one in particular?"

"Perhaps that wild English milord? They say he quarrelled with la pauvre Galoffska solely on your account, and swore he would never even see her again, because she wrote that note to your father. I hear he would commit any folly for your sake?"

"It would be a worse one than he ever committed if I were to marry him."

"I rejoice to hear you say so, ma chère. Then, if there is really no one who has engaged your young affection, what objection can you have to such an unexceptionable parti as the marquis? It is really extraordinary how he worships you! He has experienced many tender passions, of course, in his long life, but never one so strong as this — unquenchable even by your coldness. He knows he cannot expect love from you in return — toleration is all he hopes for. You would find he is a true philosopher, chère petite.”

“ Epicurean, I should think.”

“ Not at all; he eats very little ” — as if she were talking of a dog.

“ Even Paris society, which is not over particular, considers him a ‘ bad subject.’”

“ Look you, my dear, il faut être raisonnable. You cannot have perfection. Christian charity forbids.”

“ Pardon me, we will not discuss charity. Though painters represent that virtue with such abundant breasts, it is a cold sentiment to marry upon. Were you ever in love, madame ? ”

“ What a question! Of course, my dear, I adored my husband.”

“ Then you can understand my not wishing to marry until I am equally fortunate.”

We sat on either side of the fire, I and this woman, trying to read each other’s faces in the fitful light of the woodflames, for it was now quite dusk. But the tightly-gloved fingers of madame’s plump little hand, held out fan-wise to guard her from the fire, cast strange barred shadows all across her face, making the expressions there difficult to seize.

“ Ma chère,” said she, sinking her voice to an oily whisper “ have you considered your father ? ”

“ What of him, madame ? ”

“ Well, you must think of him, in this affair, as an affectionate daughter. The advantage to him will be so great.”

“ How so ? To get rid of me, do you mean ? ”

" Quelle idée !"

" Perhaps he intends taking up his abode at the Hôtel
d'Ofort ? "

" No; but the marquis's wealth, as you know, is very
great."

" And you think he will feel inclined, after he is married,
to feed my father's extravagance ? "

" Perhaps not; but it might be possible " — a pause —
" to come to some little arrangement. The marquis, I *know*,
would be willing and happy to — "

" In other words, I am to be sold to pay my father's
debts."

" Ma chère, you see these questions in a very coarse point
of view."

" I endeavor to see the *truth*, madame; and truth, like
nature, *is* rather coarse sometimes."

" We must not be selfish, chère petite, in this world.
You will be doing a good action — supporting your father,
like the Roman daughter. And, after all, if you have not a
handsome young husband, il faut bien se passer de quelque
chose dans ce monde, n'est-ce-pas ? You will console yourself in your philosophy, as I have done."

" I am afraid of such philosophy, madame, and the con-
solations that spring from it."

" Besides which," she continued, dropping her voice,
" you see, he is very old, my dear. It will not last forever,
and then you will be free."

If she could have seen my face, she must have read the
loathing and horror I felt for her at that moment; but it
was too dark. I leaned back, and pressed my hands before
my eyes.

" No, no," I murmured after her, with a very different
meaning, " it will *not* last forever ! "

She rose to go. " I hope you will be wise, petite, and
think over this." She approached and held out her hand.

At that moment I experienced one of those strange and awful sensations which remain indelibly impressed on the mind of any one who has been similarly situated. I cannot tell whether it was only the effect of an overwrought imagination, — I cannot argue about, or account for it, — but, as I looked up in the dim twilight of the chamber, I distinctly saw the figure of my mother glide between Madame de Barrènes and myself, and thrust back the hand of the former. brushing me with her long black garments as she passed between us.

I gave a sharp cry, and started up.

"Mon Dieu! qu'est-ce que c'est?"

"Stand back! — stand back! There! — do you see nothing? — How can you venture to stand there? — How dare you remain in her sacred presence? Mother — mother — mother!"

And the next thing I remember, was hearing Madame de Barrènes call loudly for Betsy, saying she thought I had a fit. The good creature ran in, and madame remarked that I was in a highly nervous state, and fancied I had seen something — she was afraid I was ill; I must be watched with care; sickness was very prevalent in Paris just now. And with similar exordiums she left me to the good offices of my faithful nurse.

*   *   *   *   *   *

After a sleepless night, during which I was haunted by the image of my mother, I rose; and my father soon after entered the room. He expressed his concern to hear I was so unwell, " because I wanted to try and persuade you to go to a ball at the Hôtel de Ville to-morrow night."

" Father," said I, seizing his hand, " I will do any thing, if you will promise me that I shall no longer be persecuted by that hateful old man. Say that you will go *alone* with me, and I will go to this ball; though God knows how little my heart is in tune for it!"

"There's a good girl. Yes, we'll go alone, Rita — alone!"

"And you promise that, if I go into the world with you, I shall be no longer intruded on as I have been in my own home? And you will not urge me to marry a man I hate?"

My father turned away his head.

" Promise me."

" Idiot! You will drive me to take the last step by your obstinacy — one I had hoped to be saved from. Consider what you are doing — before it is too late."

"You speak in riddles, father. But one thing only is clear and certain to me — that I shall go mad if this sort of life continues much longer. In one way or another it must end. Either I must leave you, and endeavor to get a livelihood somehow in honest industry, or —"

"On your own head be the consequences of this," interrupted my father, with an unsteady voice, as he turned towards the door. "You will go with me to the ball tomorrow, and *I* shall never urge the Marquis's suit upon you again, nor shall Madame de Barrènes be again *an intruder in this house.*"

As Betsy was brushing my hair, she suddenly suspended her operations in looking out of the window.

"It do be a curious thing how often I see that man a-prowling round the house here, miss. Look opposite, under the port-coach-ear. I wonder — um — whether he can have anything to do with a gentleman as has stopped me two or three times near the door, quite promiscuous, as I was a-running to get half a pound of tea at the corner — and shocking bad it is, which is n't here nor there, only six francs a pound for sich sloe-leaves! and I in a hurry — and he stops and says, ' How is your young mistress?' ' Nicely, sir,' says I. ' Tell her I am always watching over her,' says he — or words to that defect — and slips some money into my hand. ‘I’m obliged to you, sir,’ says I — but he was gone! And now I think of it, there’s something else I’ve had it on my mind to tell you since yesterday.”

“What is it, Betsy? — go on.”

“Why, you see, it be rather a hawk’ard thing — and a painful:” with a great tug at my hair, and waiting still further encouragement.

“Come, dear old Betsy, don’t keep me.”

“Nasty creature! I could ha’ torn her eyes out!”

I began to tremble violently. “Go on — go on!”

“Well, if you will have it” (suddenly dropping the hair about my shoulders), “I should like to know what business that Madam Barrou has a-poking of her nose in here and there, and opening the door of that blessed saint’s room, your dear mamma as was, and a-rummaging among her dear blessed things in the wardrobe?”

“What!” I almost screamed.

“Yes, when you was ill a-lying down, after she’d been here, I was passing the door of that room, and I hear something like the opening of a drawer, and I looks in, and sure enough there was madam a-turning and a-tossing over of everythink. That tasty satin, with the Mahometan lace, as your mamma wore at Miss Rose’s wedding, on the ground! So I asks, respectful-like, what she was a-doing of. ‘Oh!’ says she, ‘je ne vole pas,’ and draws out a Napoleon, and puts her finger to her lips, the which I refuses indignant; and jus’ then the colonel looks in at the door, and I were that angry I near told him a piece of my mind, — only for you, Miss Marg’ret, and he your father, and it would break my heart to be sent away from you. Deary! don’t cry. I were a great stoopid to tell you; only, says I to myself, the less she sees of sich folk the better, and the sooner she show that she won’t stand sich condict, the better!”

“This passes all bounds! This is outrageous!” I cried. “How can my father — Thank Heaven! he has promised me that this woman shall not intrude here again. What unparalleled insolence! Oh, that warning, my mother!" I sobbed, and the desecration of her memory affected me more powerfully than all my sorrows hitherto.

"Betsy," I said, some hours later, "I feel a longing to visit my mother's grave; I must go. Don't be afraid; I will be very calm, and it will do me good, it will, indeed. Get my bonnet, dear Betsy."

It was near four o'clock, a mild February evening. Wrapped in thick veils and cloaks, we left the house, and, stepping into a fiacre at the corner of the street, drove to the city of tombs, stopping only once on the way to buy some *immortelles*. We made our way through a labyrinth of marble monuments, gilt crosses, and graven images, to the spot where my mother's remains lay buried.

At first I thought I must have mistaken it, for the humble grave was crowned with a wreath of fresh violets; but there stood the words, still black and sharp from the stone-cutter's chisel:

"Sacred to the Memory of Marguerite, the beloved wife —"

Alas! what mockery it seemed! Her earthly home knew her name no longer. The stone wore not away so quickly as her memory had done in the heart that here proclaimed its grief in set phrase. Whose, then, was the hand that had scattered loving thoughts in flowers? God be with them, whoever they might be! I knelt down and kissed the cold damp stone, and Betsy moved away to a little distance. There I lay, my head buried in my hands, while my soul communed with that purified spirit who, I knew, beheld, with the angels, every secret of my heart.

"Mother," I cried low, "you know all now; speak to me and show me how to act : guide me through this dark valley, mother, for my footsteps slip, and I am very weary."

"Lean on a loving heart," said a deep voice in my ear.

It was now dusk, and as I looked up, a figure, or rather a shadow, stood beside me. But I had no fear, for I recognized the voice at once. I brushed back the tears, and held out my hand.

"This is your doing;" I pointed to the freshly-strewn flowers. "By what gift of prescience did you know I was to be here to-day?"

"I did not know it. I watched you leave your house, as I have done every day; and I followed. As to the flowers, I have often come up here of late. I have felt as if it were my own mother's grave. Had she lived, she would have pleaded my cause with you, Marguerite; for she felt kindly towards me, and thought less hardly of me than the rest of the world."

"May God reward you, Lord Rawdon, for the respect you have shown my poor mother's memory."

"Marguerite, we meet in a fitting place — beside the grave to which we are both hastening — for, mark me, you will not long survive this struggle. If you do not speedily break your chain, you must sink under it."

"Better so," said I, in a low voice. "But you are wrong. I shall not die, though my nerves have been so much shaken that I feel sometimes as if my mind were giving way. We do not die so easily; joyless, withered lives, are commoner than broken hearts. And you, my friend, have, I hope and pray, brighter things in store for you than an existence wasted in —"

"This is mockery, Marguerite!" he exclaimed, violently. "You must feel that my whole life is bound up in you. If you die — if you sacrifice yourself to that man — if you destroy your happiness for life by one fatal step, I have nothing left to live for. You think I am a passionate nature? So I am. And yet, so little is my passion a selfish one, that I swear before God, if I could secure your happiness by it, I would blow out my brains on the spot.

Life, indeed, has *only* one attraction for me; and it is only lately I've found it. Do you think I can easily give it up? Since I saw you I have spent days and nights — I have employed secret agents of all kinds — in discovering the workings of that vile conspiracy that surrounds you. Shall I tell you what it is?"

"I know it, Lord Rawdon — at least, I know *enough*. I had rather not hear any thing upon this painful subject. I hope my father at length sees the futility of forcing this marriage on me, as well as the society of persons I abhor."

"Never! do not believe it; he *can't*, if he would. He is inextricably tied to them. You will awake to this fact soon. Oh! Marguerite, you would pity me if you knew all I have suffered these past weeks for your sake! — scenes I would not shock your pure ears by repeating. Alas! I bear the part-burden of another heavy sin upon my head since I last saw you — a wretched woman's death by her own hand. God knows if it were my words that drove her to the deed! She had played a foul part — and yet it was for love of me, Marguerite! — some of that love I crave so vainly at your hands!"

"This is very terrible; but you speak as men always do, of *self*. *I*, too, have suffered; shame and agony, bitter revulsion of all feeling for my own father, — these are not light crosses, and she who lies under this stone knows they have been mine — do not add to them. It has been a heavy aggravation to think I was the indirect cause of that poor woman's death. Leave me to go *alone* on the path God shall see fit to clear for me henceforward; indeed it is best."

"By the memory of that mother who sees us now, Marguerite, I conjure you to hear me. She knows what perils you are in. I fancy I hear her voice now, pleading for me, and bidding you not to reject a heart that loves as mine does."

I shuddered as I looked round on the crosses and white monumental figures that gloomed like spectres in the dusky light; the evening wind sighed and trembled, like thin voices, through the trees. Then they died away, and in the silence that followed I heard my own heart speak plain.

"There is one for whom you know, in spite of all, you would still give up every other hope on earth; and this is not he. Though the cloud of darkness be on you, *this* is not the light of dawn. Never think that a voice from the tomb can plead for false vows."

And I said slowly, "Lord Rawdon, I know your strong and loyal heart. I do believe your attachment is no light thing, to be swept away to make room for another. And because I believe it, I will take a step that costs any woman dear — that few, indeed, can bring themselves to take. I will show you the great obstacle to my ever loving you as you deserve. It is that *I* also have loved, even as you love me — without return! Is this humiliating? I think your devotion deserved it at my hands, and I have outlived all false pride. I do not blush for the truth: my love was no crime any more than yours. And now, you know better than any other words of mine could tell you —"

"No!" he cried, passionately, "it cannot, *shall* not be. You have loved — so be it. We build up an enduring love from the ashes of our dead ones. I, too, once thought — Oh! how different was that from my devotion to you, Marguerite. In time you will love me, I hope and believe — but I can wait; *you* cannot wait to be saved! Of two courses your father must speedily take one. If he pursue one of these courses, a lawyer will come to you with bills, promissory notes, etc., of your father's, to the amount of many thousand pounds. The lawyer will ask whether you consent to become Marquise d'Ofort, or prefer seeing your father sent to prison, all his furniture and every thing he has in the world seized. It will be represented to you that

you will be left utterly destitute, and your father ruined for
life! Now, if this comes to pass as I anticipate, will you
make me one promise?"

"What is it?"

"That you will ask for two hours' reflection. Then open
your window — there is some one placed always in sight of
it — and wave your handkerchief. Before the two hours
have elapsed, I swear to you this money shall be paid, even
if it be to my last farthing. You will then be free, Marguerite — free as air!"

"Ah! no — bound fast by ties of gratitude! Your noble
heart is worthy of something warmer than this, Rawdon.
But I believe your fears for me exaggerate the evil. I
have promised my father I will go into society again with
him, if he will free me from this persecution at home.
To-morrow night I am to accompany him to the Hôtel de
Ville."

"Monsieur," said the gardien, approaching, "it is the
hour for closing the cemetery. The gates are being
locked."

*　　*　　*　　*　　*　　*

"Miss Marg'ret," said Betsy, as Rawdon handed us into
the fiacre and shut the door, "that's the same gentleman
as —" The rattle of the wheels over the stones drowned
the rest.

CHAPTER XXIII.

I slept that night more peacefully than I had done for weeks. Whether from complete exhaustion, or the effect of fresh air after several days' confinement, it was late in the following day when I awoke. The return to consciousness of suffering from oblivion is like nothing else in the world. The aching sense of something weighing at my heart — I scarce knew what — when I opened my eyes on the faded curtains and well-known furniture of my little room, I remember now, as I do every circumstance of that day, with a curious particularity. There are moments — moments of mental suffering, as well as of acute bodily pain, when we are more than ever alive to the minutest objects that surround us. All our senses are sharpened, as it were, and when we look back to the hour of trial, we find the picture that was before us then return with singular vividness.

I rose: the day was wild and threatening. The sky hung gloomfully over the opposite roofs. Gusts of wind drove a few dried leaves and sticks against the window-pane, and now and then sent a tile rattling into the street below. I looked out. A pedestrian or two scudded along, holding their cloaks across their mouths, and bending their heads before the bitter wind. One figure alone remained under the shelter of the opposite porch, sending forth clouds of smoke from a pipe, and beating on the stones with his frozen feet.

Presently a carriage drove up to our door. I recognized the white horses at once. A servant jumped from the box,

and in less than a minute my father appeared, wrapped
in a fur coat, stepped into the carriage, and it drove away.
The man opposite immediately left his post, whistled twice,
and then walked leisurely down the street. I lost sight
of him; but a few minutes after, when I looked out, he had
returned to his position.

As the afternoon wore on, the sky grew wilder, and the
wind more fierce and loud. I am not given to presentiments,
but the weather seemed strangely in harmony with my fore-
boding heart, which listened and waited for something, I
knew not what — but I felt that a crisis in my life was at
hand.

By-and-by Betsy came in and laid my black crape dress
for the evening on the bed.

" I 've something for you, Miss Marg'ret. What 'll ye give
me for it?" said she, with a clumsy playfulness intended to
divert my thoughts. There was that in my face which told
her I could not bear any long suspense. I held out my hand;
a letter dropped into it. My agitation was such, though I
saw at a glance it was only from Miss Lateward — a cover-
full of good advice, no doubt — that it was some minutes before I could break the seal, and read as follows:

"MY DEAR YOUNG FRIEND, — I was more pained than
surprised at the contents of your letter, being *in a measure*
prepared for your statements by letters which Lady Janet
Oglevie (who is an inmate here at present) received from
Paris a day or two ago. These letters contained (as I *firmly*
believe) most cruel and malevolent reports concerning your
' way of going on ' — to quote the vulgar phraseology used —
to which I strenuously refused to give credence. Yet we
all know the homely proverb, ' That to emit smoke there
must be *some* flame,' and I was forced to confess that these
reports could not be *wholly* groundless. Mrs. Oglevie
Fisher — I do not scruple to name the writer — had her-

self seen you in constant and close intimacy with the Marquis d'Ofort, whose society is shunned, she says, by *all* respectable females (though Lady Janet opposes to this that her daughter-in-law invariably *invites* the said Marquis to her *parties*), and his creature, Madame de Barrènes ; and she further adds that you are to be married to him in a few days. Then follows the worst portion of the tale, which I am only induced to repeat to you that you may take some *energetic* measure to show its *falsity,* and prove how unwillingly you have been forced into this *disreputable* society. ' Miss Percival,' says the writer, ' has shown so little regard for her reputation, that many people believe the marquis does not intend *really to marry* her. The effrontery with which she parades her intimacy with that notorious woman, no less than her conduct with respect to Lord Rawdon, has been offensive to all right-minded persons. Poor Madame Galoffska, at a party only a day or two before she died, said openly that she knew for a *fact* that Miss Percival had been the cause of that duel last year in which Lord Rawdon was wounded, and that she herself had seen her walking alone with him that morning in a retired part of the Bois de Boulogne ! No wonder, then, that a young woman so lost to all sense of decency should be spoken of as she is.' You can imagine how *indignant* I felt on perusing the above, which Lady Janet gave me into my own hands, saying, at the same time, with great warmth, she did not believe a word of it. She further added, that her daughter-in-law had always been *jealous* of you, and she pointed to a passage further down, where Mrs. Fisher *congratulates* herself that *her* daughters were never very intimate with you, though their grandmamma *had been* so blinded to your real character. This is very mean, petty, and contemptible, but it does not render these rumors the less *aggravating ;* and you must do every thing in your power, my dearest Marguerite, to set them at rest. Is there no lady of unblemished char-

acter, and of position, in the circle in which you move, to
whom you could apply for countenance and aid? Have you
spoken to Colonel Percival, firmly but temperately? The
moral obligation of opposing a parent is the most cruel duty
a child can be called on to perform; but, in this case, I see
no choice. The narrative of your domestic annoyances is
such, that, while affording an agreeable testimony to the
integrity of your *heart* and the purity of your *motives*, it
leaves me no room to doubt that you should have resisted
his wishes more decidedly in this matter. The trial is not
of your *own* creating — let this be your consolation, my dear
young friend — and it might be more severe, were your
affections in any way engaged. But, fortunately, your
young heart is as yet free from the tender passion, having
too frequently the unworthy for its object. The consort
proposed by your father is no less *personally* distasteful to
you than he is publicly objectionable. Here, then, is no con-
flict of sentiments. The judgment sanctions the decision of
the heart. In this matter, you alone can assist yourself;
but let me counsel your writing at once to your sister, Mrs.
Murray. Though giddy, I hold her to be a young person of
good disposition; and, if her husband is as amiable as he has
been represented, they will concur in wishing you to take up
your residence, for the future, with them. I shall anxiously
await tidings of you, my dear child. Before I close my
letter (though such indifferent matter cannot interest *you*), I
must inform you that an event is likely, before long, to inter-
rupt 'the even tenor of our way' here. Mr. Rochford is
engaged to his cousin, Miss Neville. This alliance which
has been long ardently desired by Mrs. Rochford, and has
been the talk of the county for the last two years, is now for-
mally announced. On Wednesday — the very morning, by
a curious coincidence, that Lady Janet received that scandalous letter, and showed it to Mrs. Rochford and me at the
breakfast-table — Mr. Rochford had a long interview with

his mother, and then rode over to Neville Lodge, which is some twenty miles distant. In the evening, Mrs. Rochford, who had been in *unusually* high spirits all day, announced to us that her son had proposed to his cousin, and been accepted. Miss Neville, I am given to understand, is a very superior person, and has, moreover, a considerable fortune, having only one brother. You may imagine that my thoughts have been much too painfully occupied to sympathize as *heartily* as I should otherwise do in the joy of this admirable mother, for whom I entertain the most *sincere regard.* Lady Janet I do not fancy *quite* approves of the marriage — perhaps on account of the near relationship. She is, moreover, peculiar and idiosyncratic in many of her views ; but she always evinces the same interest in *you,* and a lively concern in your truly distressing position. I will not add more to-day, than the assurance that I am ever

" Your faithful and sincere friend,

"TABITHA LATEWARD."

I had kept on saying all along that I was prepared for this. How did I meet it when it came? The blow fell heavily. My heart had clung pertinaciously to one fond hope — none the less so, that the roots had struck down deep and out of sight, coiling themselves round the secret fibres of my being. And now that it was torn violently up — O reader, dare I confess — no, let me shut my chamber-door — the secret of my agony shall remain sacred — not even faithful Betsy must see me now. She shakes the door, and there is no sound but as the fluttering of some poor bird within — low, smothered sobs. Enter two hours hence, reader, and you shall find a young girl with flushed face, unnaturally glittering eyes that terrify her, as she sits before her mirror — looking "uncommon well," so Betsy thinks, as she plaits the hair around her young mistress's head.

It was a night such as I hardly ever remember. The wind

was at our back as we drove along the streets, and saw the hackney-coachmen vainly urging their horses against the storm, which drove the foot-passengers like sand before it, and which hardly any could face. We were quite silent, till suddenly my father made the obvious remark, repeated, no doubt, many thousand times that evening by comfortable gentlemen on *terra firma:*

"What an awful night this must be at sea!"

At sea! Yes, but I would far rather have beheld the blue mountains of the watery world rising up around me, and have felt myself in the valley of the shadow of death, than have been sitting there, safe and dangerless to all outward appearance.

The contrast, when we passed into the Hôtel de Ville, radiant with light and flowers, from the howling tempest without, was striking; but I walked through it all as in a feverish dream. The ball-room, as I entered, for a moment or two, reeled round with me, and I caught my father's arm tightly. The crash of trombones, the shrill laughter of the gibbering mass, rang through my brain: chandeliers, dancers, and orchestra, the whole heaved like one great bosom decked with jewels. Then my senses righted themselves. I was conscious of a figure near the door: it approached and extended its hand.

I had almost forgotten the existence of Madame de Barrènes for some hours — that was saying much, for she had been very constantly in my thoughts of late, until driven out by one yet more powerful image — and here she stood. Our eyes met: on my part there was no other recognition, and the extended hand dropped clenched at her side.

By an evidently preconcerted arrangement, the Marquis d'Ofort, groaning under stars and ribbons, now came up and offered me his arm; my father taking Madame de Barrènes's at the same moment. I turned my head, and saw Rawdon near me in the crowd. The temptation was too great, though

I had predetermined to avoid any conversation with him that night. I made him a slight movement—he was at my side, and my arm within his. We were following my father through the crowd before the marquis had recovered from his astonishment. When my father turned his head, and saw with whom I was, his face became livid.

"I am going to dance with Lord Rawdon." And we moved on.

"How brilliant she looks!"—"Really one would never think—"—"What a horrid position!"—"Poor thing, so young, and looks so innocent! though people say—"—"Tiens! c'est la fille dont je te parlais tout-à-l'heure."—"C'est affreux!—ça fait pitié!"—"Que voulez-vous? elle a pris son parti!"—"There she is—really too shocking, and her poor mother only dead a month!"—"Oh! it is seven; but still *that* is bad enough!"—"Me dear Mrs. Borrage, what can you expect, as I say, from such bringing-up? I always thought her very bold, and discouraged any eentimaey with me girls." I turned round, and stabbed the speaker—Mrs. Oglevie Fisher—with a look. My ears caught these and many other fragments as we passed through the crowded rooms. Rawdon said nothing; but his brow was thunderous, and he bit his lip till the blood started.

"Come," said I, with a ghastly sort of laugh, "let us dance. Don't lead me off to the conservatory as you did the first time I met you. I can't sit still and talk. Do you hear them say how well I look? Of course—in such capital spirits—ha! ha! Why, if I sit still and think—I say, if I begin to *think*—"

"The time for thinking is past. You must *act*. A word with you here; we shall have time enough for dancing by-and-by." And he led me through a suite of small *salons*, occupied only by a few whist-players and a politician or two, to a small room at the end which was quite empty. He drew me into the deep embrasure of a window, which looked into the great square, having a side-glance at the river, where the lamps were, reflected like floating fires in its perturbed waters. The scene in the square was strange. The moon shone out every now and then, between great gusts of black cloud that drifted over it; the wind blew out the linkmen's torches, drove carriages against each other, and almost swept the heavy-cloaked dragoons from their saddles; it shrieked and rattled along the windows, and seemed to plough up the very ground; and through it all rose the shouts of coachmen and gendarmes. Rawdon pointed towards the bridge.

"Do you see a solitary dark figure standing under that lamp?"

"Close to the river? Yes. Some poor wretch, perhaps, weary of his life, and thinking what repose he would find from all his troubles there."

"On the contrary, a man full of spirit and vigor — a man devoted to my service, Marguerite — who is watching this window now, as he has watched yours for many and many an hour."

I was silent, and he continued:

"Do you know why he is there? On the other side of that bridge a post-carriage is waiting. At a signal from me — at this window — he will bring it over here. At the barrier four other horses will be in waiting all night. Now or never is the moment to free yourself — to decide your fate. Listen: do not shake your head, Marguerite, but listen to me."

"How can you urge it, after what I told you yesterday? Leave me — pray leave me — never mind what becomes of me. Do not —"

"My God! Marguerite, do you know what the terrible life in store for you is? Has not this last blow been sufficient? Will you consent to remain under your father's roof after it?"

"What do you mean? I am wretched enough, God

knows! but my position is no worse than it has been for many weeks."

"Is it possible, Marguerite, that you do not know — Hush! some one is coming in here." And he drew me further back into the recess, over which the heavy velvet curtain fell.

Two persons entered: they spoke low, but with great vehemence. The moment I heard their voices, I shrank yet closer to the window; my heart beat so fast and loud, it seemed to me they must hear it. But the speakers were too much engrossed in their conversation, and though the lady seated herself opposite a mirror, and began adjusting the lace on her dress, she still spoke and gesticulated violently. How different from the well-oiled tongue I had been accustomed to hear.

The first observation I caught was from her companion.

"I tell you, Charlotte, you don't understand the girl. Instead of coming round, she is more determined than ever. We must leave it to chance. Now you've got all *you* wanted, and our score is clear, Charlotte, I won't have you bully the girl; we must leave this marriage to time — and, perhaps, her affection for you."

"Mon Dieu, Percival, do you think I am a woman to be cheated by an impertinent child like that? I have sacrificed 80,000 francs for you; shall I leave it to *chance* when I have the opportunity of getting it back, and more besides? Do you take me for a fool? She shall marry him, if my name is Charlotte Barrènes."

"With all my heart, if you can manage it peaceably; but I believe myself, knowing how devilish obstinate she is, that she'll sooner go into a convent, or go out as a governess — in short, disgrace herself in any way — rather than marry *le vieux*. And, as I told you before, I won't —"

"Bah! mon cher, you don't suppose I am going to beat this dear daughter of yours? She refused my hand just now, so I suppose it will be open war between us — and no one ever insulted me without suffering for it ; but mine are *pattes de chat*, you know — I never show the claws but to *you*."

" And I suffer in proportion for your hypocrisy to the rest of the world. Understand me, Charlotte. I've done the poor child harm enough already — harm enough this very day, without —"

" Que veux-tu dire?" cried madame, starting up, and her eyes flashing. " Ha! is this your gratitude, Percival? Do you forget how often I have saved you from Clichy? Have I not singled *you* out from all others to heap my benefits upon? Have I not given up, for the last three years, the whole of my annuity from the marquis to you? which you have gambled away every farthing of? And you talk to me of *harm?* I should like to know, too, who is to support you now, if I do not? Who has obtained for you the large loan from *le vieux*, upon which you are living? Truly, sir, you forget how much you are in my debt!"

" And you've exacted devilish heavy payment, Charlotte ; but don't make a scene. We shall be having people in to see what is the matter, if you talk so loud. Of course, I am indebted to you, and very fond of you, and all the rest of it —"

" Ah! mon cher, nous avons passé par là. Let us talk about business, and not waste our time. The only thing I am afraid of, to tell you the truth, is *that Milord Reardon.* He looks as if he were a desperate man in love — or in war!"

" She does not care for him. I am afraid of her running away to become governess or companion — and the deuce of it is, I suppose the world would give it against me."

" There are ways of obviating these little difficulties." said madame, with a sardonic smile I could see perfectly reflected in the glass. " C'est grand dommage, mais il court déjà des bruits — they do not take young girls of doubtful repute into families, as governesses or companions. I shall be very sorry, but if she thwarts her own interests and your desires in this way, we must take steps to prevent it."

"By G—d! Charlotte, this is really too bad. I believe you have already industriously circulated stories about the child, and " — (he swore a terrible oath, not to be rendered in English) — "if I find you using any foul means of that sort —"

"Bah! You have a poor idea of my intellect, Percival! Such stories would come ill from me; du reste, no one would believe them! There are other ways you men don't understand. I should be the last person to have recourse to such extreme measures. Leave it all to me, mon ami." She smoothed her Brussels lace flounces as she spoke, and pulled out the folds of her dress behind, with as much care and attention as though she were not withering up my fair fame, and blasting my whole future in her heart of hearts.

A cold creeping horror seized me. I felt as if I must cry out: as if I could no longer assist at the revelation of this woman's appalling wickedness, without denouncing it, and calling down God's wrath to overtake her. I believe I almost expected to see her struck dead upon the spot. While I gasped and struggled to suppress the cry that rose choking in my throat, the speakers passed, and were sauntering on into the next room.

"Do you hear? Is that enough for you?" said the deep voice beside me. "This is but the beginning. Will you go back and form one of this respectable household?"

"Oh, horrible! What is to become of me? My own father — my wretched father! It was enough without this. What has he done? What is this bond he has entered into? I am in a thick darkness. I see nothing plainly."

"I thought you must know it already, Marguerite. Your father was *married to that woman this morning.*"

Rawdon caught me in his arms, or I should have fallen.

"Merciful God!" I murmured, "is this some frightful dream? Oh, my poor mother! to think of that woman — to call her — Oh! no, no! this is too bitter. It cannot be! It is n't true — say it is n't true. I feel — oh! Rawdon, Rawdon, take me away from her — hide me — kill me — do any thing, only save me from that terrible woman!"

Thus I raved on. I thought then, and I think still, that I was very nearly insane. I had no control over my thoughts or words. All my brain was on fire, and Rawdon himself was alarmed at the state of excitement I was in.

"Come, dearest, let us fly from here. Calm yourself, dear Marguerite. Before you are missed, we shall be far away;" and he drew from his pocket a small taper, which he lit. The wick, as soon as it ignited, shot up a bright blue flame. He held it at the window-pane. A sudden rush of recollection came over me.

"No, no! not that — it cannot be. I did n't know what I was doing — I was mad. If I said any thing — forget it. It cannot be, Rawdon — leave me, if —"

"Never! I will not leave you now to your weaker self, Marguerite. I will take you from this hell, in spite of yourself. You shall bear my name, and as soon as you are my wife, and beyond the reach of these vile, defaming tongues, I will kill myself and rid you of my troublesome presence. You know as well as I that these are not mere words. I will do what I say if your happiness requires it. But it now requires that you should leave — I will not call it your *home* — your father's house for ever. It is no longer a safe place for you."

"Don't say any thing more — you see the state I am in — on the verge of madness. God help me! I no longer seem to see right from wrong. Only I know that I have nothing to give in return for this devotion. I cannot — ought not — don't press me."

"Enough. I am content that you *should* let me devote my life for you. Come, madame will be sending soon to look for you in all directions. Remember, she has now *authority* to do so. Just think, if your life has been miserable hitherto, what it will be henceforward under the same roof with that woman. Her influence with your father will be greater than ever. She has got from *him* all he had to give — his name! wherewith she intends to get a footing in society, and being rich with the spoil of her former lovers — the marquis alone allows her a large annuity — your father's interest will make him obedient to her wishes. You understand this notable plot now. Your father has married this woman, not that he any longer cares for her, but because he was enormously in her debt. Had you accepted the marquis, your father hoped to have got off his own marriage, as the old man had promised to pay madame and every thing else. Now she and that old devil together have you in their power. You will be closely watched. Your little maid, because she is too true and faithful, is to be sent away. This, Marguerite, is your last chance of escape."

I was seized with a violent trembling.

"Why am I lingering here? She may be coming. There she is! I feel her hand on me. Off! off! Keep her off, Rawdon."

"Come!" — and he gently drew my arm within his — "this way; I know another exit without going round."

Half-dragging, half-carrying me, he opened a door, and we descended a small stair, communicating with the vestibule below. A servant was waiting there with a large and heavy fur cloak and hood, in which I was enveloped. I had no longer any power of volition — mind and body were equally prostrate — I could not have crawled along the floor alone. We passed swiftly through the crowd of officers and lacqueys, and stepped out into the wild black night. How we threaded the labyrinth of carriages and dragoons I know not.   The blast every now and then carried me off my feet. But for the strong arm round me, I should have fallen under the wheels and horses more than once.

At the corner of the bridge stood a carriage.   There, too, lay the river, swelling turbulently along under the dark arches, and as I looked over the parapet, a horrible suggestion crossed my mind.   It was only an instant ; but my companion guessed that thought, for he grasped me firmly by the arm, and led me to the carriage.

"We are driving to your old home," said he, seating himself beside me. "for your maid must come with you.   Tell her to put up a few things quickly.   Every moment is valuable now."

CHAPTER XXIV.

Betsy's face, when she opened the door, was flushed and swollen. She looked at me for a moment, and then sobbed out:

"You've heard it, miss? Oh! Lord, oh! Lord!"

"Hush! don't cry; we have no time for tears. Be quick!"

"But you don't know as they've sent me away — they won't let me stay with you. It's cruel, it's in'uman, it is. The colonel was 'shamed to speak himself, so he writes it, with my wages, and as how I was to leave to-morrow! 'Services no longer required!' Services, indeed! ugh! ugh! and I — "

"Betsy, if you wish to remain with me, you must leave this house to-night — *now* — at once."

She stopped crying at once.

"Whatever do you mean, dear? Your eyes look awful wild. Why, you're not a-going — "

"But I am, Betsy. I am going to leave my father's house forever. Don't desert me, dear old Betsy." And I threw my arms round her. She was in no frame of mind to combat my resolve.

"I'll go with you all the world over, my poor babby!"

In five minutes, with her usual quickness and energy, she had selected and put up some few necessary things. I would not wait even to change my gown. I did not give myself time to hesitate. The moment for deliberation was past.

18

I tottered with feeble steps into my mother's room. The faint light of the gas-lamps from the street dimly defined the white bed, and the forms of all the dear old furniture. I bade them, hallowed as they were by so many associations, a solemn and eternal farewell. It was the last link that held me to the past—the only relic that remained of my mother and my *home*. I turned: Betsy stood there with a couple of night-bags. We stole down the stairs like thieves, though indeed there was nothing to hinder our exit, and crossed the court.

"Quick! quick!" said Rawdon.

The carriage-steps were let down. He handed me and Betsy in, and jumped in after us; the servant mounted the box. In another moment the old house — the well-known windows with their green shutters, the walls which had witnessed all the joys and sorrows of my life — had rolled by, and passed from me forever.

I threw myself back into a corner of the carriage. Rawdon was silent. There was no sound save a frightened, stifled sob from Betsy in the opposite corner, and the rain which now began to descend in gusty splashes on the carriage-roof. Though the wind had somewhat abated, it now and then drove with such vehemence that the horses swerved across the road and threatened to overturn us.

At last we came to the barrière, where they examined our passport (which Rawdon had taken care to provide), and where our horses, already fagged by long exposure to the elements, were exchanged for four fresh ones. This time, we made good way in spite of the storm. The long rows of poplars that gloomed spectrally on either side of the road under the flash of the carriage-lamps, sped rapidly by. The postilions cracked their whips defiantly, and urged the horses forward mile after mile of flat, straight road, plunging over the uneven pavement, the mud dashing impotently up against the windows. The rain began to descend with fury.

The black heavens, from which shone no ray of moon or star, seemed emptying themselves in wrath around us. Truly an awful night!—a drive never to be forgotten!

For the raging of the storm without, reader, was as nothing compared to the scourging tempest within me. To the necessity for action, the maddened impulse, the momentary delirium, had succeeded complete inaction. And now, with ever-increasing intensity, an agony, a horror of my own self and of what I had done, seized me. There I sat, silent and motionless. Rawdon's large, firm hand held mine, and every now and then he turned to look into my face, on which the light of the carriage-lamps fell; but with rare tact he forbore to speak, for he knew what a wrench my whole system had sustained. And I commanded back the hot and bitter tears that rushed to my eyes, as I drove along through the darkness beside one whom I must henceforward study and consider, though I could never love; for my whole heart and thoughts, alas! still belonged to another. The inward voice, that is not to be stilled in such an hour as this, cried aloud, " Thou art about to perjure thine own soul! Was it all to end thus, that vow registered in secret long ago? " — The words seemed burnt into the air; I could not hide them; there they stood written on the darkness in characters of fire.

The wind had dropped altogether. Nothing was to be heard but the rain tearing up the road on either side. Heaven seemed holding its breath, and then, suddenly, from its mouth emitted a sharp tongue of fire. The vivid flash quivered through the carriage, and Betsy's scream was drowned in the thunder-clap which broke instantaneously over us.

" The horses are beginning to flag, Rawdon. Where do we stop? — we can't go on much longer."

" We change horses very soon. We don't stop till we get to Amiens, where there is an English clergyman. We shall be there very early. No time is to be lost till then — until that final step is taken. After it," he added, in a whisper, "we will idle on the road as you will — when the door is well fastened between you — between *us* and the rest of the world."

I leaned back, sick and weary.

I did not forget the fate I had escaped — oh, nó! I did not forget that here was a noble and true heart — the only one devoted to me in all the world, and over which I should possess large influence for good. Some, therefore, would justify — some even rejoice — at the course I had taken, though many, again, would mouth, and moan, and shake their heads. But what mattered it what they all thought? Praise or blame was to me alike indifferent. How much of the reality did any of them know of what was passing below the surface of the complexity of passions that stirred the very deeps of my being? Ah! it was truly said, " C'est dans les profondeurs de l'invisible que se passent les événements heureux ou malheureux de la vie!" * I did not think of what the world would say. I only listened to my own heart's fierce and bitter upbraiding.

A church clock struck four. The cracking of whips and the redoubled efforts of the horses announced that we were entering a village. Presently we drove up to the post-house, the only house in the street where a light still burned in the window. A poor place enough; but as the door opened, and I saw the wood fire blazing on the kitchen-hearth, it looked like " home." There was a crib with a child in it, near which a woman sat. It recalled my little brothers, who would have no one now, when they came from school, to stand between them and their father's coldness and neglect. How had I acted on my mother's dying injunction as regarded them? It was morbid self-reproach,

* Victor Cousin.

for had I been leaving home under happier circumstances, the poor boys would have been left no less unfriended. But there are states of mind in which we seem to try and aggravate our misery by heaping fuel on the fire. It was so with me.

There came another woman out with a lantern, and thrust it up under the carriage window, asking if we would have some coffee. Then followed a good deal of shrill swearing, and clatter of hoof and harness, but the fresh horses were already put to, and no time lost. The last thing I saw was the old postilion, inside the kitchen, dripping at every tassel, and regaling himself with a *petit verre* at the hands of the lanterned lady. Then again we plunge into the darkness, with nothing but the elf lights and shadows we bring with us dancing along upon cottage walls, and apple-trees, and long reaches of flat land.

The fury of the storm was over, and in half an hour after, spite of the excitements of that night, nature and habit proved too strong for Betsy, and she fell asleep. How I envied her, honest creature, as she lay snoring in the corner opposite. Oh, that I could only sleep and forget it all, and never, never wake again! Rawdon's eyes gleamed on me out of the deep shadow with such woeful, passionate expression, that my heart smote me as I thought how often, in the long years to come, I should find that same look bent on me — that silent, touching rebuke so impossible to answer.

This longest night in my life is drawing to an end. We have changed horses twice again, and now the dawn is breaking in a pale and misty light. The rain and wind have alike died away, and the sobbing of wet leaves and branches, and the flutter of an awakening bird, are the only sounds. The sky is heaving peacefully, as a child that sleeps after a turbulent passion of tears, while the robe of night drops gently off. A rook wheeling its flight above

the brown fields is defined darkly against the glimmering
grey. A cock crows his reveille in a farm-yard as we pass,
and the peasant, in his blue blouse, is already yoking his
oxen to the plough.

The reign of darkness and of dreams — of crime and
mystery — was past. The hour was come when terrors take
a real shape, or fade into vain shadows, that have but disquieted the heart for a while. What was past was no phantasmagoria of the brain. I was here in the body: it was a
terrible reality defined in the hard steel-light of day.

The sun is up, and we are entering Amiens. I see its
cathedral tower in a blue mist — but, indeed, every thing
passes in a mist before my eyes: the faces of the houses
thrust close to us as we crash along the narrow streets; the
market, with its scarlet umbrellas, white handkerchiefs, and
green and purple vegetable-baskets — things my strong
natural habit of observation alone forces me to see at this
moment. They present themselves like shapes in a kalei-
doscope, only seen through a gauzy film.

We drive into the inn-yard with a flourish of horn and
whip. A great bell rings, and the landlord, in a velvet cap,
backed by a chorus of waiters, cringes forward. The
carriage-steps are let down: Rawdon springs out. I try to
move, but all my limbs seem as if they were of lead. Rawdon lifts me gently out, but I have scarcely set my foot to
the ground when I reel forwards, and lose further consciousness in his arms.

CHAPTER XXV.

I OPENED my eyes in a spacious, raw-looking room, the walls of which represented the adventures of Telemachus in progressive order; the figures nearly life-size, painted in the brightest body-colors. A pile of damp wood seethed and spluttered on the hearth. Upon the marble chimney-piece stood a huge ormolu clock; a secrétaire, a table, and a few hard chairs, formed the only furniture of the apartment. The cold was intense. Rawdon and Betsy stood beside me, and the landlord, cap in hand, was near the door. I suppose Rawdon had been remonstrating, in no gentle terms, on the discomfort of the room, for the former was assuring him, in a deprecatory tone, that he was *désolé*. His best rooms — his rooms to the front — were occupied; had been already engaged before milord's avant-courier arrived. *Du reste*, the rooms were convenient — milord's on one side of the *salon*, miladi's on the other. Did milord propose remaining in Amiens that night? He would find the *cuisine* excellent.

"No, certainly not — probably not. Where does the English clergyman live?"

"A little outside the town — une petite demi-heure — would milord like some one to show him the way?"

"Yes, directly; and send up some breakfast at once. Marguerite, my beloved, I must leave you here for an hour in Betsy's charge. Remain quiet till I return, and lie down: you are exhausted. Betsy will bring you your breakfast."

"I want nothing but perfect rest — not food, but rest. I shall be better when you come back. You will bring the clergyman with you?" I added, eagerly.

"Yes."

"Betsy, go and get something to eat, my good creature; do not mind me. I am better alone."

"Lock the door, then," said Rawdon; and when Betsy had left the room, he took my cold hands in his, and looked into my face. Ah! such a look as I can never forget. "I feel a dread at leaving you, dearest, even for an hour, but I cannot help it — dread of something unforeseen stepping in between my happiness and me. I struggled *against* it so long, and since that I have struggled *for* it so long, I can hardly believe in its realization now. God bless you, my Marguerite, my own bride elect! I can pray now, you see — that is the first step you have worked in my reform."

He hurriedly pressed his burning lips to my forehead, then strode towards the door. He turned back for one farewell look. "God forgive you and me!" I muttered, with averted face. They were the only words my lips would frame. When I looked up, he was gone. I dragged my feeble steps after him, and drew the bolt of the door.

Then, at length, I was *alone*.

I breathed a long, deep breath. Though only for a brief space, this liberty was as an opened window to one gasping for air. No need to choke back the tears — to repress the agonized cry of my heart. Not an eye could see me. I threw myself on my knees and sobbed aloud. And then, for the second time, perhaps, in my life, I poured out my whole soul to God. It was one of those moments "when the soul is left passive and helpless, gazing face to face upon the anticipated and dreadful moment, which is slowly moving on:" when, finding "ourselves powerless, as in the hands of a destiny, there comes that horrible feeling of insecurity which forces us to feel out into the abyss for something that is mightier than flesh and blood to lean upon."* I prayed as the shipwrecked do — as men do in all cases when human aid is unavailing. O God! was there no turning back? no door of escape possible — any thing, any thing but this?

Yet I rose from my knees calmer, and, in some sense, stronger. My way was dark, indeed, but when the soul lights the way the understanding must see clearer to follow. I walked slowly up and down the chamber, revolving in my mind how it were possible — The clergyman? Yes, that was the first step. I must see him alone, and tell him all. I must brace my coward heart to meet Rawdon, and show him, even at the eleventh hour, that this must not be. I would implore the clergyman to find me some means of working for my daily bread, here in this town. I could never return home, of course; but was not this even a worse thraldom? I was about to bind the fetters on my *soul* which no tyranny could fasten on. They might deprive me of all that is most precious in life, friends and fair fame, but I should still have that which was dearer to me than all. We women think of these things so differently! To me, the prospect of sitting down for life beside one whose presence never made my heart hurry one beat faster — to whose thought my own never sprang up responsive — from whose tenderness I shrank back, — in short, to give only one half myself, while the other was turned to stone, this was a life-solitude compared with which almost any other fate, which I might *voluntarily accept*, would be preferable.

I had approached the window, and, almost unconsciously, stood looking down into the court-yard below. There stood the *berline* which brought us, covered with mud; and there

* Robertson.

too, a dark travelling-chariot, ready packed, and upon which a servant was strapping some night-bags, assisted by the ostler. A lady's-maid, carrying a parrot, came down, and the cage was hoisted on an imperial. Then followed dressing-cases, air-cushions, a medicine-chest, and sundry books. An old gentleman now appeared, who walked carefully round the carriage, examining the axles and fingering the springs; no strap or buckle escaped him, I am sure. Then he went up to the *berline* (his hands were now behind his coat-tails), and inspected the small coronet and arms on the panel with minute attention. I watched the old gentleman's movements with growing curiosity. Surely I had seen him before, somewhere? So I had many hundred faces in Paris. What then? Better not see these. Nevertheless, if I could but remember where I had seen him! The broad-brimmed hat (I seemed to recognize even *that*) concealed the eyes.

He looked up, and it all flashed upon me at once. The garden at Grandregard — the sick lady and her devoted brother — yes, it was certainly Mr. Bisset.

Was this the answer to my prayer, pointing to a door of delivery? I ran to the bell, and pulled it violently. I unlocked the door, and met the astonished waiter in the passage.

"Where is the English family who slept here last night?"

"They are just leaving, madame."

"Where is their room? Quick."

"Number 2 — there, at the end of the passage."

"Go and say that an English lady desires to speak with them instantly."

I waited trembling in the corridor. The man knocked. I heard a soft voice say, "Entrez." The man went in, and gave his message. Then followed two or three questions from Mr. and Miss Bisset alternately. Then a slight altercation.

“My love, you had much better send out to say you are sorry, but you are just starting, and have n’t time.”

“My dear, the horses are not put to yet, and it may be something, you know, in which one could be of use, and really in a foreign land — Demandez à la dame de entrer.”

I stood in the doorway. Miss Bisset sat at breakfast; the same little brown curls and tidy arrangement of the whole person.

“Do you remember Marguerite Percival, Miss Bisset?”

She dropped the piece of toast. “Good gracious! Why, of course!”

“Bless me!” said Mr. Bisset. “This is curious, quite a coincidence. Who would have thought of our meeting here, my dear young lady?”

“And we ’ve so often talked of you, have n’t we brother?”

“Thank you; I’m glad you remember me. It makes my task easier. Oh! Miss Bisset, I hardly know how to begin what I have to say.”

“Why, dear Miss Percival, what is the matter? You look dreadfully pale — not ill, I hope?”

“No, no, not ill; but I must explain to you how I came to be here. I am a stranger to you both — you know nothing of me. How shall I induce you to believe the truth of a very improbable story?”

The brother and sister looked at each other in mild wonderment. All their customary conventions of kind phrase were baffled. I told as rapidly and concisely as I could so much of the past as was necessary to understand the strait I now stood in.

“My conduct seems inexplicable to you. It must; for it is almost inexplicable to myself. I have fled from my home with a man I do not love — whose wife I never ought to be. I know it must shock all your ideas of propriety, but do not, Miss Bisset — *do* not condemn me too severely. You don’t know what it is to be goaded, driven to desperation — what

a life of constant terror and humiliation will do in the end.
But I have awoke from this fearful dream before it is too
late, I hope. I come to you as one Christian woman to
another, and implore you, on my knees, to save me. Take
me to some convent or house of refuge here; do any thing
to save me from this. I am strong and have energy, though
you see me now so weak and unhinged. There is nothing
—no work I will not do, to escape from my present position. But alone, I cannot break this chain. Of course I
must be married *at once*, or leave him. I dread my own
power of resisting his passionate, energetic remonstrance, if
we meet again. Even the clergyman will, perhaps, side
with him, or urge my returning home, and *that* is impossible
—quite impossible. My only hope is in you. For God's
sake help me!"

The brother and sister again exchanged looks, and Miss
Bissett, beckoning to her brother, walked to the window. A
few minutes' whispered consultation followed (and I am
bound to add, apparently no contradiction). Then they
came forward, their kind faces beaming with satisfaction.

"As to your remaining here, my dear young lady, in a
Roman Catholic establishment, or any thing of that sort,
with the risk of becoming a Papist, it is out of the question.
We couldn't lend ourselves to it. My brother has strong
Protestant principles. It is very shocking that you can't go
home—very sad indeed. Do you feel really quite determined in your own mind that it is impossible?"

My heart sank within me during this speech. I shook
my head resolutely.

"Well, we will hope that it will only be a temporary
absence. In the mean while, my brother has thought of a
plan" (it was *she*, I know, but this was her way), "which
will be the safest and most respectable thing you can do, I
think. We will take you with us to England. There is
plenty of room in our large chariot, if you don't mind going

bodkin. And then, when we get to London, you know, we can think of something. You said you had a sister married, I believe? Well, at all events, the great thing is to get you away safely and quietly. A terrible piece of business, really! If we can start before the gentleman returns, so much the better — it will prevent a scene. Don't cry, my dear Miss Percival, please don't — it makes me nervous; and don't thank me, there's nothing to thank me for. It can be no trouble or inconvenience to anybody, but quite a pleasure to brother and self to have you with us."

As I recall, at this hour, the unutterable relief, the thanksgiving of my heart to God, at that moment, something of the same deep and solemn feeling of gratitude wells up within me. What would my subsequent life have been but for that window overlooking the court-yard!

My eyes were brimming over. I could not speak. I threw myself on my knees, and buried my head in her lap.

"No, no, my dear, pray don't; there is no time to be lost. You've got a maid, haven't you? There, now, calm yourself, my dear. Well, she can go in the rumble with Sarah, and John will mount on the box."

"My love, it would be much better if Sarah were to mount on the box and John go in the rumble, because then he can keep an eye to see that no ill-disposed person (shocking scoundrels, these foreigners) cuts off my hat-box, or ——"

"My dear, it's perfectly impossible. Nothing would induce Sarah to give up her place in the rumble. Sarah must not be disturbed. *Any* other arrangement you please to make but that. Now, Miss Percival, if you wish to write, as I suppose, here are pens and paper. I will go and speak to your maid, and see that your things are moved into our carriage."

I hurriedly wrote two notes, which, as far as I can remember, ran somewhat as follows:

"Forgive me, Rawdon; do not curse me when you read this. Your prognostication has come true. I fly from you even at the hour of our marriage, because what I suffered last night shows me with fearful distinctness that life would be a long martyrdom to us both if we were married.

"In a moment of delirium I consented to accompany you: I alone am to blame. You have shown yourself all that is noble and devoted: be still more so; do not follow or attempt to trace me: in short, try and forget my existence from this hour. You have repeated several times that you would sacrifice yourself for my happiness, and I ask that sacrifice of you in this way. It is the last request I shall ever make you in this world. Return to Paris with all possible speed; let my father have the enclosed note; and refute as soon as possible, by your presence in public, the rumor that will connect your absence with my flight.

"A kind family, known to me, who are in this hotel, have offered to take me to England. There I shall gain an honest independence somehow, and in this independence I shall be happy, Rawdon — as happy as I can ever be again. This should not displease you. Believe me, we never could have been happy together. You deserve a better fate: and that you may find it, shall be my earnest prayer. Above all, let not my life, which has been sufficiently unhappy already, carry to its grave the bitter thought that it leaves you a more desperate man than when we crossed each other's path a year ago — readier to drown in dissipation the better instincts of your nature.

"God bless you. I have no heart to say more.

"MARGUERITE."

Enclosed were these lines to my father:

"Your own heart will have told you why I left home, father. But it is my duty to let you know where and with whom I am, as well as my unalterable determination for the future. When you receive this, I shall be far on my road to England, under the protection of my excellent friends, Mr. and Miss Bissett. On my arrival in London, my future course will be guided by circumstances, but at all events you will, henceforward, be relieved from the burden of my support, as well as from the restraint of my presence. I shall inform you when my plans are more formed. At present, my feelings are too painful and bitter to allow me to write more."

By the time I had finished, Miss Bisset was standing in nervous impatience beside me. Already had her brother twice announced that the horses were put to. He was too anxious to be off, to dispute the bill, as he generally did. Betsy's face, bewildered with the rapidity and unexpectedness of this last move, not knowing " whether she stood on her head or her heels," but strongly disposed to remonstrate with me, presented itself at the door. Behind her stood Rawdon's confidential servant, and the gaunt courier who had preceded us. I believe there was a suspicion on the minds of all three that compulsion, or at least energetic persuasion, had been used with me, and the two latter looked as if they were disposed to offer every resistance to my departure. I saw it was necessary at once to speak.

" Give this letter to your master," said I, stepping up to the servant, " and tell him that I left this of my own free will, in company with this lady and gentleman."

" Nous allons nous en aller," said Mr. Bissett, as he gave me his arm, and conducted me to the carriage. The tale having got wind, a couple of *sergents de ville* were at the door to witness my departure, backed by chambermaids, ostlers, and scullions.

First the sister steps in, then I, then Mr. Bissett. The parrot screams " Bonjour" from his cage on the imperial, and we slowly emerge from the shadow of the great archway. We are actually off. Brother and sister lean back with a long-drawn breath of relief.

Farewell, Amiens! I have never seen you since. Years have elapsed, but even now it would be painful to me to revisit the scene where I passed those few hours of my life.

THE train from Dover brought us into London late on Saturday evening. We drove to a private hotel in Dover street.

As I looked out of window the following morning, my infantine impressions of the metropolis revived within me. A gloomier prospect it would be difficult to see. Outside our windows, upon a rickety iron balcony (never intended for any one to stand on), were three cypresses, like mementos *mori*, in funereal pots or urns; ghastly reminiscences of departed greenness in pleasant gardens, that beheld the rise and set of sun. Flakes of soot were encrusted in their close branches: they were petrified trees, standing for years past, probably, as they now stood, stoical and grim, heedless alike of winter snows that melted from the roof upon thin blackened tops, and blistering summer rays that peeled the stucco from the wall. The face of the houses opposite was begrimed with thick tears of dirt. They seemed weeping their melancholy condition, as though they felt that seven dippings in the Jordan would be required to wash away their uncleanness. Upon one of these houses was what in my ignorance I took for the painted sign of a warehouse or shop. When Mr. Bissett informed me, at breakfast, it was a hatchment, the association of ideas did not enliven the character of the view.

The only living things that presented themselves for a long time, were a house-maid sweeping down the steps of a

door, and a cat peering through the area-railings. The only
sound, a bell tolling dismally from a neighboring church. I
checked a sense of depression I felt at the cheerless aspect
of the great city in which my life would probably henceforward be passed. I had gone through too much not to be
thankful for freedom alone, and comparatively indifferent to
every thing else. I would not disquiet myself about the
future beforehand. The kindness of Mr. and Miss Bissett
prevented my feeling that I was indeed *already* alone in the
world. To-morrow the fight must begin in earnest.

I must mention that at Calais a messenger had overtaken
us from Rawdon. I do not give his letter, though I have it
before me, and shall always keep it. In spite of the despair
it breathed, there was a manly and noble spirit throughout.
He saw, at length, that fate was against him — it was no
use; but far from regretting the past, he rejoiced in it, as it
had liberated me, though I had dashed aside the cup of happiness forever, just as he had raised it to his lips. The latter part of the letter, which he had evidently tried to make
as calm as possible, was much blotted and erased. Knowing his wild, passionate nature so well, I felt what it must
have cost him to write thus. He said his life henceforward — which he prayed to God might not be long —
should be more worthy of the only pure love he had known;
and that he would do as I requested, by returning to Paris
at once, etc. There was no resentment, no reproach; but
so much the more did the tears blind me as I read it.

Mr. Bissett, standing before the fire and rubbing his hands
after breakfast, said,

"Where shall we take Miss Perceval to church, my
dear — St. Paul's, or Westminster Abbey? Sound doctrine
at Westminster Abbey, ain't it, my love? Or the temple —
what do you say to that? We must show you some of the
sights before we leave — we shall only be here two days,
you know. By-the-by — hem — hem —"

"I hardly know whether it is right to discuss business on Sunday, but — hem — hem — brother and I have been talking over your plans — and — it struck brother that the best thing you can do is to come and spend a month down with us in the country."

"Until your sister and her husband return to England. You wrote to them, I think, from Dover? Well, that will give you time to look about you. As to remaining here in a lodging, my dear young lady, and consulting those trustees you talked of, and so on — why, you know, lawyers — confounded rascals! — never did any one any good, and you'd much better see some of your friends, or, at all events, hear from them, before you do any thing decided."

"Dear Mr. Bisset, what can I say? I thank you both from my heart, I am sure, but I think it is better I should at once set about looking for some employment. It must be done; so the sooner the better, for I never will live on my brother-in-law's bounty, or any one else's, if I can help it. I am afraid you think that wicked pride, Miss Bissett, for you shake your head. My sister had not a penny when she married — is it fair to lay an additional burden on her husband? If I could be of use to her, it would be different, but I should be only in their way. They have no children, as yet, whom I could teach, and I should be a kill-joy in their gay existence. Believe me it is so: I have thought over it much. I had better set bravely to work at once; nothing like hard work for making one contented, is there?"

"No, no, my dear; it is all very creditable, your wish to be independent, and I am sure we honor it exceedingly, but you really require rest for some time. Your nerves have been shaken — you don't look as a young girl should. Your energies will be all the better for lying by. And the spring, as I always say, is such a very trying season!"

"Lord! you don't know what spring in the country is,

Miss Percival! The finest sight in the year to see all the hedges bursting, and the lambs sporting in the fields, and the wheat sprouting up thick !— a sight you can't see in that land of *Mounseers* you've lived in. *I* never saw such farmers ; it's my belief they only know how to cultivate frogs ! "

" Brother, you carry your English prejudices to a ridiculous extent, as I often tell you. Besides, young ladies don't care about farming. But I flatter myself, Miss Percival, that we can show you as sweet spots near us as are to be found in England. The Peak is not many miles distant. You've read ' Peveril ? ' With your artistic eye (you said you were so fond of drawing) you would find plenty of food for your pencil — if you don't think you would be bored with our very quiet, humdrum life."

" Please don't say that. It sounds as if you thought my foreign education had unfitted me for a quiet English life. I have never tried it, but I can fancy nothing happier."

" Come and judge for yourself," said Mr. Bissett. And they succeeded, at last, in persuading me to accept their kind invitation.

I wrote to Miss Lateward the following day (Sunday being devoted to two churches and the Park). It was, for many reasons, a difficult and unpleasant task, and I made it as short as I could. I begged her to spare me any advice about returning home. I told her I was with friends, and had consented to pass some weeks in the country with them before returning to London, where I intended commencing my career as an artist. I concluded by saying,

" Be good enough not to name me, nor allude to this letter or its contents, among your circle. You will oblige me greatly by attending to my wishes in this respect. I have suffered much, and I had rather, henceforward, be completely forgotten — never spoken of, nor canvassed in any way. I have no desire, now, but to drop down the stream unobserved — to glide as quietly as possible onward to that peaceful sea towards which we are all hastening."

During the days we stayed in London, desirous of raising the British character in my eyes, Mr. Bissett kindly wished to take me to every sight the capital afforded at that season. I lived in hourly apprehension of museums and zoological gardens. Fortunately, his sister saw how ill-disposed my thoughts and spirits were to answer these active calls. Many were the amiable bickerings on the subject I over-heard; but it ended generally in my being left quiet. Mr. Bissett (notwithstanding his abuse of the profession) had to see his lawyer in Lincoln's Inn, and Miss Bissett her doctor. Then there was an old aunt in the Regent's Park to be visited, and sundry purchases to be made, such as garden-seeds, and books for the school-children, besides presents from the Soho Bazaar for all the members of the Exton household; so that the time of both brother and sister was pretty well employed, and in a delightful and pleasurable fidget they both lived.

I called at Sir Charles Murray's, in Brook-street. He was in Suffolk. Mr. and Mrs. Murray were not expected home till the beginning of May — nearly two months hence. The only visit I paid was to my brothers, who were at school near London. Their joy at the unexpected sight of me was the cheeriest thing I had met since I landed in England. But it was painful having to break to them a knowledge of the changes that had taken place in their home since they left it six weeks before. I said that as our father was married again, I was come to live near them and Rose. I dared promise they would spend their summer holidays with her in the country, if they were good and worked hard. I was leaving London, but they must write to me very often, and I should be back before long, and then we would spend a long half-holiday together some-where.

"Perhaps Greenwich, where the old sailors are?" suggested Roger.

As we returned in the cab along the Strand, and I looked down some of the dark and narrow streets that lead to the river, I thought how it was possible I might soon be a dweller in one of those dismal houses. I pictured myself on a hot summer's evening looking out of a second-floor window, while wherries on the river bore holiday-folk to pleasant gardens far away, and an organ in the street below played old tunes, full of memories of the long ago!

I was to begin existence anew. New scenes and faces — new interests and aims. Only no new hopes: they were buried with the old life. Or, at most, one arose, of doing some small good in my generation — that my life should not be confined to a round of selfish toils — that I might find some work beyond the daily task for bread apportioned for me to do.

Sitting in the grim London room, upon a black horsehair sofa, with the *Times* supplement in my hand, my eye resting vacantly on paragraphs beginning, "Landscape-painting: six lessons for one guinea," etc.; "Pictures and sketches for sale," my thoughts too often strayed from the practical questions I had sat down to consider. The mind is a strange, sensitive plant. It answers to touches of which we are scarcely conscious. When we fancy our attention fixed, a chance word is enough to unloose a whole chain of thoughts, and send them wandering up and down the face of the earth. He is a wise and happy man who can say he has absolute control over his restive imagination. I found, to my sorrow, at this time, how little I had over mine. I was constantly referring my motives and actions to *his* standard — asking myself what *he* would have thought on such and such a point; though I struggled very hard to forget his existence, and tried to think I did so.

The night before we left London, I told Betsy it was

probable that **I** should be returning in a few weeks' time to take up my abode in some small lodging, and I begged her to say honestly if she still wished to remain with me under these circumstances — whether she had no desire to "better" herself, or, perhaps, to return abroad? She had been spending the day with a cousin in Long Acre, and declared that she was sick of *foreign* parts. She would stick by me, *that* she would, so long as I were a lone child, the which, however, she foresaw, would not be long. Though I *had* disappointed his lordship — and a great pity, too, *she* thought, for he was a fine gentleman, and spent his money like one ; and that, for herself, if she ever was to marry, for sure it were like time, when I were settled, and there were those, perhaps, as *would* — However, she should n't more particularly delude to that, for it was neither here nor there. Putting these things together, had my palm been crossed with silver, I should confidently have predicted matrimony on the Long Acre horizon.

We started by an early train next day. About three in the afternoon, Mr. Bissett, suddenly starting up and rubbing his eyes, announced that we were not far from the station where we were to get out. Whereupon, a folding up of shawls and dispersion of the crumbs of sandwich lodged in fold and flounce.

"Fine land this, eh? Very fine land, Miss Percival?" Mr. Bissett has been in the land of dreams for the last hour, but it is not of this land he speaks. "To think of those confounded fellows wanting to give us free trade, when one looks *there!* It will be the ruin of England if Peel ever succeeds."

"Sir," said a plethoric man, with "cotton" written all over him, who had not yet spoken, "you should look at the question from a broad point of view. A long-sighted policy — "

"Don't talk to me of long sight, sir. I have long enough

sight to see those fields. I say, that you will bring down
the farmer to the level of his laborer. It's the beginning
of Socialism, sir. You'll have England just as bad as
France."

"In the present day," said the free trader, with a sarcastic manner, "the greatest good of the greatest number is
supposed to be the aim of legislation, not the greatest good
of a very small number, which the farmers are. If, by the
cheapening of bread, you better the condition —"

"Nonsense, sir! I beg your pardon, but you make me
angry. How are the laborers to get employment — how are
they to buy bread *at all*, if it is not from the farmers? And
how can the farmers afford to pay them when there is such
a monstrous competition in the market? I say it's impossible, sir."

"Nay, then the fields must lie uncultivated," said the
other, with a smile. "But you will find things don't quite
come to that pass, though we *shall* have free trade as sure
as I sit here, sir. You will find that the only difference
is, that your farmers, instead of sending their oats *only* to
Anchester (you live near there, if I am not mistaken, sir?),
will — "

"Anchester?" said I, turning to Miss Bissett (and from
this point I lost the Protectionist discourse). "Are there
two Anchesters? I thought it was in —shire?"

"So it is — on the borders: but yet it is only fifteen
miles from us. Why do you ask? Do you know any one
there?"

"No — that is, I believe an old governess of mine is living with a family not far from there. That is the post town,
at least."

"What is the name of the family?"

"Rochford."

"Oh yes! They are the other side of Anchester. I
don't know them much myself, but brother does. He meets

Mr. Rochford on the grand jury, and so on; but they live much too far for visiting acquaintance."

"Oh!" A long-drawn breath of relief.

"But their cousins, the Nevilles, are our near neighbors. I have seen Mr. Rochford there. It was thought at one time he would marry Maud Neville. She is a great favorite of mine — such a nice girl! Since we've been abroad, I have heard nothing more of it; but, indeed, I am quite behind-hand in county news. I believe I must have lost some of dear Mrs. Deane's letters."

What would I not have given to return to London by the next train! Had I but known this, nothing in the world should have tempted me down here. While Miss Bissett ran on about Mrs. Deane, and a thousand other indifferent things, my visit to Exton was being prospectively curtailed to days instead of weeks.

I asked carelessly what the Neville family consisted of.

"There is the father, Mr. Neville, who is reckoned a clever person. He has written a book. He has one son — a young man at Oxford, who is, in the slang of the day, what you call rather *fast*. Maud is his only other child, so she will have a large fortune. Her mother was an heiress, sister of Mrs. Rochford's. She died only two years ago, poor thing! She was devoted to her daughter, and took great pains with her education. Mr. Neville did, too; though, somehow, I never can fancy he is as clever as they say. He *has* written a book though (something too learned for me, however). Little Maud and I are great friends. I call her little, though she's a big girl, but having known her since she was —"

"Come, come, my love, don't sit there talking; here we are! Quick, now — that basket. Miss Percival, take these shawls, please. Good day to you, sir. I hope we may *never* see your free trade in England — that's all."

It was dark as we drove down the narrow lane that led to Exton. I leaned forward and said,

"Mr. Bissett, I have a singular request to make to you. You are so open and straight-forward, that I hardly know whether you will grant it. During the short time — for it must be a very short time — I am with you, I have most urgent reasons for wishing to remain unnoticed — *unknown* — in your house."

"But, my dear Miss Percival, nothing is more natural. God bless my soul! worried and plagued to death as you seem to have been — and I dare say I don't know half — you, of course, want to be quiet. You need n't be alarmed; we are very quiet; we 've hardly any visitors, and you need n't see *them*, if you don't like. My house is Liberty Hall."

" Dear Mr. Bissett, there are reasons that I cannot enter into exactly, why I am very anxious my name should not be known in your neighborhood. I assure you there is no terrible secret under this mystery — it is only a matter of feeling — of false delicacy, perhaps; but I dislike its being talked of, that I am staying in this particular part of the country. Do you mind calling me by any other name?"

I do not think Mr. Bissett at all relished the idea. A change of name was connected in his mind with the magisterial bench, swindling, and the county gaol. It was "such a very odd thing" — he had never heard of such a thing — except — really — well, if it was particularly to oblige me — for Miss Bissett was nodding and winking significantly at her brother all the time, and those cabalistic signs he never long resisted. She, I believe, would have acceded to any proposition of mine, for I was beginning to have a great ascendency over her.

So it was settled that I entered Exton as Miss Hope.

CHAPTER XXVII.

It was a long, low house, with a homely English face, and pleasant irregular features : bay-windows, trellised porch, and conservatory. The evergreens, which shut it in on two sides, were of the most luxuriant growth, such as one never sees in France ; sweeping the gravel with their broad-leaved branches, and forming an emerald wall nearly as high as the roof. The greenest of velvet lawns, brocaded in knots of flowers, sloped down to a clear stream: on the other side of which the pleasure-grounds extended for some distance — Mr. Bissett would never allow it to be called a park — with a large farm beyond.

I looked from my window, the morning after my arrival, on that happy home-picture : the lawn, glistening under its veil of dew, the rooks cawing in the bare top branches, the partridges freckling the farm-fields, and the blue ridges of the hills behind. Under the wide-armed elms, whose trunks, with all their moss-enamellings, lay clearly mirrored in the shallow water, the sheep and cattle were come to drink ; the only sound of human life was the gardener's scythe upon the lawn, and that in no way disturbed the sense of peace and repose that came over me as I stood there.

Of course the brother and sister found enough to do after their year's absence from home, to enable me to be many hours of the day alone, and these I spent mostly in the library. A fire was lit there once a week, nominally to keep

the books dry; but the south sun fell full into this room,
otherwise it would have been untenably chill and damp.   A
mouldy smell of books struck on one as one opened the door.
I took down volumes from the topmost shelves, that, save
by the housemaid's broom, had probably not been touched
for years.   The leaves clung together from long companionship in damp: for, excepting the works of Mrs. Hannah
More, I do not think Miss Bissett was much given to literature, and her brother certainly never read any thing but
the newspaper, the Bible, and the Book of Common Prayer.
Here I spent some very happy mornings: here I made
acquaintance with many of the treasured classics of our
language, hitherto only known to me by name — the courtly
verse of Pope, the polished prose of Addison and Steele.
In such company I often forgot the anxieties of the present,
and the tranquillizing effect of this life was very beneficial
to my health and spirits.   The family at Neville Hall were
from home ; and as my assumed name prevented any
rumor of my being here from reaching Rochford Court,
where all the party were assembled, I was comparatively at
ease ; though I still determined only to remain at Exton a
fortnight.

The approaching marriage was, of course, the first piece
of news Mrs. Deane, the clergyman's wife, had to communicate to her dear friend Miss Bissett.   I was obliged to make
Mrs. Deane's acquaintance, notwithstanding my request to
be allowed to slip away unnoticed when any visitors were
announced : but it would have been impossible to escape this
lady, for she popped in and out, at all hours of the day ; at
breakfast, at luncheon — no hour, or meal, or room was
sacred.   An active, benevolent, shrewd, inquisitive woman,
invariably seen, with a basket or a bundle, trudging to and
fro in all weathers ; indefatigable in her charities, which were
no cold matter of duty with her ; a patient listener and judi-
cious counsellor; a right good gossip (which, in a genial

sense, is a most commendable village weakness); a warm, comfortable body, in short, inexhaustibly supplied with the caloric of human sympathy. She was the dispenser of Miss Bissett's charities during the absence of the latter, and her prime minister when at home. This accounted for her constant little dartings in and out of the house, charged with flannel petticoats and cordials. I hardly ever crossed the hall without finding her rubbing her feet on the mat, in a glow of benevolence and sharp walking; or taking her departure with a cobwebbed black bottle protruding from her basket. Our acquaintance progressed rapidly. At first, indeed, I found her rather disagreeably curious to know where I came from, who my parents were, how I came to know Miss Bissett, whether I was related to the Hopes of Shropshire, etc. etc. But we got on together capitally, when she had satisfied herself that I was a " young person" whom Miss Bissett had met at T—, that I had no family, no home, and that I intended earning my livelihood as an artist, in London. My kind hosts had laid injunctions on their two faithful old servants to say nothing about me whatever; and, to their honor be it spoken, they never yielded to the strong temptation of a strange tale to tell " in strict confidence " to all their village friends. The possession of this secret, and their having travelled in foreign parts together, tended greatly to their intimacy with my Betsy. This triumvirate of the " upper table," as I learnt from her, had a sort of freemasonry between them, and their often ambiguous talk inspired the others with great awe.

Of Mr. Deane, I have little to say. He was a character of secondary importance in the village : a good man, but dull and slow. I often wondered how his sharp, active wife could resist slipping on the surplice, and taking his place in the reading-desk. For in every other emergency, even to the delivery of a slow joke at dinner, she came to his rescue, and carried him briskly through it. But in church he always sent his congregation to sleep.

Ten days had passed; I was beginning to feel as if I had spent all my life at Exton, and to look forward to leaving it with great regret. I sat in the library window one morning, a book on my knee, thinking how I should broach the subject of my departure to Miss Bissett, when, on looking up, I saw her standing on the terrace, talking to a young lady in a riding-dress. The latter, with one hand held up the long habit from her feet, while she pointed with the other to some flowers. Not a look or gesture, not a fold of the cloth escaped me; immediately my eyes fell on her, there they remained greedily fastened. I instinctively felt that it was Maud Neville; a fine, well-grown young woman, dark-haired, fresh-colored, with agreeable features, clear eyes, and a remarkably firm mouth and chin. The term " good-looking " just suited her; she was *good-looking* — something solid, sensible, pleasant to the eye if not strictly handsome. The manner, and the expression of face, were frank and rather eager: the movements more quick than graceful. I watched her for full five minutes with intense interest.

" Well," I sighed, as they moved away, " this then is she! I am glad to have seen her. Strange! she is not the sort of person I fancied that he— We know so little of men's tastes. She has character, I am sure — consistency. Was that the charm? I am better looking, I suppose. Pshaw! what a fool I am, to think that has any thing in the world to do with it! Well, now I must be up and doing. They must have returned to Neville Hall, and it is time I were gone."

" Excuse me, my dear," said Miss Bissett's small voice, opening the door ajar, " but I must break through your rule for once, in favor of my friend Miss Neville, whom I am so anxious you should know. She only returned home yesterday, and has ridden over to see me. Maud, my dear, come in; allow me to make you acquainted with Miss Hope, of whom I have been talking to you."

The young lady entered. I had no means of escape, and felt myself growing red and white as I bowed. She looked at me in her rapid way from head to foot: not the impertinent stare of fashionable life, but a searching, intelligent glance, surprised at something unexpected.

She held out her hand. "I am glad to make your acquaintance, Miss Hope. Our neighborhood doesn't abound in young ladies, and Miss Bissett tells me so much about you" — (I shot a look at that lady, but she screwed up her lips tightly to signify discretion) — "that I am very anxious we should become friends. I hope you'll come over and see me."

"Thank you — but I must return to London the day after to-morrow."

"Nonsense, my dear," said Miss Bissett. "Brother will never hear of that. But you will not have much time, I suspect, to cultivate friendships *now*, my dear Maud," she added with a sly smile.

"I am not to be married for three months, if you mean that, and Hubert will be with us very little, I believe. He has so much business, and lawyers are so slow. By-the-by, you don't know Aunt Rochford, I think? They are coming over, if Violet is well enough, on Tuesday, and you must really come and make their acquaintance. Do, now."

I was filled with dismay; and when Miss Bissett accepted for herself and me, could only repeat that I should have left Exton before then, and were it not so, that I was unfit at present to mix in society.

"By-the-by," said Miss Bissett, as if she had hit suddenly on a bright thought, "you know one of the Rochford party! — the governess, Miss What's-her-name? — an old friend of yours you told me, I think. You would like to see her, I'm sure."

"You know Miss Lateward? You met her abroad, I suppose? An excellent woman — but still. However, she is

bringing up Violet capitally, and my aunt is really fond of
her, and she does n't *easily* like people, so there must be
good in her ; but she bores me dreadfully.   I begged that if
they came, Violet might have a holiday and Miss Lateward
be left behind.   It is n't very civil saying that, if she is a
friend of yours, but I can't help it.   By-the-by, did you ever
happen to meet my cousin, Mr. Rochford abroad ? "

"Y-yes — I have met him."

"You never told me so, my dear," said Miss Bissett, looking surprised.

"Did n't I ?   Oh! it was n't any acquaintance to speak of.
He has forgotten my name long ago, I am sure."

"He never forgets a face, at all events," laughed Miss
Neville.   "I am sure he won't have forgotten *yours*."

I shivered and turned aside to the book-case, under a pretence of replacing the volume in my hand.

"Come, there is the luncheon-bell.   We won't wait.
When brother gets any one to his farm, there is no knowing
when he will come away."

We were crossing the hall.

"Will you excuse me, Miss Bissett ?   I don't feel —"

The words died away on my lips.   *There he stood before me.*

The hall door was open.   Mr. Bissett and he were just
entering.   My knees seemed to give way under me.   I
caught hold of the marble table to prevent myself from falling ; and by a strong effort I managed to retain some semblance of composure.

He turned deadly pale, and stood looking at me as if I
were an apparition.   I will confess that a spasm of joy shot
through me, and my courage, strange to say, overcame my
emotion when I saw that his self-possession was even more
upset than mine.

Miss Neville was occupied in receiving the hearty salutations of Mr. Bissett.   His sister had passed on to the dining-
room.

It was necessary to speak, and at once.   Miss Neville had turned towards us.

"I see, Mr. Rochford, you do not remember me — Miss Hope."

"Come, brother!" cried Miss Bissett, from the dining-room, "don't stand gossiping there.   Luncheon is getting cold."

Rochford said nothing, but offered me his arm; then he asked abruptly,

"How long have you been here?   What does all this mean — Miss — Hope?   How is it that the brilliant capital has spared you?"

It was with great difficulty I replied in a low voice, as we seated ourselves at the table,

"Paris has *not*, indeed, spared me; in another sense, heavy sorrows — heavy troubles of many kinds.   That is why I am here.   I do not expect you to spare me, either.   You find me in a strange position."

Miss Neville threw off her riding-hat, and said, carelessly,

"I was sure you wouldn't forget Miss Hope, Hubert.   She said you would.   You must join in trying to persuade her to come over to the Hall for a few days, instead of returning to London.   I'll mount you on my little bay mare, Miss Hope; and when that gentleman is busy with deeds and lawyers as long as my arm — I mean deeds, not lawyers — you and I will have some pleasant rides over the country.   If this weather lasts, it will be charming."

"I hope it won't, my dear Maud," said Mr. Bissett; "it will bring every thing much too forward.   We shall suffer for it by-and-by.   Miss Hope, a slice of brawn?   That field of Farmer Smith's you passed on the road, Mr. Rochford, why the wheat there is already —"

"Barley, brother, isn't it?   Well, it don't signify, to be sure.   Maud, how are your anemones coming on?   Those splendid ones I gave you before I went abroad?   That was a great piece of generosity on my part. I can't bear giving away my flowers. It is the only thing in which I believe I am really stingy."

"They are your children, dear Miss Bissett; no wonder. My children are my birds and my dogs. Unfortunately, Hubert can't bear them."

"That is an exaggeration, Maud. I think there are places fitter than a young lady's boudoir for three or four pointers and grey-hounds. And when one is talking, or even reading quietly, there are pleasanter things than an aviary in the same room; but in their proper place —"

"Ah! that is what people always say when they don't like a thing. Now, I think your books, and poor-laws, and petitions, and all the rest of it, very well in their place; but when you are with me, I prefer your conversation."

The door opened as Mr. Bissett was laughing, and Mrs. Deane appeared.

"Good morning to you all. Just run in for a moment. My dear Maud, welcome back! Mr. Rochford, how d'ye do, sir? Hope your mother is pretty well. Any news from Anchester about poor John Hurst? When is he to be tried? His wife just laid in of twins. I've come, my dear, to ask for some wine for the poor thing. Is there any chance of her husband's being acquitted? May I give her any hope?"

"Unfortunately, Mrs. Deane, as far as actual law goes, there is no doubt he is guilty. In a very similar case, last year, a man was transported."

"Yes," said Mr. Bissett, looking judicial and severe, "and these petty thefts have become so common of late."

"Dear me!" said his sister. "After all, to think of transporting a man for a few miserable turnips!"

"Potatoes, my love — a sack of potatoes; you can't be too exact in cases of this sort."

"His wife was starving at home!" burst in Mrs. Deane. "And then, to think of an infamous wretch like that Scroggs, who beats his wife and nearly kills her, and is sentenced to a month's hard labor, and fined five shillings. It is shameful!"

"If Hubert gets into Parliament next year," cried Maud, "I shall make him bring in a bill to redress the wrongs of women. That wife-beating makes my blood boil. Don't you agree with me, Miss Hope, that American women are quite right about the emancipation of our sex?"

"Emancipation from what?" I stammered.

"Oh! from the swathing-bands that society puts round us. There is my cousin, for instance, who thinks that a woman ought to be brought up in a dull routine, like Violet, and me. As to any knowledge of life, or a foreign education, or a woman's having any independence or ambition, or being any thing, in short, but a sheet of white paper, he can't bear it."

"You draw a pleasing picture of my liberal views, Maud."

"It is only the truth, Hubert. You think a girl's education ought to be made up like a prescription, so many grains of literature to so many of housekeeping; and when made up, to be kept in a cool place until required."

"At all events, my dear," said Miss Bissett, laughing, "you ought to be glad that he approves of the way in which *you* have been *made up*."

"Perhaps he finds now it is not so good in practice as in theory. I'm a painful instance, you know, of what is called a solid education. I have never been allowed to read a novel, or any other poetry than Milton, and that I thought a bore."

"My dear!" cried Miss Bissett, much shocked. "'Paradise Lost' a bore! Impossible!"

"I did, really. I suppose I have no imagination: at all events it has never been cultivated. Papa taught me the Latin Grammar, and said I should find it very useful. Perhaps I may when I have a house of my own; at present I rather regret not having learnt to play and sing."

"I wish you did most heartily, my dear," said Mrs. Deane, who, having finished luncheon, was again in full possession of her tongue. "I wish you did, for then you would see after the singing in church. It really gets worse and worse. I dread *you*, Mr. Rochford, with your critical ear — and your mother, too; I remember how she used to play. But we have really no one here who is musical. By-the-by, Miss Hope, perhaps *you* are? No? Sorry for that. Well, I mustn't stay. You will excuse me, I know."

"I want to consult you, my dear Mrs. Deane, about how many yards of flannel it takes to make — "

"Come, my love, if we have all done, we may as well go into the garden. I want to show you my Cochin-China fowls, Miss Maud."

Mr. Bissett opened the window, and they all stepped out.

This was the moment to escape. I turned to leave the room.

"Stop! I beg your pardon, Miss Hope — since you wish to be known by that name — may I speak a word with you?" said Rochford, in a low voice.

My fingers twitched nervously round the handle of the door. I looked back, but did not speak.

"I have to apologize for the way in which I met you just now. I was quite unprepared for this. Pardon me if my manner seemed unkind. I assure you I was wounded to the quick when you referred to your great sorrow — for I sympathized heartily with you when I heard of it; but we since heard that you had recovered your spirits, and were going again into the world, and latterly that you were — in short *false rumors,* no doubt. May I now take the liberty of an old acquaintance, and ask you to tell me how it is you come to be here, and under a feigned name? I feel that I have no claim on your confidence, but I ask it because — because — "

" There is nothing to apologize for, Mr. Rochford," said I coldly. " If you believed those rumors, you are perfectly at liberty to do so still. I shall not contradict or explain any thing. I have left my home, and am living under another name. These are facts: to which you may add, that I intend earning my bread as an artist. But I wish you very distinctly to understand that in accepting my friends' invitation down here, I had not the most distant idea that I was coming into the neighborhood of — that I was likely to meet *any one* I ever knew before. However, I leave this in a day or two, and to avoid a great deal of gossip, I think you will agree that it is better to say nothing about me. Mr. and Miss Bissett know all the painful circumstances that have led to my being here; and that, Mr. Rochford, I suppose you will consider sufficient."

His cheek flushed, and he looked annoyed.

" You speak with resentment: but it was from no distrust I asked for an explanation, but because you are here in a false position, and because I would vindicate you from those very rumors you allude to. I know much of what you had to suffer. I can guess more. In memory of some happy hours, Miss Percival, let me be of service to you if I can, in any way. My mother — "

He hesitated, and that firm face actually quivered with the strength of some repressed emotion.

" You can do me no service, thank you," I replied, gently. " We shall move in very different paths henceforward, and it is not probable that we shall cross each other again. Allow me, therefore, in return for your expressions of sympathy, to offer you my sincere wishes that your marriage may prove happy, and your future be as bright as it, no doubt, seems to you now. Good morning."

I turned and left the room. To linger, to prolong this

interview, was impossible. I could only trust my self-command up to a certain point. When I got to my own room I turned the key of the door, and did not come down stairs again until some hours after Miss Neville and her cousin had ridden away.

CHAPTER XXVIII.

It was dusk, and I had paced the shrubbery with a rapid step. Yes, I must leave Exton at once — why not to-night? To linger in this neighborhood, with the chance of another such meeting, was positive torture to me. He was right. I was in a false position. The very last person who ought to have been, necessarily *was* the sharer of my secret. If it should accidentally be discovered now — if it should reach Mrs. Rochford's ears — that I, Margaret Percival, was come into her son's neighborhood — my pride revolted fiercely at the bare idea.

I nearly ran against Mrs. Deane in the impetuosity of my self-absorbed walk. She was crossing the shrubbery, and stopped short.

" Bless me, Miss Hope! why, where are you going at that pace? Only walking up and down? Well, I don't mind if I take a turn with you before dinner, as all my work is done for to-day. Now, tell me what you think of Miss Neville. No fool, you know, under that off-hand manner. Plenty of determination and good sense, eh ? "

" She has a frank, fresh character, apparently, which is always pleasant."

" But that very frankness prevents her being generally appreciated. Many people don't like her."

" Do you think that signifies, as long as the few — the *one* — appreciates her? If she is wise, that will be quite sufficient for her."

"Ah! hem — don't know — can't say. I doubt the *one* appreciating her as she deserves. However, it is no business of mine."

"You are not serious, Mrs. Deane? They have known each other from children, have they not? and now that Mr. Rochford is going to marry his cousin, why should you doubt his appreciating her good qualities?"

"Well, perhaps I am wrong; but I know she never had an idea he cared about her until he proposed, and if she didn't believe him to be too highly principled to marry her while he is in love with somebody else, I'm sure she wouldn't have him."

"Oh! So then there was some other attachment, was there?" A pause.

"Well, it's all past and done with now, my dear Miss Hope, so I suppose there's no great harm in telling you that his mother was for some time very uneasy about his marrying some half-French girl he knew in Paris. She had been very badly brought up, and was in shocking society, and, altogether, Mrs. Rochford was naturally in a great fright. The idea of such a daughter-in-law, coming down here to turn every thing topsy-turvy, was dreadful, of course, for she likes exercising her influence on her son. She is an excellent woman, but she has that little failing — and though she wished him to marry, she also wished to choose his wife for him."

I stopped to gather a primrose. "Well, and how did it end?"

"Oh! I believe she wrote to him, imploring him to do nothing rash. But he was very much infatuated for a long time, and declared that the girl would be very different if she were in other circumstances; until at last his eyes were opened to her real character, and, to his mother's great joy, he unexpectedly returned home. How she managed it I'm sure I don't know; but the great wish of her life was realized at last, and he proposed to his cousin Maud. He told her what she knew already — that he had loved, and been disappointed; and as she did n't care for any one, she accepted him. She is really fond of him in her way, too, and I dare say they will get on very well by-and-by, only I *don't* think they are particularly suited; and certainly he is not very like an ardent lover, is he? Now, just fancy his riding off again to Rochford to-night!"

I drew a long breath. "Oh! indeed? And does he not return to Neville Hall?"

"He is to bring his mother there next week. But he is very little there himself, always having business or something that takes him away. Really, it is very good of Maud to stand it."

"Ah! very. By-the-by, you were kind enough yesterday to propose writing to a cousin of yours, who I think you said is a printseller in London, relative to my boarding in his house. It would be doing me a great service if you would do so, as I must leave this on Monday."

"Why, my dear Miss Hope, I sha n't be able to get his answer. This is Saturday. If I write by this evening's post, I can't have an answer before Tuesday. And, indeed, I think it would be a very great advantage to you in all ways being in a respectable house like my cousin's. His wife is an excellent woman, and he could be of such use to you in your profession. You must just put off your departure till Wednesday, my dear; it really is not respectable your going to that great Babylon alone, and getting into you don't know where for lodgings. No, no; better wait another day, and have John's answer. There's six o'clock striking, and dinner at a quarter past! What will Mr. Deane say to me? Good-night, Miss Hope, good-night!"

I was left alone there upon the bench. My eyes were opened now. I no longer doubted that he had loved me — nay, that he loved me still. Did I exult in this? No. His love had not been strong enough to resist the pressure from without — a mother's solemn warnings and tender supplications, and the world's calumny. The love I dreamed of was no weak infant-passion, to be weaned like this. Oh no, oh no! my heart cried aloud. I, the poor, despised girl, of such poor moral training, found strength, even at the eleventh hour, to resist this heart-perjury, while *you*, Hubert Rochford, the man of pure life and lofty aims, trampled under foot that sacred fire of love. The world can never accuse you — *I* even have no right to do so; no word ever passed between us. But through the long years to come, how will the secret monitor at your heart speak to you in the watches of the night? Do you choose your wife as part of the great social scheme? a mere helpmate in the outer vineyard, not a home-refuge from the disappointments and unfruitful labor there? If, indeed, she be content with such a lot, well; but if, having asked for bread, she finds she has no teeth for stone — beware, Hubert Rochford, beware!

The following was the first day of the week, essentially one of peace at Exton, and as unlike the brilliant Paris Sunday to which I had been accustomed, when all the frivolities of the past week come to maturity and burst into blossom on the Boulevards, as it was unlike the jaded London Sabbath, where dingy streets seem mourning that another week has commenced.

I sat in the little church, and looked down, probably for the last time in my life, upon that peasant congregation. Happy and tranquil life, how much to be envied! I thought to myself. That good gray head, in horn-spectacles, reading his Bible on the same oak bench where he stood, as a child, beside his mother, listening in decent reverence to the minister's discourse, is not his round of labor, and the rest that labor sweetens, better than all the feverish wants and struggles of the world? Though Mr. Deane's discourse be marvellously dull in our ears, though we hold the choir to be somewhat harsh and nasal, they are not so to that old man. In the fulness of time he will be laid beside his faithful wife in the green churchyard where his fathers sleep before him : and another generation will grow up, and pass away as he has done, and the same psalm will be sung on Sunday mornings, and swallows will twitter as they do now, under the eaves of the old church porch.

I never felt so strongly drawn to the country as I did then, so loth to exchange it for the crowd and hurry of a capital. I would willingly have gone to live in any obscure village, where among the poor I might have found a field for exertion. But I felt it was not to be. I must work hard for my brothers and myself, and this could only be in London, where there was, no doubt, misery and sorrow enough in all shapes to be sought out. The peace of the country was for others : the happiness of listening to wind-stirred boughs and quiet field-sounds was not for me.

But at the earnest representation of my kind hosts, backed by Mrs. Deane, I consented to remain at Exton until " Cousin John's " answer should be received, which, at latest, must be on Wednesday. Had Hubert Rochford still been in the neighborhood, I should have held firmly to my original resolve ; but he had returned home, so there was no chance of our meeting, and on Wednesday nothing would prevent my being on my road to London.

Miss Bissett came to me early on Monday morning, with a note in her hand.

" Maud wants us very much to go over there to-morrow and spend the day, if you won't sleep, my dear. You will come with me, won't you ? Do, now."

" Pray do not let me prevent your going, Miss Bissett, but I cannot. You see how I behaved the other day. I am not fit for civilized society."

" Well ! it will be a great disappointment to her. I know. This is what she says about you in her odd way." She

opened the note and read: " I took a fancy to your friend
Miss Hope, though I suspect it is more than she did to me.
If I were a man I should fall desperately in love with her
(only desperate love is out of fashion, I am told). I want to
see her again, and I want Aunt Rochford to see her ; so do
bring her over on Tuesday.' I suppose Mrs. Rochford
comes to-morrow too, then. Now, my dear, do let me
say —"

"Thank you, it is quite impossible. I am very much
obliged to Miss Neville. I should have no objection to see
her again, but it is out of the question. I cannot meet
strangers, Miss Bissett ; pray do not urge me."

The amiable but obstinate little lady, however, was not to
be baffled even now.

"Well, then, my dear Miss Hope, will you let me drive
you over, quietly, this afternoon ? I should like you to see
the old Hall, and as you say you do not mind Maud, why
you *can* have no objection?"

What will not a steady persistence achieve ? I lothfully
consented at last.

Neville Hall was four miles distant. Miss Bisset drove
her gray ponies, and was sufficiently occupied in keeping
them in hand, while I silently enjoyed the fragrant breath
of spring as we drove along the lanes. At last we came in
sight of the mansion, a fine old building, belonging to an
age when men knew not architectural shams, before Grecian porticos overshadowed our doorways, and stucco had
superseded honest scarlet bricks.

Miss Neville met us on the steps. She was surrounded
by five or six large dogs, who alarmed me somewhat until I
understood that they only meant to be friendly when they
thrust their great cold noses into my hand.

" Down, Ponto ! Be quiet, Nep. Ain't you ashamed of
yourself, sir, eh ? Are those your manners to company?
Miss Hope, I am glad to see you at our old house, though I

wish you would have come to-morrow. 'Better *soon* than never,' though. Don't be afraid of the dogs, they won't hurt you. Will you come in and see papa? and afterwards we can walk about."

We passed through the hall, round which were stuffed birds in glass-cases — the trophies of a departed race of sportsmen — and entered the library. Mr. Neville was standing with his back to the fire. He bowed with great formality to us both, and then extended his hand frigidly to Miss Bissett. It was easy to see, as Shenstone says of some one, that "he was the dread of all jovial conversations. . . . . and yet he had acquired the character of the most ingenious person of his county; not that he had ever made any great discovery of his talents, but a few oracular declarations, joined with a common opinion that he was writing something for posterity, completed his reputation." Mr. Neville had indeed done *his* work for posterity, for which it was to be hoped that posterity would be as duly grateful as the present age was indifferent; and instead of "a few oracular sentences," his conversation was inexorable as fate. You saw it coming on; you felt that nothing could stop or change its course, or mitigate it in the smallest degree. Nothing less high-spirited than his daughter could have retained any elasticity under such circumstances. Mr. Neville quoted Virgil at us on the subject of the weather, but seemed very indifferent when I admired his old house, and asked some questions about the fine portraits on the wall. One, indeed, of the late Mr. Neville, with periwig and snuff-box, he pointed to, informing me that he, his father, had built a church and endowed an hospital; but when I learned that this was the same gentleman who had painted all the oak wainscots a pale salmon-color, my wrath was kindled against him, and I immediately saw a strong family likeness to the present proprietor. We were shown the Blue Chamber in which his Majesty King Charles, of blessed memory, once slept; and the haunted chamber, in which no one had ever slept since a certain Neville was said to have roasted his wife there. Then Miss Neville took us to her own private room, where an aviary of singing-birds occupied one entire window, and passing through a glass door, we descended into the gardens, and visited the fish-ponds, and the peacocks, and the owl in his solitary grotto, which were Miss Neville's peculiar charge.

"You must be very happy in this charming home of yours?"

"I suppose I am—I never thought about it. When Willie has been at home and is gone back to college, I find the difference, and am rather lonely. We suit each other exactly, Willie and I. Do you know, Miss Bissett, I used to think once that we should always live together, like you and your brother."

"Humph! my dear. I am afraid Mr. William would hardly like such a quiet life for very long."

"You think him very wild and extravagant; so he is, but he has such a good heart, and is so fond of me. I understand him better than papa does, and I intend him some day to marry Violet, which will be what historians call 'a double alliance.' I am so sorry poor Vi is not allowed to come here to-day. She is left with that excellent old dragon Lateward (beg your pardon, Miss Hope), as my society, I suppose, was considered to be detrimental to the studies."

"I thought Mrs. Rochford was to come to-morrow, my dear."

"Oh! no, this afternoon. Hubert brings his mother, and leaves her for a day or two. Do stay and see her; they ought to be here before long."

The stable-clock struck four.

"Dear Miss Bissett, you don't like driving at dusk — had we not better be starting home?"

I plucked the good lady's sleeve so imploringly that she resisted Miss Neville's efforts to detain us, and the carriage came round.

The ponies were very fresh, and as Miss Bissett stepped in, a shot in the wood close by startled them.

" Bless me, my dear Maud, what is that ? "

" The gamekeeper having a battue in honor of our guests. But take care of those little grays, Miss Bissett, they want a tight hand. Good-by, Miss Hope ; something tells me we shall meet again very soon."

I had just seated myself; Miss Bissett was gathering up the reins, and the boy had stupidly left the ponies' heads to clamber into his seat behind, when there was another shot, still closer than the first, and the little animals began rearing. Miss Neville sprang forward, but it was too late. The traces had broken : the ponies set off full gallop down the avenue.

I was terrified, but sat quite still. Miss Bissett displayed more nerve than I should have expected, but the reins had slipped from her hand. Nothing could stop us now but the lodge-gate. Trees and bushes flew past : all the blood seemed rushing to my head. I could no longer see. I have a confused impression of Miss Bissett's giving a horrified cry, and of seeing some dark object coming on the road towards us.

The next moment, crash we came against it ! There was a piercing shriek, and I felt a shock as if every bone in my body was broken. The gravel flew up into my eyes, and I remember nothing more.

We had driven against the Rochford carriage, and the concussion had overturned us upon the side on which I sat. I remember opening my eyes once and recognizing the anguished gaze of the person in whose arms I lay : then I relapsed with a pleasurable sigh into darkness, and remained unconscious for several hours.

CHAPTER XXIX.

A STRANGE room, round the walls of which hung rods and fishing-tackle, and two figures, equally strange to me, standing by the bedside. This is what I saw when I opened my eyes.

"She is coming round, ma'am. The head has bled a good deal, so we shan't require to take any blood. The ankle, unfortunately, has begun to swell up, so that I can't tell whether there is any thing broken. I am half afraid; but you can't do better than continue lotioning it; and I'll ride over in the morning, ma'am."

I knew now that I was not dreaming. I felt a throbbing, burning pain all up my right foot and ankle. At last the door opened, and a familiar face approached the bed.

"Betsy, tell me where — " I began, faintly.

"Hush! You mustn't talk, not on no account. Drink this, there's a dear, and keep quiet."

I felt cooled and refreshed after taking the draught she brought me, and fell asleep. Several times in the course of the night I woke, and one or other of those women was sure to be in the room: moving stealthily about, under the tremulous spotted shadows of a rushlight. I never wondered, or asked myself who that other watcher might be. My brain was in too confused a state to do more than passively admit impressions. When I opened my eyes in the gray of the morning, Betsy alone was with me: I began to collect my scattered thoughts.

"Tell me where I am, Betsy. What has happened? I can't rest any longer without knowing."

"You are at Neville Hall, Miss Marg'ret, but not on no account to speak, if you please. I were sent for, and came direct after the haccident; and Miss Bissett, she escaped miraculous! She were a good deal decomposed, beside a slight confusion of the face, and lost her front, but nothink to speak of."

"I want to ask you particularly —"

"There's the doctor's ring, and you're not on no account to speak, miss."

"Stop! I insist on it, Betsy. I have been delirious — light-headed! Have I said any thing —"

"No, no, deary, not a ha'porth. Never spoke a word."

"And who is the tall lady in black?"

"Mrs. Rochford."

*   *   *   *   *   *
*   *   *   *   *   *

It is a marvel I had not a brain fever, such was the state of strong but suppressed mental excitement I was in on finding that I was an inmate of the same house with Mrs. Rochford and her son, and that here I must remain. The doctor authoritatively pronounced against my being moved; and said I must make up my mind to be a prisoner for some weeks probably. The injuries to the head, indeed, were slight, but the inflammation to my ankle continued unabated; it was a very severe sprain, if nothing worse, and my pulse was so high, added to my extreme restlessness, that the doctor looked grave. He was deeper-sighted than most country practitioners, and he soon perceived that more was to be apprehended from the irritation of the brain, caused by some secret anxiety, than from any local injuries.

The room was kept dark, and for days Mrs. Rochford and Betsy were the only persons, except the doctor, who entered it. The former little suspected how her presence tended to increase the state of feverish excitement in which I lay. She was the one object of my study and speculation : my eyes followed every motion of that gaunt figure about the room. She seldom spoke; when she did, it was in a whisper. The third morning she opened the Book of Job, and read part of that glorious poem in a low, sonorous voice. What was it about her that reminded me of my Aunt Mary? Certainly not her face or figure. She was harder-featured and a larger woman; but the expression of her eyes, and certain expressions of mind shown in peculiar movements and intonations, were strangely like my aunt, and drew me more towards Mrs. Rochford than even her tender and motherly care.

Once, through the stillness, I heard a step that came softly down the passage and stopped at my door, and when Mrs. Rochford had opened it, I thought I recognized the voice that whispered without ; but it might have been fancy.

Gradually, more and more, in spite of my deep-rooted dread of Mrs. Rochford, I felt that there existed one of those inexplicable sympathies between us that every one has experienced, at some time in his life, towards a perfect stranger. I had not spoken to her ; and yet I could have fallen on her neck and opened all my heart to her — under other circumstances !

Maud Neville was allowed to see me on the third day ; I was much better, though still very weak, and forbidden to talk much.

" You frightened us dreadfully, my dear Miss Hope. I really thought you were killed when Hubert carried you into the house. He rode off instantly for the doctor, and we were in such a state till he returned ! You see it was decreed by Fate that you *should* stay here ! You wouldn't yield, and Fate is not to be thwarted with impunity. Now Miss Bissett, who was more amenable, came off very easily. So odd, being such a weak little creature, that she should n't be more hurt."

"Have you heard how she is to-day?"

"Oh! as well as ever; only dreadfully distressed about you—sends over twice a day. The old gentleman rode over himself this morning, like Count Ory, he said (in some opera they saw abroad), come to invade our conventual solitude! You know that we are three lone women here? Papa and Hubert obliged to go up to London about those horrid settlements."

"Ah! Will they be long absent?"

"A week, I suppose, or more."

"Your convent is very quiet. I'm afraid you've hushed even your birds' voices on my account. Where am I? In what part of the house?"

"On the ground-floor, opening into my boudoir. This is Willie's own den, and these are his trophies and implements of war. There is his rod, and below it the outline of a trout weighing eight pounds, he caught last summer. Dear fellow! he never had his room so honored before; but it was more convenient to carry you in here; and, when you are well enough, we can wheel you on the terrace, and into my room, so easily."

I assured her I should be able to walk about in a few days. I was, indeed, sanguine of being well enough to leave the Hall before Hubert's return. But, although the following day I was strong enough to sit up for a few hours, the doctor gave me no hope of being able to put my foot to the ground for three weeks at least. He said (at Mrs. Rochford's instigation, I suspect) that I must give up all idea of being removed to Exton, or elsewhere, for the present. The slightest movement of the ankle might retard my recovery for months.

One of the few things that had, by accident, been thrown into my box the night I left home was an old sketch-book, and I tried to give myself the semblance of employment, as I lay near the window, by sketching some beech-trees near the house. But the fingers moved listlessly: the pencil lay idle between them for the half hour at a time, while Mrs. Rochford plied her energetic knitting-pins beside me. There were times when it seemed as if all the vigor of her mind could not shake off a certain gloomy preoccupation; and then the long lapses of conversation were only interrupted occasionally by a deep sigh. She would suddenly turn round after a while, as she did one morning, with the question,

"Where were you born and brought up, Miss Hope?"

"In Paris."

"Ever been to school?"

"No;—excepting, perhaps, in that of adversity."

She looked at me for a moment in silence. "The best we can go to, and we are never too old for it. I am an old woman, and have had plenty; and yet, perhaps, my schooling is not done." Then, after a pause, she added, "But you are too young for that, my dear. Don't get into a sentimental way of talking about sorrow. It comes soon enough."

"I am only saying the truth, Mrs. Rochford. I have had an unhappy home, and I am alone in the world."

"It is strange how unequally troubles and crosses are allotted in life! There is Maud, for instance, who is just your age, and, except her dear mother's death, has never had a grief. Still, I am not sure that—"

"Miss Neville," said I, hurriedly, "has such a bright disposition by nature, that it would be difficult to cloud it."

"She is a very good girl—few like her for sterling worth—and capitally constituted for the kind of life she will lead when she is married: visiting the poor, and taking her full share in the work of a country life. She has no nerves or sensitiveness. Very few girls are fitted by their education for the kind of thing, and they get soon disgusted with coarseness and ignorance. They would like, perhaps, to have a model school, and trellised cottages, with old women in red cloaks, but they shrink from dirt and disease. Is n't it so? Don't you feel that?"

"Perhaps. I don't think I should; but I have never tried."

"And you are one of the few girls to whom I *would* give a trial, Miss Hope, though you *have* been brought up abroad, against which I have an old-fashioned English prejudice."

"Does Mr. Neville interest himself about the poor?" said I, anxious to change the subject.

"Mr. Neville is an upright, worthy man, Miss Hope; but he cannot be said to *interest* himself about any thing except dead languages and dictionaries, which I don't understand. He does n't know a turnip from a potatoe, so how can he care about the country? and though I've tried to get him to exert himself in improving the intellectual condition of his peasantry, he only shakes his head and quotes some Latin, to the effect that they are all swine, which is true enough, but is that a reason we are not to try and elevate them? My dear sister, whose nature was warm and genial, never had much sympathy with her husband."

"Why did she marry him?"

"She had seen very little of the world, and had had no opportunities of comparing him with any one else. It was a very suitable marriage in worldly respects, and my father had long wished it."

"It tells against a secluded youth; don't you think so?"

"Perhaps," she replied, gravely; and then added, "The responsibility of parents in these cases is a very grave one."

Miss Neville stood beside my sofa in her boudoir that afternoon, as I was finishing my sketch in the window.

"I wish I could draw. I can't do any of those sort of things, unfortunately."

I offered to give her such instruction as I could. She sat down with a smile.

"Do you think people without talent can ever arrive at doing any thing, Miss Hope?"

"Hardly any one is without some talent for some one thing, however small; but it may lie dormant."

"I don't think all the teaching in the world would make me a musician, or make me draw really well. I wish it could, for Hubert's sake — more than for my own. He ought to have an accomplished wife."

"For his sake, then, try and become one," I said, in a low voice.

"Do you believe in what is called 'improving oneself?'"

"Of course. Why not?"

"Well, I don't. I am speaking of the *dulce*, you know, not the *utile*, as papa would say. One must have a natural gift for these things, otherwise it is vanity and vexation of spirit. I dare say you drew from your cradle?"

"I did: but a talent often lies dormant for years. Bernardin de St. Pierre, for instance, never wrote till he was near fifty: besides many others."

"Still the disposition must be there. Now really your drawings are good enough to be an artist's."

"What do you understand by an artist?"

"Oh! any one who makes it their profession, I suppose — who sells their things."

"In that sense I *am* an artist, though not in the higher sense, I fear. Did you not know this?"

"No. I hadn't an idea of it. I should have thought — I mean, I should never — no, what I *do* mean is, that I never met any one about whom I felt so much curiosity as I do about you. I beg your pardon, but I can't help it. You seem to have seen so much of the world for your age, and — but I see I am paining you: forgive me; I am inconsiderate."

There was a pause, and then Miss Neville asked abruptly,

"Have you any sketches of Paris in that book? That is where your family live, I believe?"

"I have no longer any family, Miss Neville."

She took the book on her knees, and turned over the sketches, examining each with great care. She had gone half through them with little comment, when she suddenly uttered an exclamation of surprise.

"How very curious! Did you do this? 'A window in the Hôtel Cluny?' Hubert has the exact fellow of it. I know the drawing well. He has been having the school windows at Rochford made from it. It is *most* singular. I could have declared this was the same sketch."

"Really!" I felt the color mounting to my temples under her frank, steadfast gaze. "It is a popular subject. Dear Miss Neville, would you give me that screen? the fire is so hot. Now, if you have cut your pencil, let us begin. You must hold it like this."

* * * * *

A window in Miss Neville's room, as I have mentioned, opened into the garden below. This garden communicated with the village by a path through the shrubbery, which every one used who had business to transact with the young lady, instead of going round half a mile, by the great entrance. My sofa was drawn up near the window, which stood open, for it was a warm April day. Miss Neville had left the room for a moment, and my head had dropped upon the pillow, and was shaded by my hand. A step came along the gravel; it ascended the steps, and a shadow fell across the room. Not till then did I raise my head and look up.

The person who stood there gave a sharp scream.

"Good God! what do I see? *You?* Marie Dumont! Hush, hush! for Heaven's sake! What are you about here?

Pray, pray don't appear to know me — my name is Hope — don't—"

" What was that scream?" said Miss Neville, running into the room. " Surely some one screamed?"

Marie was leaning, pale as death, against the window-sill.

" I twisted my foot, mademoiselle, coming up the step. It is nothing. I brought you home the embroidery, and I thought you would like to know I have two more scholars."

" That is famous. You will soon have more than you can manage. Mr. Rochford was inquiring particularly how your boy was getting on. I told him that he was already half English."

The fierce look I had once before seen there came over her face; but a gentle and subdued expression quickly succeeded it, as she said,

" Let him be *all* English, so that he be like Mr. Rochford and you. All we have we owe to you, through him. Mademoiselle, I pray to the good God my boy may never forget it."

When she was gone, Miss Neville said,

" A singular parishioner for our quiet little village, I dare say you think? The fact is, Hubert was interested about her, and asked me, some months ago, whether, if he rented a cottage for her here, I thought I could get her employment in embroidering and teaching French. Rochford Court is so isolated — so far from any gentlemen's houses — that this populous district seemed to offer a better chance of success. I promised to do all I could for his protégée, and she came over, and it has answered beyond our most sanguine expectations. She has now seven scholars, who are too glad to avail themselves of a real French accent, instead of the — shire version of Clapham-Seminary French, which is all Anchester affords. Besides this, she teaches the art of embroidery to our school children, so that in process of time we shall be populated with a generation of *brodeuses ;* and she makes a great deal by ministering to the vanity of our far- mers' daughters in worked collars, etc. Her boy goes to our village school, and Hubert means to put him into some trade by-and-by. That is the history, present and future, of Marie Dumont. What her past may have been I never inquired, but it was a sad one, I am sure."

CHAPTER XXX.

It was dusk when Rochford entered the room, on his return with Mr. Neville. He came up to my sofa, and said a few commonplace words. We shook hands like people tolerably well acquainted — a greeting more cold than coldness itself.

Well, I had dreaded it so long and now it was over! Candles were brought. I could not but be struck by the alteration in his appearance during the last fortnight. His face was very worn and pale; the least observant would have remarked, "There is a man bowed down by some secret care!" and the struggle to cast this aside rendered his manner almost irritable at times. I glanced at Mrs. Rochford. Was it possible that a mother's eye should be blind to this? Her back was towards me; but presently she rose, and walking up to him with her firm step, she put back the hair from his forehead and kissed it. Then she left the room without a word.

'Maud drew a stool near Rochford's feet, and sat there looking up into his face every now and then with an inquiring glance, not without a shade of disappointment in it. He appeared unconscious of her presence : he never spoke or lifted his eyes from the fire on which they were fixed. At last Maud spoke, and in her usual vein ; but I fancied it was with some degree of effort, as though she were resolved *not* to entertain any foolish fancies.

(330)

“You have brought down the London fog with you, cousin Hubert.”

No answer.

“Come, tell us some news, sir. What have you been doing in town?”

“Law and lawyers — nothing else, Maud. And you? Riding and amusing yourself, I hope, while I —”

“Oh! don’t flatter yourself you were the least missed. We have been very busy in all sorts of ways. To begin with, Miss Hope has been giving me drawing lessons.”

“She is very good, I am sure.”

“Yes. *You* would ’nt take the trouble.”

“My dear child, I never knew you had any taste for it.”

“Neither did I, sir; but you should have found it out, as Miss Hope did. Perhaps you ’re not aware that she is a great artist? I intend the walls of my boudoir at Rochford to be hung with her pictures. You shall be her first patron — do you hear, Hubert?”

I heard *him* writhe in his chair, but Maud, quite unconscious of the effects of her words, continued,

“You must see her charming sketches after dinner. There is one of a window in the Hôtel Cluny —”

Rochford suddenly darted forward from his chair to poke the fire. In doing so, a small case fell from his breast-pocket.

“Oh! by-the-by, I forgot it. That bauble is for you, Maud. Say nothing about it, my child — not worth thanking me for. What’s o’clock? It must be time to dress for dinner.”

He leaned his head between his arms against the mantelpiece. Maud held the bracelet just as he had given it into her hand, her eyes fixed, with a peculiar expression, on her cousin. The painful silence was broken by the dressing-bell; and in a few minutes I was left alone.

The Deanes and the Bissetts dined at the Hall that day.

After dinner the ladies adjourned, on my account, from the drawing-room to Maud's boudoir, where Mrs. Deane gossiped over all her neighbors, high and low, with pre-Raffaelite minutiæ of detail. I remember that a certain Mr. and Mrs. Hunter were under discussion when the gentlemen came in for their coffee. Sometimes a subject which has no interest for one bears indirectly on another which has: it was so in the present case.

"Is there no chance of her recovery?" asked Maud. "Poor man! I'm very sorry for him. He is perfectly wrapped up in her."

"No hope of her living another six months, I'm afraid. Sad thing — very sad! — and he such a reformed man, too, by his marriage! A shocking character, I'm told, before, but impossible, I'm sure, to find a better husband. Such an attached couple!"

"It is very strange," said Miss Bissett, shaking her virtuous little head, "but I always considered that a permanent affection must be founded on *esteem*."

"A very just remark," said Mr. Neville, who had just entered. "*Conciliat amicitiam et conservat, virtus.* A profound truth, which the ancients did well to recognize — "

"Oh!" interrupted his daughter, quickly, "I'm not at all sure of that. One hears of very bad people inspiring very strong love. I believe, on the contrary, that no one ever made a great sacrifice for *esteem*. It is a sort of sentiment to lend money on, not to give up a life to."

"Well, certainly," observed Mrs. Deane, "there is William Hunter, the brother, who is a most estimable person, and so is his wife, and yet they're any thing but happy — quite unsuited. That is in favor of your argument, Maud."

"But then, you know, he was attached to some one else, and both parents were very much against it, and it was broken off. I don't think he was ever quite the same afterwards."

"Ah! *vetitum ergo cupitum* — true, very true, from our first parents downwards. The Roman law — "

"Poor Bill Hunter!" cut in Mr. Bissett (in nervous terror of the Roman law, which was inflicted, with all its severity, on Mr. Deane for a full hour afterwards). "A cheery good fellow he used to be, but since he married his rich, psalm-singing wife (beg pardon, Mrs. Deane) he is the most melancholy, chapfallen man in the neighborhood."

"My love," remonstrated his sister, "a more virtuous, kind, and charitable woman than Mrs. William Hunter does not exist. If her husband is not happy, surely it cannot be *her* fault."

"I am of the opinion of the Dutch philosopher," said Maud, "who declared that people were like cheeses cut in half and rolled down hill, and that very seldom the right halves came together, but more commonly two that don't at all match. When, by any chance, the proper halves *do* meet, I think nothing in the world ought to prevent their joining."

Miss Neville laughed, and walked to the further end of the room to cover up her bird cages for the night. As she passed the lamp, I remarked that her cheek was flushed, and the full, firm lips more firmly set than ever. Neither Mrs. Rochford nor her son had spoken; and I suppose it occurred to Mrs. Deane as ill-advised to protract the present discussion, for she speedily unravelled another skein from her inexhaustible wallet of small-talk; and soon afterwards I was carried to my room.

Several days elapsed. An indescribable weight had fallen on the spirits of the little party since Rochford's return. For myself, my sole thought and desire, of course, more than ever, was to escape from the singular and humiliating position in which I found myself. But the very intensity of this longing operated against my recovery. The feverish and harrowing anxiety to which I was a prey prevented my sleeping at night, and I grew more wan and wasted every day. My position would have been even less supportable had I seen much of Rochford; but he never entered Maud's room until the evening, when my health was a very plausible excuse for retiring early. His manner on these occasions was constrained; but towards his mother and Maud it underwent many variations: indifferent, pre-occupied, and sometimes considerate and gentle as his former self, only always tinged with a profound melancholy. Poor Mrs. Rochford! her brooding fits were daily longer, her brow more and more contracted with the lines of anxious thought. Expiation had already commenced for the terrible mistake which, in her affection for her son, she had committed. It is forever going on around us, the same mistake and the same expiation, and some of the best men only learn too late that human hearts are not to be squared and measured according to a given plan, as they lay out their houses and their grounds!

She and I were generally alone together now, for Miss Neville had taken to longer rides than ever across the country — fast and furious gallops, from which the grooms complained that the horses returned as tired as after a day's hunting. If Miss Neville herself was tired, at all events she never complained: her face had a hard, indomitable look, under which it was difficult to see whether she suffered any thing. But I caught Mrs. Rochford's eyes more than once anxiously bent on her: and as she sat there, apparently tranquil and absorbed over her embroidery, I think a close observer would have detected that she was working in secret the solution of some difficult problem.

One wet afternoon, when she could not ride, this was especially the case. The rain falling silently outside, the voices silent within; the dogs shaking the water from their backs on the terrace, without so much as a cheerful bark; the very birds in their cages hushed, — no wonder that Miss

Neville, submitting to the influence of the day, was unusually preoccupied. Mr. Neville at last came in with the day's *Times*, and instructed us as to the foolish nature of that journal regarded from a classical point of view. He talked a certain number of pages off, and though no one knew exactly what it was about, we all felt it a relief, I believe, to hear an uninterrupted flow of words after the oppressive silence.

But the longest afternoon will come to an end, and the dressing-bell at last rang. I had not been alone five minutes when the door opened, and Hubert Rochford entered.

"Pardon me," said he, rapidly, "I thought it well that you should be prepared for a death which I have just seen in the paper, and that you should learn it when you were alone. It is that of a person you had no cause to love ; but so awfully sudden a death will shock you." He pointed to a paragraph :

"At Algiers, on the 20th instant, of cholera, after a few hours' illness, Frances, Lady Greybrook, in the 51st year of her age."

I dropped the paper.

"Poor, unhappy woman! dying in that way, without warning or preparation ! God, in his mercy, forgive her !"

"Can *you* forgive her all the grievous wrong she did you ? If so——"

"Yes, yes, Mr. Rochford. What am I, that I should judge any one? I have forgiven her from my heart already."

"It is almost more than I *can* do," he exclaimed violently. "She was the cause——" He broke off suddenly.

Maud stood in the doorway.

She was returning to fetch something she had forgotten, and, arrested by Rochford's excited voice and manner, seemed, for a moment, irresolute whether to advance or retreat. Her clear, searching eyes pierced through and through me. She came quickly forward, took some work from the table, and left the room; but her cousin had passed out before her.

That night, when Miss Neville came into my bedroom, as she always did, to wish me good night, she said, in her straightforward, fearless way,

"I never saw Hubert so much excited as he was to-day, when I came into the room. Do you mind telling me what he was talking about?"

"He was showing me the death of — of some one I knew well — in the paper."

She considered for a moment. "May I ask who?"

"An unfortunate person, of whom it is not probable that you ever heard — Lady Greybrook."

"On the contrary, I have often heard of her. So you knew her then? And why do you suppose my cousin was so moved in speaking of her?"

"She destroyed the happiness of some one Mr. Rochford once knew."

"Of course you mean Miss Percival."

I trembled to think how long my strength would stand this sort of ordeal. She continued,

"I suppose you knew her also? Don't be afraid of talking to me about her. I know the whole story : he told me every thing himself, and I felt very much interested about her, until she married that horrid ——"

"Married?"

"Did'nt you know that she is now Marquise d'Ofort? We heard very lately from Paris all about it. I believe she was really to be pitied though, for that dreadful father of hers made some disgraceful match, and she was almost *forced* to accept this old man — they were married the same day. Mrs. Fisher wrote to us next day, and said Paris was talking of nothing else."

"I think you will find in this case, as in many others, that

Paris tongues are far in advance of truth. Miss Percival is certainly not married, though her home was wretched, as you say. Whatever you may hear about her, let your kind heart, Miss Neville, remember that she was severely tried. Do not be too hard upon her."

"So you think she is not married?" said Maud, at last. "What, then, has become of her?"

"Who knows? What becomes of the leaf drifted from the tree? I believe she has left her home, and sought for an asylum somewhere."

"Have you no means of finding out where she is?"

"None, at present."

"Do you think ——" She broke off, and after a pause, said, "Tell me all you can about her character. I know she is brilliant and attractive, and all the rest of it. Men, of course, are ensnared by that; but I want to know more —her *character*. What did you think of it? Hubert was not a fair judge."

"She was full of faults which needed severe discipline, and she has had it, in sorrow and disappointment of many kinds. Let us hope that they have produced some good result."

"I like that: I was afraid you were going to tell me she was a saint. I like her the better for her faults. I mistrust phœnixes — religious ones particularly. I dare say you think it odd, now, that I am not furiously jealous of this girl; but really, I don't believe I am. I should like to ask you — I have a great curiosity to know — whether she cared for my cousin?"

"How could she, if he did not care for her? You would have a poor opinion of her, would you not, Miss Neville?"

"Oh! but his heart was *there*. Well, it is difficult to know men, as you will find out some day, my dear Miss Hope. I don't know how it is that I am drawn into talking with you thus, and so is my aunt, she says. It is curious,

for I am sure you don't seek it; but I suppose we both feel
instinctively that you have judgment and penetration — and
there is something in your being so perfectly unbiased that
makes one able to talk with you about these things. I have
a great deal more I should like to say, but I must n't keep
you up any longer now. You look tired. Good-night."

What Miss Neville said of her aunt was curiously confirmed the very next morning.

The post came in late at the Hall. Mrs. Rochford and I
were together when the bag was brought in: there was a
letter for her, and one for me. Mine was from my sister at
Genoa, written a fortnight before, and announcing her
speedy return to England. She affectionately expressed
sorrow and surprise at the step I had found myself obliged
to take. Charles was shocked to hear of my father's marriage, and, as I was not in Paris, they had given up their
intention of stopping there, but looked forward to my being
with them in London, where Rose expected to be confined.
This was the essence of several sheets of foreign paper,
crossed. The letter was directed to Brook-street (as I had
desired her, when I wrote from London), and the housekeeper there, in conformity with my written instructions
from Exton, had forwarded it on, under cover to " Miss
Hope." Strange, upon what trifles hinge the greatest events
of our lives! Had it not been —— But all in its proper
place: other things of that morning must first be told.

Mrs. Rochford had read her letter twice before I had
finished my sister's somewhat illegible epistle. I stuffed it
into my pocket as Mrs. Rochford rose and drew a chair
towards my sofa with a grave, perplexed air. She knitted
for some time in silence. At last she said,

" When one has committed an error, one ought to repair
it by every means in one's power."

I did not see that this self-evident proposition required
any reply, and she continued, after a minute,

"I have a letter here which will gravely affect my son. It is a question of rendering justice to a person who has suffered great injustice. Unfortunately, a knowledge of the truth will not tend to make him happier, poor boy! rather the contrary ; and yet I must not hesitate : my conscience says I must not — but it is a cruel thing. If I could be sure that he — "

She waited for a moment, and I said, gently,

"Truth is the only thing in this world we *can* be sure of, dear Mrs. Rochford. Opinions change, but that is unchanged. The nearer we can get to it *always* the better."

"You say well, my dear, opinions *do* change. We live, sometimes, to see the events for which we prayed turn out curses instead of blessings. It proves how miserably weak our judgments are. It should teach us humility : but it does not prevent keen self-reproach at the same time. I was always too proud, and now, in my old age, I am being taught this."

"However much you may have been mistaken, Mrs. Rochford, I am sure that you thought you were acting for the ultimate happiness of — of — your son."

She shook her head. "I was too ready to take my wishes for convictions. I am sure you knew Miss Lateward's old pupil, Marguerite Percival, though you have never mentioned her. You know that my son —— "

"Oh, yes! I heard all that — a tale of the past."

"I wish it were : it is a living and terrible reality for my poor boy. Since his engagement to Maud, far from changing the current of his thoughts, he is more depressed than ever. A month ago, when he heard that Miss Percival was to be married immediately to the Marquis d'Ofort, he told me that he believed his passion was cured — that it was no more than a sort of romantic friendship, arising out of peculiar circumstances, and that he felt sure she never cared for him."

“ He ascertained that, I suppose ? ”

“ Why, I urged him so strongly to pause, from all I heard
of her way of going on, and the set she was in, that he did
so.   He would not speak to her of love : he never allowed
her to see *how* much he cared for her.   He watched and
waited, and at last, in desperation, he left Paris suddenly.
He had every reason to believe she liked another person.
Poor fellow ! when he unexpectedly came home, he told me
all — *all.*   I thought he would get over it in time.   I was
grievously mistaken.   I have much to reproach myself with.”

“ Since your son, Mrs. Rochford, so easily transferred
himself, need you reproach yourself so much ? ”

“ Ah ! that is not a fair way of putting it.   In the first
place, it was not weakness, but strength of principle that
made him resist his love.   And it was not without a long
struggle — not until he had given up all hope, that he said
that perhaps I was right, that he had better make for himself other ties, other objects of thought and interest, and try
and forget the past.   I urged him very strongly to this
course, though I ought to have known his character better.
But mothers are jealous, my dear — unconsciously so.   They
think nothing is good enough for their children, and are,
above all, afraid of believing their son’s reports in these matters.   Had I been firmly persuaded that Miss Percival was
sensible, innocent, and high-minded, such a girl, my dear, as
you are — ”

“ Dear Mrs. Rochford, I pray, do not speak of me — ”

“ How gladly would I have welcomed her as a daughter !
But all I heard of her disreputable father and her miserable
home filled me with apprehension for my son.   God knows
now, whether it would not have been better than — Ah, me !
it was always my dream that he should marry Maud, whose
heart and disposition I knew so well — a daughter-in-law of
whom I was *sure,* and who would be content to sit down
quietly in the old house — (not that *I* shall live with them ;

I move into the dower-house, a couple of miles off) — in short, a wife suited to that sort of life not always wanting company and excitement. Well, after all, you see I was wrong — wrong from the commencement — I know it now. Hubert has a true regard and brotherly affection for his cousin : he will always be kind and indulgent to her, I am sure of that; but his heart is not hers, and *he*, at least, will not be happy, I fear. It is *done*, so I say nothing; for, of course, he would never break off his engagement. I can only hope that Maud is blind, poor child! and does not feel his coldness, and that her eyes may never, *never* be opened. You are the only person, my dear Miss Hope, to whom I can speak thus. Between my son and me there always existed the most perfect confidence and affection, and now a cloud has come between us. There is something at his heart he cannot speak of to his mother. We are no longer the same towards each other."

She hastily brushed away a tear from her eyes, and opened the letter in her hand.

" But this is the worst part of all. I know how keenly he will suffer when he finds that these reports were false, to which I gave too ready credence. My Hubert will almost hate me !"

I had never seen Mrs. Rochford so moved before. She gave me the letter with a trembling hand : the excitement of unburdening herself of the secret trouble at her heart had proved too much for her self-command. The tears were falling thick on the paper, but she rose to her full height, and looking upwards, as if to invoke strength and counsel, walked to the window, to recover her composure.

The letter was from Lady Janet Oglevie, at Paris, where she had arrived a few days previously. My eye ran down the first page and then the second, until I came to these words:

" I know, dear and valued friend, you would wish to hear

the truth, and nothing *but* the truth, concerning a certain person. No one lother than you to deny her fair play, and she has not had it. To my disgust — which I made bold to express pretty strongly — I find the tales which my relatives here have thought fit to credit and to circulate concerning the poor girl, are vile lies. Not a word of truth in any of them. She has neither married that old profligate, nor has she gone off with Lord Rawdon, as they pretended, for he has been in Paris ever since, and is a changed man, they tell me. There is no doubt he was very much in love with her. He has sold his horses and dismissed all his servants, and is going off to fight for the Hungarians, and hopes to be killed, I believe, like all disappointed lovers. Strange things people do in these days, to be sure! To return to poor Miss P., there is no doubt she *has* run away from her home, but it was to escape the iniquitous conspiracy of her father and his new wife to marry her against her will. I honor her for having resisted all their machinations, and I could really excuse her running away, if I knew that she was respectably married — even to a shoemaker. But I can find out nothing about her, except that she is in England. Whenever her father is asked, he professes ignorance, and says he supposes when his daughter is tired of wandering about, she will return to him. He confessed to some one, however, that she was with a respectable English family, and if so, she is better than she could be at home. That wife of his leads him a pretty life, I hear: I'm glad of it. It would not interest you to hear of the scenes that are said to take place in that establishment already; and I have not Mrs. O.'s pen for scandal. I try to believe it was through inadvertence she wrote as she did: unfortunately, I must confess, she was always prejudiced against Miss P., and jealous of her besides — as I told her plainly. Women's tongues do enough mischief, my dear old friend, but their pens do much more. So, lest I should wax bitter against my own kith and kin, I'll stop.

"I hope Hubert's marriage may answer your expectations. You know *my* opinion of it; so I will only say, that I shall be delighted if I am *mistaken*, and if he has really forgotten a certain person; for I know this is the thing nearest your heart, and that you are delighted now that all chance of *the other* is at an end. You'll do me the justice to say I never encouraged it. She had been brought up in such a school, that it would have been a great risk (as I always told you) setting her down as your young squire's wife in the country. But a more honest-hearted young woman does not exist, I believe: I have never had good reason to change that opinion since the first day I saw her. So be good enough just to give the lie to these scandalous tales. Though it is not likely that you will ever come across her, or even hear of her again, still truth is truth. Give my compliments to Miss Lateward, and please to tell her all this," etc.

I laid down the letter, and reflected on the strange influence this old lady, personally so little known to me, had exercised already on my life. She had now placed in my hands the power, it might be, of changing my whole future. Never was a stranger position. It needed but a word from me — and I would not have spoken it then — no, not to have saved my life!

The window was open, for it was a mild May day; just wind enough to float the dappled clouds across the pale blue sky, and to disturb the tops of the beeches opposite. The door opened to Miss Neville, and the sudden draught carried the letter from my lap, fluttering to the floor. I could easily reach it, however; and I looked for Mrs. Rochford to return it, but she had left the room. Maud sat down silently to her work; then presently she came and stood by my sofa.

"You look ill; what is the matter, Miss Hope? I am afraid you are suffering more to-day."

"No, no; on the contrary, the doctor found my ankle so much better this morning, that I may be moved to Exton, he says, in three or four days, now."

"I have persuaded my aunt to send for Miss Lateward and Violet. She says she should like my cousin to know you; indeed, I think it is your society that has kept my aunt here herself so much longer than she intended. They arrive on Wednesday — you must wait to see your old friend. But you are so dreadfully pale, Miss Hope; I am sure you are not well. That letter contains some bad news, I am afraid?"

"Oh, no! It is not even mine. Your aunt gave it me to read."

"Who is it from?"

"Lady Janet Ogilvie."

"Oh, give it me! Dear old lady! I always read her letters to my aunt. You need make no secret of it. I know that she is a great friend of Miss Percival's, and all that she has said in her favor, and I am curious to see what she thinks of her conduct now — how she explains it away — for I suppose she does so."

"This letter was clearly not meant for you, Miss Neville. Indeed, you must not read it. What relates to that other person is simply a refutation of —"

The door opened, and again the draught filled out the muslin curtains, and fluttered every thing about the room. Mrs. Rochford entered with Mr. Bissett. Maud stooped to pick something from the floor.

"Good day, little woman! How are you getting on? and when are you coming back to us?"

"I hope on Tuesday, Mr. Bissett."

"Maud, Maud! What is the matter, child?" cried Mrs. Rochford.

I turned round; but if Miss Neville's face exhibited any strong emotion the instant before, it had already completely passed, as she replied, calmly,

"Nothing at all, aunt. But let us leave Mr. Bissett to flirt with Miss Hope, for I want you to read to me some of

this letter of lady Janet's — which is n't the least intended
for me, I know."

Mrs. Rochford took the letter from her niece's hand, and
they passed into the library together.

"I say," whispered Mr. Bissett, leaning his elbows on his
fat little knees, so as to bring his face closer to mine, "things
are going on in a queer way here, ain't they? He is a rum
sort of lover, if all I hear is true; never with her, always
moping about, solitary, and looking, I am sure, as if he'd
seen the Neville ghost, who roasted his wife up-stairs. I
should be afraid of his following the example, if I was
Maud. She's not the girl of spirit I took her for if she
stands such —"

"Dear Mr. Bissett, don't you know that it is impossible
to judge for other people in these matters? Who among
your acquaintance ever married the sort of person you
expected?"

"That's true enough. Perhaps, like the old woman in
the play, you think it is better 'to begin with a little aversion?' Lord! how I laughed at that, I remember, at the
Bath theatre, more than thirty years ago. It's the reason *I*
never married, Miss Hope, I never could find a woman I
had an aversion to! He! he! But seriously now, sister
and I often talk this business over, and she persists in saying that, because they're both excellent, steady young people, they —"

"Hush! Mr. Bissett, I am afraid of your being overheard.
Pray let us change the subject. It is no business of ours, is
it? Would you kindly look on the floor, I think I dropped
an envelope."

"Not visible to the naked eye, my dear young lady."

"How provoking! Perhaps it has blown out of window.
What shall I do?"

"It is not upon the terrace," said he, looking out. "There
is nothing but Miss Maud stepping out of the library win-

dow, and the peacock strutting up and down — perhaps *he* has taken to writing, and has borrowed your envelope — the impertinent coxcomb! Well, upon my life, now, that *is* the queerest couple! There is Rochford coming up the avenue, and immediately Maud sees him, she almost takes to her heels. Very strange, to be sure!"

But I am too disquieted to listen to Mr. Bissett. Further search after the missing envelope is equally unavailing. If it has *not* blown away among the trees —

The old gentleman at last takes his departure, and the afternoon passes without my again seeing Maud. But towards dusk Mrs. Rochford comes into the room, and says, in her sorrowful voice,

"It is at last done. He took the letter more calmly than I had expected — not a reproachful word or look: he only said, 'I should have known it all along, mother.' He looked so miserably ill, poor dear fellow, I had not the heart to remonstrate when he said, soon after, that he must go to London on business, and should be away some days. 'Make the best excuse you can to Maud, for I have letters to write which will prevent my being with you this evening.' He leaves us to-morrow morning at daybreak. God knows, Miss Hope, how it will all end!"

CHAPTER XXXI

A LETTER lay upon the dressing-table that night when I was wheeled into my bedroom. Before I looked at the hand-writing I felt certain as to the writer. I knew it came from Hubert Rochford. But not until Betsy had left me, with a light upon the table by my bedside, did I tremblingly break the seal, and read as follows:

"It is impossible for me to continue living under the same roof with you, day after day, eternally parted as we are. I can bear it no longer. I leave this to-morrow, and I shall not return until all chance of our meeting again is over. But at this moment, for the first and last time in my life, I must open my heart to you, my whole heart, not to say that I have loved you with all my soul and strength — you must know that, as well as I know that you never cared for me. Otherwise I dare not write thus, Miss Percival. But it is because you never felt towards me more than a friendly indifference which has latterly hardened into contempt, and because I cannot live under that contempt, that I must speak once, before I am silent forever.

" You say to yourself — I have read it in your eyes — 'He loved me once, and yet so light a thing is this man's affection, that he could believe every vile story that was cir-culated about me, and has even transferred his love already to another woman.' Hear me in justification. Our acquaint-ance was a strange one from its commencement. Though young, I felt myself called on, in some peculiar way, to be

your mentor. I had a Quixotic desire to save you from the
dangers that surrounded you; and this I endeavored to do
partly through Lady Janet. My efforts failed, but I learnt
two things: that you had a strength and clearness of mind
which would prove good shields to you, and that I was not
the man ever to captivate your heart. If, once or twice, I
thought otherwise, you quickly undeceived me. When I
spoke of better things than you were accustomed to hear of,
you showed, indeed, some interest; but I suffered tortures
when I perceived that you took a far other deeper interest
in the conversation of a man against whom I tried to warn
you, for I knew his character too well. I believed that he
loved you as he had loved a dozen other women before, and
my heart was full of bitterness when I saw you exercising
your influence over him. I heard it often repeated that you
were vain, frivolous, worldly. I tried to believe it. You
often disappointed me; sometimes carried away by excitement, sometimes flattered by what was utterly repelling to
me. It was natural, for you were young, and it was all new
to you; but my mother implored me more and more in her
letters not to try and obtain your affections — to fly the
temptation rather, while there was yet time.

"Then began that violent struggle within me which has
been going on ever since. My rigid education, the self-con-
trol my mother taught me from a child to exercise, have
imposed a restraint on me which has passed in the world for
coldness. I am content it should be so: but to *you* —

"I will not refer to the circumstance that at last determined me to quit Paris at a few hours' notice. Suffice it, I
believed I had convincing proof of your attachment to that
other, and I resolved, by a sudden wrench, to terminate this
struggle. My excellent mother only exacted one promise
from me on my return home — that I would not see or write
to you for the space of twelve months. 'If at the end of
that time your affections are still the same, my son —' But

long before then we learnt that you were to be married!
Ever since I was a boy, my mother has talked of Maud as
my future wife. She now again urged on me her many
admirable qualities. Had I needed another proof of them,
her treatment of poor outcast Marie would have been sufficient. She was content to take me as I was, knowing that I
had no heart to give — that its fire was already burnt out at
another altar — and so I became bound to her, and am hers
for life!

"Then came the cruelest trial of all. Why did we ever
meet again? Far happier for me had we not done so.
The mystery you assumed, coupled with all the tales that
reached us, perplexed me, while I felt all the old love
within me unextinguished. And that love was now crime.
I tried to harden my heart against you — in vain! Bitter
has been the pang to see my mother growing day by day
to love you, and to think of what *might* have been! And
now that the Marguerite Percival who has been so calum-
niated stands acquitted in her eyes — now that the shadow
that overhung you has been fully cleared this day — it is
but tardy justice, most brave and noble-hearted girl, to
humbly beg your forgiveness for having wronged you in
thought for one instant. My heart is stirred to its very
deeps when I think of all you must have suffered. I
well understand now, how, going forth into the world
alone to fight your way, you thought it well to leave
your name behind, with home and its associations. I see
it all.

" Farewell! Pray for me, Marguerite, for I am very
wretched. But, happily, I am the only one to suffer. Some
day, when the present cloud is overpast, you will be happy.
For myself, I dare not look forwards — it is a dreary path.
With high aims and aspirations at the onset, I have already
broken down! I tried to teach others, and was ignorant of
the first great secret of life, myself.

" God bless and keep you. " R."

My fingers slowly relaxed their grasp of the letter ; it fell upon the coverlid, as my head sank back upon the pillow. And there I lay, in a sort of trance or stupor, which was not sleep, I believe, though it closely resembled it. I say I *believe*, for what followed, was it the working of my perturbed imagination in a dream, or an actual transaction of which I was dimly conscious?

Methought a figure clothed in white glided into the room, and pronounced my name in a low clear voice, and behold, I could not speak! The words labored in my breast, but found no outlet. And the figure came and stood beside the bed, and its eyes shone down on me with a sorrowful light. Then it knelt and prayed in the awful stillness, through which I heard the ticking of the clock outside, and the beating of my heart within. And as the figure rose from its knees, with a calm face as of an angel, methought its eyes fell upon the open letter. There was a start — a moment's hesitation — and the trembling hand was stretched towards it.

"I am justified," said the low clear voice, "for this is the only way to remove all doubt. To-morrow will be too late."

The perspiration started on my forehead. In vain I endeavored to call out — to move hand or foot. I struggled under this terrible nightmare till, from pure exhaustion, I fell into a profound sleep — oblivion, at least — dreamless, without a care.

I awoke to daylight streaming through the window, and the early chattering of birds. There stood the night-light burnt down into its socket, and there the letter on the bed as I had left it. The clock struck six.

"He is off by this time — it is all over! — a few more days now. O my heart, and all these shall have passed away, and you shall hear their name no more!"

I lay moaning and tossing on my pillow as Betsy entered. She drew back the curtains, and threw open the window.

"Oh, my! well, patience me! If there's not the young squire a sweethartin' with miss in the garding at this hour!"

"Impossible! Mr. Rochford was off an hour ago. The mail passes at half-past five."

"Yes; but Mrs. Rochford was took ill last night, and tumbled in a faint like in her room, and got a severe confusion of the cheek, which ain't of no account, and was quickly got to. But miss gives Jeames a bullet this morning to take to him — that is, the young squire — just as he were starting, so in course he stopped."

An hour later came a knock at the door. I was lying on the sofa, dressed, when Mrs. Rochford entered in a morning wrapper, pale and agitated, and yet with a happier look in her eyes than I had ever seen there. She motioned Betsy to leave the room, then silently threw her arms round my neck.

"My child — my dear, dear child!" she said, at last, "I know all, and so does Maud. How blind I have been!"

"What — what do you mean, Mrs. Rochford?"

"That my boy is free. Maud has herself cancelled their engagement. She told him that she did not love him as a wife should — that she felt herself unsuited to him — and she also told him something else. It only wants a word from you now to make you *really* my child. I felt as if you were so from the moment I first nursed you, though I never suspected the truth. Forgive me, dear — forgive me all the misery I have caused you, and let me be the bearer of glad news to my poor boy in compensation. Maud says she knows you love him, though he will not believe it. Thank God! it is not too late. Now that I know you, it seems so strange, dear child, that I should ever have thrust you from me; but you *do* forgive me and *him*, don't you? Say that you forgive *him*, at least, for it was my doing, dear — all my fault."

The strong woman fairly sobbed upon my bosom. And she was the bearer of my message, reader — of such a message as I never thought to have sent on earth, though I hoped the angels would carry it to him some day from heaven.

And when by-and-by he sat beside me, holding both my hands within his, and those deep, earnest eyes fixed upon my face, it seemed too great happiness to be true — the sudden revulsion was hardly natural. There was one test which yet remained to be made — words which I felt must be said, and which I trembled to say.

" Hubert, is there no question you would ask ? No doubt you would have explained ? Once I disdained to justify myself to you ; now the case is different. Hubert Rochford's wife must not even be suspected. Is there nothing you would know ? "

" Nothing, dearest. I desire only to forget so much of the past as has intervened since I first knew you. I believe few women are so tried, and fewer still come out of the fire unscathed as you."

" Are you sure of that ? What if I told you that I left home under Lord Rawdon's protection ? "

He was silent for a moment.

" I should only feel the more keenly how much you must have suffered before you took that step ; and I should know that you had repented of it *in time*. Against all facts I should bring the fact of your pure, candid brow and eyes, my Rita. That is enough for me. If you have erred, I desire not to know it ; so, too, have I, and with far less excuse. Let us forget this past. I am trying to do so while I hold you thus in my arms. Help me, dearest, and never let us refer to that dark season."

" If I am to be your wife, Hubert, you must know all. From my husband there must be no reserve." And when I had told him my story, I added, " These are dark and troubled waters from which to take a wife, Hubert. Have you thought well? The world's tongue has been too busy with my name to be easily stopped when —"

"Hush!" said he, smiling, and putting his hand before my mouth, "I must stop yours to begin with. You are a pearl of great price, my Rita, and they only who dive deep find such. We have gone through the troubled waters, and, with God's blessing, all now shall be fair sea."

23

CHAPTER XXXII.

It is related — and we will not question the truth of the story — that a certain traveller, on visiting a Chinese burial-ground, expressed his surprise to see that none but infants were buried there, the ages inscribed on all the tombs averaging from one to three years. "We calculate the length of a man's life," was the reply, "not by the days he has lived, but by the amount of happiness he has enjoyed."

According to this estimate, I may say I am ten years old. We have been married just that time, and each year, instead of taking from, has added something to my almost perfect happiness. We have two children, and between my husband and them I have never any inclination to stir from home. My dear mother-in-law, who lives in the dower-house a mile or so from us, smiles at my increasing laziness each year, when the time comes round for us to go to London ; for my husband is now in Parliament, and fulfils his duties there, as he does in every position, faithfully and well. If you wish to know his politics, they are pretty nearly those of Mr. Gladstone.

I take a great interest in our village, and flatter myself I am nearly as efficient in my superintendence of the school, as if I had not been a Paris-bred young lady. A never-failing source of pleasure, also, are the improvements about our old place. It is hardly recognizable since we threw down hedges and fences, and turned the swamp into a lake, and planted groves, and laid out terraced gardens round the house. Every one has his weak point; this is mine: I think my home perfection. If you come and see me, remember you say something pleasant about a place that is not richly endowed by nature, giving more scope for improvement at the hand of man.

I made up my mind that I would not write this until I could finish my story by announcing that Maud Neville was married. We began to despair of her ever finding any one for whose sake she would relinquish her liberty, and who she would believe sought her for herself and not for her large fortune. At last — and she is nine and twenty — she has found this happy some one, and who do you think he is? My brother Ernest; who returned from India eighteen months ago on sick leave, and came down to us at once to spend the winter. A very handsome man he is; and though looking ill when he first arrived, his long rides over the downs (when Maud and he galloped far ahead of us) soon restored his color and spirits. Having been long without seeing any thing so fair and fresh as Maud, he naturally fell in love at first sight: she was "just a woman to my taste," as he remarked the first evening to me, "not a flight above me, as some women are, but a jolly girl, without any kind of humbug." It did not by any means follow, however, that Maud should reciprocate this sudden flame, any more than that of the many young gentlemen who had by turns bowed down before her. She was nearly three years his senior; but Love laughs at such obstacles, and before long it became evident that Maud's obdurate heart was at length captive. I am bound to say that my brother was ignorant of Maud's fortune; when he proposed, he asked her to accompany him back to India in six months' time, and this, as much as any thing, showed her the disinterestedness of his attachment. A finer, more noble-hearted fellow it is impossible to meet; the very pattern of a soldier as he was, and of a keen sportsman and liberal country gentleman as he now is. And though I cannot say that he is of much use as a magistrate, or in carrying out our various schemes for improving the condition of the poor, he is the best rider across country, the best racket-player in the Anchester court, the handsomest man in our county militia, of which he is now major, and indisputably the most popular host in the neighborhood. For I forgot to mention that Mr. Neville died four years ago, and as the young squire entered a cavalry regiment when the Crimean war broke out, Maud lived alone at the Hall until her marriage. Poor Willie Neville was one of those who, having borne the burden and heat of the day, sank from exhaustion at the eleventh hour, just as his regiment was embarking to return home. Heavy was the sister's mourning for her early friend and companion; and it was a merciful arrangement of Providence that she should meet, a few months afterwards, that other friend and companion who will never leave her now, but has promised to share her joys and sorrows till death do part them. So she still lives at the Hall which is hers: she is very happy, and the last time I was there it was for the christening of a baby, who was named Willie in memory of the last young squire.

My twin-brothers are doing well in their several professions, partly owing to my husband's exertions, but more still to their own merits and perseverance. Arthur has a good curacy in the west-end of London. He is earnest and devoted in his labors, and an especial favorite with the female portion of his congregation, being of gentle demeanor and high church principles. He occasionally gets a holiday and comes down to us, when he and my husband have long theological discussions after dinner, from which I am always glad to escape. Roger has not yet served his time for his lieutenancy, but he writes to me in high spirits from Canton, looking forward to the hope of distinguishing himself, as there is a chance given us of "licking the Chinese."

Dear old Lateward lives still with Mrs. Rochford, though Violet has, of course, long ceased to require a governess. It is an understood thing that she will never leave her, as they suit admirably, and in the event of her daughter's marrying some day, Mrs. Rochford will want a companion in her solitude.

Rose has a very large family. She is now Lady Murray, old Sir Charles having been gathered to his fathers a few months since. The present baronet is little changed since I first knew him, except that he rides sixteen stone, and does not blush when he comes into a room — perhaps because his face is in a more continuous blush than it was then. They are very happy in their way, which, of course, would not be *my* way, but I have learnt to let people be so according to their own fashion and capacity. For though I could wish that my sister were less fond of dress, and thought more of her children's minds than of their faces ; and though when we meet I always find the conversation flags after the first hour or two, seeing that it is reduced to people and is shut to the world of books and thoughts ; and though, moreover, Sir Charles and she have many a little tiff, in which his " Rose is washed, just washed, by a shower " of tears, plentifully at command, I know that nothing could materially increase her happiness, and that few husbands would be as indulgent as hers.

It only remains for me to speak of two persons who have played prominent parts in these pages.

Rawdon was not killed in the Hungarian war, as he expected. He lives, and is still unmarried. He played an active part in the Crimea, taking out provisions in his yacht, visiting the hospitals, and serving as a volunteer at the siege of Sebastopol. He came to see me, in London, on his return. He was much changed : grown very gray and old, but calm and cheerful in his manner. He brought with him a little girl, whom he told me he had adopted after the battle of Inkermann, where its father, who was a sergeant, was killed.

"The poor fellow died in my arms. I promised to look after his child, for the mother had been carried off by fever some weeks before. I took it, and it has been with me ever since. I had no object in life, and we all want one, Mrs. Rochford, so this child has become mine now."

He smiled — that old peculiar smile of his — and we shook hands cordially.

I said I was "almost perfectly happy," but I too, like the rest of the world, have my 'skeleton in the closet.' In the sunshine of my life there stands one figure which, though from afar, sometimes sends its dark shadow across my home. That shadow is my father's. I have seen him twice during these ten years, and the object of each visit has been to apply to my husband for money. He and his wife occupy different apartments, and are strangers to one another. The effort Madame made to be admitted into society having failed, she no longer required the tiresome and expensive luxury of a husband: so she allows him a small pension, upon the express condition that he does not inflict his society upon her. His habits, I fear, remain unaltered. As in youth and middle life, so in old age; the same appetites, but with enfeebled powers. And Society, acting upon her well-known generous principle, has become virtuous and severe towards him, and nods distantly in the street to the once handsome Guardsman, now that he shuffles and is somewhat bent with time: and Society shakes her head, too, over his way of life, now that he has only himself to vent his spleen upon, though she smiled and palliated the same in that gay and pleasant gentleman who was breaking his wife's heart, and bringing his children to beggary.

THE END.

www.ingramcontent.com/pod-product-compliance
Lightning Source LLC
Chambersburg PA
CBHW030100130726
47902CB00018B/1418